SUCH A
NICE GIRL

Other Books by Carol St. John:

Taproots: Where Ideas are Born

Anchors of the Soul

Little Ways

SUCH A
NICE GIRL

a novel

Carol St. John

dedicated to the young girls in my life

Cara Buchanan
Anna Clare Harvey
Madison Travaglione
Asha Egmont
Orea Bass-Egmont
Mia Bass-Egmont

1

The disaster took place when I was seventeen in the middle of my senior year at Purgatory High. It marked the end of the world as I knew it and the beginning of another. Before it happened, I believed life was negotiable and predictable. There was a formula to follow and all I had to do was figure it out. I thought the key was obeying the rules. I didn't ask if the rules made sense. I didn't have to. I was in a comfort zone I attributed to being a *good girl,* from a *good family,* doing what I was told to do and playing my part in the daily order of things. I didn't want much more than tomorrow to be a better day than yesterday, and yesterday a little better than the day before.

On the night of the fire, all the things I had once been sure of were consumed, leaving only questions in their place. That night, as flames climbed the wall and ate the dusty roses plastered on the ceiling, no noise warned us we were in danger, no smoke alarm or barking dog. The fire was a silent beast, it had a kind of insatiable energy, a fury that needed more and more food.

Coils of putrid smoke sent the first clue. The sickening stench woke me from a dream where I was trapped in a cellar with decaying cats. When I smelled the reality, the air poisoned by melting plastics and ancient resins, I ran from my bedroom into the upstairs hallway and looked straight down at Hell's face. Then I ran to the other end of the hall screaming as I ran, "Mom, Heather, the house is on fire! Wake up! Get up!" At my brother Brent's door, I pounded and yelled, "Fire! Get up, get out!"

I turned back to my bedroom to find Ernest, but my cat was gone. Meanwhile, I grabbed the sweater that was lying on the floor next to my bed, put it over my head and opened the window, leaning into the night screaming senselessly, as if someone could actually hear me, "Fire! Fire! Help! Somebody, help!"

My voice cracked in the frosted pines and was lost to the frozen street. No lights flickered in distant windows, no cars or trucks broke the icy silence. It was too still and much too cold for a fire.

Back in the hallway, I saw the carpet runner blaze up the stairs like a yellow tongue. I ran from it, flying past the glowing stair rails. Brent stumbled into Mom's room. She held his arm with one hand and pointed to the window with the other. She turned to me, "This way, Lil," she called.

"Where's Ernest? I have to find Ernest!" I cried.

"There's no time, Ernest will save himself. *Climb out the window*," Mom gasped. "Go, go, Lily, come on, hurry!"

Heather was next, then Brent, all of us scrambling out Mom's bedroom window onto the slippery back porch roof. She took off her long robe, and turned it into a rope to shorten the distance to the ground. One by one we shimmied down its velvet cloth to jump to the earth twelve feet below. When Heather climbed down, there were three of us holding onto the robe above. Then I went, trusting Mom and Brent's strength. Brent decided he could shimmy down the drainpipe, but it came loose sending him into a snowbank, just feet from the dead Christmas tree that had been there for months.

Before she leapt, Mom sent her robe down to us. It floated, a dark green angel with its arms spread like wings. Heather, Brent and I grabbed it and tried to make an instant trampoline to break her fall. Our efforts resulted in a heap of us on the ground but Mom was unscathed.

Still, there was no sound, no snapping, popping noises or smoke escaping onto the street. The windows of the house were like jack o'lantern eyes watching while I opened the back door to let the cat out in case he was downstairs. I turned away, following Heather and running as fast as I could to the sleeping neighbor's house down the street. We flew across crunchy snowbanks and through the fir trees. At the road, Heather and I went left and Mom and Brent ran right.

We could hear Mom clanging away at the cowbell of the Kleinholz's place as we made our own noise, yelling, banging and ringing at the Horner's door. Lights went on inside and time slowed down as we watched Mr. Horner scuffing his way through the living room to see who was making the racket. At the same time, Mom and Brent managed to wake up the Kleinholzes.

Calmly, as if he did it every day, Mr. Horner called the fire department. Almost immediately, we heard the familiar horn bleating like a sick cow in the hills, 1-3-3-2, signaling where the firemen should go. We knew people would soon be scrambling out of their beds ready to help.

It was only minutes before the Kleinholzes and Mom and Brent came over to the Horner's. Mom and Brent were bundled up in blankets and borrowed galoshes; the Kleinholzes were wearing their night clothes beneath their parkas. We all watched from the safety of the living room as the fire escaped from my bedroom window and climbed the wall up to the shingles of the rooftop. There was a boom like a roadside bomb as the back porch blew up. The propane tank must have exploded. I shivered with gratitude that we had escaped in time. With the porch went the ice cream maker, the freezer and the pantry, but not us.

I went to the door and called into the night, "Ernest!"

My mother yanked me back indoors. "Try not to worry about Ernest," she said.

"It's only a dumb cat," Brent added. "They have nine lives."

"That's a myth," I cried, feeling all the more afraid. I rocked back and forth, angsting about my dear yellow buddy.

The flames lit up Mom's face and her chin quivered, "Your poor father. It's probably for the best that he's not here to see this."

Why don't you call him? I thought, although I knew someone would. He was once a volunteer fireman himself. In a town the size of Purgatory, it was every man's obligation. Mom tugged at my sleeve and I retreated back into the Horner's house leaving Ernest to the night.

Soon we heard the sirens on Rural Road and wailing at the foot of the hill. It went on and on until we figured out that the trucks were unable to make it up the slippery grade. It was too late, anyway, our house was already becoming a trophy for the fire's rage.

It wasn't the first time that trucks couldn't make it up the hill, either. Five years ago the Horner's had a chimney fire and had to put it out for themselves. The winter's nasty ice and blowing snow often make roads impassable, but this night would be seared into our brains forever. It wasn't that the firefighters didn't try. Some of the volunteers scrambled up the hill on foot to join us, while others poured sand and broke nearby branches to give the tires more traction. But all that was in vain. By the time the first truck reached us, our house was showing its bones. The firefighters tried to protect all that was left, the barn and Grandmother Lillian's studio, spraying them with huge amounts of water, and then soaking the grounds around the house to stop what couldn't have happened in the first place. I mean, I doubt the fire could have spread over the snow banks.

The volunteers worked well into the night, long after the flames were out and a few stars had begun to appear, twinkling above the red glow of the emergency lights. We were in slow motion, in a surreal black and red landscape where sounds came and went, and grim faces, reflected my own. Too much was being taken to name.

I didn't think of my prom dress, or the scrapbooks I had made since I could cut and paste, or the dozens of paintings I had saved in the back of my closet. I didn't think about the quilt on my bed with its pieces of my first dresses and jeans or the tapes and the books, the clothes I loved or the photograph albums Grandmother Lillian had saved from the beginning of time and left to me for safe keeping. I kept thinking about Ernest. He'd had a tough beginning. Was this his end?

I had found him two years ago, whining and scrawny, huddled by some garbage pails alongside the fudge shop downtown. I considered calling him Fudge but his front paws each had six toes like the famous Hemingway cats of Key Largo. So, Ernest came to mind, and somehow the silly name suited him best. Those huge paws on his skinny orange legs loomed white and clumsy. Homely things are easy for me to love, especially when no one claims them. Ernest and I seemed to have an affinity for one another. I understood he was a nervous little critter and you had to be considerate around him. A slammed door would have him off all fours heading for a shelf or a mantle or any high place. He only ate the food I offered and was discriminating about people. For example, when Brent entered the room, Ernest vacated. My unconscious excuse for a brother couldn't have cared less about what happened to Ernest; they never liked one another.

We ended up spending the rest of the night at the Horner's. They had two extra bedrooms because their kids, Amelia and Steven, had grown up and left. I think I was in Amelia Horner's bed. My kid sister Heather was in its twin. The sheets were girlie-girlie pretty. They had tiny yellow roses on them. The wallpaper had more sprigs of yellow roses in lacey rows. I lay inside the freshness of the sheets and looked at a spidery brown stain on the ceiling. No house is perfect, I thought. Amelia probably wasn't perfect, either, no matter how pretty she was. She had married her high school boyfriend and had a baby the same year she graduated from high school. Her mother and father cried about it a lot over tea in our kitchen, but now they are in love with little Henry. I saw him at Christmas. He had a bowling ball head. Perfectly round with two dark eyes and a little mouth that seemed to have come with a plug.

I turned to Heather. "Heather, you awake?" I asked.

"Of course I'm awake, who could sleep?" She was bundled up in her covers like a sausage in a bun. "I can't get warm," she said.

"I want to go out and find Ernest."

"Oh don't worry, he's watching from a tree somewhere. You can't find him now. Is that all you can think about? Geez."

As usual, I thought Heather could be so mean, a typical middle child, stubborn and self-centered. Lately I wondered if we were from the same gene pool.

Lying in bed listening to the drone of trucks and people, I tried not to swallow the fear that was caught in my throat. It felt wrong to have left the scene of the accident, to be in a strange bed trying to sleep while the real world was going on outside.

"What are you thinking about?" I asked.

"I am thinking that the cow jumped over the moon and the little dog laughed to see such a sight while that bitch ran away with the spoon. What the fuck do you think I am thinking about? My feet are frozen. We're homeless. We have no clothes, no father to give a damn. No food. No nothing. Now what are we going to do? Life sucks."

"At least we're alive."

"Sure, lucky us."

She was not available. I thought about the roses on the wall and decided that when I had a house of my own, I would put wallpaper with yellow roses in my bedroom, too.

"Doesn't it seem strange to you that we are sleeping with the Horners when Dad murdered their dog?" Heather asked.

"He didn't *murder* their dog, it was an accident."

"Mom says he did," she claimed.

"He didn't. It was awful. He felt terrible."

"But don't you think Amelia must hate us still."

"No. I don't.

It had been mid-December, and the roads were frozen and white with driveways obscured by drifting snow, not the best conditions for driving or wild things. We were coming back from my afterschool art club. Dad was in good spirits, probably because he had stopped at the inn before he picked me up. He was singing along with John Lennon, *Imagine there's no Heaven, It's easy if you try...yi...yi....* Then he interrupted himself, "A fucking nobody wasted one of the best musicians in the world. So fucking sick," he said, shaking his head, "A nutcase."

My breath stopped when I realized he had tears in his eyes. I had never seen him cry.

"I still can't believe it," he said. "He was only forty for God's sa...." Then he grabbed the wheel and shouted, "Whoa!" The car hit something as we swerved to the left, our headlights buried in a snowbank. "Jesus Christ. Jesus," Dad gasped, pulling open his door and reaching for something in the snow. I got out and saw Corker, the Horner's pup, his furry feet jerking and belly pulsing, fighting for life until he became still; his eyes frozen open and his tongue hanging out.

"Daddy, Daddy," I cried, "It's Corker! Do something!"

He did all he could do. He took off his coat and wrapped the limp little body in it. "It's too late, Sweetheart. I'm afraid he's gone."

Then the next horrible thing happened. We had to bring him to the door. Mr. and Mrs. Horner greeted us with smiles and asked us to come in. They had no idea it was Corker that we had in our arms.

Dad opened his coat and showed them what was inside. "He must have escaped when I brought the groceries in," Irene moaned. "Oh, Sweet Lord!"

Mr. Horner peered down at the small bundle. "Corker, hey, wake up little fella," he said, just as Amelia and Steven came in to see what was going on. Amelia started screaming, "Corker, Corker!"

Dad apologized as best he could. "I never saw it coming. He came out of nowhere. I am so sorry. I don't know what to do." His face was splotchy; his red eyes could only stare at the dead dog.

We stood there, a bundle of misery, wishing for magic. If only we had a button that could have taken us back in time, just ten minutes earlier.

Now I might have to say good-bye to Ernest, I thought. Maybe Heather was right, Amelia might feel we had it coming.

Even though Heather and I were only in bed a few hours, it was a long night. Wet smoke permeated the air, a revolving red light kept playing on the walls. Muffled sounds crept up the stairs. Now and then I started crying over Ernest. Heather didn't cry. She didn't sleep either. I caught her looking out the window at the smoldering ruin, hoping, I suppose, that it was all a bad dream. She wouldn't say that, of course.

To me it looked like death. Grandmother Lillian's death. What had been her history book, gone. Dad used to call his mother a true matriarch, a creation unto herself, and she was, almost to the very end. She never let a day go by without earrings, lipstick, something "sinful" to eat, a magical moment and one good thought.

As her first grandchild and namesake, I knew our closeness was special. And although I was taught to refer to her always as Grandmother Lillian, a mouthful for a little girl, it never was too formal to make her any less mine. She was not only my adoring and adored grandmother; she was a naturalist, a philosopher, a reader and painter, too. Dad spent years transforming the barn's tack room into a studio for her, just to say thank you for being his mother. I loved that place where northern light flowed through the carefully placed windows and barn planks covered the floors. Large rusty nails protruded from the high beams to hold empty frames while the rough-hewn walls provided backdrops for works in progress. Not only did Dad make Grandma happy, he made me even happier.

Grandmother Lillian was drawn daily to the art "shack" and amidst the splattered smocks and aborted beginnings, the crusty containers and dried out brushes, I shared her sacred space, honored to paint at her side and absorb her energy as we worked. When we worked. Some days she just wanted to think out loud. Some days we would explore illustrated books or she would read to me from the The Art Spirit by Robert Henri.

She had strong opinions about everything and did not believe in accidents. "Everything in life is connected to everything else," she would say. "There are no accidents."

I wondered what she would call this fire.

Then I remembered how she thought the unexpected should be treated as a gift. "If a brush should stiffen, make it a pointer or use it to carve into your paint. If water spills on your work, allow it to add movement. Perfection is not superior to spontaneity. "

And, although she was flexible, she had plenty of rules. "Place your darkest darks next to your lightest lights. Always move your colors from warm to cool. Consider every edge, no two should be the same."

She knew I loved rules and she was sure to deliver. I was her sponge, soaking up all the wisdom she offered.

I miss her, I thought, as I tried to shut out the annoying red lights moving across the walls.

How could I have not known she was leaving so soon? It was obvious. Her bones were as transparent as milk glass, when she warned me she would be graduating soon. "I am tired, now," she explained, "but you'll understand when it's your time."

I longed for my four-poster bed, the one Grandmother Lillian had given me when she was moved downstairs. I wanted to curl up in the lavender folds of its downy comforter and hide. At least she didn't have to see this cruel end.

When morning finally broke, we migrated to Irene Horner's cozy kitchen. Always the friendly neighbor, she was pouring watered down orange juice from a slim carafe into long glasses that glowed like promises on her table. Through her windows, we watched the sun lift, bringing with it a ridiculously blue sky. I couldn't sit, couldn't eat and couldn't speak. Mrs. Horner seemed to understand as she filled the space with chatter about how soon the birds would return and rebuild their nests, and more about nature teaching us all we ever needed to know.

"One thing we can always count on is that the robins return by the end of April. Why, when I was a little girl we could set the clock by the robin's return..." Mrs. Horner chatted. She was trying hard.

No words could blot out what lay on the other side of the crisp white café curtains, the smoking black punishment with its debris all over the road. The phone kept ringing and Mrs. Horner took on the role of official reporter. I believe she enjoyed it. *Yes, the children are safe, they're with us and just fine....No, no one knows how it started, but they will need everything—just everything, bless their hearts. No. Jon is still away.* I heard her say that one, again and again.

Mrs. Horner was one of those buxom women that look like everyone's great aunt. I had always liked her. I saw her as a remnant of the way women used to be and I was never going to become, because women don't have to get dowdy anymore. She canned and froze the vegetables from her garden and was perfectly at home wearing her husband's shirts and those elastic-waisted pants, the ones that stretch to accommodate an ever-expanding middle. She was homey.

Mr. Horner was a square quiet man; he seemed to be enjoying flipping the pancakes and turning the bacon while Mrs. Horner talked on the phone. They were a team, like one person split into two parts. It didn't take words for them to know what the other wanted. They moved like well-practiced dancers, unperturbed and cheery despite the circumstances.

Brent did not look out the window. He seemed preoccupied with the crispy bacon that appeared before him. I couldn't know what he was thinking or if he was thinking at all. You would have to be a mind-reader. He was like so many other ninth grade boys, non-verbal and pouty—especially around girls—even his sisters. A. Brent Woodhouse my folks had named him. The A was for Atticus, a name we were sworn not to reveal. Mom said Atticus was a handsome, gentle leader in the days when Constantinople was the center of the world. She claimed it was a family name, but Brent found small consolation in that fact and was only grateful he hadn't been saddled with Achilles or Aristotle. He also hated his other two names, the middle one, Brent, my Mother's maiden name, was sometimes converted to Bent, just as his last was often transformed to *Outhouse.* At school he was known as Woody, but that didn't work for him either. "Hey, Woody! Got one on?" the boys would call after him as he walked down the halls.

Our great house was almost as old as Vermont. After five generations of Woodhouse men increased its size from a log cabin to a virtual mansion, its total destruction seemed impossible. Brent, the shaggy-haired misery of a human, smoldering over his breakfast plate, was no longer the inheritor of anything more than a barn and a hillside.

I noticed how Mrs. Horner ignored Heather's new blue-black hair, and the metal in her nose and eyebrow. She fussed over her appetite instead. "Now the best thing to do, Heather dear, is eat a good breakfast and then consider taking a nap before the morning is through. I am sure you didn't sleep much last night."

Heather muttered something, and mashed her pancakes into her plate. She moved them from one side to the other and then upside down. It seemed impossible for her to pick the fork up and put the food in her mouth. I understood.

Brent set up his bacon strips like a defense line, then picked them up with his fingers and stuffed the whole batch into his mouth. He could be such an animal.

The volunteer firemen came in and out, filling their coffee cups and grabbing one more of Mrs. Kleinholz's homemade cinnamon buns, the ones she'd made in the middle of the night.

Mrs. Kleinholz was still hanging around the house when Ted Costa, our fire chief, came in for a break.

She was just making friendly conversation. "You know my family watched that house grow and thought it was indestructible. I grew up hearin' stories of how it became a showcase in Vermont. My word, money grew on trees for that old codger, Andrew! Yes indeed. The age of invention was just made for him. He had every luxury that came available. The tub with gold feet that got itself settled upstairs was downright legend. Even the barn grew to be a story for those who built it. It was a fortress of the same stone as was used to build fences 'round heah. Must have been fifty years ago that the elms were planted along the dirt road leadin' to the house, 'though they died with that awful disease. Whole forests were cut down to clear the fields and build enough wings to the house we thought it might take flight. Ayah, that old relic should 'ave lasted foreveh. Makes me want to do oveh the wirin' in our place, I can tell you that."

Ted Costa said, "I don't think it was the wiring, Martha."

Looking at the ruins, I wondered how anyone could possibly know what caused the fire.

2

After breakfast we kids needed to go outside. Even though the firemen and police wouldn't let us go near the smoldering ruins, we wanted to stand witness. Since we were still in our pajamas Mrs. Horner found odd things for us to put on—sweatpants, boots, a ski cap, a silk scarf. I was thinking we looked like refugees when it dawned on me that was exactly what we were.

While I hunted along the edge of the woods calling for Ernest, I couldn't help but face what was left of the house. A sick wet smell hovered in the air. Drops were plopping from the roof of the barn. For the first time I thought it fortunate that we didn't have one of those classic Vermont barns, the kind that are attached to the farmhouse. I had never liked having to shovel my way to the horses on a snowy morning. But now I was grateful that it stood a safe distance from the house.

The day was warm for March. How strange that the spring thaw started twenty-four hours later than it might have. Inside the barn, I could see our car's headlights reflecting the sunlight. They looked startled and surprisingly clean, peering out from beyond the huge barn doors which the firemen must have opened.

In the rubble I recognized a fragment of Grandmother Lillian's mahogany loveseat. It used to sit at the foot of her bed. Some iron pots and pans were tucked inside one another in a neat arrangement where our kitchen may have stood. Corpses of dolls with their body parts melded together lay near Brent's semi-buried collection of metal trucks. Our antique sewing machine had melted down to an abstract shape and some picture albums with lifetimes of photographs looked no different than decaying leaves.

The fire also destroyed the portrait of Grandfather Sheldon Woodhouse in its gilded frame. He would no longer stare anyone down. A black film was all that remained of his aristocratic face. It struck me that I would never see that face again, the last vestige of our family's distinguished moment in time. I thought about my banished father, Sheldon's only son, who should have been called to the scene of the fire right away. The house was still his family home and it was *his* family's dust that went with the walls and the hand-me-downs. He was staying near enough by that he could have been there in no time.

Then again, I had been waiting for him to come home from the day he left and a year had already passed. The one good thing about his leaving was that I didn't have to listen to the fights that erupted almost daily. Mom called their separation a *time out for healing*. I certainly noticed that she seemed more in control and more relaxed with him gone. Heather acted much angrier than I felt, but she was often angry. I thought she used their problems to justify her anti-the-universe self.

Brent was a squall on the horizon. You could see it growing, but not smell it, hear it, or know its depth. If I were to describe Brent in a word, I guess I would have called him a *secret*, a precious secret, yes, but a secret known only to himself. My mother always loved him best. She'd never have said so, but I knew. He was her baby. When he was little she would sit with him stroking his pale skin and weaving his long fingers through hers, telling him that his hands were meant for flutes and piano keys. I can still picture the tiny miracle of him wrapped in her cashmere shawl, his yellow-tipped head against her breast. She would sing and rock him to sleep in front of the fireplace. He needed special attention because he had asthma back then.

With time, it seemed to go away. But asthma wasn't the only thing that threatened him. She tried to block his ears from my father's occasional rages. Brent was Mom's shield as much as she was his savior.

Dad had been mean to Brent from time to time. I remember when Brent was little and attached to a doll he had found abandoned in the shed; he bathed it, dressed it, took it to bed with him and named it Willy. My father took it away from him, saying, "Willy is going to a nice farm in the country."

Mom was wiping Brent's tears and really fuming, "What is wrong with you?" she scolded Dad. "You know he loves that doll?"

"You want him to turn into a fairy?" he shouted back. "If that's what you want, why don't you get the girls' ballet costumes out and give him their tutus, for God's sake! What's the matter with you? We finally get ourselves a son, let's let him become a man."

I couldn't understand why he was so angry. It wasn't as if Mom had done something awful. Don't boys become fathers? Wasn't it a good sign that Brent loved a doll? I mean, exploding over a toy was just weird. But that was the whole problem with Dad, we never knew what was going to make him pop-off. Usually he was madder at Mom than the rest of us, but that didn't help.

My mother has a way of becoming very quiet when things go wrong. But she's not weak. She's strong. Not someone I want to argue with. Once you say the wrong thing she is likely to bring it up over and over again, at least that's what Dad and Heather say. I make a point of not crossing her. She has enough to deal with.

Mom has always been different with Heather than with me. Of course, I don't give her a hard time and my sister can't seem to help herself. Mom says *up*, Heather says *down*. It's just their way. I thought Mom would die last week when Heather took her allowance and dyed her honey-colored hair black. "Lil, why don't you tell her it looks just awful?" she asked.

I knew better. The best thing to do with Heather was to pretend not to notice. Even Mrs. Horner seemed to know that.

When Dad showed up, late in the day after the fire, Mom walked over to meet him and I saw him wrap her in his arms and her body collapse into his. It was the first time she had really let go and sobbed. He may have cried, too. At least, I thought he was crying as I watched them wander around what was once his family's castle. The two of them walked around and around the remains, pointing, leaning into one another, stopping to blow their noses. A gust caught Mom's long blond hair and he gathered it in his hand, took off his hat and put it on her head, tucking her hair inside.

He was wearing his navy blue down vest and the brown and blue plaid wool work shirt that I gave him for Christmas. I realized all his clothes were saved, while all of ours were gone. He looked so much better than any of us felt. Mom always said his good looks were part of his charm, but he didn't seem to know it. He was at least six foot three with the square shoulders of a swimmer. I was proud of the sight of him, the furry brows, his strong nose with a distinctive hook that made him look aristocratic. His new beard was okay, but no one wants their parents to change too much.

With our house lying like a crime scene across the road, we needed to get away as quickly as possible. I hated the way its presence pulled me like a magnet and that I kept searching for anything in its dark face that had color or a recognizable shape. We were told to stay away, stand back from the yellow tapes around the remains.

After a few days with the Horners, we moved into two rooms in the guest house in town. It was right next to the Quick-Stop Market and a long walking distance to school. Our celebrity was an awesome thing. People from all over

Windsor County brought us stuff. Most of it was too big, too ugly, or too small for us, but Mom told us to thank everyone and anyone who showed up. *Charity is a beautiful thing,* she said. Honestly, so much came our way we had to hide the piles in the Inn's basement and then take it to the Good Will in Springfield at night, far enough away so no one noticed or thought us ungrateful.

I did find a cool white ski jacket in one of the black plastic bags that arrived anonymously. It looked like it had never been worn and fit me like a glove. I kept the gifts from my girlfriends because they each gave me something blue. They knew I wore mostly blue. But didn't know I loved blue because Harry Weaver, back in eighth grade, had told me I had pretty blue eyes and I should always wear blue. Maggie gave me a blue sweater, Carrie a pair of blue mittens and a blue ski cap. Trish gave me her blue flannel peejays.

We were seniors at the centralized high school. Our school felt huge to most of us when we came together in tenth grade, but it didn't take long to find those who would become our friends and create a safety zone within the noisy halls. We had classes together, ate together and looked at boys together. We also shared a moment in history together.

Our entire school watched the lift-off of the space shuttle Challenger. Seared into my mind was how innocently we carried our journals into the common areas, one class after another, giggling and snorting to watch the launch. One of the astronauts, Christa, had visited our school before she left because she was friends with Dr. Lydell, who had applied to be an astronaut, too. She was so excited, all smiles and confidence, and so much like other teachers we knew, particularly our English teacher, Mrs. Anderson.

"Today we are going to write history as it happens..." Mrs. Anderson began.

By the time the countdown began, the whole school was tuned in. The kids throughout the school shouted, 10-9-8-7-6-5-4-3-2-1- *Blast off!* My voice was part of that. Then the Challenger soared, the crowd in Houston cheered and so did we until, 73 seconds later, the ship seemed to explode like a bad firecracker, falling in a lot of directions at once.

Most of us knew that something had gone very wrong, that its parts were headed down and none were going up, and still we did not believe what we were witnessing. Dr. Wolfe hugged himself; Mrs. Anderson covered her face and turned away from the monitor. I was waiting to see parachutes or floating devices appear to return the astronauts to earth.

"They'll be all right, won't they, Dr. Wolfe?" I asked. Dr. Wolfe shook his head no, but did not speak. His jaw was locked, tucked as far into his neck as it could go; his lips sewn in a fine line.

I guess that's how it is with disaster. We can't really look it in the eye, even when it's undeniable—our house, for example, with its roots exposed and gaping wounds. It was something I wanted to avoid, an embarrassment, something I wished was plowed under, but remained raw as a wreck on the highway for a long time, a dark reminder of how suddenly things can change.

Ours wasn't the first fire in town that anyone had called mysterious. There had been the fire near the tennis courts, in a garbage can filled with papers and grasses. Kids said it was set on purpose, but I thought it was an accident, just some kids looking to warm their hands. It was, at worst, a prank and it didn't do any more damage than let the middle school out early.

Then there was the fire near Tanner's market in Grafton igniting oil cans, twigs, dead leaves and newspapers thrown in the parking lot's dumpster. Maybe someone threw a lit cigarette on it, who knows? But the thing was, it could have set the pumps on fire and blown up the cars in the parking lot and that might have grown into a fire that burned the whole village down. Maybe even the hillsides. The Grafton fire happened within eyeshot of Griffith's old Farmhouse where Dad lived, just yards from Tanner's. At the time he said he *would* choose a village with a pyromaniac living next door

I looked for Ernest for weeks following the fire, even asked the fire inspectors to look for a carcass and they did. No bones were found in the process, no kerosene or suspicious fire starters either. Nevertheless, the newspapers listed the cat as a casualty and the fire's cause as *unknown.*

The yellow tape outlining our house and the adjacent property remained, making it inaccessible to the curious public. It would stay there until criminal intent was ruled out and the search for the cause completed. The air still smelled like old wet wood but the inspectors had been on the job since the fire stopped smoking.

It was a balmy week for March, not even near freezing when the inspector met with us at the inn.

"Looks like the house went up pretty quick once the fire got started. We think it mightta started in the TV room," he said. "In the couch, most likely. You smoke Mrs. Woodhouse?" he asked. "Could have been matches or a cigarette," he added. He was writing things down on a pad as he read from a list of questions.

"No. No, I don't," Mom answered. "We have a smoke free house."

He didn't point out the irony of her comment.

"Anyone visiting the day of the fire? Sleeping in that room?"

"No. We were all in bed upstairs when the fire broke out."

"Mr. Woodhouse, Jon, was he here at that time?"

Mom made a fist and tapped her knuckles on the table. "No. He was not."

"I see. So it was just you and the kids. It looks like the fire mightta started in the couch."

"It's a daybed," Mom corrected.

"Looks like it ignited the curtains, they ignited the walls and the old window casings. Then spread to the rafters and the rugs and ran through the first floor and up the stairs."

"It was Lily who saw it first. She saw it before it reached the upstairs and woke us up."

"Is that so?" he asked, and turned to me.

"What exactly did you see Lily?" he asked.

I felt very important recounting the story with the inspector treating me as an adult. He was big and in charge and I was glad he was there. He seemed like a hero and we needed a hero.

When he left, Mom sat down at the kitchen table and put her head in her hands. "This is so frustrating, with this *Mr. I. M. Important* running the show, things will never get settled." Mom did not like him. She called him *presumptuous.* "I don't appreciate his insinuations, either," she added. "Isn't it bad enough our house is gone and I don't know where we will go, or how I'll manage?" she complained. "It's a good thing we have a bank account. What would others do if their insurance money was tied up by such ridiculous suspicions?"

I watched Mom's every move after that, she was just holding on, distracted, and not her ordinary self. Sometimes she would be standing around looking as if she didn't know where she was. When we were in the grocery store and Mr. Caldwell said something nice to her, like, *we are so sorry,* and when pizzas arrived at the inn and she didn't know who to thank, she cried. She cried because the barn was still standing and our bicycles and lawn furniture had survived. She cried when she found Dad's black and red check hunting jacket hanging on a hook. I saw her rub her face in its sleeve.

The barn still had some hay left over from better days when we had the horses. It was very old dry hay and would have gone up like a torch with so much as a spark. It was probably a good thing that ten months ago, Mom had sent the horses to live elsewhere. No matter how much she nagged and threatened to take the horses off our hands, neither Heather nor I rose to the responsibility it required to keep them groomed, fed, and exercised.

Meg Flanders, my American Saddlebred Pinto, went to live in South Woodstock, at the private school on the edge of town and Wiley, a russet quarter horse, went to a horse farm outside Rutland. The pinto's first owner's thought she was a pony when Dad bought her for me, but when she grew to over 5'6" at the withers; we knew she was no pony. Meg is still going strong, happily toting disabled kids on her back and thriving in her new role. I didn't deserve her.

Heather has never forgiven Mom for taking the horses. But if I were to be honest, both Heather and I had ignored her warnings; we didn't believe that she was serious until it was too late. Heather still believes Mom did it for spite, just to make us more miserable than we already were.

3

As I said, no one wants their parents to change too much, but I knew Dad *had* to change to return to the family. I heard Mom say it plain and clear. "Jon, there is only one way back, and that is clean and sober. You must be willing to change." She was right. It was his drinking that led to all the arguments and made him say and do things he'd never do otherwise.

Dad didn't push himself on us, but he came to the inn for dinner a lot after the fire, and that meant he made long trips to and from Grafton just to be with us. "You know," he said, to Mom, "Ol' man Clarendon has a place where he thinks you might be comfortable. It's a chalet near the slopes. Want to take a look?"

Well, of course we all did. Living at the inn was no one's idea of feeling good. The walls were paper thin, we had only one bathroom, and the wood trimmings were splintered and old. The place was a matchbox.

Within a few days we were in the glass chalet, a modern, gleaming A-Frame, furnished in ski country glitz. It had large posters of skiers, ski ropes for balusters, a living room swing with gondola seats and all in all it was fun. The only old things that could be found were a pair of wooden skis that crisscrossed over the front doors. "I hate this phony shit," Heather announced upon entering the living room.

The rest of us liked the heated floors in the bathroom, the big white kitchen and the views of the slopes. What Mom liked most was the absence of evidence that other people had been there in the past. It felt like a beginning.

I could almost hear Brent's sigh of relief when we sat down for our first meal and no one was watching us from another table and no waitress waiting to ask him, "Is everything okay, Sweetie?"

One night, about a week after we moved in, Dad came for dinner and the table felt right with him at its head and Mom directly across. Our conversation went way beyond school, movies and weather. Dad began talking about his drinking problem and how he knew it affected all of us. Brent sank in his seat, but Heather leaned in. "It's *your* problem, Dad, not ours," she said.

I think that was the opening Mom and Dad were waiting for. "Drinking is a family problem," Dad said, and Mom agreed. They both began to sell us on Al-a-Teen. Heather and Brent had no trouble saying no. Heather actually sneered in her typically obnoxious way. "Are you kidding me? Al-a-Teen is just another mind-control middle class manipulation. People need to think for themselves. If Dad needs to drink then he is no different than most of the rest of the world. Let him drink. He would rather be in la-la land than here and who could blame him?"

My stomach turned and Mom's eyes rolled. Dad's head shook in a woe-is-me fashion and sighed. Brent whined that he didn't want to talk about his family problems with a bunch of people he didn't know.

The truth was, Brent wasn't talking much to anybody. Mom tried to convince him the group was about learning to take responsibility for his own life, being his own person, within his family. She didn't get that Brent was more about being removed altogether than becoming more responsible; that her son was not only stubborn but had drawn himself in like a box turtle. Didn't she know turtles do not grow up to become swans no matter how hard they stretch their necks? I hated the whole idea of group therapy myself, but someone had to go, we had to support Mom and

Dad. So, as the oldest and most responsible child I decided to be that person.

It was yet another rainy spring night. Sloppy ruts in the road made any outing a challenge. Mud season in Vermont should really be called suicide season. Just when you're thinking daffodils and warm air, the rain takes over and then Canada dumps a cold front on you that's worse than mid-winter. Frustration and depression set in. If you can get away, Florida or any tropical island calls, and those who can, answer.

Dad picked us up in the pick-up, which was no longer white but a dripping brown creature that looked like it had been salvaged from a riverbed. He had named it Mavis after a woman in town who could only be called a survivor, a derelict of a soul, who still marched on, attending every town meeting and making herself known. Mavis, the truck, gave you a heck of a ride, especially in the back seat where I bounced all the way to East Chester.

We went to what should have been called the Last Gasp Methodist Church. Dad was sure it had more alcoholics visiting mid-week than visitors on any given Sunday. Grace Methodist was a traditional country church with a white steeple and the typical Chester fieldstone foundation. From the vestry, we walked down a hallway leading to the Sunday School rooms. Children's work covered the bulletin boards. Some of it was mimeographed coloring book pages of halved apples with cores exposed like stars, a metaphor for the star over Bethlehem. Square hand-cut letters of fading poster paper defined the display. GOD PROMISES NEW LIFE. I figured this referred to the seeds that would be sown from the apples after they fell from the tree. Also on the wall was a colorful picture of a long-haired, blonde, blue-eyed Jesus sitting on a rock with his arms outstretched and saying, "Suffer the little children to come unto Me, for such is the Kingdom of Heaven." I wished for a second I was one of those children and someone or something could cure the soreness in my gut. It would be wonderful if Jesus came back in my lifetime, that is, if there ever truly was a Jesus.

Mom tucked her chin in her collar and stuck her hands in her pockets as she left me and walked downstairs to the lower level. I was left outside the empty Al-a-Teen room looking for the teen version of the same stuff she was going to hear. "You just relax and go with it," Dad said, as he turned into another meeting room across the hall.

I waited, leaning against the white plaster wall outside the brightly lit space. Finally, a group of kids arrived and went inside to sit around the large round table. They took their seats and quietly waited for a leader. When I entered the room, they all looked at me expectantly, like maybe I was to lead them. Uh-oh, I thought, this is not my comfort zone. Not one of the six or seven kids appeared any smarter than I, and I couldn't help but wonder how a meeting such as this could make any difference in my life. I seriously doubted that this bunch of ordinary kids could know what I didn't. I wanted to leave, go home, go anywhere else, when a girl tapped my elbow and said, "Hi, I'm Nancy."

I smiled. "Lily," I said.

"This your first time?" she asked.

"Yeah," I said, wondering if *she* was the leader. But no one in the room was looking at her. I figured this might be her first night, too.

"Mind if I sit next to you?"

She was around my age, maybe younger, because she still had braces on her teeth. They were the worst kind, huge blue metal clamps that left no room for popcorn or kisses. I was grateful I didn't need such miserable contraptions and relieved to have her next to me, blue teeth or not.

A young guy eventually arrived to lead the group. He couldn't have been more than sixteen; he still had pimples, no beard to speak of and a shape lost to loose fitting sweats. He swore us to secrecy and then asked us to introduce ourselves. We were seated in a circle and I realized I would be expected to speak right after Nancy. I practiced in my head. *Hi my name is Lily and I am the daughter of an alcoholic.* Oh how I didn't want to be there. Heather was probably munching on pretzels and watching *The Dating Game.* The first boy told how his father had woken him in the middle of the night when he peed in his bed. Another boy told how his mother had walked into the high school and started screaming that he had stolen her car when in reality she had forgotten where she had parked it the night before. My situation was nowhere nearly as bad as the seven other kids'. Some of them were slapped around, some living with strangers, some crying as they spoke and some very angry. When it was my turn, just saying I was the daughter of an alcoholic sounded awful, disloyal, untrue and exaggerated. I had no stories to tell.

After I sat back down, I heard laughter coming from my father's meeting on the opposite side of the hall, along with clapping and cheering. I wished I could be with them, the troublemakers, instead of in this miserable place where unhappiness and blame were running the show. We were working on a step of some sort. I listened as again and again we were told that we had to accept the fact that alcoholism is a disease.

We finally took a break, and Nancy hung out with me the whole time. She was real nice, trying to help make me feel comfortable without asking personal questions. We lived just far enough away from one another that our paths hadn't crossed. We bought Cokes from the vending machine at the end of the hall. It was then the door to the happy room opened and a cancerous cloud followed a ghost of a man limping toward the men's room.

"Geez," I said, waving my thumb toward the AA meeting's room. "A person would need an inhaler just to sit in there."

"Like, better here than in a bar or on a bench somewhere," she said. "That was my scene. I used to wait outside bars until my mother was, like, totally smashed and then I got to ride hell-bent for home with her, holding my breath the whole way. That was before I learned to say no. Now she drinks at home and alone."

I told her I didn't think my father's drinking was that bad, but my mother was always pissed off at him if he was late or loud or a little high. "She's the reason we're here."

"You're lucky to have both your parents willing to get well." Nancy said.

"My mother isn't sick, but if she starts hanging out here, it won't take long. Sitting in a fog of nicotine can't be that good for you," I said, remembering the black lungs of smokers Dr. Lydell brought to science class to compare to pink healthy ones.

"How come the church lets people smoke in their holy temple?" I asked.

Nancy shrugged. "The church probably wants them to come inside. Like, they're into healing."

"Well smoke isn't going to get them well. Anyway, all these people aren't really sick. I'm not. My mother's not."

"We're all sick. Like, anyone living with an alcoholic is sick," she said.

After the meeting, Mom, Dad and I had coffee at the Chester Diner. When they asked me what I'd learned, I said I learned that alcoholics have more fun than the rest of us.

The work on what was to become our new house started shortly after that. Dad showed up early in the mornings with treasures from The Home Station piled in the back of the truck. He had taken a night manager's job with the store that gave him discounts on materials and plenty of daylight hours to work on our place. He liked his job well-enough, claimed its reward was never having to put a *noose* around his neck again, "No more suits or starched shirts or shoes that need shining!" he said. According to him, the life of the law was far less desirable than managing a store that was neither corrupt nor compromising.

Since his legal practice had ended three years ago, he had wanted to find a job that didn't follow him home or ask more than he wanted to give. I never knew the whole story of what happened with my father and the Clarendons, but I think he was charged with some infraction of the law and it cost him his license.

The Clarendons were the other voices of Purgatory's history, what with their entire lives spent in the village and family roots that traveled as far back as the Woodhouse's.

Grandpa Sheldon Woodhouse and Howard Clarendon had been friends from the cradle. That may have been why the case against my father remained a secret. All I knew for sure, was that the outcome changed things in a big way around our house. Mom was nervous and angry most of the time and Dad began drowning himself in booze. I wasn't sure which came first.

Spring rains helped us plow what remained of the old house into the earth and soon the sun blessed the barn's steady transformation from an equine to human habitat. The whole family was obliged to work on it. Because it was a post and beam construction, we worked from the inside out. Where there had been horse stables there would be a living room, a kitchen and dining room. Grandmother Lillian's studio would stay the same except for a few skylights. What was once the hay bin would become a hobby room with a vaulted ceiling; the four bedrooms would line up behind the loft. The barn's original two-story stone walls would be sand blasted and freshly grouted to make them look like new.

Mom and Dad were totally involved with the re-creation. It was the first time in years that they had worked together without bickering and tension. Even Brent worked alongside without making excuses. His hair had grown long enough to put in a ponytail, and his shoulders were squaring while his voice got deeper by the day. He might have been becoming a little handsome.

I had taken an after-school job at the village's boutique, Pandora's Box, so I only worked on the house at the end of the day. But on Sundays, I was the grunt. *Lil, fetch me the hammer will you? Lil, go grab some Coke from the fridge. Lil, take the end of this beam like a good girl.* I didn't mind. It felt purposeful, the kind of work that had meaning and hope attached to it; a new *us* in the making. Unfortunately, the whole togetherness thing was too short-lived. An opened letter from the fire department was lying on the picnic table we were using in our future dining room. *Suspicious* was the word Mom underlined.

After the tools were put down and the tea kettle was singing on the Bunsen burner, Mom held the letter out to my sister, "You know, Heather, this report suggests the fire may have been started by human carelessness. You surely weren't smoking were you?"

Heather, overreacted. There was no build up; her fury just went ballistic. "There! You have finally said it! I knew all along you thought I started the fire! You blame me for the fire, just like you blame me for everything else around here! I told you I don't smoke. If I should ever smoke it is to forget I am from this crazy family where you can't breathe without someone peering down your neck. Why don't you ask Lily if *she* smokes? Why don't you ask your baby boy? I hate you. I hate you!"

"Heather, I..." Mom waved the letter her way, but Heather didn't even look at it.

"I know you hate me. I know you think I started the fire. I didn't start it. I can't make you believe me, but I didn't."

My father rose from the table and moved toward her. "Well, that's all you have to say then, Heather. You don't have to shout for us to hear."

"I am not shouting," she screamed, cartoon tears popping out of her eyes.

It was like all the poison inside her was trying to get out. Mom seemed cemented to the bench on the other side of the table. Brent stood up as if to leave and Dad said something like, "Now, Princess, calm down. You aren't being blamed, and you don't hate your mother."

"I am. I do," she blubbered.

Her eyes caught mine. *Snitch bitch. Did you tell Mom I smoked? You are such a freak. Miss Perfect. Miss I-Never-do-Anything-Wrong.*

"I'm outta here," Brent said, and disappeared.

I didn't say anything. She was out of control. I knew she pretended to smoke now and then, and had tried marijuana, but I was sure she hadn't started any fire. It was only the suggestion of the fire investigator that put the idea in Mom's head. Heather's hysterics were typical; her way of spoiling things, turning a nice evening into something mean and ugly. I wanted to believe we were doing well, that we were making some progress at being a family again.

But we were walking on unknown ground, and beginning to blame one another when things went wrong. I was just as guilty as anyone else. It was scary to think how a good safe knot had come unraveled so easily. Was it really just Dad's drinking that did it? Was I guilty too?

Don't we want to think someone or something is to blame? When Chernobyl's nuclear plant melted down, Mom was quick to say she knew it would happen. "Those people don't build things with integrity. Now, the whole world is contaminated."

"It's easier to blame the Soviets than accept the idea that we are all vulnerable to a nuclear accident. The good ol' USA built their plants on fault lines, for Christ's sake!" Dad argued.

"Oh what do I know?" she said. "You're the one with the degrees, I am just plain scared."

Giving up, handing over the authority to Dad had been Mom's way. I saw it now. In fact I was paying closer attention to everything they said.

He loved to tell us how he had picked her from the vine before anyone else had the chance. He said he fell for her the minute they met, when she was selling tomatoes at a roadside farm stand. A few words and he knew he had found the love of his life. "She was the hottest tomato of the bunch!" he'd say, and each time she'd laugh. He claimed he proposed to her right there, on the spot.

"Not a true story," she would say. "Your dad was a spoiled kid with a sports car and an attitude. He thought all he had to do was ask and he'd be given."

"That car was an old Mercedes with the bends," he'd laugh. "It was taking its last breath."

Work became synonymous with family. Nothing seemed as important as finishing the house, although we weren't exactly a team. Heather, Brent, and I made a point to stay out of each other's way. We did as we were told and asked few questions. We weren't warring but we weren't exactly making play dates. I was hoping Mom and Dad were doing better than we kids.

My feeling of disconnect was proved when my high school graduation took place in June with little fanfare. I believed the fire's cloud was to blame. We were still trying to find our way back to "normal."

We lived day to day. I made a point not to ask for anything, or hope for too much. I ignored my college applications until it was too late. But I didn't care very much, even considering the fact that the year ahead loomed wide and empty. I must have been content with nothingness and my life going nowhere.

4

The renovated barn was livable by the end of August. Dad moved in before we did. I was pretty happy about the whole thing. Brent wasn't talking and Heather, well, Heather was caught up in a gothic clique of one. We hardly communicated. At school she moved in different circles and pretended not to see me on the rare times we passed in the halls. It was fine with me. It seemed unlikely we were real sisters anyway. How could she be so tall and myself so average? Why were her eyes green and mine blue? She looked more and more like a young Morticia Addams and was happiest in front of the mirror with Cyndi Lauper screaming in the background that she just wanted to have fun.

Nancy and I, on the other hand, had become close. We bonded over time spent at meetings and our shared love of horses. She had two horses and deigned to let me ride the little gray mare, Bliss. I became friends almost instantly with that mass of sweetness. She would trot over to the fence as soon as I arrived, ready for her carrot or apple or whatever gift I had to offer. I suspected Bliss knew I lived in a barn, too. Whatever, we nuzzled easily and were comfortable together.

Nancy's mother was not an obvious drunk. I could see how much Nancy suffered, but she never said much about her, except to refer to *the disease* and *the battle.*

Nancy had a kind of steadfastness I could only hope for; she faced up to her problems, which were real and difficult.

Maybe that was why I wanted to talk to her about mine, even though they were small and self-centered.

I was afraid of something I couldn't see, and needed answers to questions I couldn't name. Sometimes I was jittery and imagined the smell of smoke. Other times, my stomach felt tight and hard. I would think about Grandmother Lillian and ask her advice, but she didn't answer. I wondered about prayer but that was like going to a foreign country.

I was operating in a strange margin the spring and summer of that tumultuous year. I put in more hours at the boutique while my friends busied themselves getting ready for college or falling in love. My closest high school friend, Carrie, the one who had been crowned Homecoming Queen at the Senior Prom, was madly in love with Drew Piersall, who just happened to be crowned King. They were a pretty couple. I wished I was as much in love as they were, but it was also sad because they would have to separate in the fall. They clung to each other constantly as if that would make the year ahead easier. My other close friend Trish was down with mononucleosis; my sister called it *the kissing disease*. She didn't look to me like she was doing any kissing. She was sleeping her summer away, thin as a rail, and worried she'd be too sick to start school.

I began to spend more and more time with a boy I met at Pearl's named Strange. I thought he might be one of those kids whose parents move to the *country* to save them from a big city's temptations. But after our talks and our time at the shop, I learned his parents were dead, and that he and his brother had come to Vermont to start life on their own.

"But why Vermont?" I wanted to know.

"It wasn't so much Vermont as the name of the town. I mean, Purgatory? What kind of bizzarro name is that? It sort of suited us. We joked that the walking dead probably came out at night."

"Do you know where the name came from?" I asked.

"The Catholic Church?"

"Nope. It came from a carving on rock at the fork of the two rivers. Some old boulder that rolled out of the ice age. The story goes that the name came before the village, a kind of hand-me-down from a trapper who marked his trading spot long before Vermont became Vermont."

"Very cool. How come they kept the name? This town doesn't have a Catholic in sight."

"According to my Grandmother Lillian, whose ancestors were among the first settlers, they probably thought the name was divinely planted. She said people were real superstitious back then."

Strange nodded. "They still are. Ever see anyone walking under a ladder?"

"Or choose a town because of its name?" I teased.

"Or like your name because it's weird?" he said.

From that moment, I no longer cared about his drooping pants, spiked hair, and pierced ears; instead, I admired his independence and how he seemed to choose being different. He was a lonely sort, and yet we had a great working relationship. He seemed unaffected even though everything about him looked the opposite. He liked black, wore chains, and sprayed his dyed hair until it was as stiff as porcupine quills.

But the major thing was, we talked about serious things. I told him my mom and dad were separated, and that while he was gone we had all climbed into worlds of our own and built little cocoons around ourselves. I added that we weren't the same family after the fire. Our house burning down was like losing the glue to our family. We were becoming new people.

He said that after his parents died, he became someone different. When his brother sold their house, and bought an

RV, they took off to settle somewhere else, traveling around *like nomads from nowhere* until they decided on Vermont.

"We're not together anymore, since I turned eighteen. I stay in town, now. It works better for me."

"But what will you do later on?" I asked. "When you're older?"

"Oh man, you sound like my brother. I'll figure it out when I'm ready. I mean, you don't know what you want to do yet, do you? Hey, there's no script out there waiting to explain your life—is there?" he asked. "Well,   I   always wanted to be a veterinarian, 'cause I love horses," I said.

"And I want to write the next great American novel, 'cause I love to read," he teased.

"What kind of novel?"

"I dunno," he said. "I think I might take to the road like Jack Kerouac or go to Alaska like Jack London."

Some afternoons Strange shared his poetry with me. I pretended not to hear the paper rattle, knowing he'd hate to look nervous. I always told him it was good, really good.

"I might put it to music," he'd said more than once. He had a guitar and was teaching himself chords when business was slow, and it usually was.

The day he asked if I wanted to have a new experience, to go someplace where he had never taken anyone before, I thought he might be referring to acid or pills or something wicked.

"I don't know," I said. "Is it dangerous?"

"Yes. Definitely, yes," he said, "but I want you to see what I have had to deal with every day of my life."

I couldn't imagine what he meant.

"I want to take you to see the wackiest show on earth— my brother's church. It is so far out; it should be in Ripley's, *Believe it or Not."*

Instinct told me he was sharing something big with me and therefore I had no choice but to go.

On the following Saturday, Heather, Mom and I were doing the great fall ritual of gathering leaves. "Leave that pile for Brent," Mom said over her shoulder as she headed back to the house. "You know how he loves to watch them burn."

"Whatever," Heather agreed.

As we raked the war-torn acres around us, I was thinking about Strange's invitation, and spoke out loud. "I'm going to one of those alternative churches tomorrow with a friend," I said. (What idiot told me such news would make for good conversation?)

"And what friend might that be?" Heather asked, looking up from her pile of reds and browns.

"Strange Barry. You know, the guy at Pearl's that I work with?"

"What? You with that Deadhead? I don't think so," she said, as she yanked the top of a leaf bag together and wrapped it with a twistie.

"He's not a Deadhead," I said. "Just shows how much you don't know."

At that time I didn't have any idea what music Strange liked, but I didn't appreciate any of Heather's assumptions, especially when she looked like a bad version of the Wicked Witch of the West most of the time. In fact, she and Strange looked like they were made for each other.

Mom came back with more black plastic bags. "Here," she said. "What's up with you two, anyway?"

"Like, you wouldn't want to know," Heather said.

"Why do we remove the dead leaves?" I asked. "It's good mulch."

Mom smiled. "Spring is just around the corner."

"More like a lifetime away," I grumbled.

"Lily is going out with a weirdo," Heather announced with her evil smile.

"Excuse me?" Mom said.

"I'm taking off tomorrow morning to go to Woodbury," I said over the racket of summer's waste.

"I see, and what do you expect to do there?" Mom asked.

"I'm going to a church thing with a friend."

"Church? Well, that's interesting," Mom said casually. "Who with?"

"Strange."

"What's that, a rock group?"

"No. Strange is that friend of mine I told you about. He's new in town. He lives on South Main right near the store."

"Strange what?" Mom asked.

"Strange Creep," Heather answered.

"He goes by one name, Strange. I like it. His real name is David Barry but that is too ordinary for him, I guess."

"What is it you're going to? Some kind of musical thing?" Mom asked, pulling impaled oak leaves from her rake's teeth.

"His brother is into...a religious thing. Strange said I should see it. It's like a freak show for Jesus."

"Your intentions sound pretty shallow, Lily," Mom said. "Something tells me the people there don't consider themselves performers. Are you and *Strange* Whatshisname driving there alone?"

"Yeah. He's already promised me that I can call it quits whenever I want to. I just thought it might be cool. He said sometimes they talk in a kind of mystical language. I want to see if they fake it." I paused. "Geez, what's with all the questions, Mom? I'm eighteen, I work. I should be able to go to a church if I want to, without anyone's approval. It's not like there's anything better to do in this town. "

"Well, I suppose that's true," Mom said, as she attacked yet another swell of leaves. "What is the name of the church?"

"I don't know. Really, what's with all the questions? I'm old enough to get married and have kids if I want." My friends didn't have to put up with such interference. They were long gone.

"Just interested, that's all," she said.

"Like, why don't we all go?" Heather suggested.

"Crap. Forget it."

"Hey, have you lost your sense of humor, Lil McGil?" Dad asked, returning with an emptied wheelbarrow.

"There's just not that much to laugh at around here," I said, throwing down my bag and marching to the barn. I was overreacting, I knew it even then, but I needed space. I needed something more than being heckled.

"Well maybe when you come back from the freak show you can entertain us," Heather called after me.

Mom laughed, "Now, Heather..." she said.

It was three against one.

Sunday morning Strange met me down where Rural Road meets Woodhouse Hill in his sorry excuse for a car. He was extra quiet on the way to the meeting, like he was in some kind of trance. I liked him like that, when we could be together and not talk. I studied him from the side, with my body at an odd angle from the door, trying not to press on it in case it was unsafe.

He had interesting looks. His body was long and lean, a modern D'Artagnan, that famous musketeer, who Mrs. Anderson force-fed into my memory bank last year. Lately, Strange had softened his straight black hair and the new version framed his pale face and accentuated its angles. His upper lip was now defined by a pencil mustache, giving him a kind of shady beauty, like that of a dark angel or a foreign prince.

I imagined that Mom and Dad would not like him. I was surely not going to test the water to find out. What they couldn't know was that he was the only boy I'd been with that didn't maul my breasts or ask me to do things I chose not to, like those stupid boys from my high school who kept scorecards.

I looked at the old Chevy's steering wheel. By old, I mean decrepit. The wheel was wrapped in silver electric tape. The floorboard had a massive hole in it, so big you could stick your foot through, and there was an unfortunate odor of sweat that rose from the upholstery. Seeing the blacktop fall away beneath us as we went, gave an exaggerated sense of speed, but no sense of protection should a rock fly up from the unpaved roads below.

"Let's stop at Dreyer's Store and get a Coke," Strange said.

"Sounds good to me. There's never any soda in my house."

We rattled into the tiny parking lot, parked and he hopped out, his long legs sprinting to the door. The door on my side didn't open, so I sat and waited while he shopped.

I noticed the woods were getting as thin as Dad's hair. Winter was probably a minute away, although it was only mid-October. Between two tall beeches, myrtle and rhododendron had already folded their leaves against the early frost. Nearby, poison oak screamed danger. I was always scared of that stuff; it took only a nanogram of oil to give me a miserable rash.

An old yellow dog lumbered out of the thicket, no doubt looking for food near the garbage bins. He had no collar and plenty of ribs.

Strange reappeared with an opened can of Coke. He stood next to my window motioning for me to roll it down so he could pass it to me. I took my first swig.

"Cold enough for you?" he asked.

"Tastes good," I replied. "Strange. Look at that poor old dog. His ribs are showing. Should we pick him up and take him home?"

"Hell, he knows better than we do what he needs. He'll be okay. He's a vagabond. All labs are."

I nodded, hoping he was right.

"You know you don't have to go through with this church thing," he said.

"No, no. I want to. Don't worry, I have an open mind."

"Yeah, well my brother will try to close it for you, if you let him."

"I am just curious, that's all. Why did you ask me to go with you if you really believe I'd get weirded out?"

"That's just what I was asking myself."

We talked back and forth as we traveled down the road. At Christmas Tree Forest, I saw a doe poised at the edge of the woods. She was probably on the run now, knowing the days of the hunt were near. Her femaleness would protect her later, but for one day, the first day of the hunt, every grown deer in Vermont is at risk. "Good luck," I thought.

In the little village of Woodbury we came to the make-do building. It was a worn brown box with a wooden cross nailed to its side. Surprisingly, we had to park a short distance away. We saw a mixed array of people entering, but I was sure they were people I had never met. We were far enough from Purgatory for that to be so.

"Are you ready for some hootin' and hollerin'?" Strange mumbled in my ear.

"I suppose so," I said, not at all sure, now that we were at the door. Part of me wanted to back out.

He pulled at my elbow. "Come on, we can go back. You don't have to go through with this."

"We're here, let's go."

"We'll sit in the back so's we can get out if we want to. This can get pretty crazy once they get going."

Strange was not helping the situation.

The church was bare-boned. Between the wall studs, batts of insulation were being installed to fend off the winter's cold. Blue-gray folding chairs were lined up on either side of a central aisle. A low platform pretended to be an altar at the front. A simple cross leaned against the wall and no handrail or pulpit, no chairs or choir loft existed to block its simple shape. A small Yamaha synthesizer sat to the side of the raised area, but no one sat on its bench. Wireless and waiting, a microphone lay on the floor where the aisle met the platform.

I checked out the crowd. There were at least twelve kids, scattered throughout, all with shiny faces and dressed in Sunday clothes; clothes like a grandmother who didn't know any better might buy.

We sat down in the last row as close to the door as possible.

"How long do you think this will last?" I asked Strange.

"You mean like, how long until we leave? Like, man we can, like, leave right now. I am warning you, this is a freak show with my brother the top freak of all."

At that very moment the doorway was filled with a presence. A tall, bearded man stood silhouetted against the backlight of the morning with his hands raised toward the ceiling. His sleeves were rolled up and his jeans faded. He was beautiful.

He boomed, "Do you love Him? Do you love the Lord? Do you want him for your lover, your friend and your everlasting Father?"

Like a chorus, people sang, "Amen." Then the man walked down the aisle singing, "Praise Him, Praise Him, glory hallelujah."

Everyone seemed to know to repeat the tune and the words. My mouth stayed shut but my ears were wide open. I felt Strange tapping the floor like a colt at the gate. Energy filled the room and put goose bumps on my arms. The voices rang out clear as a school's choir. They had no director and didn't seem to need a hymnal, but then a slide projector was turned on and slides splayed the words on a white screen in the righthand corner in the front of the room. A boy with a guitar appeared and the pastor drew him up to his side, then scooped up the mike from the floor.

They smiled at one another and began to sing, "Arise my soul arise. Shake off my guilty fears. The Savior's sacrifice, in my behalf appears."

"Now you know. That's my bro'," Strange said in my ear. "It's him at his best. Marshall Fucking Barry, the one and only."

I couldn't believe he was Strange's brother. He was over six feet tall, large shouldered, fairer and larger than life. The microphone was lost in his big hand and his voice, rich and strong, dominated all the others. In the midst of his dark lashes his eyes blazed blue. The fingers on his left hand moved like messengers of the word, pointing, cupping, reaching, enfolding. He leapt onto the stage and embraced the room with his smile and the stretch of his arms. He was a one man group, magnificent to watch; a singer, a dancer, a magician and as in charge as a person could imagine.

After the singing he called over our heads, "Bow! Bow your heads unto the Lord who loves you. Know the Lord who has claimed you for His own; the Lord who made you and will give you comfort; the Lord who knows you as no one else can. This is the Lord who brought you here today. This is the Lord who calls you to His side. We are in the army now. We are soldiers for the Great Father, the Gatherer of Souls, who gave us life and will just as surely take it away. He is the breath of the world. He is yours for the asking. Yours, just as you are. His, whether you like it or not, whether you know it or not. *As I am Lord, as I am,*" he sang. The others echoed. Over and over they sang the same words.

I noticed I was bowing my head. I could not, not bow it. I felt a force pushing my chin to my chest and the top of my head no more than a funnel as I heard the words like blasts of steam. My hands began to sweat and the air in my lungs wouldn't travel on their regular route. The room began to implode, pressing on my skin. I opened my eyes and saw it merge together in a pink wad in front of this tawny-maned lion.

"Amen," he cried.

"Amen," his worshippers cried back.

"Amen," he sang.

"Amen," they echoed until the amens became more and more beautiful, elongated, illuminated and harmonized. Altos and sopranos found their tones, a deep baritone played against a woman's high c. The music rose from nowhere, and lifted the roof off the building. My knees went weak. I unconsciously reached for Strange's arm, which was hard and cold but held me as I tried to right myself in the midst of the others.

When it grew quiet, I felt relieved, like I could go into my mind and breathe again. But that time was short. His sermon began, a bold knowing came forward. He said an enormous earthquake in San Salvador had swallowed the people where they stood. Without warning, the earth's great mouth had opened and taken them where they slept and where they worked, the young and old, the rich and the poor. "Were they ready? Were they right with the Lord?" he asked. "Are you ready? Are you right with the Lord? Will you have taken the Lord as your Father, your Friend and his Son, Jesus as your Savior. Ask yourself, where are you, who are you, will you be ready when he calls?"

He walked over to the front row. "Now, Bobby Jay is ready, aren't you Bobby Jay? He has been touched by the Lord's own hand! Haven't you Bobby Jay?"

"Y-yes, Bro-oth-ther." The boy said.

A large woman rose and pulled Bobby Jay's hand as he stood, and then she led him to the front of the hall. She had big purple tears cascading over her bronze cheeks. "The Lord has given my boy his tongue," she cried. "He know now how to speak past his stutter. The angels has taught him how to sing. Praise God he met the Pastor Marshall Barry! His life be changed now forever!" The teenager stood before us, a human rubber band, with legs too long for his pants and hands too big for his arms; a head too large for the spindle of a neck.

The pastor placed the mike in the boy's hands and I saw the miracle of his transformation with my own eyes, and heard it with my own ears. He smiled like a saint from his lofty view, and nodded while his mother went to the synthesizer and played a few notes. "I, I am a child of the Lord. I know who I am," he sang in a clear happy voice. "Just as I am Lord, just as I am."

His performance was followed by another chorus of amens from the congregation, more beautiful than the first.

I didn't know there were tears behind my eyes wanting to come out, but at some point water was streaming down my cheeks and snot was dripping from my nose. I had no handkerchief, no tissue, so I had to let it soak my face. I was really embarrassed. Why this goofy boy's singing affected me, I couldn't know; except he was kind of pure and sure and willing to expose himself to all these people. He was probably the same age as Brent, but so different. Luckier. I wished someone could lay hands on Brent and bring him back from whatever Hell he was in. I missed that little boy with his endless questions. Why had we teased him with dumb answers when all he wanted was to know?

A disfigured girl came down the aisle walking very carefully. She approached the edge of the stage and surprisingly, no one helped her up. Instead she was introduced as Maddy, the Lamb of God who had been blessed with scoliosis. It was clear that Maddy was not put together like the rest of us. Her left shoulder reached down toward her hip and her back bone was distinctly curved. It made it difficult to wear a dress and walk and who knew what else.

"Maddy, here, could barely walk before she met Jesus. Could you Maddy?"

"I have made peace with the Lord," she said to him, her eyes shining as she answered.

"Maddy is born again into the spirit. She has made her peace with the Lord."

"Yes. Brother Barry, I have," she responded, "Now I am full of Jesus, I am one with him. I can even dance with Him. He is leading me wherever I go."

She took a step towards him and then began turning around in a slant of twirls, moving in little awkward motions, glowing like a Christmas ornament. It stopped my breath as she fell at his feet, hugging his legs and smiling all the way down. Gently, very gently he lifted her up and held her tightly as she clung to his waist. He looked to the ceiling and thanked the Lord.

Strange leaned in, "Want to leave now?" he asked. "This is getting you spooked more than I thought it would."

"No, no. We have to stay," I said.

Then his brother lifted his arms toward the congregation. "There are no accidents," he said. "No one is here today that was not called. You are here to see the power of God to cast light on what is dark. You are inheritors of that light. It is in you to save the world from darkness, the darkness that Satan himself spreads. You are here to save yourselves Brothers and Sisters, heal! Get ready, fall down and ask Jesus what you must do to be ready for the Lord. There is no more that he asks than that you believe in Him. Humble yourselves. He will make all things right. He tells us to beware the wages of sin. Satan loves sinners. Look how he seduces us, waits for our resistance to grow weak and then strikes.

"Satan laughed as he led the sons of Cain to the fruit that would poison them and then cast them out upon the world. Beware, my brethren, beware. Take hold of what is right, resist the easy way. Do not allow yourself to fall away from the Lord of Light. Trust and He will show you how to do His work and be self-sufficient. You will find joy in His love. He is Love."

He wasn't done yet.

"You are here today to pick up your shield and wear it in the war against darkness. It is waiting for you, asking you to shine in the truth of who you are. You are the descendants of Abel, the lost tribes of Israel, found. Ask yourselves, 'Is it me Lord, Is it me?' Stand. Raise your hands, close your eyes and listen. Listen for the answer. The Lord will tell you. 'Yes. Yes, it is you, I love you, completely and forever, but you must give Me your will and trust'."

We all stood, and a girl started singing, "Is it me Lord, Lord, is it me?" Then another and another joined her. I felt heat traveling from my head to my toes. I forgot Strange sitting next to me, the ugly room, and the homely assortment of people. All I knew was my whole body felt like it was being drawn to a new place.

"Come to the altar, come and receive Jesus Christ, be one with the Blessed Spirit."

"We're outta here," Strange said. He grabbed my elbow and drew me away from my seat, pushing open the door and delivering us into the sunshine.

"You could have waited until it was over," I said.

"I just couldn't take any more of that bullshit," he said. "He's getting off on the show. It's all about him."

I stayed silent. It took a lot of steps for me to keep up with his near run to the car.

"All he wants is their money. It's all about money and power. I'm telling you, I'll be moving away as soon as I know where it is I want to go. Maybe L.A. Maybe New York. All I know is it won't be anywhere-near this sideshow."

I knew enough to let him rant. I wondered if he might be jealous, if he wished he could change people's lives as easily as his brother was able. I felt sorry for him.

5

It was the week after Thanksgiving and things at the boutique were slow. Every shopkeeper in town knew sales wouldn't start again until last minute Christmas shoppers were forced to shop locally. Nevertheless, Polly Appleby was going door to door selling homemade Advent wreaths and finding folks to buy electric candles for their windows. As the days grew darker, the Rotarians were hanging street decorations to add color and cheer since Purgatory in early winter is no poster child for Vermont Life. It suffers an in-between-seasons gout unless, of course, there is a significant snowstorm.

Strange was rearranging leftover Halloween items; wax teeth, bulging eyes, cans of fake egg spray, plastic vomit, fart pillows. "You know my brother thinks Halloween is devil worship," he said, toying with a pair of zany glasses with pupils on springs.

"Isn't it a national holiday?" I asked.

"Hell, Halloween's not legal, it's just tradition. But, it might as well be legal it's such a hit for junk like this." He picked up a rubber bat and shook it at me. "Holidays are great for retail."

"I plan my year around them," I said. "Well, the ones that close schools, anyway."

"Yeah, I always loved Jewish holidays in New York. They don't celebrate them here like they did in New York. The schools actually close down there."

"You're kidding?"

"Nope. I think it's time to make a new holiday."

"Whose?"

"Madonna! They should make August 16th a national holiday. She's a goddess. The fearless one. Queen of the World! It would be no more bullshit than Columbus Day."

"Well, don't hold your breath. Madonna will be probably be replaced by someone else next week. I still don't get what's not to like about Halloween. I suppose the sugar highs are bad but how does your brother come up with it being the work of the devil?"

"He's a bona fide genius and an honest to God crazy dude. He has memorized the entire Bible and has an answer to everything. You have to know none of his opinions are out of his own head. Somewhere he learned that Halloween is Satan's season. As far as I can see Halloween is just another one of those Arab myths from the first century. Maybe the Druids thought it up. Unlike Marshall J. C. Barry, I find the most ancient gods a hell of a lot more interesting than old JC." He picked up a wig made up of multicolored snakes and jiggled his head to make them dance.

He was just not like anyone I had ever known.

"Myths are my hobby. They're inside all the great stories. I like figuring out how they got reinvented from one religion to another, like the Virgin Birth: Chrisma, Maya, Mary—there's a shitload of virgin births out there. You know, girls still swear they have miraculous conceptions? You read about them all time. Like, they think someone will believe them! Myths are my favorite way of telling Marshall off, but it doesn't work. No matter how many times I point out who did what, first, he won't go there."

"Where does he live?" I asked. "I don't think I've ever seen him in town."

"He lives in his trailer—hey, lookie here, a pipe cleaner tarantula!"

He set the fuzzy creature on his shoulder. It was completely unscary.

"Marshall's my legal guardian, and I owe him something. In the beginning I wanted to *be* him, walk, talk, read, sing, play ball like him. I was only twelve when our folks died. He had hair on his face and knew how to talk like a lawyer, even though he was only a whopping twenty-one. I might have been sent to a foster home or with my bald Aunt Sarah in some hick town up north. But he went to court and fought for me. I was lucky they let me stick with him. Maybe he won custody because he said he was a pastor."

"How did your parents die?" I asked.

"Car crash."

"Geez," I said, not knowing whether to ask more. "So, you two still officially live together?"

"Nah. Not really. At eighteen I became a liberated man. My bank account is full, but I don't know what I want to do with it yet. I'm outta here as soon as I do. One thing's for sure, I'm not going down Marshall's road any further than I have to. I stick around half-hoping he'll wise up and come out of the trance. He was once a normal person, whatever that is."

"It's really that bad?"

"Are you kidding? He thinks he's Jesus reincarnated. I know better. He may have the memory of a squeegee but he has a warped intelligence. It's kind of amazing how he's given up reality and replaced it with some dead dude's raving. And not only that, he manipulates it all to suit himself."

He shook his head, stretching a rubbery rat's tail in his hands. "Lots of cheap shit here to get rid of."

"Kids love that stuff, though," I said. "Let's make a basket of stocking stuffers out of them."

"Cool! Capitalism at its best."

"Do you believe anything your brother says?" I asked.

He tossed the rat in a waste paper basket. "Nope. I only believe in not believing. My truth is the Mu."

"The Mu?" Strange loved to throw out words no one had ever heard of. He obviously had to live up to his nickname.

"The Mu. M-U. The Big Nothing. No here, no there—a wash of atoms."

"No me? No you?" I laughed.

He stepped in front of my face, with his hands on my shoulders and said, "You may not buy this, but, we don't really exist."

His dark brown eyes, shaded by a curtain of lashes, were beautiful and intense. Instinctively, I stepped back. "You're serious! I don't know what you mean, my mind won't go there. If we can't trust what we see and feel, what can we trust? There must be a reason for our senses."

"They aren't real, just one big illusion, like a lake in the desert. The only thing is the All, *the oneness.*" He picked up a little bottle. "Hey, here's some disappearing ink. What do you think ink has got to do with Halloween?" he asked.

"Magic?" I suggested.

"Gee, maybe I should get some for my brother. He'd figure out something manipulative to do with it," he laughed. "Like, smearing graffiti or hate words on the church walls and praying for it to disappear, and then claiming another fucking miracle when it does. He'd say the big magician of the sky did it."

"So you think nothing is real? Nothing is up or down or in or out or right or wrong? It's all the same to you?" I asked. "Nothing is sweet or sour, hot or cold, true or false? That's pretty strange thinking, Strange."

He opened the disappearing ink and wrote STRANGE on his hand. "Yeah. It's just your perception and only your perception. Look, a hill is flat when you look down from a plane. A mouse is huge to a gnat and small to an elephant. Something like that. I mean it's what your mind tells you. Some people can walk on coals, stay under water for ten minutes, ride sharks and survive a face-off with an alligator. For them, anything's possible." He waved his hand. "I bet you think that ink should have stained my hand but look—I can wave my hand and abracadabra it's gone!"

He grabbed my hand. "Here, let me do you," he said.

On the back of my hand he wrote, *BEAUTY*. It was maybe the nicest thing anyone had almost said to me.

I tried not to blush. "I have to admit you're the only person I know who talks like this, the only person who thinks like this, or thinks at all," I said.

"And my ideas seem freaky to you, but they aren't. There are only about a gadzillion other people in this world who agree with me."

"Well, I only know one such person and that's the big You, Y-U that rhymes with Mu that sounds like Moo and is New to me!" I rhymed.

"So, you're a poet." He took down the plastic masks that hung on tacks at the end of the shelves.

"I wish. I love words. Maybe that's what I liked about your brother's service. I would like to go again. It interests me. He seems to know something I don't. Something really, really far out."

He put on a sad faced pumpkin mask and stuck his tongue through the mouth's opening. "So that means you hate me," he whined.

"I didn't say that. I just don't understand you well enough to agree to this Mu stuff."

"But you agree with the crazy guy? What have I done to deserve this? I hope you don't want me to drive you there again?"

"Only if you want to."

"Well, I don't."

"Okay then...I understand. He's your brother and brothers are hard to take. My brother, Brent, is so spaced out, I don't know who he is anymore. He's mean one day and quiet the next. Sometimes I think he hates everyone and everything," I said, trying to fit one plastic mask inside another for easy storage.

"How old is he?"

"Almost fourteen."

Strange shook his head. "Thirteen's a bad age. His brain is like a racket ball hitting all four walls and not winning a point for shit. He'll come out of it. As soon as he gets his wheels he'll be better. When you're thirteen you live in a kind of a green cloud. That's when you catch on that the world is not as you would like it to be, and there's nothing you can do about it but smoke some good weed and wait for Fabulinus to materialize and teach you how to communicate all over again."

"You're sounding really dark today. Why are you so angry?"

"I'm not angry. I just don't want to see you and Jesus getting it on."

I guess that's why he decided to take me to the second service after all. He must have decided to chaperone. Then again, we knew the days were short before the first snow fell and almost any excuse would have served to get out of dull gray Purgatory on that particularly dreary Sunday. I was bundled up waiting at the end of the road, away from my family and wondering if Strange was really going to come for me or not. He showed up just in time for us to get to the service on time. We parked near the door, so we could make a quick get-away when it was over.

Sitting in the back of the room again, Strange was more fidgety than I'd ever seen him. It was as if he had no-see'ums under his clothes. The place was as crowded as the first time, and this week I recognized a couple of people from our last visit, but I knew no one by name nor did I think they knew mine—which was reassuring. I didn't want anyone to get the wrong idea.

The moment Brother Barry entered, the air moved. I swear I could almost see it happen. This time he placed his hands on people's heads as he walked down the aisle and I watched them look at him like he was a God. They bowed their heads when they were touched, like holy water had been poured on them. "Amen, brothers and sisters, amen," he said. "How the Lord loves you for being here today! Thank you, Jesus, for your everlasting love. Let no man put this love asunder. It is yours to choose and yours to own and yours in the face of those under Satan's rule.

"Have you made yourself ready in the eyes of the Lord? Have you cleansed your soul by asking for forgiveness? Repentance is such an easy task. Love Him, who loves you, turn away from the Devil and live life anew. It is the avenue of joy and peace. It is the street of well-being and promise. All things will be righted when all doubts are banished. Go forward into the arms of the Lord and leave the wicked to their own Hell! You are the anointed ones. God's Beloved is soon to be born in the spirit once again."

The tiny electric organ at the front of the room sounded and the words of a hymn projected on the screen. "The Lord is my Redeemer," the people sang, "I shall not suffer loss."

I tried to sing, too, but I couldn't hear myself well enough to know if I was on key. Strange was jerking around beside me. I looked at him and questioned him with my eyes. He shook his head and continued to scratch.

Brother Barry delivered a long prayer after the hymn and then some people offered up their own. Few were without a need and none short on words to tell it. I found myself listening carefully to each person, the sick mother, the job that was needed, the lost love, the guilty conscience. "My grandmaw she has the cowlic. She needs Jesus to lay hands on her. She's so mean she might as well have swallowed the devil."

"Amen, Jesus!" the people cried. I had never heard people speak so openly about how much they hurt and never seen a room more ready to heal them. Brother Barry lifted his hands with the weight of the prayers apparently on them and gave them to the heavenly spirit. "Take these cares, oh heavenly Father, this pain, and these confessions to your bosom, oh, Lord, and bring your people peace."

As more song, more praise, and more testimonies continued, more tension grew beside me. Strange was almost dancing with nerves. His face was twisted with anger. He growled, "Gotta go. Now!" between gritted teeth.

Just then Pastor Barry made a call to the congregation to come forward and accept Jesus as their Savior. I was fixated on the people who stood up with tears on their cheeks and lights in their eyes. One by one they rose and, with each new saved soul, a chorus of *Praise Gods* cried out with relief.

Pastor Barry looked right at me, his arms raised in my direction. "Just a few steps, an open heart and your whole life will start over." My feet had stakes in them attaching them to the floor. It seemed like hours that his eyes bore into mine but it was probably only seconds. They told me I could have what he had, that there were answers and I could learn all I needed to know, if I would just get up, give myself over and trust.

In the midst of the shuffling of feet heading for the altar, Strange leaned into my ear. "Now," he begged, yanking my arm and practically pushing me out the door. We popped into the smart, cold air like twins escaping the womb, his hand pulling mine, racing over the grass and down the gravel driveway to the car. "Whoo-whee!" he screamed. "Free, we're free!"

He revved the motor and I climbed inside. "Lord Almighty that guy deserves the Oscar. Honest to God he's got the best show in town!"

"How come you couldn't stay until the end then?" I asked.

"It's a tragedy. The hero dies at the end. I can only take the comedy part. The part where everyone believes they are going to live happily ever after."

His fingers gripped the steering wheel like more pressure would get us out of there faster.

"Your brother is very powerful. I suppose that's hard for you, especially when you don't agree with what he says," I said, not mentioning that I thought the man oozed a kind of maleness that Strange could only dream about. They were polar opposites physically as well as mentally.

Strange looked at me like I was crazy. "He's a joke, dude. A bad joke. Don't you get it? He is a one man freak show."

"I think he means what he says."

"Yeah, sometimes I think he actually takes himself seriously. But how could he? How could he go out there and tell people what they want to hear and get away with it? People are assholes and he's delusional."

He pressed his foot on the accelerator and we took off kicking up enough stone and dust to startle the squirrels and turn my ankles gray. Curves didn't slow him down; nature was at risk.

"If God exists, he's a sadist. What is religion but trying to kiss-up to the great trickster? He has too many forms of torture to name. He not only crashes planes, sends tornadoes and tsunamis, plagues and murderers to wipe out innocent people like they're flies on a wall, but he also wipes out whole species, civilizations and ultimately kills every poor fucker who takes his first breath. And Marshall calls that love?

I decided not to talk about the sermon or the church until he had calmed down. As it was, he was driving too fast. The cranky barrel of rust was trying to keep up with the pressure of his foot, grinding its gears in the effort.

With a blur of browns and greens on each side, I kind of thought of praying, but then I thought it might be better if God didn't notice us at that particular moment.

6

"Where have you been Lily-Vanilli," Dad called from the couch, his nose deep in the *Sunday Globe.*

"Strange and I were just tooling around."

"You out with the weirdo again?" Brent asked.

"What do you care? He's no weirder than you," I said.

"He's a faggot," he answered.

"He's my friend," I said. "No one is asking you to like him. You might try being decent now and then, just to see how it feels."

I had poured myself some cocoa and was trying to get the last spurt of Ready-Whip out of the can. I shook it a few times and noticed that my wrist was silent. Grandmother Lillian's clunky silver bracelet was missing. I panicked, realizing I might have lost the one precious thing of mine that had been salvaged from the fire.

It was a heavy silver bracelet with cloisonné lilies linked together in leafy loops—a family heirloom. Lilies for the Lillians in the family, handed down many generations. Ted Costa had retrieved it from the wreckage, but now it was gone again. Why were the things I loved most getting away from me?

On Monday, I checked to see if it was in Strange's car. I asked him if he remembered seeing it. We rummaged through the car, dug into the seats and felt underneath them. I found some change and old napkins, a few receipts but no bracelet. It was possible the bracelet had fallen through the hole in the floor and was lost to the highway. I wanted to cry. My only hope was that it could have fallen off

57

at the church. Then I thought this was something I would take care of myself. I'd go to Woodbury, search the church, comb the grounds and see if anyone had returned it to Brother Barry.

The next day, a Tuesday, I drove back to the meeting hall alone. The church was empty but I saw what I figured was Brother Barry's truck out back, parked next to a disconnected five-wheeler resting on some concrete blocks. I figured the RV was his office. Where else could it be? There were no separate rooms in the meeting hall. Nervousness fluttered inside me at the thought of knocking on his door. I reminded myself he was only human, simply Strange's brother, a mere mortal.

It was only a little after three and warm despite the long shadows that crossed the path. Just beyond the aluminum stairs in front of the door, I could see a gold light defining the river's bank and hear yesterday's rain rushing downstream. As I rapped at the door, I noticed grass cuttings sticking out from the soles of my sneakers.

"Just a minute," I heard from inside.

Now a banging pulse in my ears overwhelmed the river.

I saw his shadow behind the door and had to step back as the door opened out, instead of in. I stood there, dumber than the grass stuck to my shoes, trying to exorcise it from my soles.

"You're here," he said, smiling, as the door opened. "I hoped you might come." His smile was very wide. I thought his teeth looked too white, too big to be real.

"My bracelet," I said, stupidly, surprised by his warm welcome. I leaned on the door frame because my legs had turned to noodles incapable of supporting weight.

"Come in, come in. It's Lily, right? I felt God reaching for you this Sunday and hoped He was opening your heart and sending it my way. You're my brother's girl, right?"

I liked that he knew my name and didn't want to correct him but said, "We're just friends."

"I felt your heart moving, at the service on Sunday," he said, guiding me easily into the room.

"Maybe that's why my bracelet fell off. Some kind of message that I better get back here, after all there are no accidents, as you and Grandmother Lillian have said." I smiled apologetically for the not so witty person I am.

"Come in and sit down." He nudged my arm a little. I felt his heat.

"My feet are dirty."

"No problem."

"I mean my sneakers are covered with dead grass."

He laughed. "Believe me this little trailer has seen more problems than a little grass. Take your shoes off, if it makes you feel better."

I did, and lay them side by side inside the door.

He patted a chair for me to sit. I sank down in it, too easily, too far. His big hands ran through his hair and he took a deep breath as he sat down on the shabby plaid sofa, across from me, stretching his legs out so they filled the room. His body looked relaxed and hard at the same time. It was as if ions of energy sat right on top of his skin. The soft hair on his arms glowed. I wondered if he was electric. Maybe his normal temperature was 102 degrees.

"You didn't come to me during The Call. What was holding you back? I felt you might make that walk."

How could he know that *The Call* was my favorite part of the service? Both weeks I had been fascinated by the people who went forward, but I would never have left my seat. He had it wrong. I may have watched the faces of people, saw their tears or relief or belief as they made their way to the front of the room, but I never thought of being one of them.

"I don't know...I am not sure if I could do that. It's pretty scary."

He laughed. "Not as scary as Hell. Once you give yourself to God you never have to be afraid again. He loves every hair on your head. Jesus said, *I say to you, do not worry about your life, what you will eat or what you will drink; nor about your body, or what you wear. Is not life more than food and the body more than clothing? Look at the birds of the air, for they neither sow nor reap nor gather into barns; God feeds them. Consider the lilies of the field, how they grow: they neither toil nor spin; and you in your natural beauty are more beautiful than these.* Imagine how God loves you and waits for your love?"

He was poetic. Profound. I had never heard a man speak like this before. I looked at his face looking at mine. It was without a doubt the most confident, shining face I had ever seen. His eyes were so clear you could almost see Heaven. I felt my own gaze lower and focus on the floor. I couldn't look at such depths, couldn't take a chance of being blinded. I should have thanked God that Brother Barry's eyes were powerful enough to stop my tongue from blabbering like an idiot's.

"Maybe you and I need to have a talk. Why don't you let me tell you a beautiful story? Would you like that?"

He sounded like a gentle father and yet I knew I wouldn't be able to hear his story. My heart was drumming and my ears plugged, I wrapped my arms so tightly across my chest I could hardly take in air or exhale it. My hands were hot and clammy. I could only imagine how they looked at the end of my arms, stiff and red as lobster claws.

"Oh, I can't stay, not today," I said, stuffing my hands in my armpits. "Really. I just thought maybe, if, you found my bracelet. Did you? Did you find my bracelet? It was my grandmother's. One of the only things I have of hers except for some earrings. Well, and then there are some half-burned books. We had a fire you know."

"A fire?" he asked.

"Our house burned to the ground. It was like our history was wiped out in one awful night. I don't know why such a terrible thing happened, I just know it did." From out of nowhere big tears started slipping down my cheeks. I hated myself for crying. Couldn't believe how easily the dam broke.

"Fire is a spiritual thing, Lily. It's fed from God's breath and it wipes the slate clean. You could think of it as a new beginning, an opportunity for new life. Perhaps the Lord is calling."

I felt five years old, looking like a drooling blathering toddler for all I knew. Everything in me was trying to calm down, trying so hard to be relaxed I couldn't hear most of what he said. Obviously he thought the fire more significant than the bracelet. He handed me a tissue.

"Fire cleanses and punishes. It asks you not to look back."

"So you haven't seen my bracelet?" I asked.

"No, but we could take a walk and see if it is on the grounds."

"Okay," I said, with the voice of a kindergartner.

We went to the building and looked around the seats where Strange and I had sat. Then we revisited the area where I thought we parked the car. We poked among the brittle white grasses, the corn flowers and confusion of dead leaves.

We found sparkling mica stones, metal tabs from soda cans and, here and there, shards of broken bottles, but no bracelet came to light.

"I am sorry, Lily," he said. "Just place it in God's hands. It will be returned to you if it is meant to be. Jesus is your best friend. He will give you whatever you ask for if it is right for you. The Bible promises, *"Seek and ye shall find."*

He touched my arm ever so slightly and gold appeared around the pewter clouds of dusk. I didn't begin to breathe normally again until I was miles down the road.

The ride home was all about Brother Barry. I thought about his jaw, the space between his incisor and front tooth on, his one point of imperfection. I thought of his large hand touching me and I ached for something too big to name. It twisted my privates, left me nervous, excited. I turned on the radio and the religious station was pumping out a song about Jesus. The hymn made him more of a lover than a savior. It didn't take much for me to catch on to the tune and the verses. *And he walks with me and he talks with me and he tells me I am his own.* I started belting it out like I'd sung it all my life. I tried harmony and repeating the words on the heels of the words. The road from Woodbury to Purgatory was a lonely road, but I crowded it with energy.

I saw the gentle Green Mountains more sharply. The hills were still studded with the last red leaves of autumn on the southern sides, and turning to burnished browns and deep umbers on the north. When the tops of the hills darkened to silhouettes, a radiant Venus appeared on the northeast horizon, and soon an even brighter Sirius. The cold winter moon moved quickly above the horizon, as though on a celestial string. Its size, its apricot color, its timing was amazing. I was sure it had never been as remarkable.

I drove slowly down Rural Road and up Woodhouse Hill to the barn we now called home. A swirl of smoke was emerging from the new chimney. Dad had designed the fireplace himself out of the same stones as our original chimney. Not only did the chimney and its streaming smoke make the barn look cozy, so did the warmly lit windows and well-lit front door. Dad had transformed what had been only fit for horses into a beautiful home. Well, sort of. A home is more than a structure, more than a wide hearth and warm temperatures.

My siblings were becoming increasingly weird. Mom was obsessed with Dad's every move, and my father was obsessed with the house. Except for rare moments, we remained tenuous, each in a separate universe.

As I walked in the front door Brent said, "Saint Lil is home, Mom. Now can we eat?" I was sorry I had told anyone where I was going. But then again I had to borrow the car to justify the trip.

"Did you find the bracelet, Honey?" Mom asked.

"No," I said. "But I'm sure if someone picked it up they will get it to Pastor Barry."

"Sure," said Brent. "Like all those losers that go to that place are honest. They go there to get forgiven."

Mom gave Brent a disapproving look. "Since when have you been so cynical, Baby Boy?"

Brent spun around and glared. "Don't call me that."

"O dear, I think you must be hungry. Well, it's all ready. Lentil soup and fresh bread. How does that sound?"

Brent could never really do anything wrong in my mother's eyes. Even his moodiness didn't get to her, whereas Heather just looked at her funny and Mom would be off and running. Maybe that was why Heather was home so little. I liked her absences. It was a relief to have her attitude out of my face.

A huge pot of soup was placed in the center of the table. Its sides looked like they were bulging out from the weight of it. Heather lifted the lid and looked inside. "No meat for a change?" she complained.

"We don't need to eat meat to survive, Heather. I will not apologize," Mom said.

"Well, I happen to be from a long line of carnivores. Can I help it?" Heather asked. "My great grandparents were Vikings weren't they? Their meat is my meat. My blood runs thick with their slaughters. My desire for flesh is congenital." She clawed her darkly polished nails in Brent's direction.

"Gross!" he groaned.

"So, Lil how was the road? Leaf peepers still cluttering the highways?" Dad asked cheerfully.

"No. I think it's over, but the moon was just amazing tonight."

Dad smiled. "Cold winter moon," and started to sing, "By the light of the silvery moon..."

Heather leaned on her right cheek and farted. I don't mean a little fart but a big rude blast.

"That's it Heather. Leave the table." Dad said. "I will not have my crooning interrupted."

Heather fell over her soup laughing. Really, nothing in the world could make her laugh harder than basic crudeness. She obviously found something riotously funny in a burst of methane. A true intellectual. No wonder she was skipped in school.

As she shoved her chair back to leave, Mom said, "I thought we were working on adulthood Heather. I am sure there's a lady in there somewhere."

Heather burped. "Oh, excuse me," she said quickly, "I think you have me confused with my brother." She patted her lips demurely with her napkin, then wiped her underarms with it.

Mom's lips pursed, her face got red and she lifted her bowl to retreat to the living room. Dad stood up, too, following Mom with his bowl, to sit on the fireplace's hearth. He sat facing her, his profile towards us. I noticed how his shoulders hunched, as he pulled his old pilled gray wool sweater up and over his head in the face of the heat. My appetite disappeared. "Good soup, Mama," he said.

"How many times have I told you not to call me Mama?" Mom said.

"But you are. You're my earth mother. My angel. What could be wrong about that?"

Later, lying in bed, looking through Dad's perfectly placed skylight, I watched the clouds skitter across the now distant moon. I needed to make my own life.

7

I don't know when I started believing in miracles. It should have been when I found my lily bracelet in the weeds, after living without it for almost a year. It was sparkling in the grasses at the side of the road, right where I had waited for Strange on that autumn day when we first went to his brother's church. I was thrilled to have it back, of course, but no angels blew their trumpets or rainbows appeared. The one thing I realized was that I had been looking in all the wrong places. At services, I regularly checked women's wrists and continued to kick aside pebbles in the parking lot, but it appeared when I happened to be walking along Rural Road looking for katydids.

During that long stretch following graduation and the mass exodus of my friends, I applied and was accepted at the University of Vermont for a January entrance, but I decided to wait until the September of '88. We finished our house during the fall and winter, and while I was home I kept working at Pearl's, alongside Strange. I wasn't entirely bored despite the many slow days that winter brought. But April was tough; it took May's sunshine to rescue me from the doldrums of a very gray, wet April.

One of my favorite places to hang out on our property was beyond the crest of Woodhouse Hill, past the cow pond, the hardwoods and the family *campground*. The campground held a number of tilting stones meant to mark the names of the ancestors who lay beneath. Unfortunately, their inscriptions are now beyond recognition, smoothed by weather and time. Beyond, the emerald mosses of the graveyard's rocky wall, on the far side of the hill, hyssop, poppies, coreopsis and rudbeckia spread like a heavenly carpet. It was a perfect spot to think. I loved the silence of the pasture and the knowing that, as Grandmother Lillian used to say, this was nature's garden, a gift, with no purpose other than to be. I felt close to her in this spot.

It was a place to consider things like mortality and reality, whether we go somewhere else when we die. Is there a Plan B that we can't see? Would life still be interesting if we had all the answers? Pastor Barry has them. Should I?

Not much seemed to make sense in the world, at least in my fuzzy world. I was not such a bumpkin that I didn't know about wars and starving children and the natural disasters that kill thousands each year. With a world so cruel, I was ashamed that I worried so much about myself. But I didn't know enough. I mean, what was I supposed to do tomorrow and tomorrow and tomorrow? I was born with parts that worked, a decent brain and parents who fed me well and made sure there was a roof over my head. In truth, I had almost nothing but good fortune, but...but what? Why must life end? What is it for? I just didn't get it. Meaning felt out of reach. Anxiety started and ended too many days.

Purgatory's social life was as exciting as dry clay. Not a single boy from town interested me in a romantic way. My friends from school were inaccessible and busy discovering new lives and new people. It felt awkward to get in touch with them because I had nothing to share. I was growing duller by the day. The sad fact was that the one place I felt something happened each week was Al-a-Teen and I hardly wanted to reveal that piece of embarrassment with anyone, including myself. Nor could I reveal the secret little trips I made to the Woodbury church on Sundays to revel in the dangerous Brother Barry. Strange would have called me a traitor and my family would have thought me nuts.

Nancy Kimball and I continued to grow our friendship,

what with our problem parents and her letting me ride Bliss and helping her out at the stables. Our times together managed to fill my otherwise non-eventful life.

Like me, Nancy had decided to wait for a while before going off to college. Unlike me, she wasn't in the throes of preparing to replace her old life with something new. She seemed content to be where she was needed most. As the only responsible adult in her household, leaving meant risking the horses' well-being. She deserved a blue-ribbon for her faithfulness, which I appreciated because I was a loser in that field. I had loved Meg Flanders but loving didn't prove to be enough. Keeping her was more about sacrifice and I hadn't been up to that.

Throughout the summer, Kimball's Farm became my second home. Nancy and I usually hung out in the barn where the beams were going soft and the hinges of the old paddocks needed to be replaced. I asked why her father didn't help and she said her father would rather see the house fall down than show up to fix anything. While she was committed to keeping it clean and taking care of the horses, I soaked up the pheromones of hay and horse and would have been happy to move in. Some days we would saddle up early and ride for hours, down logging roads and across pastures where we often flushed out pheasants and turkeys. Back at the barn we'd lather up *the girls* and scrub them down, brushing their coats until they shined like satin. We worked well together.

I particularly remember one afternoon. We were sitting on some newly cut bales of hay, watching the horses in the corral, sidling up to one another with their equine snorts and affectionate nose knocking. Happiness was having them trot our way every now and then, whinny at us and playfully move away. It was in this setting I felt most comfortable; with a close friend, near horses, a corral and killing time under a warm sun.

Nancy's mares each had distinguishing characteristics. Sadie's long eyelashes were as seductive as any diva's and the white on Bliss's mane and tail combined with the black accents on her face gave her stunted self a certain distinction. She wasn't as tall as Sadie but she held her head high with an air of dignity. The two girls were obviously best friends. Knowing Bliss, I couldn't help but be reminded again and again of what a soul mate I had lost when I lost Meg Flanders. We had understood each other's language and fit so well I hardly had to use reins or stirrups. Although Bliss was a great horse and we were getting on well, I had to remind myself she wasn't mine and never would be.

"I wish I had been better to my sweet Meg," I confided.

"I understand, truly, but then I wouldn't see you as much and Bliss wouldn't get such good workouts or attention. Like, I'm kinda glad you need us."

"Meg had that sixth sense they talk about," I said.

Sadie approached and shook out her mane. Nancy patted her nose.

"Kind of like Sadie. Don't you think animals know us better than we know ourselves? Sadie always nuzzles my neck when I'm feeling down."

"Yeah, a horse's instincts work better than that *Give up and let God stuff*," I said.

Nancy jumped at the reference to AA. "Are you getting sick of Al-a-Teen's jargon, too?" she asked. "I totally know why! Like, it's the same old thing over and over. I don't think I am getting much out of it, really I don't, but if I give it up I won't have anything else to turn to, and I would miss seeing you."

The horses started to play racetrack, running side by side along the corral's fence.

"I do the best I can to manage around here, but the situation seems to stay the same. Sometimes I feel completely alone, like I am the only one who cares. Father comes by every month, but stays, like, minutes. He's only interested in Kimball Lumber. My mother loves her Vodka, my father loves his business. What can I say? It's like I hardly exist for anyone but you and the girls. You're my best friend, Lily, you really are."

I wanted to tell her she was my best friend, too, and the only reason I kept going to the meetings. But I didn't because I noticed her eyes were filled up and I was afraid she would cry. If she started, we might both lose it and start bawling. I tried to think of something else to talk about.

Looking up, I saw the most amazing formation of clouds in the sky. "Look at those clouds coming in! Geez, they're racing just like the horses. Do you see the horses' manes? They're flying," I said. "They're awesome."

Her eyes followed mine, and saw what I saw. "I see them. Wow! Like, the air is really moving fast up there. It should cool off soon."

"*Farmer's Almanac* says we're going to have a late summer, but it's never right," I said.

Nancy continued to study the sky and as if she was thinking out loud said, "Clouds are like art. We see in them whatever we want."

I nodded. "Yeah. There's no predicting them. They come in waves and then, poof, they're gone."

"My life is looking too predictable these days," Nancy said.

"Not mine. I feel just the opposite. I feel mine is about to undergo some major changes and I don't know what I am doing or why. Going away to school is something I have to do and yet right now I am thinking of it as signing off to the young folks home."

"Are you scared?"

Bliss had slowed to a trot and was ambling toward me, looking for her usual treat.

"No," I said. "*I am turning it over to my higher power.*"

I retrieved a carrot for the girl.

"Like, seriously?"

"Only kidding. I don't know my *Higher Power*."

"You don't believe in God?" she asked.

"I don't know. No one in my house believes in God. Dad calls it the great crutch. A case of man manipulating man, designed for the masses who can't see the joke."

"The joke?"

Bliss took the carrot carefully from my outstretched hand.

"Yeah, the big lie about heaven and hell and obeying laws that should have been dead and buried long ago."

"But they don't really think it's a joke? Like, I mean, they don't actually laugh about it do they?"

"They do. They laugh at religion of any sort; although they seem to be using the words from the program. Their new mantra is *Turn it Over*. Turn it over to what? That's what I want to know. I want something more than a thought; I want something I can see and touch and count on. I want something real, something that won't leave me or disappear like those clouds up there. I want it to take ahold of me and last forever."

"You mean you want a miracle? Maybe you should try my church and become a nun!"

"Oh, so you're Catholic?"

She turned, and crossed herself. "A Roman Catholic. But, not really. I don't know. After going to Catholic schools and being brainwashed into the world of saints and sinners, it just doesn't add up. Like, how come, in a world of five billion, only a little more than a billion are Catholic?"

"You mean why didn't God save everyone? I've had the same thoughts myself."

"Yeah. I don't go to church anymore, and I don't believe in saints...well, except, like, maybe, Joan of Arc and Bernadette."

"Who?" I asked.

"The girls that saw visions. Bernadette spent her whole life locked up in prison because she claimed Mary spoke to her. Joan believed God told her to lead the French to victory. And she did. Like, with God at her side and all."

"I bet they were nutcases," I said. "Imagine if we saw the Virgin Mary and told anyone about it? They'd put us in a crazy house!"

"Yes, well they didn't believe Bernadette, either. I mean that girl was like serious! Even if what she saw was wishful thinking, she stuck to her story. So did Joan, who was rewarded with death by fire."

I slid off the hay bale. "I would love to see a vision."

"Well check the char on your toast or the frost on your windows. Jesus is known to show up in some strange places," she laughed, joining me on the ground.

"I want the *real* thing."

"Like, just how real? People believe things and then their imaginations take over," she said.

"If I saw Jesus, I'd fall down at his feet. If I knew God, really knew Him, I would give up everything and do whatever it took to be holy." I was saying words I'd never said before. She was looking at me as if I had painted my face purple.

"Well, I suppose if God was that handy the whole world would pay attention."

"I want to believe like people do at this little church I go to now and then. They seem to really be into it, whatever *it* is. It's half magic and half true. They have these miracles that happen all the time."

"Miracles? Church? I didn't know you went to church! Geez, Lily."

"I feel weird even trying to talk about it."

She jumped down from the straw bale and came closer to me to give me a hug. We walked arm in arm down the driveway. "I suppose there's lots we don't know about each other," she said.

"So, do you think I'm crazy? I mean, I'm just curious, that's all!"

"No, I don't. Really, I hope I didn't hurt your feelings."

"Hey, don't worry. I am actually not into churches. It's just that I can't help wondering what's real and what's not. I've been visiting this little church with no name in Woodbury once in a while. It meets in an old barn. Out front the sign says, **God Loves You** in big hand painted letters. It kind of interests me."

"Wow," Nancy said, "I can't imagine going *inside*! I don't think I'd dare go in a place like that."

"Oh, I went for fun. Strange, you know, that guy I work with, took me there to watch his brother preach. He thinks it's all an act, a performance. I guess I was expecting to agree, but I didn't freak out at the service the way he does. I was amazed at the power his brother has. It's like you can see electricity popping off his skin. He's a big handsome guy, a movie star pushing God."

We had walked to the end of the road. "I should get on home," I said.

My bicycle lay in the golden rod and as I pulled it up she asked, "Would you take me sometime? I mean, I'm curious, too."

"Sure," I answered. "That's why I went there the first time and the second and the third—I guess it's why I will go again."

I felt flattered that she would even consider going. It was more proof of our closeness, and besides, she had her mother's yellow bug, so that would solve any transportation problems.

At first, I thought it would be interesting to see her reactions, but, then I had second thoughts. Maybe I didn't want to bring her along. We had both changed a lot lately, and her changes were most evident. With her braces off, she was more beautiful than ever, and without a bit of make-up. There was something about her softness that made you feel safe and drew you in. Did I really want to introduce her to Brother Barry? I wasn't so sure I wanted to share his attention.

As I rode my bike home, I considered how things happen in the most unusual ways. Strange, who hated churches, had introduced me to one. Nancy, who was questioning her life, managed to add meaning to mine. My parents were together again because their house with all their history burned down. It just didn't make sense. How could anyone figure it out? Just when you think you are going one way, the road turns and you're going another.

I was pushing hard on the pedals climbing up Woodhouse Hill when a bona fide reincarnation happened. I saw something moving in the apple orchard on my right. A big rabbit, a puppy, a fox? I hopped off my bike and saw the unbelievable. There was a cat, squatting in the roadside lace. It was a pale orange, the color of Ernest, hugging the ground and as pathetic as a tarred rabbit, not that I'd ever seen one.

"Ernest?" I called, squatting down, hoping the creature would come closer. Its ears went back and its tail stood tensely on end. As I moved slightly in his direction he stayed crouched, studying me with those big yellow eyes opening and shutting. "Ernest!" I cried, "Is that you? Come here, come to Mama."

He stretched his head forward, put up his rear-end, waved the tip of his snarled tail a little and then took a few steps. I waited as patiently as I could for the next step and then the next. Suddenly, he ran and pounced on my chest, purring into my neck, winding himself across my shoulders. It was Ernest, wonderfully alive. I counted his toes. Six on each foot! He looked fine. Not hungry, not wild-eyed, just a mess of stickers and straw. "Where have you been?" I asked. "Where have you been?"

I left my wheels on the side of the road and walked the rest of the way home with Ernest nestled in my arms. It had been a long time for me; well over a year of adventure for Ernest.

Soon it was late summer at its worst, hot and still, with air as heavy as a horse blanket. It weighed on my shoulders, made me too lazy to think, but I took time to get together with Carrie and Trish. I wanted to touch base before summer was over. They were going to be sophomores soon. It was too obvious they were happy to have lives beyond Purgatory and anxious to get back to them. Living in different worlds for the last year meant our realities had changed. I felt like they had new priorities and I was the odd girl out.

We sat in Carrie's car drinking soda at the Carvel stand with the car's air-conditioning running so we could stay cool. I was in the back, barefoot and as undressed as I could be without breaking the law. It almost felt like the old days.

"It isn't that I don't like Purgatory," Carrie was saying, "It's just that it's so boring. There's nothing to do here but drink and get stoned or take a hike. No surprises."

I asked her about Drew. It used to be she wouldn't talk about anyone else. "Oh, I don't know," she said. "He's still sweet as rain but he's *so* Purgatory, and I want something new."

I had heard from Trish that Carrie and Drew still had a thing going, but she insisted they were just trying to make summer more interesting. Trish, meanwhile, had been running to Boston to visit new friends and I suspect there was a boy she was more involved with than she admitted. The good news was Trish was healthy and happy, her mono long gone.

Over the course of the year, those who had not gone away to school were working, getting married, pregnant, falling in and out of love and turning their high school cliques into another generation of Purgatory locals. Their giggles and gossip made me uncomfortable, I had withdrawn into romantic books, poetry, horseback riding and looking for God in the strangest of places. My September exodus seemed less and less of a choice; it had become a must.

From the small wages I'd earned at Pearl's Boutique and the monthly dole of my trust fund, I managed to have enough to start school unburdened with loans. Once in school, I pictured a full life in Burlington, finding a part-time job, new friends and hopefully a clearer direction into the future. The idea of becoming a veterinarian wasn't as fixed as I pretended. I was glad Carrie was going to be my *big sister* on campus and she promised we would have nothing but fun. Like Carrie, I was ready to leave Purgatory behind. Most of it, but not all.

8

I'd started having a secret life that summer by borrowing the family car on Sundays and taking off for church in Woodbury. It was easy to get away on Sunday mornings because Mom and Dad slept late, then usually indulged in their ritual pancake breakfasts, too many cups of coffee, devouring the *New York Times* and hanging around until mid-afternoon—their idea of a day of rest. Heather preferred to sleep late and was left undisturbed, while Brent may have been there physically, but was usually lost in his ongoing space cadet game of Dungeons and Dragons.

On the last Saturday in August, I received a phone call from Brother Barry. I wasn't home, but he left a message saying he hoped he could have a talk with me before I left for school. Would I stay a few minutes after the service? I replayed the message twice before I erased it and prayed no one else had heard it.

For weeks I had meant to call Nancy to come to church with me, but I didn't. I was preserving it for myself and perhaps a little afraid of her judgment. I didn't even tell her about Brother Barry's call which I considered comparable to having an audience with the Pope.

On the following Sunday, I dressed carefully, putting on my favorite yellow t-shirt, a potato-print wraparound skirt and the tiny blue turquoise earrings Strange had given me for my nineteenth birthday. Grandmother Lillian's lucky bracelet sparkled on my wrist.

Driving up the bumpy road beyond the Woodbury Common, the words of last Sunday's sermon began reverberating in my head. "There is no fear in love," I'd heard. "Love takes care of itself. Perfect love drives out fear."

I wondered if the tightness I was feeling was excitement or fear. Each week I felt I was getting to know Brother Barry better, mostly through his sermons which I thought were directed at me. Sometimes he would hold my hand at the door a little longer than he held others and say how much he appreciated my coming.

"I can see a light around you wherever you sit," he'd said last week.

My foot inadvertently leaned harder on the gas pedal as I thought again about his surprise phone call and its curious message. Why had he called and asked me to visit with him after church? Was he going to pressure me to join? Was he worried about Strange, who was no longer in his life? Was he going to make a pass at me? My heart jumped just at the thought. He was a grown man and I had yet to date a boy seriously. How could I possibly think such a thing?

I wished I knew who I wanted to know more, Brother Barry or Jesus. Brother Barry was so clear about who and what came first. I also knew where his clarity came from. He told us in one of his sermons that God spoke to him at a time when he couldn't even think to pray. His parents had just died violently and his world had disappeared overnight. He said it was an abandonment too terrible for fixing, too hard to try to understand. He and David, his brother, were left with only each other, and a rickety clapboard house that asked for a lot of maintenance, along with a garden that wanted tending.

One day while he was sitting on his back steps, wondering what to do next, whether he should send his brother to a foster home, sell the house, rent out the spare rooms or clean up the vegetable garden, he felt the heat of the Holy Spirit enter him. "Like a sword descending from on high, God pierced my heart and love coursed through my veins, pushing out the poison and pain that were about to close me down. I heard God's words, 'You are blessed my son, you will never be alone'."

He believed this experience was a calling. He had no one, no religious education, no background or affinity to explain the phenomenon. But he was changed in that moment, and knew he had been chosen by The Promise and called to do God's work. Doors continued to open from then on.

I believed his story was true, and it made it easy for me to understand why he was so fervent. It also explained why he set up his life as a preacher first, before he worried about his education. He said his congregation ordained him week after week, proving he was on the right path, and that God continued to reveal to him everything he needed to know; it was all there right on the pages of the Bible.

He reminded us that, like himself, the Apostles were simple men. They didn't get degrees or look beyond Jesus for permission to spread the Word. God took his hand and ruled his mind when he read scripture. The Lord helped him just as He did all his true disciples. When he named himself Brother Barry and held meetings in the Episcopalian church basement and people began to come to hear about his experience, he believed God sent them. He was not shy about reaching out either. He made notes to leave on windshields in parking lots, brought messages to the local hospital, visited the local court and attended hundreds of funerals and weddings where he handed out invitations like candy. And people came. As more and more people started attending the evening meetings, they began to outnumber those that attended the church upstairs, and soon the gift of space from the Episcopalians came to an end.

He didn't give up. The following week God led him to an abandoned store in Brattleboro and when he asked if he could hold meetings in it until it was rented, the realtors were agreeable. With an investment in folding chairs, a second hand podium and a new SONY microphone, the store space became a meeting hall until an Avis Rental car dealer took it over six months later. Now, he was feeling more settled as he transformed the old barn in Woodbury into a house of worship.

Not only did the faint scent of horses make the place more comfortable for me, but I liked its simplicity in contrast to the musty velvet covered pews of the Methodist church. Purgatory's stodgy old church left me cold, with its dark glass windows and dead people's names hammered in brass at the head of each row. The barn's old wooden exterior, its wide open doors and fresh air flowing through the windows were more inviting. That, and the way people went there to find Jesus and not just out of habit. More important, I thought it was wonderful to know a person who believed in Christ completely. For me, to meet someone God had chosen was as amazing as meeting Edison or Bon Jovi or Princess Diana. Marshall Barry's Christianity seemed like the real thing. He not only asked us to think differently, to learn and trust God's laws, he offered answers to questions I had never named.

Like I've said, churchy people were jokes in my house. Dad would say things like, "Old Lady Smithwick has her Sunday trappings on, I hope Jesus likes pink." Or Mom would say, "Those old biddies think putting a steeple over their heads makes them right, I think they'd be better off with a subscription to *Mother Jones*." Heather called the Christian girls at school the future *Stepford Wives*. I knew everyone in my family would feel superior to Brother Barry.

A blazing branch of maple against a sun-bleached field flagged an early reminder that autumn was approaching and in only days I would be heading north to start school. I was considering how much I would miss my forays to the church when the weathered building appeared on my right at the bend of the road. Brother Barry was standing outside the door wearing a new long burlap robe. He looked monastic with a rope at his waist, a wooden cross hanging across his chest, and heavy leather sandals on his tan feet.

I pulled into the side parking area, fluffed my hair and checked my teeth for raspberry seeds in the rear-view mirror. As I walked to the door, I saw him see me and meant to look away, but ended up at his side among a few overly adoring teenage girls and some little boys, a bundle of numbers in oversized sports shirts.

"Good morning Brother Barry, nice to see you," I said, hoping I sounded cool and confident.

"Glad you made it, Lily." He smiled, his fathomless sea blue eyes full of welcome.

"Do you still want to see me after church today?" I asked.

"Yes, Lily, I was looking forward to that. Would you be willing to wait until the other parishioners leave?"

My name sounded almost musical coming from his lips. Did he need an answer? I would have waited 'til the snow fell to find out what was so important that he needed to talk to me about.

The sermon was all about trust and intimacy, the need for loved ones to stay true. He taught that an obedient love for each other was no different than our love for God. "Love must come first. Love begets love. Two are better than one, because they have a good return for their work: If one falls down, his friend can help him up. But pity the man who falls and has no one to help him up! Also, if two lie down together, they will keep one another warm. But how can one keep warm alone? Though one may be overpowered, two can defend themselves. Love is the greatest power." His eyes grew moist as he spoke of The Most Profound Love, the gift of Jesus and the covenant with all who believed in him to have everlasting life.

At the end he instructed us, "Do right. Walk with God. Love one another. Trust. Amen and Amen."

After church, I had to busy myself until the last of the sheep took off. It was warm and humid, so I walked down the path behind the church to the river where some trees offered shade. The backs of the leaves were up, rain surely on its way. My hair was hopelessly limp and pulling it back would be a wasted effort. On the river bank, I found a large flat rock beneath a willow and sat with my espadrilles tucked beside me. With the cool water running over my feet and away from the chatty church folk, it was quiet and peaceful.

I saw a turtle scrutinizing me from a granite perch in the middle of the stream. As soon as I caught his eye he slid into the safety of the water. Little did he know I represented no danger; I would only protect him. Tadpoles swirled around my toes. I looked for evidence of how big they would grow, what colors they would wear in the spring, that is, if they survived winter. Smooth gray stones were transformed into yellows and greens in the water. From the top of the silver ash across the way a cardinal called. Downriver, glimpses of fall's colors lit the woods. We hadn't had a frost yet, not even a cold night, but the leaves were starting to turn anyway, ahead of schedule. Top-heavy heads of Queen Anne's lace nodded among stalks of black-eyed Susans. Blue asters lit the dark tangles of brush with periwinkle stars.

Brother Barry's shadow darkened the river at my feet. I said, "Hi," and his deep voice asked if there was any room for him on my rock. I moved over and smiled, patting the space I had made. He removed his sandals, put them next to mine and sat down beside me, slapping the water with his feet. "Hmm, feels good," he said. We stared at the ripples running about and around our feet. He was very close, we almost touched. I became a sponge soaking up the nearness of him; inhaling the scent of his maleness and trying to recognize the soap he must have used that morning. I was heady from his mild, musky fragrance, his heat. His arm hairs touched mine and set them on end. I don't think I ever felt so alive.

"Thank you for waiting," he said. "Is this the last week for you, Lily?"

Again, my name sounded musical spoken from his mouth. "Yes. I guess it is," I said.

"I don't want you to lose what you have found here. College is a dangerous place for an uncommitted Christian, Lily. You can be led away. I would hate to see you led away. I would hate to see that happen to you."

"I can't imagine how it could be any more dangerous than the rest of the world," I said.

"Well, it is. College professors have a great deal of cynicism and may seduce you away from the simple beauty of Christ's message. They don't see the light that pours out of the Bible or believe the truth it reveals. They prefer to intellectualize it and break it down to cast doubt on the Word. They think it is their job to make every student question the most basic ideas they arrive with. It's a sad situation, Lily. I want you to remember every minute you are there that God loves you, and so do I."

I turned and forced myself to look right into his eyes. I wanted to make this moment something to remember until I died. "I will," I said, hoping he heard how I had turned my promise into a sacrament of some sort.

"I am sure. You are a very special girl," he said. His head was tilted up, catching a stray slant of sun, something like a halo seemed to form around him.

"I want to be," I said softly, a deep truth in my own words making its mark on my newly discovered soul.

"But you must remember that *in much wisdom there is much grief and increase of knowledge is increase in sorrow.* These are God's own words."

I couldn't help but thrill hearing him speak so directly to me, from the Bible or anywhere else. I was never quite sure where Scripture left off and Marshall Barry began.

"I want, I want to love God. I want to trust that what you know is something I could know just as well," I said.

He seemed to like that, and leaned into me a little more. He placed his hands on my shoulders and I felt the strength of his big hands burn into me.

"Of course you can. You are God's daughter. *You are the temple of God and the Spirit of God dwells in you.* Have you been baptized, Lily?"

I was almost embarrassed. "Baptized? Me? No. My parents don't believe."

"Well, then, why don't we baptize you, today, here in the river, out in the open under God's gracious sky, in His unspoiled waters. Let's do it right now. Are you ready?"

He was so sincere, so caring and wanting to share this wonderful thing he knew with me, I felt honored and shy. Strong and weak. It was a moment that could change my life, forever, if I chose to do as he asked. "Here? In the river?" I asked.

"It won't be the first time anyone was dedicated to the Lord outside, under the sun. After all, Jesus was baptized in a river by John. What could be a better example than that?"

"What do I do about my clothes? I mean, do I just bow my head or something?"

"Imagine that we are at the River Jordan. You are delivering yourself into God's hands just as he delivered you unto the world, naked and trusting. Take off your clothes and enter his waters. He will make all things right."

I had no idea that Christians were baptized this way. In a kind of dream, I lifted my t-shirt above my head and folded it neatly placing it on the rock. Then I untied my skirt and draped it on a bush nearby, its sash hung down and teased the water. Then he turned me to him and put his thumbs on either side of my cotton panties and pulled them down, placing them atop my shirt, neatly. His hands then took my shoulders and moved down over my arms and found the fasteners to my bra. Without moving, I ended up standing before him completely stripped and not afraid. All of heaven might have been watching and I felt like I was in a trance, ready to be lifted up.

Then Brother Barry began to caress my breasts and move his lips from my hair to my forehead to my lips, and then moved from my face to my neck and downward. I had never been seen in my woman's body by any man, and was trembling and amazed at what was happening. I didn't ask myself whether it was right or wrong. I was giving myself completely, my trust and love and the thrill of it all tangled up into one thing. His strength, the rock hard maleness of him that secured me as he tipped me on my back and lowered me into the water.

"God loves you, Lily," he said as he made the sign of the cross with his fingers on my brow and moved me to a deeper part of the river. "I baptize you, Lily Woodhouse, in the name of the Father and Son and Holy Ghost. All your sins are forgiven and you are born again into the house of the Lord."

I lay like a lotus flower, my body relaxed into ecstatic peace, with my arms spread out like petals and my hair floating like roots beneath the cool water. Ripples danced over my breasts and knees. I was suspended in time and place. Any sin I had ever committed was washed away. Wonder and beauty filled me and I was one with the spirit.

His arms lifted me and carried me from the water just as they had laid me in it and as far as I was concerned they might have been the arms of Jesus.

My feet didn't touch the ground as we moved from the river to his mobile home. He carried me to his unmade bed, dropped his wet robe then covered me with himself. Our bodies met and melded together with a heat that I didn't know existed. He kissed me, all of me, my eyes my hands my belly and then he opened my legs and placed himself inside me. It was what I wanted. All I wanted.

I suppose there was some pain, but nothing compared to having the son of God giving himself to me as I offered myself to him. It felt like the most natural and holy thing that had ever happened. It was as if my whole life had been waiting for this moment and now everything made sense. I was no longer a me but a we. I was part of something too big to name. I burned with pleasure and wept from the relief and beauty of it all. He groaned and collapsed on me. Salty tears rolled off his cheeks and merged with mine. We both were found.

I couldn't speak, I was wet with emotions and the cataclysmic commotion of our body fluids. He slowly rose and soaked a small towel in warm water and returned to me to wash me like a baby. Tenderness passed from his hands through the pores of my skin and became lodged in my heart.

This was love.

After a few intimate moments together he dressed and went outside to retrieve my clothes. Shyness swept over me as he returned and I put back on the clothes I had so willingly abandoned.

We said little as I staggered somewhat dazedly from the trailer to the car. Everything in the real world was changed. Nothing I saw or tasted, smelled or touched would ever feel the same. I spent the rest of the day reliving those miraculous moments with Brother Barry, behind the closed doors of my room. Had we made a baby? Would Strange ever forgive me? I didn't care. My new life was spread before me and God was going to hold my hand. I wanted to be as far away from my family as I could be and school was last on my list.

9

The next day Brother Barry called me at the store and asked if I was all right. I spoke with my hand cupped around the mouthpiece and my back to Strange. The store was too public for me to have any real conversation, not that the bubbles in my brain would have allowed it.

"Oh, I'm fine. How are you?" I replied, trying to ignore the blood throbbing in my ears, the wetness of my hand.

Of course, I was all right! I was very all right. The only unthinkable problem was that I would be leaving town in six days. I needed to see him and I didn't know how to tell him how much. "Could we get together someday this week?" I asked. "I really want to see you. You know, I'll be leaving soon." Was I whining? I could not whine.

"I know you are leaving soon. I want to see you, too, Lily. But I have to do a funeral tomorrow in Londonderry," he said, "and there is a family event afterward. Wednesday, I have to help plan a religious retreat at the Putney Independent Church with their board. We are doing a program with our combined youth groups next weekend." He paused, "How about Friday? Can you make it then?"

Disappointment struck me. Friday? It was a hundred years away as far as I was concerned. "But...I...I am leaving on Sunday. That will only give us one chance to be together."

"Lily, I have to do what I am called to do. You are one of the most precious creatures on earth as far as I am concerned, but when Jesus calls, I have to answer. I would love to spend every day, every minute with you, except that

I am bound to these other things. This is a very, very busy week for me. It must be the same for you."

My arms ached. My legs ached. I wanted him so much. I knew he had important work and that many people depended on him, but I felt like my whole body was screaming, *Me, me, take care of me!* "Okay, if you can't see me I suppose I have no choice but to wait. I understand," I lied, trying to cover the wave of disappointment. The difference in my urgency from his was clear.

"I *see* you Lily. I see you in my arms. I feel you too, your skin, your long legs, your sweetness letting me come in."

"Oh. Oh, I see you too," I said, almost melting at the thought of us in those unbelievable moments.

"Believe me, Lily, I am with you. Remember this. *Wherever two come together in my name, there am I.* These are God's words and we have come together in his name. Just as He loves us, I love you, Lily. We have a beautiful thing that is going to grow only if we tend our responsibilities. I have a job that I cannot deny. You are preparing to go away. Please don't let your feelings make you sad. I will see you on Friday. Would you like me to pick you up or will you come to the trailer?" His voice grew softer, "I want to hold you."

The phone just about burned my hand off. I was weak with want. I needed to be with him. I needed to know he was real, that we were real.

"I will come to you," I promised.

School was supposed to be number one on my priority list. I knew that. But how could I take off in the face of what I was feeling? Life had just begun. Every color was brighter, every minute more urgent. The skies opened and closed only for me, for us. The one thing that existed was this new desire. My family dissolved into a group of actors on a stage. Heather and Brent did not annoy me as much as they normally did. In fact, I wanted to tell them that I was born again, but that would have been stupid.

Ernest slept with me at night. I felt his tenderness and attachment as I had never done before. He was my proof, my very own proof in miracles. I made Heather swear that she would take care of him for me. Make room for him in her bed if he was missing me. In a weak moment she agreed. Maybe it was because she was about to take over everything else I had once considered mine. My room, my bed, my closet and probably any clothes I left behind. I don't know that I cared. My attachment was to Pastor Marshall Barry and nothing could compete for the space he now filled.

One night during that final week at home, Mom was preparing dinner and the smell of her homemade pumpkin soup and browning popovers pulled the whole family to the kitchen. She asked me if Pearl had found my replacement yet?

"No. I don't think she's looking very hard," I said, as I took another spoonful of the thick orange froth. "Hmmm, this is so good."

"I could do it," Heather said, twirling on the kitchen stool.

She might as well have said she was trying out for the cheerleading squad. "You? You would work for Pearl? But you've never even walked in the front door of Pearl's. Why would you want to work there?" I asked.

"Simple. I need the money," she said.

"You could make more waitressing on weekends," Mom pointed out.

"I refuse to serve Cokes or anything else to the kids in this town."

"Oh, are you too good for that?" I asked.

"How about babysitting?" Mom suggested.

Brent snorted, "Heather? Heather tucking kids in at night?"

She agreed with him. "I don't really like kids that much and they're worse with a babysitter. Remember how we used to torture Amelia?"

I did. I remembered how we told her the old house was haunted and Woodhouse ghosts lived in the attic. Amelia was a very young jittery fourteen year old when she sat for us. We recognized a patsy for our pranks. It was great fun to spook her with strange sounds, faking fear, running to the basement and dragging her with us, piling stuff around us to build a safety zone.

Mom pointed out that all kids were not as imaginative as we were. "You could win them over, Heather, with some good story-telling and treats."

"Are you kidding? It's the parents I'd have to win over. Haven't you noticed how the people in town look at me? It's like I'm a drugged-up vampire or something. No conscientious mother would leave her kids with me!"

"Well, Heather, maybe it's time to change. I mean, you don't have to stick with this Goth nonsense," Mom said.

"And why would you want people to distrust you?" added Dad. "It's not a bad thing to be a pretty woman. You have good ankles and nice feet and then you cover them up with those big combat boots. And what's more, I hate to be the one to say it, but you don't look that great in black."

"I happen to like it, and I don't give a shit what you think."

Ouch. The nasties were coming on, her nails getting ready to scratch the blackboard.

I was foolish enough to try reason. "What about Strange? Do you really want to work with Strange? You've always made fun of him. You called him a creep and a weirdo."

"I don't have to marry the guy. God, are you jealous or something, Lil? Do you want me or not want me to have the job? Is this some kind of family intervention? Let's all get in Heather's face?"

"No, not at all. I am only pointing out that Strange is my friend. I don't want you to push him away. You need to consider that the two of you will be in a tight space and you'll have to get along. I could speak to Pearl and maybe help you get hired, but you'll have to promise me that you'll figure out how to get along with Strange. He's a really nice guy and smarter than most of the boys you know, which of course isn't saying much. And, maybe, if you are serious, if you really want the job, you could tone down the heavy black eye shadow a little."

"If Pearl likes Strange; why not me?" she argued.

"You might be right. Just don't try to be so morbid, so snotty, okay? Try niceness. Smile a little, if you're going to dress like a Goth you don't have to act like one. You need to bring people into the store, not put them off."

"You can be such a bitch," she sneered, forgetting to say thank you, as usual.

When Nancy and I got together for a cup of hot chocolate at the coffee house on Purgatory's green, I couldn't wait to tell her about the possibility of Heather and Strange working together. "It'll be a love or hate relationship, that's for sure," I predicted. "I imagine Strange must feel like it's his place now that he's fixed up the back room into a studio apartment. You should see it; it's pretty cool. Black ceilings with sticker constellations that glow in the night. Big posters of tattooed music men; a life size photo of Madonna; a strobe light and black pinstriped striped sheets on his bed."

"Black sheets! Like, not good if he has dandruff," Nancy said. "Let's go to the shop. I need a scrapbook. I've been taking pictures of the horses and shots of the barn, playing with angles of light on horsey things like reins and stirrups. It will be a kind of memory book around *the girls*, like a photo essay."

"I can't wait to see it!" I said. "I love photography."

"I have to get into something that's going to interest me while you're away. Like, I am really going to miss you."

"Pearl doesn't sell albums. We have an odd mix of inventory, everything from crazy hats to birthday candles that you can't blow out, and clown noses that squeak when they're pinched. Pearl goes to outlet places and brings back what she calls *exotics*. It's mostly stuff that nobody needs but work as gag gifts or something unique for the person who has everything. She's a character. Let's go over there, anyway. I want to talk to Strange and you can meet him and see his space."

"Sure. He's the one with the holy brother, right? The brother with the kooky church that I have yet to see? Like, we never did go," she pointed out.

I ignored the hint. "Strange is different from any guy I know. He's his own person. He reads heavy stuff and actually thinks about things like philosophy and science. He's not a person anyone would date, but he's a person anyone would like once they got to know him."

"Do you think Strange is too strange, like, for your family?"

"Oh, I don't know. My family might like him, if they knew him well enough. Brent teases me about him. Heather makes fun of him, too, but she would make fun of anyone who was my friend."

"Even me?" Nancy asked.

"Probably. That's why I've kept you all to myself."

We walked across the road and down Main Street to the front of the shop. Inside, Strange was perched on a high chair at the counter reading *Mad Magazine*. He didn't lift his eyes above the page when the Indian bells tinkled.

"Oh, so it's St. Lillian," he said. "Soon to be among the departed."

"Hey, David, I want you to meet my other best friend, Nancy Kimball."

Nancy smiled and said, "Hi."

"Call me Strange," he said, eyes downcast, voice as dry as old bread. His lips were covered by the curl of his thin index finger, which wore a coat of metallic black polish. He stroked his chin while his eyes remained glued to the page.

Then he snarled, "Pearl says you are trying to replace yourself with the bitch of the century. Are you actually going to sic your sister on me? What have I done to deserve this queen of the dark? I'll bet she doesn't know shit about the Goths other than black! Has she ever heard of Beetlejuice or Sisters of Mercy? Bauhaus? I mean she doesn't even know the meaning of the stupid costumes she wears."

"You'll have to teach her," I laughed. I couldn't help but wonder which one of them would be the first to mess things up. They were both very capable.

"Do you have any scrapbooks?" Nancy asked, nonchalantly.

"You want to see my scrapbooks?" Strange responded, finally looking her way.

"Not exactly. I want to *buy* a scrapbook, but, like, if you want to share your own, that's cool too."

"We've got a few inane photo albums, is all," Strange said, rising from his chair. He poked around the shelves and came up with a little plastic picture album meant to amuse people unable to think of captions for themselves. "Butt Ugly, Serious Mistakes, Momma's Favorite, An Excuse for a Friend." They were full of inspirational titles for idiots.

Later, in the afternoon, when Nancy and I were back out at the farm riding Sadie and Bliss across the field, I mentioned my fear. "Heather better treat Strange well. He doesn't have any family or friends to speak of, except his brother and that is like a dove trying to love an eagle."

"Who's the dove?" Nancy asked.

"Definitely Strange. He's delicate, can't you tell? He's wants to keep life simple and keeps to himself. He's beautiful, but not like most guys and nothing like his brother."

"I thought he was a little stuck-up," Nancy said. "Sounds like you understand him, though."

"He was just putting on an act. I'll miss him more than I'll miss Heather," I said.

"Oh, I bet you'll miss her more than you know. Like, I'd love to have a sister. It's hard being an only child."

"You wouldn't want Heather for one, I can promise you. Sadie makes a much better sibling, even though she whinnies a lot."

Nancy laughed. She was sunny that day, like most days, really. No matter how miserable she may have felt, she was good at acting happy. We could ride and hangout and talk for hours or not talk at all. When we talked, we were honest with each other and she was a good listener, what I thought a true sister should be.

Bliss was trotting along next to Sadie and seeming to enjoy the cool outing as much as I. Her reins were slack in my hands as I turned to Nancy. "I want to tell you something and I need you to swear not to tell a soul. It has to be secret for a zillion reasons. Number one—no one will understand."

"Geez, what is it?"

"Well, I met this man. I never thought anything like this would happen to me. It's all kind of mystical and scary. He's the most wonderful person I could have imagined. It happened so fast, so miraculously, I know God put us together."

"God?" she asked.

Color came to my face. "It just happened, Nancy. Big time. One minute I was just a me and the next I was his."

She stopped trotting and so did Bliss. "But when did this happen? How come it happened so fast?" Nancy asked, gripping Sadie's reins, Sadie looking at me through her long lashes as if she, too, wanted an explanation.

"I'm totally in love with him. He's all I can think about. I keep wondering how I can go away to school feeling this way. We're meant to be together. It can't be an accident that he showed up in my life just before I was to go away. Now I don't want to go. I think maybe I shouldn't."

"Wow! I don't know what to say," Nancy exclaimed, just as Sadie raised up her head and front legs and neighed. We all saw what she saw. A black snake slithered away, disappearing in the grasses.

"I hate snakes!" I cried.

"It's just a plain, old, harmless garden snake. They're good to have around."

"Maybe you think so, but they're scary to me," I said. "I'm going to go back, okay?" We turned our horses around and trotted slowly toward the barn. The road was rarely traveled by anything other than logging trucks and cross country skiers. Occasionally a mountain biker found it. We loved that it was mostly quiet and undiscovered. I was nervous because of the snake but mostly because I had told Nancy my secret. She was more concerned than happy for me, I knew. I could hear it in her voice.

After a few minutes of silence, she spoke. "Lily, I'm your friend and I am going to give you advice because I really, really care about you. I know you haven't asked me for any but...."

"I just hate snakes," I said.

"No. No, it's not about you and the snake, it's about you and that guy *God* sent."

"You think I am making it up. Is that it? You think I'm just dreaming, that's there no such thing as love at first sight?"

"I didn't say that."

"I haven't made it up, Nancy. I love Brother Barry and he loves me. He said so."

"Who? Is that who you're talking about? The minister? Strange's brother? But isn't he too old for you? I am not questioning you, Lily, it's just, I just wanted to say...."

"Don't, don't say anything."

Why did I want to cry? I was frightened to hear what she thought. All I meant to do was let her in on what I was going through; to tell her about the most important thing in my life. I shot back, "Don't say anything because you don't know him. He's not old, he's less than ten years older than I, the same age difference between my father and mother. He's mature and special. Anyway, how you could you know what I feel? Have you ever been in love?"

She blushed. "Not really. There was this boy from Brownsville, but the timing was wrong."

"But don't you see? You blew it. He's gone!"

"We weren't ready. I got over it. I did. The same might be true for you."

"I am almost nineteen years old. He's got his career going. He doesn't have anybody to back him up. I could be that person, Nancy. God even says two are better than one. You know in the olden days girls got married at fourteen and fifteen. The Virgin Mary was only fourteen."

"Married? Geez! I hear you, Lily, but it's so quick. Have you talked to your mom and dad about it?"

"How can I? My parents won't want me married, especially to a minister. I can't even go see him without my parents pestering me about where I'm going. If I come home for visits, they'll ruin it—ruin the best thing that has ever happened to me. They can't know. They wouldn't approve. I know they wouldn't. It makes it so difficult. They think Christians *should* be fed to the lions. Dad says they should be eliminated for the sake of human progress, that they are the world's troublemakers. He would never understand Brother Barry or be willing to try."

"Maybe your mother would understand a little better."

"She doesn't seem to feel any differently than Dad. She laughs when he starts ranting about the far right's righteous thinking."

She shook her head. "Listen, you have to go to school. It is not like you are leaving for a stint on the Voyager. If you can get a ride home, you can stay with me when you come. Come to my house and you will be able to see him now and then. I know I must sound like somebody's grandmother, but you don't want to jump off a cliff for this guy. If this is it, this is it. Just take your time, try to get to know him a little better. You shouldn't have to worry about losing him."

"I know him now. I am so sure this is it."

After I had absorbed her wonderful invitation, I realized she could not have said or done anything kinder. Life was going to work out after all.

What I did not realize was that I had yet to call Marshall anything but Brother Barry. Nevertheless, Friday was in sight and then I would call him what he was, my love, my life, my everything.

You can imagine my heartache when he was called away and I couldn't claim him after all.

10

I was barely settled in at school when I got a letter from Heather. If she had parachuted onto the quad, I wouldn't have been more surprised. Her words raced across the pages in run-on sentences.

I'm choking on Ernest...he sleeps right in my face. Mom and Dad are fighting again and even though he's still in the house he's not sleeping in her room....Brent is his miserable self....I'm working weekends at Pearl's and Strange is introducing me to music I never heard of before. My favorite, Sisters of Mercy, goes like this—

Departed or gone
They were waiting for me when I thought
That I just can't go on
And they brought me their comfort
And later they brought me this song—
Yes you must leave everything
That you cannot control
It begins with your family,
But soon comes round to your soul...

It's deep, isn't it?
p.s. I am thinking of changing my name to Jezebel.

How smart of Strange to connect through his music! Her letter closed with thanking me for my bed as it was proving to be more comfortable than the swishing waterbed she had begged for and hated from day one.

I read and reread the letter. It was full of energy, like she was dancing on the page. My going was the best thing that ever happened to her, that was clear. Well, good! If it took my absence to make her happy, so what?

I was living in a pastel dream, far away from everyone and everything, including my roommates. Four girls in a suite is not exactly comfy, cozy. We shared one small window, a single toilet and had no privacy except for a lock on the bathroom in the event of those times when absolute privacy was necessary. Two of us had computers that hogged the desk space. Our only telephone was the one we shared with everyone else in the hall.

All I wanted was to be in that little travel trailer beside the church. I had taken a part time job at the school store that gave me a break from obsessively wishing for Marshall's arms. I found myself praying he would come up for a visit, knowing he wouldn't, that it would be awkward and he would feel out of place.

I called him during my second week of school. It took restraint to wait until then, but he needed my number and my address so he could reach me when he chose.

"How's my precious bird," he asked.

"I want to be with you," was all I could think to say. Feeling the want running through me."

"So, are you lonely?" he asked.

"Only for you," I said.

"You be a good girl, now," he said.

Good girl? What did that mean? I was not a child.

October was coming fast and would be my first excuse to go home. Carrie offered me a ride. She and Drew were going to be featured alumni at the OctoberFest, and not only ride on the royal float, but award a few scholarship prizes. As the fall of 1988's Homecoming Queen and winners of the Rotary Scholarship at graduation, they represented Purgatory's glitterati. I thought having to go backwards in time for local celebrity told you everything.

Funny though, we don't know what a hometown is until we leave it. Coming back in October with the big old maples and oaks dressed in their outrageous colors, the overstuffed scarecrows on the front lawns competing for best design, porches trimmed with pumpkins and cornstalks tied onto posts with homemade ribbons and raffia, the place looked prettier than I had remembered. I wondered why I had once been so anxious to leave.

On Saturday afternoon, Mom and Dad drove us to town for the homecoming game. Brent and I rocked and rolled quietly in Mavis's clumsy backseat and as I could have predicted, we split up as soon as we arrived in the high school parking lot. Brent announced there was no way he wanted to watch the football game, the parade or any of the rest. I claimed a need to connect with old friends.

"Back here at the lot by four," Dad ordered, clearly disappointed.

"Don't wait for me," I said. "Someone will give me a ride home." I was as sure Brother Barry would deliver me, as I was that he would be waiting for me somewhere in the parking lot.

I had called him as soon as I got home and we planned to meet.

I could see the top of his truck only yards away. My breath was short as I fought the urge to run to him, but I moved on, walking in the opposite direction. Little puffs of steam escaped from my mouth as I moved away from my parents, and quickly got lost in the crowd, feeling light-headed, a little queasiness of tension in my stomach. The town square, crispy as green apples, was warmed by the bright leaves of the maples. I loved their hot, happy splashes and dots, dancing one way and another in the last of their glory days.

OctoberFest is an annual tradition, fixed in the town's calendar. It's hallowed by most of the locals, old and young, including those in transition. Events were coordinated with the high school's Homecoming Weekend. With or without the weather cooperating, it brought out loads of people, many of them I almost knew; people to whom I could tell how much I loved college and that my family was doing fine, and our new house was almost finished, and real nice to live in. And, yes, we were lucky this year that the weather was awesome. And doesn't Carrie look beautiful? And oh I have to go say hi to Billy and so on. That's all I had to do for a half an hour to touch base and make sure folks would remember seeing me.

When I had done the rounds, I headed back to Brother Barry's truck. He was leaning against the cab, his strong arms folded across his chest, his feet crossed in a casual way. His plaid wool shirt, jeans and workboots were not at all like his Sunday self. He looked more like a tall John Denver. A wide-brimmed felt hat sat slightly askew on his head, shading his handsome face. That face, those arms. He was talking to a young girl, she must have been twelve or thirteen, kind of a goofy smile on her face as she talked, and he was listening intently, acting like she was the most interesting creature on earth. I wanted to stamp my feet and cry, "Mine!" but I knew better. I waited my turn and moved as nonchalantly as I could to his side. "Oh, Brother Barry," I said, as if I hadn't expected to see him, hadn't counted the minutes and planned every possible moment we would have alone. The girl could have been air.

He looked over at me, real calm and sure of himself. "Well, look at who the good Lord has sent this way." The girl smiled and stepped backwards. She knew her time was up.

"I saw you walking across the parking lot," he said.

"Yeah, I had to make the rounds. I couldn't show up and then not. Thank you for waiting for me. You know how it is." I was doing my best at acting relaxed.

"We should get out of here," he said. I clambered into the front seat ready to go anywhere on earth. It didn't matter where.

We headed north, on roads that wound through the tiny hamlets of Grafton and Hoosick Falls, over wooden bridges past inns and vegetable stands with pumpkins by the thousands. The Green Mountains seemed to be celebrating along with us. Bright branches laced in their autumn best arched over us. Roads opened and shut as we looked for the perfect logging road to lead us deep into the woodlands. At least that's where I prayed we were going. All the fancy words I'd planned had disappeared. I was like a cat at his side wanting to be stroked and more.

We found the perfect spot at the end of a dirt road, near an old foundation that spoke of a time when a person might have been forced to give up his dreams; when a winter may have been too hard and loneliness too harsh to build a home in the middle of nowhere. A cathedral of branches knotted overhead, walls of myrtle, hemlock and spruce surrounded us on three sides.

It took no begging for me to leave the cab and go to the blanket he spread on the rusted pine needles. He embraced me and we soon lay down. His kisses were like warm rain, turning me into a state of want I had never known. He was in charge and I was willing to let him have his way. It wasn't like he didn't give me a chance to say no.

He asked, "Lily, do you want this?"

"I do. I want it as much as I have ever wanted anything." I said. "It's just that, that..."

"Are you unprotected?" he asked.

"Yes," I said.

"I do not believe in protection," he said. "Sex is a sacrament, Lily. My semen will do what it is meant to do. I can only act as God's faithful servant. I am no Onan."

"Onan?" I asked. "What's an Onan?"

"Onan was the man who wasted his seeds in the soil and was killed for his disobedience to God's plan," he explained. "When sex is interfered with, it becomes a lurid act, denying God's design."

All I knew at that moment was that Onan had no meaning to me whatsoever. I loved this man and wasn't afraid to have his baby, dozens of them, as unlikely as it seemed.

He gripped each of my arms tightly and stared into my eyes before I shut them. "We are in God's hands," he said. "The Bible asks us to procreate and grow His kingdom. It says that is how a woman will be saved. I don't think we should try to outguess God's laws. Why would He have had them written down? Christians from the very beginning have honored them. Love is meant to bless us with babies and teach those babies to love and build the faith. If God chooses us, and He does, Lily, He will protect us and guide us and sustain us. You have to trust that."

"I do," I nodded. "But...." I said, as he put his lips on mine and my body careened into his with the heat of a branding iron. It had to be right, I knew it. God wouldn't have put us together if it wasn't.

We made love until we fell asleep all tangled up on his silly blanket with its infantile design of teddy bears holding hands. I awoke with my head on his broad furry chest. I licked the sweat from his neck, burrowed my nose in his mane. It was as if we had known each other forever.

"Marshall?" I said.

"What?" he asked.

"Nothing. Just, Marshall."

"We have forever and ever," he said.

The trip back to Purgatory was quiet, almost sad. *How can I go back to school?* I thought. An hour or two with him the next day was not going to be enough. I needed more, much more of Marshall Barry.

I wasn't ready for him to meet my parents, not yet, so, I asked him to drop me off at the end of Woodhouse Road and I climbed the hill alone. I was in an altered state. It was well after seven; my path, illuminated by only the moon and stars, seemed clear enough. The cool air felt pure against my face.

Our house was lit but looked ominous. An unexplainable wave of anxiety passed through me; a sense that things were not right. Inside, the house was stone dead. The coals in the fireplace had a pungent unpleasant odor as if some animal had peed on them. I called out to see who was home. Only Ernest answered, wobbling toward me on his huge feet, his furry presence reassuring. "Where is everybody?" I asked, on my way to the fridge, where I took out a tin of opened cat food and the jug of Clarendon's Apple Cider. After Ernest was fed, I poured the cider into a tall glass.

It seemed reasonable that the family had stayed in town after the game, that they met some old friends or something. Then again, on second thought, that seemed unlikely, with Brent along and Heather's comments about things not being so good between my parents. They should have been good. They had worked on their building project well enough. I saw how finished the house looked, as finished as it needed to be; the log walls thickly mortared, the wide stairs to the second story polished and solid; the big loft strewn with signs of activities in its large open space.

Like an intruder, I wandered about, going in and out of the bedrooms, knowing none of the four would be occupied. I even checked the huge built-in closets just in case—of what—someone hiding? Everything seemed normal, but prickles of worry persisted.

Could there have been an accident? Wouldn't we have passed it? Why were the Saab and the truck both missing? Heather should have come home hours ago.

Without a fire in the fireplace, the house was chilly. I stepped outside and got some kindling and saw car lights coming up the road. It was the Saab. Mom and Brent got out before Heather. When Heather walked into the house she threw her parka on the couch and collapsed into it. Brent ran upstairs and slammed his door shut. Mom stood still, staring at me with the strangest look. Then she asked where I'd been all day and took the kindling from my arms. In one big swoop she dumped it into the fireplace.

I looked to Heather. She rolled her eyes and shook her head as if to warn me not to speak.

Flopping down next to her, I whispered in her ear, "What happened? Where have you been?"

"Brent disappeared after Dad castrated him at the festival," she said.

"Your father got into the hard cider and after that I don't know what all he drank," Mom said, obviously overhearing Heather's explanation.

"It's a sickness," I reminded her.

"He's cruel and vulgar and I just can't do it anymore," Mom answered.

"Whatever happened was just the liquor talking," I said in my best Al-a-Teen voice.

Heather made a slash across her neck with her forefinger. "Dad was tossing the football with Drew and acting like a kid," she said.

"It was horrible, just horrible." Mom choked, angry water escaping her swollen eyelids.

"Gee, it doesn't sound that bad," I tried.

Heather went on. "When Brent came up to ask Dad to go home, I guess Dad put him off and asked Drew to help teach his son how to throw a ball."

Brent doesn't generally toss footballs around and probably would never think of tossing one to Drew. I mean Drew was the super jock of Purgatory. Brent would not have been interested.

Mom said, "That is not how it went. Your father insulted Brent. He asked Drew to teach his son not to be such a *Mary*. Said it was time for him to learn how to be a man. In front of everyone, in front of half the village!"

Heather nodded. "Brent took off."

"He was humiliated," Mom said.

"Dad and Mom had a fight, right there on the Green. Afterwards, she walked to the store and asked Strange and me to help find Brent. We figured he probably didn't want to be found, but we looked everywhere; went to the graveyard, the river, took the roads from town in every direction."

My shoulders ached. It didn't seem possible to make things right in our family. Poor Brent. No matter how much he annoyed me, he was still my baby brother. Dad wasn't usually mean but when he was drinking there was no telling what he might do or say.

Heather went on, "I guess he walked until he was too tired to take another step and then he tried hitching. Strange figured that might happen, so we went to the highway, travelled about two miles North, and then three miles South and there he was, thumb pointed towards Springfield. We told him to get in the car and we'd talk. For some reason, he listened and got in. He sat like a wad of wet tissue while Strange talked at him saying, 'Let it go, Man. Let it go.' Brent looked pretty bad, his eyes all red and the hairs on his chin and upper lip sticking out like he was in shock. He'd been crying, but I didn't see any tears."

Mom began to weep, "My poor baby. My poor boy."

11

Sunday morning Mom was standing in the kitchen when I came downstairs. She had all the produce she'd bought at the fair spread out on the new table. By *new* table, I mean the Carnegie Library's well-used, heavily scarred, oak reading table. The pine picnic table we had been using since the fire was now back outside.

I said good morning but no response came my way.

The kitchen wall phone rang. I ran to answer it and heard Nancy at the other end. "Where are you? Are you home and, like, actually not calling me? I thought we were best friends."

"We are! I have just been so busy. Can you possibly come by this morning and take me to that place in Woodbury I told you about?" I asked.

"Well, sure. The little church that holds the love of your life?" she answered, sounding like she was just waiting for the invite. What a life saver she was!

"I'll be over in a jiff, okay?" she said.

Mom looked at me with detachment. She was definitely in some other zone. Her hair was hanging on either side of her face like blinders.

"Going to town with Nancy and then to meet Carrie for my ride back," I announced. "You okay, Mom?"

"You aren't going to that peculiar church again, are you?" she asked without looking up.

I didn't answer. There were times I thought she was psychic. I never talked about the church or Marshall Barry. How could she possibly think I was going there?

She took a handful of green beans and threw them in the colander, sloshing them under hot water in the huge soapstone sink, turning them over and over until her hands turned red.

"So, I guess things are not too great around here, huh?" I asked.

"Not your worry," she said.

I thought, okay, I guess my father, in or out of the house, shouldn't matter to me.

"You know your father is drinking again. I will not tolerate that behavior. It's bad for everyone, including him. Just devastating for your brother."

"Mom, it's his first slip, right?"

"A terrible, hurtful one, and not his first."

No words came to mind I dared say. What good would it do to point out that she had been much happier while he was back? Why rub that in, as now he was gone again? I sat dumb as a potato watching her whack the fresh green beans and carrots with the cleaver. Nothing told me to work at her side. A mountain might as well have stood between us. She chopped away angrily, her mind lost to itself.

After a few minutes, I retreated to pack my bag and place it by the door. Despite my excitement to see Marshall and Nancy, I felt strangely guilty about leaving the house and its sorrows so soon. I had to go straight into town after church to meet Carrie and go back to school.

However, guilt vanished when Nancy beeped her horn and stepped out of her yellow bug grinning and waving like a happy playmate. The sight of her made me feel better immediately. She looked warm and comfortable dressed in a big gray wool sweater with a red turtleneck underneath and a pair of baggy jeans. Her hair was piled on her head with wisps of it framing her fresh, open face. I had almost forgotten how beautiful she was and how much she meant to me.

I awkwardly hugged my miserable mother good bye and went outside pulling the big oak door shut behind me.

"Ready to go meet Jesus?" I sang.

"Promise?" she asked.

"Up to you," I laughed.

Our happy moment was short lived. I gagged when I took a whiff of her car. The same horsey smell I used to love overwhelmed me. Even after I opened the window my stomach was behaving like a broken garbage disposal. "Whew, I need that fresh air. Don't know what hit me!" I tried to explain, adding, "Did you go riding this morning?"

"Like, what else is a girl to do on a beautiful autumn day?" she asked.

Driving to church she brought up the fact that I hadn't called her as soon as I got back in town again. I told her about how time was taken up from the moment I arrived until the disaster of the fair and my family's upset. Then I kind of mentioned that I had been with Marshall the day before for a while.

"Oh, time for him and not for me, eh?" she teased.

She filled me in on *the girls,* admonishing me for leaving and saying she wished she had another friend to take my place who could work out the horses. It was hard to keep them happy with me gone, etc. I noticed she showed exactly no interest in my new life at school. Not one question. But I told her a little about my roommates, anyway, that they were nice enough, although I still didn't know them very well, considering we shared the same space and used the same bathroom. I explained how they were involved in being freshman, going to frat parties, drinking too much, studying too little and doing all the things that freshman do to orient themselves. I added I was simply not interested in that kid stuff.

When we pulled up in front of the church I saw Marshall standing secure as an anchor by the door. "There he is," I said.

"Hmmm, yummy," she said.

Before I introduced them I felt his eyes graze over me. I went weak from their knowing. It was Nancy, however, who he reached out to touch as he welcomed her with a warm smile.

We took seats in the back. A heavyset woman in the row in front of ours was wearing a pink flowered tent and perfume that stunk like dead lilacs. I scrunched my face at Nancy and put my index finger under my nose. She giggled. I was glad she was with me, glad she would soon understand why I loved Marshall.

The music from the little Yamaha started and Nancy copied the others as we stood for Brother Barry's entrance. He walked down the short aisle past the twelve rows of folding chairs with his hands raised, exclaiming, "Glory be! This is the day the Lord Hath Made! Glory be to the Father! Be glad and rejoice!" He joined the congregation as they sang *Amen*. Quiet followed as he lowered his eyes and collected himself before he held up the Bible.

"Let us open our ears and our hearts to the holy words. John 12:27, 28."

I saw and heard Bibles opening and pages fluttering to find the words that would be spoken.

Now is my soul troubled. And what shall I say? 'Father, save me from this hour?' No, for this purpose I have come to this hour. Father, glorify Thy name.

Then a voice came from heaven, 'I have glorified it, and I will glorify it again.'

"I have heard that voice and so will you," Brother Barry promised. "You are here to meet your Savior. He is waiting. Once you open up your heart to your true Father every step along your way will bring you closer to Him."

The sermon was powerful and as usual I was sure it was for me. "We are all children in the eyes of the Lord. He is our Protector. He loves us and we need only to love him back. Our service is all about living in His name, doing his commandments, fighting for what is right and following His word. He knows who we are. He wants our total devotion. He asks us to love him more than our fathers or mothers, and says those unwilling to carry the cross are unworthy. Unworthy! Only by your willingness to share in His suffering can you be made whole. He knows where we are from. He loves us, every hair on our head, every breath we breathe is proof. Give Him your devotion. Live for Him and your life will have meaning. Rejoice and be glad!" He paused. My heart was beating. Nancy pinched my arm and just as I was turning to look at her face he spoke again.

"No matter what your sin, you are forgiven. Love forgives you. Love forgives the perverts, the thieves, the whore, Love rules in the house of the Lord. But beware the temptation to stay with the familiar. Fear not the mockery of others. When you walk in the light of the Lord, there will be enough to sustain you. Jesus preaches that we must leave all that is safe behind. We must take a new path, the higher road. This call takes enormous courage. Compare the letting go to that of a trapeze artist, suspended on a swing high above the circus ring, propelled back and forth, going higher and higher, building up momentum and then letting go. The only way to do this is to have an absolute trust that another pair of hands will be there, exactly at the time they're needed. And in that moment, the moment of letting go, the moment of transition, the most amazing twists and turns will take place. Those of you who have been there, you know. You know the courage it takes to let go. It stops the very breath of the audience. I am telling you that all of you can find the momentum to fly high, you, too, can let go of the old and trust that Jesus will be there waiting for you. He will be there to save you, to take your arms and embrace the whole of you and your life will be changed forever. Forever and ever. Praise Jesus. Praise Him. Amen."

When we stood to sing the final hymn written on the sheet we were handed on the way in, Nancy and I started out on the wrong note and a disastrous bubble of laughter rose up between us, made us snort and giggle until tears fell. It took ages to stop. By the time we recovered we were among the last to leave the sanctuary.

When we solemnly exited the hall to face Pastor Barry in all his dignity, he didn't smile. "I hope you enjoyed yourselves," he said. "I am sure you can appreciate that the House of the Lord is sacred, perhaps not as casual as you may think."

I stood closer to him and he leaned into my ear and said quietly, "I would like it if you would wear a skirt the next time you come, Lily."

I looked down at my jeans and felt ashamed, ashamed because he had seen my outfit as disrespectful. It occurred to me he was already thinking of me as a pastor's wife. I had to make sure to learn the etiquette, even though he preached God loves us just as we are.

Nancy was funny on the way back. "Whew, I am glad I'm not you," she said. "He and Jesus have the whole world in their hands. He's almost like, scary, that Reverend Marshall Barry."

"So, you think he's as fabulous as I do?" I asked.

"He's pretty hot."

"I can't believe how he's in my mind all the time. He's so fervent, so full of God's grace. You know if we all thought like Marshall the world might actually work. It could be so simple if everyone had the kind of faith he has."

"Well, they don't and they won't." Nancy said.

"It's possible that something could happen that would bring the world together, though, don't you think?"

"You mean, like Martians or a pandemic?"

"Maybe something spiritual. Maybe a Second Coming. A lot of people believe in that."

"You mean another visit from Jesus and another what? Crucifixion? Witch burning? Inquisition? Crusade? Geez,

Lily, like, hasn't the world suffered enough from Christianity? Is this guy getting to you or what?"

"Maybe. Maybe he is. It's just that I am taking these courses that analyze everything to death. I have to memorize all sorts of boring sociological statistics and psychological patterns. Rural, white, middle class, female, IQ, family origins, ya-da ya-da. They take away our souls and turn us into statistics. I don't want to be categorized this way. It's...it's offensive."

"So, like, what are you wishing for—that everyone worships this God of the Bible that your Brother Barry is pushing? How likely is that?"

"I know it's wishful thinking. I am just saying that it would be so much easier if we all could find a common belief. If people accepted that there's one God who loves us all."

"Lily! There are zealots who blow planes out of the sky, fire on our ships, kidnap our people in the name of Allah. They believe there's only one God, too. Their love for their God asks them to destroy us, either that or send us back to the seventh century."

A sportscar whizzed past, a couple of rich boys trying to cut us off. New York plates. They probably thought we were hicks.

"They need to be loved and saved, Nancy."

"I don't think so. I think it's best we leave them alone. They're serving their one true God, who they think is the Right God. Like, the time for religious wars is over, don't you think?"

"I don't think we should fight over anything, I just wish we could all agree."

"But, Lily, life isn't ever going to be simple, no two people think alike. We all come from different places, have different realities and interests. How can anyone think we should think alike? Does your Brother Barry really believe we should all believe what he believes?"

I felt kind of stupid trying to take a stand on an issue I knew so little about. "He knows what he knows. God has spoken to him. What if we trusted that the Truth will show itself to everyone in their own language, in their own time?"

"This guy is not in the real world. There's no God and no Truth," Nancy said, shaking her head slowly and sadly. "I've read and read. It's all, like, wishful thinking. The great minds of literature have known that all along. Asimov, Chekov, Twain, Baum, Nadine Gordimer...there's no end to the big brains who have been willing to stand against so-called Divine Authority."

"I hope they're wrong," I said, "I hope there's more meaning to life than some biological accident. I mean how can we explain miracles and the power of faith?"

"What are you reading right now?" Nancy asked.

I knew she had an advantage over me. She was intent on educating herself. I had to admit to my limitations. "The truth is, I don't have time to read anything other than the books on my reading lists. They're about history, you know, theory and scientific breakthroughs. I'm stuck with these texts even though I'm more interested in what came first. Didn't God set it all in motion? Why is He left out of the textbooks?"

"He? How about She? You need a little feminist philosophy, Lily, read women like Germaine Greer and Simone de Beauvoir. Then we can talk about Mr. Wonderful and his Bible." Her knuckles were holding onto the wheel so tightly they were stretched to white. "The horoscope would be less dangerous."

I hardly understood what was heating her up. "I don't think so," I said simply.

"Uh-oh! I hear you. Now, I'm thinking we are on completely different tracks. Maybe we should stop talking about this."

"Maybe," I said.

She softened her voice. "We can't let this come between us, Lily, you are too important to me to let some possessed guy do in our friendship."

I felt a white heat rising from my belly to my throat, burning at the insulting way she referred to Marshall. I regretted bringing her to the church; regretted allowing her question my love life, to ridicule my man. I regretted acting like two silly goons in the church. All I wanted to do was to say good-bye and get away from her.

But I was trapped in the car, so we proceeded silently across the hills, until we arrived at Pearl's. I didn't even say thank you as I grabbed my bags and went inside the store. She knew I was upset, I knew she was not sorry; she couldn't understand.

Carrie was late. I poked around the store with Strange and Heather. Pearl's was now an extension of Strange's home. He had made the most of his room in the back, and the black ceiling against the white-white walls looked great. There was a bed built into a corner of what also served as a kitchen and living area. His tiny bathroom now sported a plastic shower stall meant only to bathe a stalk of celery. But, you would have thought he was a Vanderbilt he was so happy showing it off. He told me his next move was to buy a motorcycle and an Apple computer. I mean, he was feeling flush and more up than I had ever seen him. Heather seemed relaxed, busying herself with rearranging items while we waited for Carrie. It was a cozy domestic little scene. The odd couple. Who would have guessed?

"So, Strange, are you still writing?" I asked.

"Travelling through time," he said.

Then he brought up Brent and we talked about what had happened the day before. At some point he said, "Brent is miserable." Then he promised, "He's definitely going to stay on my radar."

12

Carrie chatted all the way back as she rehashed the weekend, what went right and what didn't. She was more confused about her relationship with Drew than ever. Being with the town hero again affected her more than she had expected—would she miss him more than she had before, now that she was with him again? Being caught in that high school romance was not what she intended—she liked to think of herself as moving on.

I let her ramble, knowing she was thinking out loud. I was doing my own share of thinking, quietly, in another world, checking in and out of Carrie's monologue, imagining Marshall's hands in my hair. I came to when she asked how Brent was doing.

"Brent?"

"Yeah. I felt so sorry for him when your father called him queer. I don't think any boy could laugh that one off. At least that's how Drew felt. I mean, he felt so bad."

"I don't think he called him queer, did he? "

"No, not queer, but he might just as well have. He called him a Mary. I could see how it hurt him."

"Well, whatever he did or said it *was* awful. Brent took off and it took hours to find him. Then my parents had a big fight and Dad left. It must have been the booze he drank at the fair. My father wouldn't do anything that mean in his right mind. He's a mush, you know. He always roots for the losing teams, blames the rest of the world for the poor man's problems and makes excuses when you mess up."

"In other words he's a liberal?" she asked.

"If being anti-war, distrusting big money and avoiding anyone who wants to tell anyone else what to do is being a liberal, I guess he is. He calls himself a Libertarian. He's for homegrown, homemade everythings. He's for being whatever it is you want to be."

"I guess he's different when it comes to his son," Carrie said.

Although I had a quick defense for Dad, words got stuck in my head, caught in the confusion of Mom's sadness, all those trips to the AA meetings, poor Brent being the brunt of name-calling at school and his own father now being as guilty as the school bullies. Where did it all begin and end? What could I do? I was lucky to be leaving the scene of the accident. "I guess my dad does have his problems," I admitted.

Carrie was probably embarrassed for all of us. She dropped the subject.

A memory of words between my mother and father came to my head. "Jon, you are impossible. I can't take much more. I feel like a puppet with you pulling the strings." And my father's answer, "No. *I* am the yo-yo and it's you pulling me close and pushing me away. I can't take it anymore." What was going on between them, and who was to blame, confused and escaped me.

As we drove onto the campus, past the tall elms and the ivy covered buildings, I wished for a feeling of belonging, for a positive connection, but it wasn't there. Instead, a heavy cold cloud turned the world into dismal gray. We pulled in and parked near the side door. I zipped up my parka, took the duffle bag from the trunk of the heroic old Datsun and was about to go into the dorm when Carrie reached for me. I hung onto her for a minute giving her a special hug goodbye. What I really wanted to do was beg her to be my confidante and ask her to listen to all my most private thoughts. But I couldn't. I couldn't even form them in my head no less attach words to them. Besides, Nancy had failed the test when it came to sharing. She was judgmental and skeptical. I wouldn't be confiding in her anymore.

Back in the dorm my roommates were eating a pizza and watching Jeopardy on our small TV set. They barely reacted when I came in. God, I thought, I'm invisible here.

"Who was King George?" one of them shouted. "Who was Henry the eighth," called another. "No, no! Who was Prince Charles?"

Who am I? I thought.

Exhausted, I lay down on my bed and my hard thin mattress felt incredibly good. Sleep took over despite the girl talk, the TV's drone, the lights and activity around me. When I woke in the morning and saw I hadn't even changed my clothes or opened my duffle bag, I got up quickly to make up for the lost time. As I did, a great fish seemed to rise in my throat. I needed the bathroom but it was occupied and I had no time to run down the hall. The only receptacle I had was a waste basket which I grabbed just in time.

"Gross!" Ellie said. "Who poisoned you? Where did you eat on the way back yesterday?"

I couldn't remember. Even the thought of a hamburger was enough to make me sick again.

"Save the evidence. You can sue them and spare the rest of us," Ellie suggested.

I had to laugh.

Jennifer found some saltines in her purse and Ellie got me a Coke out of the machine in the hall. Before long I was feeling better.

A shower, fresh clothes and my roommate's consideration helped.

Soc.101 was the first class of the day. I raced to the Annex to be in my seat before the door to the lecture hall was closed. Joke on me was the professor was late. I took advantage of the extra time to peruse the chapter we would be discussing. I am not a brilliant student. Not as smart as

Heather. Not as intellectual as Nancy. I think one would call me average with a few gold stars to my credit. Teachers generally liked me because I did my homework and didn't make trouble. Being a good girl has always come easily because I don't like being bad or watching other people acting out. I suppose I'd always believed that good was preferable to bad.

I looked down at my book. The subject for the day was deviance. The first paragraph left a lot to learn: *Deviance is a term that describes actions or behaviors that violate social norms and formally enacted rules. This includes violations of social norms which are subject to change depending within the context of social morés and paradigms.*

Huh? I wasn't sure what a moré or a norm was, not sure about paradigms either. Actually, I didn't much care. I was more concerned with the sense that something was wrong. I felt unsettled, queasy again. I wished I could go back to bed.

The issue of social power cannot be divorced from a definition of deviance because a group in society can criminalize the actions of another group by using their influence on legislators.

Are we talking about animal rights, pesticides, or standing up against higher taxes? I asked myself.

Deviants justify their behaviors by denying responsibility for lack of choice, claiming helplessness, as if a force outside themselves propelled them into their actions. They (deviants) may also claim that no one was hurt by their actions so no moral wrong was committed.

Was this about driving without a license, self-defense, or over-spending?

Marshall had warned me about this stuff. It makes life so much more complicated than it needs to be. If you have a rule book like the Bible and accept God's laws, you don't have to worry about deviance or differential associations. I groaned with boredom and just as I was putting my books and papers together to leave, the very tardy Professor Blackman walked in. "Sorry, sorry, sorry," he said. "Incorrigible kids, impassable roads and not enough spare time built in to make it on time, but here we are and no worse for the weather! Shall we begin?"

I almost laughed thinking about his excuses. It wasn't his fault, we weren't hurt by his lateness, and all was perfectly okay. He couldn't possibly be one of those deviants we were about to discuss.

I don't know when I felt comfortable enough to criticize what Blackman was saying, but it had something to do with Foucault and post-modern society. I wondered how being in the present could be post anything modern, but no one else seemed to have a problem with the oxymoron.

"Foucault theorizes that, in a sense, the postmodern society is characterized by a lack of free will on the part of individuals. Institutions of knowledge, norms, and values are simply in place to categorize and control humans," he said.

Gee, I thought, *if only Marshall was here with me to clarify what I am supposed to learn from this.*

I projectile vomited in the bathroom the following morning. Jennifer exclaimed, "God, I know my shit stinks but it can't be that bad!"

I spent a half an hour between cleaning up one mess and making another. It was humiliating. Then when I was taking a nap in my bunk that afternoon, all balled up in my comforter and tucked into the wall, Jennifer and Ellie came in. They obviously didn't know I was there. "She could be pregnant," Ellie said.

"I don't think so. She's not one bit interested in boys and doesn't get letters or calls. I think she's homesick," Jennifer argued.

"Homesick doesn't mean you throw up your breakfast," Sarah said, as she walked into the room and dumped her books on the already overloaded study table. "I am so pissed off! The phone is out of order again. I can't call Richie or my mom to have her send my boots. The girls are staying on the phone too long, taking collect calls and not paying. What's up?"

"We're just worried about Lily."

"She's got something wrong, that's for sure," Sarah said. "I remember at camp that a girl was sick to her stomach from homesickness. Maybe that's what's going on."

"Ellie thinks she's got a bun in the oven, that the dye is cast."

I lay perfectly still, hearing every word, but too embarrassed to reveal myself.

When I could wait no longer, I simply sat up and yawned like I wasn't quite awake and asked what they were talking about.

Sarah was quick to answer. "I know someone who caught worms from her dog. They were honest to God worms and she could see them in the toilet when she pooed. She was sick to her stomach for months."

"Yuk!" the girls screamed and cracked up.

"I don't have a dog," I said lamely.

"Well, do you have a boyfriend?" asked Ellie.

"Yes," I said. "But he doesn't have worms."

They laughed.

"Are you homesick? Jennifer asked.

"I am. I miss him so much."

"What's he like?" she asked.

It made me happy just to talk about him, to have their interest and be able to speak his name.

"He's a man, not a boy, and he is very handsome. We knew almost from the minute we met that we were meant to be together."

"So, he's old then?" Sarah asked.

"No. But he's very mature and definitely beyond the college scene."

"Love at first sight? Is that for real?" asked Jennifer.

"Yes, it was like that. Amazing."

"When is he going to come for a visit?" Ellie asked.

"Well, it's very hard for him to get away. He's a minister and works seven days a week and the most on weekends. I have to try to be patient, but it's hard."

"So, I guess we can scratch off pregnant then. I mean priests, like, they don't fuck around, right?" asked Ellie.

"Remember Hester Prynne!" Sarah blurted.

"Remember Richard Chamberlain in The Thorn Birds," added Jennifer.

I just smiled. I wasn't about to try to tell them the difference between fucking around and making love; I could only hope they found out for themselves. I didn't choose to say that if I was actually pregnant it would be God's grace that made it happen

Their interest in me changed my feelings about our relationship. It was as if now someone knew who I was, and what I was about to do. From that day, they behaved as if I existed. Still, I counted the days until Thanksgiving and prayed that my phone calls would be answered and that just once, he would call me first.

13

Home at last, I thought, as I rolled over for another half hour of precious sleep. When I finally came to, I was hit with the aromas of Thanksgiving, a barrage of smells; onions, celery, rosemary and thyme. Nauseating. How could I survive the day? Luckily, the upchucking session was short lived. As usual, once I had smelled something long enough, I adjusted.

Lying in bed, waiting for my strength to return, I began to accept the idea that I might be pregnant. All signs were pointing in that direction. If so, I would have to leave school and marry Marshall right away. I didn't need a degree to be a pastor's wife, and marrying Marshall, along with being a mother, would be full-time work.

I couldn't help but think of Grandmother Lillian's trust, she wrote it in a way that ensured my higher education, but it stipulated that if I was to leave school, the amount would be relegated to the next in line. *You are a Woodhouse,* she would say, as if I had royal obligations to higher education. But, wasn't it she who gave me that baby doll with the pouty lips and fat cheeks to love? A baby so realistic I could dress her in newborn hand-me-downs. How many happy hours had I spent dressing and feeding and walking that facsimile? From dolls to Dad to Brent to Mom to Strange and school and physics and my condition, my thoughts went round and round; sometimes full of joy, mostly full of anxiety. What I really wanted was clarity; clarity about making things work out. I tried to believe as Marshall did, that whatever risk we had taken, it was now in God's hands.

After a hot shower, I wiped the steam off the long mirror on the back of the bathroom door and examined my body. My figure seemed to have stopped becoming itself. My waist was as tiny as it had been a year ago. My hips weren't changing as far as I could see. What was added were the raccoon rings around my eyes. That, and my darkening hair. My breasts were somewhat fuller but I liked them that way. After-all, I was now a woman.

I put on a t-shirt, a big plaid flannel shirt and some jeans. Downstairs, Mom had started a fire in the living room making it cozy, despite the frost on the window panes. It was very cold outside, even for late November. The thermostat by the window read nineteen degrees. It had been going into the teens at night for days.

"Where is everybody?" I asked.

"Brent has gone off to the cow pond with his skates to test the ice and Heather is still asleep. Your father is probably on his way. Did you know Heather invited your friend Strange to join us for Thanksgiving? He'll be here about one."

"Wow, I wish I had thought of that. Good for her. I hope she's out of bed by then, since she was the one who invited him," I pointed out.

Mom put up her hands. "Let's not tackle that issue. Why don't we get started dressing the table?"

It was mid-morning and the teen queen was still sleeping. Mom seemed unbothered as she handed me a tablecloth and we began to set things up. I carefully placed her huge bouquet of chrysanthemums in the table's center, then gathered the napkins, glassware, plates and utensils. I loved our new dishes. They were Pottery Barn bright, happy colors just made for holidays; not the old bone China that gave me the creeps when I learned it was actually made out of bones—human skeletons included. Not only were the old dishes trimmed in gold, we had to treat them that way.

Forget the dishwasher—boneware was too precious for a machine.

It was only eleven when Dad arrived. He came in huffing and puffing as if he had run all the way from Grafton. His cheeks were red and he looked a lot better than the last time I saw him.

"Lily-Vanilli!" he said opening his arms for me to step inside. After a big hug he turned to Mom. "Hey, Leslie, sweetheart," he said. "I hope you'll forgive me for coming a little early. I thought I might be of some help." He put his arms around her with a little less confidence than he had shown me.

Mom stood still, offering no hug in return. "You know perfectly well we can always use some help around here."

Heather must have heard the door opening and shutting and Dad's voice booming. She appeared in the kitchen sleepily surveying the scene, her new hairdo standing on end.

Dad's eyes went straight to her head. "Well, look here! It's Blondie! What happened to you Princess? Did you fall in a tub of bleach?"

No one laughed. Heather turned and said she was going to get dressed.

When she returned she looked like she was dressed for Halloween instead of Thanksgiving. She wore a huge orange and black bowtie around her neck, no doubt one of Pearl's items, and a very short houndstooth black and white skirt topped with a yellow sweater. The black tights on her legs were enhanced with yellow knee warmers made of ostrich feathers. She looked fresh out of Sesame Street.

Dad laughed. "Well look at you. Our very own Cyndi Lauper—all you need is an electric guitar! Or maybe you are going to be the next Coo-Coo Chanel."

Heather ignored him and turned to me as I handed her the potato peeler.

"Jon, some of the doorsills seem to need adjustment," Mom said cocking her head toward the stairs.

They took quite a while up in the bedrooms where the doors had been sticking.

When they came downstairs Mom made a pot of cocoa and Dad cleaned the hearth. Brent came back from the pond around noon, a little blue at the gills from the cold, and eager for the cocoa Mom had made for the rest of us. He squirted whipped cream in his cup until it spilleth over.

"Geez, Brent, you are such an oink," said Heather.

Dad walked into the kitchen to greet Brent. "Hello, on, Happy Thanksgiving," he said.

Brent nodded and moved away from him like he might be contagious, but then he helped build a roaring fire and seemed to relax.

By the time Strange arrived, we were doing pretty well at behaving like a family. Heather took responsibility for the introductions and I was surprised she called him by his proper name, David. Was it for my parents' sake or his? I never asked.

He was dressed in his black costume, a few chains and a pair of stud earrings, the nail polish was still on his index finger but he had combed his hair back into a ponytail. I thought he was a little nervous, and who could blame him? It had to be weird, joining up with the whole family when he had known only a few of its parts for so long. We sat down at the table and soon he appeared to become more comfortable.

"Leslie is probably the best cook this side of the Green Mountains," Dad said to Strange. "We met at a food stand, but neither of us knew how prophetic that was. The poor woman has been feeding me ever since."

"Wouldn't count on that," said Heather.

Dad ignored her and turned to Strange. "So, David, tell us about your family."

I suppose it was a perfectly normal question. Dad could have no idea who Strange was or where he came from. We hadn't taken time to prepare him.

Strange was blunt. "My mother and father died in a car accident ten years ago."

"Christ!" Dad said. "That's a hard one." He took a breath as the words sank in. "Who brought you up?" he asked.

Heather raised her eyebrows, and cocked her head like someone who wanted to know.

"Pass the 'taters please," she said.

"My brother."

If you knew Strange, you heard the closure in his voice.

"Must be quite the guy!" Dad said, pouring more water into his goblet .

"Hmm...wants to be,"

"Where do you two live?" Dad persisted.

"Well, we don't live together anymore. I'm in town. Pearl let me have the space behind the boutique. Marshall's living near his church."

"His church?"

"The rolls! Did you take out the rolls, Mom?" I asked, pushing my chair from the table.

"They're out and right in front of you, Lil." Mom said.

Strange went on, "Yep. Out in Woodbury. He's a crazed Christian."

"And you? Not so into it, eh?" Dad noted.

"Nope."

Dad was just being social but this conversation was going downhill fast. I had to stop it.

"What denomination is he?" Dad asked.

"He's a Bible freak. He's under his own dominion."

Strange was about to bad mouth Marshall before my father even met him.

I interrupted, "Dad, is that old man over in Grafton still alive? You know, the one we bought Meg Flanders from?"

"Damned if I know Lily-Vanilli. I don't talk to anyone over there. I just tend to my own business. Why?"

"I don't know. I just thought you might see him around."

Dad turned back to Strange, "David, I hear a fellow wants to open a tattoo parlor, right in the center of Purgatory? Is it true?"

"Who's going to keep him alive?" Heather asked. "I mean it's like selling ice in Alaska."

"I might give him some business," Strange said. "Maybe get a big Star of David on my arm, just to get Marshall riled up. He says tattoos should be forbidden, 'they're un-Christian'."

"Un-Christian?" Dad asked.

"Yeah, he says they mess up God's work."

"Tell that to the Maori," Dad laughed.

"I think they're cool," Heather said.

"The Maoris or tattoos?" Dad asked.

"Tattoos! Well, maybe the Maoris, too. They have funny droopy butts, though."

"I think they're fads," I said. "What if you change your mind or you get infected?"

Dad nodded, "I'm with you, Lil. What if you get flabby? When it comes to tattoos, I'm pretty sure that more than half the folks who get them when they're young regret it later on. What we think is 'cool' one year isn't necessarily *cool* the next. Tattoos are forever."

"Nothing is forever," Mom remarked.

Dad's reaction was fast. "No nothing is forever, but we can damn well try to hang on to what is good. We live in a throwaway society. Don't like it? Return it! Buy the new, dump the old. Need new shoes? Buy twenty pair. Excess and waste, that's America these days. Once we had a vision. It held us together."

"I don't throw things away," Heather said, "I just pile them up."

"As in the rat's nest on your bed, under it and around it?" Brent smirked.

"There are lots of good people who try to make the world better, Dad," I said, thinking of Marshall's love for his church family and how much he was needed by his congregation.

"But they aren't interesting," Heather said. "It's the bad guys that make the news and keep the world awake."

"Back to you, David," Mom interrupted, "How do you like living in a little village like Purgatory? Do you see yourself staying here long?"

Strange put down his fork and looked at Mom. "No. No, I don't. It's good enough for now, but I won't stay much longer. I plan to travel. Maybe go to school and study writing."

He was being super polite, I wasn't sure I knew him so well after all.

"And what would you like to write about?" Mom asked.

"I'm really into sci-fi. Maybe I could write for TV or film."

"Well, hell, now there's a plan," Dad said. "Sounds like you have a dream and that's what you should follow. I followed mine, she's sitting right here at this table."

"Oh, stop, Jon," Mom said, picking up the bowl of turnips and passing it.

He didn't stop. "No, seriously, where's the passion these days? Jesus, when I was your age," and he pointed his knife at Strange and me, "I was out marching for freedom and justice. My generation had a dream bigger than Jesus or nationalism or capitalism. We believed in peace and equal opportunity. We stood up and were counted."

"Gee, thanks," Brent said under his breath. Heather snorted and covered her mouth with her napkin.

"We stood up to the Establishment who wanted to control our lives, but now we've got the same damn pigs back on the chessboard, with their dirty players back in place."

"Jon, for Heaven's sake, it's Thanksgiving, why don't we think of things we're grateful for. Lily, how about you?"

I didn't have a chance to speak, as Dad wasn't through. "Well, I'll tell you what I am not grateful for! I am not grateful for the fools who re-elected this damn pro-oil President. The greatest country on earth is now run by a man who can buy the job and destroy the earth at the same time. He's another God-damned Alie, not only a Yale man but a party man in the worst way; the world's air and water be damned. We're watching a disaster unfold that will take a century to fix, if ever. He'll sell out in the Middle East, continue the arms for money, arms for power, arms for oil policies of his predecessors. He's in bed with the bad guys. The Middle East is a cauldron and we're going to pay the price for sticking our greedy noses in the pot."

Heather rolled her eyes at me, Brent looked at Strange and crossed his.

Throwing up his hands Dad said, "Okay, okay. I guess we can do without politics today, Sorry one and all."

"Good, because Daddy doesn't just angst about Bush, he worries about Monsanto, the World Bank, the Mafia, Halliburton, Christians, Muslims, Israel and Palestine—corruption everywhere, and we just can't take care of all those folks from little ole Purgatory, now, can we, Daddy-dearest?" Heather said, sweet as a sticky bun. God, she was a witch at heart.

"Well, my little girl has been listening to me after all. I never would have known! Hey, pass the gravy, Princess. This turkey wants some sauce."

"Would anyone else like some gravy?" Mom asked. Brent had sunk so low in his chair he was almost under the table, but he rose for the gravy.

Mom said, "Personally, I'm grateful that we are here together, in our beautiful new home and all in one piece."

"I am glad you are glad, Mom," Heather added.

I thought that I might be in two pieces and Brent might be in a thousand, but I said. "I am grateful that Stra...David is here."

Strange looked like a kid when he said, "I am glad to be with you guys."

"Brent?" Mom asked.

"I am gratefully working on gratitude."

"Now that might be the most intelligent thing I've heard come out of your mouth," Dad said. Then he turned to Strange again. "So, son, what do you remember of your parents? That was a terrible thing to happen to a boy when he was what? Nine? Ten?"

"I only remember the good things. Mom speaking Russian to me, so I'd grow up bi-lingual; Dad teaching me crossword puzzles, how to ride a bike, the usual stuff. They were not very interesting people, I guess."

Dad said, "You know my grandfather was an unbending idealist but my father, Sheldon, was even tougher. He's is probably turning in his grave right now watching what is going on in Washington. I wouldn't be surprised if that old portrait of his isn't going to mysteriously show up on our mantle one of these days. Between the liars in the White House and the kinds of pranks they're up to, he's got to be trying to find a way to come back."

"Jon! Really!" Mom said. "We are talking about being grateful. I don't think we have to dwell on how bad things are. David do you want more squash?"

"Thanks Mrs. Woodhouse," Strange said. "It's really good." He held up his water glass. "To the chef," he toasted, "and to Brent and gratitude."

Heather laughed, "I'll drink to that!" She lifted her glass of cider and clinked it against Brent's. He was smiling. Actually, smiling. I felt it through my skin.

We were breathing in thin air. I was afraid things would get worse but they didn't. By dessert we were remembering

Thanksgivings of the past; the ones when we feasted in the old house. We got into our family stories, like the one about Dad telling Brent that chocolate milk came from cows and brown eggs from bulls. He never questioned; he was only five, too young to challenge his dad. We were all in on it and it was funny until he went to kindergarten and told his classmates. We laughed about Grandmother Lillian's malaprops, too, the man who spoke like he had a frog in his nose and the car she called a lime instead of a lemon. For our guest, we ran down the familiar list and laughed like we used to, a lifetime ago, in a house we had failed to appreciate, with a family we thought was forever.

The following day, Friday, brought an ice storm. I was imagining I would be trapped in the house along with Brent and Heather, but they went out in the treacherous glare to cover the shop for *the biggest shopping day of the year*. I tried to read and couldn't concentrate. My tummy was fighting the feast of the day before, my heart aching for Marshall but my head refusing to call him.

Mom asked, "Are you feeling alright, Lily?"

I said, "Yes. I'm just worn out from school and all the pressure."

"You're looking a little bit under the weather."

"Oh, I've had a small problem with my stomach lately. I'm not used to eating prepared foods. You've spoiled me for dorm life, Mom."

"It was my pleasure," she smiled. "I hope you're not getting the flu. There are a number of cases in town."

"No. I don't have a sore throat or a fever."

"It usually starts with the chills."

"I don't have those either."

The two of us drank tea and made turkey pot pies out of the Thanksgiving leftovers. She was relaxed and thoughtful, more relaxed than I thought she should be. Here was Dad living on his own, punished and in exile, and here she was having to handle life on her own. Wasn't she upset about all the extra responsibilities, the loneliness? Why wasn't she grieving? I would grieve awfully if something happened between Marshall and me. I'd probably die.

"I hear they are giving flu shots at the drug store but I'm not sure I believe in them," she said, her expert hands tucking the pot pie's top crust into the lower to form perfectly crenulated edges.

"We need to have a talk, Mom," I said, hoping for her confidence, for room to tell her about Marshall and tell her about my love life. But she must have thought I was asking to be *her* sounding board. The space between us was soon filled with Mom's new truths. I heard that Dad was not the man she'd married, alcohol had burned out his brain, he hadn't grown up yet and had no idea he might destroy us with his compulsiveness.

"Don't you mean destroy Brent?" I asked.

"Yes, I mean Brent," she answered. "Your father has been so much a part of me, it took a terrible incident for me to realize who he is. It's only when he's gone and returns that I can see how much we've changed. The truth has finally broken through and I must move on. This is it, the time for a change. With everything in flux around here, I might as well start to find myself, find out who I really am."

I considered telling her right then and there that truth turned my life upside-down, too. But I waited.

Brent and Heather were different people than those I'd left in September. In just a few months their feathers were in and their wings flapping to leave the nest. They were not as stuck on themselves as they used to be, either, at least not as stuck as I had thought they were.

Nancy called at three and said the roads were passable, would I be willing to come over to her house for a visit. I was glad to hear from her, hoping we could get past our differences. But, I couldn't go, the car was unavailable. She offered to come my way instead. I wished it was Marshall who had called, however, I knew he was busy with a wedding rehearsal.

Mom seemed real happy to have company. "Nancy, it's so good to see you!" she gushed. "Tell me, did you get those shoes on the horse?"

"I did. Like, we're ready to trot."

"And how's your mother doing?" Mom asked.

"No changes, since last week, or the week before or the week before that."

I hadn't realized how often they saw one another at the Al-Anon meetings. It was nice they were comfortable visiting, but I wanted to have Nancy to myself. My hopes were thwarted when Mom put on a pot of tea and we sat down in the kitchen as a threesome. Well, I told myself, at least this is neutral territory, no room for arguing over what is true love or not. At some point I envied how easily Mom and Nancy got along; horse talk about Bliss and Sadie, then healing talk about Al-a-Teen and Nancy's mother's non-progress, even news about the Kimball lumberyard seemed to interest Mom.

A cramp sent me to the bathroom and lo and behold I saw a spot of blood on my panties that explained my swollen tummy and cramps. My period brought on mixed emotions. It was welcome and not. I had been preoccupied with how to tell Nancy and Marshall about the miracle taking place inside me; and now there was no baby, no marriage, no huge event on the horizon, and this didn't seem as much a relief as it should have. Marshall would never know how far I was willing to go for him. I'd have to become the student I was supposed to be, heading toward a profession I couldn't name. My family would remain my homeland, with all their frayed edges and bad behavior. Without the child I thought would frame the future, my fate was no longer sealed. It is no wonder they call pregnant women "expectant mothers."

I had been living in a dream, expectant and ready to let the role of mother seal my fate. I felt stupid and sad.

These feelings must have shown. "Want to go for a ride?" Nancy asked when I returned to the klatch.

"No, I'm kind of tired, but thanks, anyway."

"Actually, Lily hasn't been feeling well. We should have called the doctor this morning. Why don't we do that now?"

"You know, I am already better, Mom. I just got my period and I don't want to take up the doctor's time for no good reason. Maybe I've been off because school is stressful—all that studying after a year of freedom."

I felt peculiar, empty, alone, alone in the company of my mother and best friend.

14

Saturday night with Marshall had been as I hoped. We made love, ate good food, read to one another, and it was easy to put aside my foolish sense of loss over the non-existent baby. Marshall treated me like the most special person on earth, surprised me with a tiny gold cross on a slender chain which he placed around my neck and declared his love over and over again. What more could I ask? I was disappointed when he sent me home early, but understood, because he had to work on his sermon. Besides we had Sunday night and eternity beyond that.

On Sunday morning, I arrived at church early, taking a seat in the rear of the sanctuary where I meditated mostly on the night before. When he entered he brought with him the same light as usual but that quickly disappeared. I wanted to disappear, too, because what I heard next was no post-Thanksgiving sermon. Something very dark had happened between our parting in the moonlight and the morning's hour of worship. He was fuming. His message was not like any I'd heard before. With his forefingers pointed at the congregation like gun nozzles, he accused us of foul play, said we were being duped by the Devil, and warned that our self-indulgence would be our destruction.

"The Ten Commandments begin with, I am the Lord Thy God, you will have no other gods before Me. No graven images, no idols, nor will you use my name in vain. Can this be any clearer? It is the fundamental law of your faith that you will love and honor your Father, first, last and always. Hollywood and its icons are corrupting our young people and our nation. Pay attention to the people your children idolize. Madonna. Michael Jackson. Doom. They are spreading the word of the Devil."

Some man in the second row called out, "Amen."

"How dare anyone worship a woman who usurps God's mother's name, who dares to demean God in the face of promiscuity? Listen to her words as she calls on women to forfeit their divine purpose for profit of the flesh...*they can't see the light, the boy with the cold hard cash is always Mr. Right, and I am a material girl living in a material world.* She's telling your daughters to go for the money and use sex to get what they want! She is without the Spirit and she's proud of it! She's about taking the money and running.

"And who else are our children worshipping? They love that narcissist Michael Jackson dancing backwards, holding himself and singing *beat it.* His words? *Beat me, hate me, you can never break me. Will me, thrill me, you can never kill me.*...Now I ask you, does this man know Jesus? Does he think he is beyond the power of the Lord? Is he threatening or is he begging for trouble?"

I could only see the backs of most of the congregation's heads and they were bowed low or fixated on Marshall's face. I felt uncomfortable. Embarrassed. He was not himself.

"Beware, my brothers and sisters, movies, television and computers are spreading filth. Christian values, American values are being trampled, ridiculed, and undermined by people who call themselves names like Venom and Doom. Without censorship, our children are at the mercy of these anti-heroes. We are watching the money-makers of an amoral industry, run by Jews and communists, harm our youth and ultimately our country. Hollywood's messages mock the good and the sacred and they are everywhere; on billboards, film, in schools, libraries and in our museums. Yes. Even the art world is contributing its trash to this disgrace.

"Do you realize what your tax money is funding? Do you realize the federal government gives grants to spread obscenity? You may not know, or maybe you do, an award has just been given for a replica of Christ, floating in a sea of urine. It's called the Piss Christ!"

Marshall lowered his head and raised his arms and opened his hands. "Forgive me Father for exposing this disgrace, this mockery with a name too offensive to be spoken ...but I must tell *you,* my brethren," and his fiery eyes looked down on all of us, "so you will know what is happening. Don't hide yourselves in ignorance. Stand up. Arm yourselves with righteousness. Protest this obscenity, this blasphemy in the name of art. How far can it go? Hasn't our Lord suffered enough? Wasn't the crown of thorns enough? The cross? How much debauchery must happen before we Christians stand up and demand to be counted?

"Christ's beloved ones, these are signs that we are fast approaching the Endtimes. Soon we will be witnessing the prophecies as foretold in Revelations. Our battle will be terrible and our choices difficult. We will see the anti-Christ riding against Christ himself. Who will you follow? Will you be able to recognize good from evil?

"The Ayatollah is here, the anti-Christ Islamic forces are rising, Satan's slave, and he is going to take us into the Endtimes. The Apocalypse is at hand, starting the Holy War of holy wars. Why aren't you down on your knees five times a day begging God for forgiveness like the people of the Koran? Why aren't you seeking God's Grace? Why aren't you humbling yourselves, bowing this very second, praying for all those people trapped in foreign lands without the cross to lead them home?"

He fell to his knees himself. "Kneel with me!" he ordered, and we followed, our knees pressed to the hard boards of the floor. We prayed aloud, beseeching God to forgive us. He shouted. "Lord have mercy upon us," and the congregation echoed him. "Louder!" he called. "Make a loud noise unto the Lord with me, all ye who need mercy!" We raised our voices. "Lord forgive us our trespasses!" he said. Again the echo. "Hear our transgressions!" he begged. And one after another the sinners around me called out their confessions until the sound of the many drowned out the sounds of the few.

"*Blessed be the Lord, my rock, who trains my hands for war and my fingers for battle,*" Marshall read. "You need fear only your own transgressions. God will make your path straight and you will be saved, for it is the kingdom of Heaven that we seek. You cannot be conquered if your soul is saved, that is the Promise and that is what no battle can take from you. Death need not be feared. Everlasting life is yours when you place your hand in God's. If we must go to war then so be it. We will fight until every last enemy of God is slain and peace can reign forever. *Where the wolf shall dwell with the lamb and the leopard shall lie down with the young goat, and the calf and the lion...*so says the Holy Word. Amen."

I touched the gold cross that he had given me. It was another man who stood before me that morning, a man wielding the crook of an angry shepherd frightening the sheep he saw before him.

"Beware the theaters, reject the music, cast off the debauchery that celebrates the profane. These instruments are the seducers of the innocent. Go to your knees instead of your computers. Beware the technology that is corrupting the information highways of the world. The age of pornography, of greed, of cynicism, perversion and hedonism is upon us. Beware the seal of heretics who profess the righteousness of false gods."

He was an angry giant—a man who could find words to say when others had none. And yet, what would he think if he knew I loved *him* more than God? He would not love me as much if he knew I sang along to Michael Jackson, that I thought Michael was brilliant and exciting. I didn't believe the Devil had anything to do with fame, with money or music, with failure or poverty, either.

What was going on in his head? Something had set him off.

After church I went to the trailer and timidly waited to find out what triggered his outburst. A fifth wheel trailer is usually made of metal, a metal and plastic answer for a place to live. Marshall's version was bigger than some but still a small, inconvenient place. I looked around and considered that our baby would have had to sleep in a dresser drawer. There was no room for a crib, that was for sure. On his papered walls he had teapots in the kitchen area and a laminated wood design in the living room. Last night's plates were still piled in the tiny sink.

I washed them. Then pulled up the covers of his unmade sofa-bed and gathered the scattered clothes needing to be laundered. I should have helped more the night before, but he made me leave. Thing was, he was so happy then.

When he came in the door, windblown and flushed, but one hundred percent calmer, I asked, "Marshall, are you all right?"

He shrugged his shoulders. "Of course, I'm all right. Did you see how many came forward this morning?"

I piled some dishes and placed them on the open shelf above the sink. "Maybe they all felt guilty," I said casually. What made you write that sermon? You sounded so angry."

"I am angry. I am afraid the whole world is going straight to Hell."

"But you were so happy with the world when I left you last night," I said, shining the glasses.

"I revised what I wrote, after you left. I needed to write a new sermon this morning."

"What happened?" I asked, putting down the cloth and turning toward him, milk glass in hand.

"David. He came by late last night. I did not like what he had to say. I do not like what he reads or how he thinks. I am not sure if he is using drugs or experimenting in other ways. He is rude and mocking. Ungrateful! This is the person that has been like a son to me since our parents died. I have always tried my best to be responsible for him, but I have failed. He does not care about what God wants. What I want. We cannot find one another. We cannot communicate without hatred filling up the space between us. He is not going in the right direction, just further and further away from me. I see only trouble ahead."

All sorts of advice flooded me, but it was not a warm safe place for us to talk about issues of parenthood. I wanted to speak to the difference between raising a brother and a child of one's own. But he was too distracted, and so was I. There had been the spot at Mom's, and yet only that, no more. I wanted so much to share what I had suspected could be true—that a tiny person was growing at lightning speed inside me, being fed through my body's pipelines, building a life of its own for us to love unconditionally. I wanted to make such an announcement, to make his life more joyful, however I still wasn't sure it wasn't wishful thinking.

Had I known more, I would have realized that at that point my baby had a heart and lungs and the makings of eyes and ears and the bud of a brain. Inside me a reality was blossoming that would change the world forever.

I decided to tell Carrie about my circumstances during our drive back to school. Cars are like closets, a safe space, where no one can overhear. She was pretty shocked, not by the fact that I might be pregnant but that I had a relationship. She was used to being the one with the drama. Carrie's curiosity helped me decide to keep Marshall a secret until I knew what I was going to do next. But Carrie had no intention of dropping the subject for a minute.

Of course, the great question loomed, was I or was I not? I explained why I couldn't buy a pregnancy test in Purgatory and she pointed out that it was easy enough to find out. She said in Burlington it would be easy. So, we went directly to the drugstore and scanned the multitude of tests. They were interestingly packaged in baby colors and lying next to every kind of condom imaginable. Carrie told me what the differences in the condoms were to educate me, and then pointed out that everything that prevented pregnancy was available to men, but nothing for protection was available for women.

"We're supposed to know better," she scoffed. "You see? There are no pills or devices for women on the shelves in any shape or form. Our choices begin and end with a pregnancy test."

Back at her dorm we studied the little package I had bought. It had a few directions and a simple tool to insert. After only three minutes the sign appeared and it told me all I had to know.

"But they're not always accurate," Carrie said. "You still have to go to a doctor. Call the campus infirmary and get an appointment right away. I'll take you. And don't worry. Your life isn't over. You still have lots of choices."

My heart was racing. I just shook my head and said that I needed to be alone. She took me back to my dorm without saying how impossible it would be to be alone in a suite with three other women and a baby exploding inside.

Ellie was the first to ask. "Lily! Welcome back. How are you doing?"

I must have looked different, I surely felt different. I said, "I'm feeling a lot better," and I was, I was just a little distracted.

"You look better. Maybe now you'll start having some fun."

She seemed innocent compared to me, now that I was the bearer of secrets. Partying was the least of my wishes. But she didn't need to know.

Two days later, Carrie and I went to the medical center where I met Dr. Bomson. He was a small, kind, soft-spoken person and I felt his compassion when I told him about the test. He listened carefully while I described my symptoms, his small hands tapping their fingers against one another. He had me lie down for an examination and asked for the dates of the first time and the last time I'd had intercourse.

He guesstimated my baby was three months along. That would mean I conceived when Marshall and I first made love. It made sense to me; our lovemaking had been so intense.

"Do you want to keep the baby?" he asked.

What kind of a question was that? I was shocked that he would imagine I would not. Before I could answer, he said, "You don't need to worry about confidentiality. All doctors respect their patients' privacy."

"I...I love the father."

He must not have heard me. "There are doctors here in Burlington that perform terminations every day. I can give you their names and you can decide what to do. But you need to act quickly. Most physicians won't perform an abortion past the first trimester."

Carrie had waited for me in the waiting room, and of course I had to tell her the mind-blowing truth.

"I just knew it. Now what are you going to do?"

"What do you mean what am I going to do? I suppose I will get married and become a mother and live happily ever after."

"It's just a little wad of phlegm. You don't have to keep it. No one will ever know but me, and I swear I will never ever tell. I had to have one in high school. It's not that bad. Not painful and life goes on as usual."

"I love the baby and the father. I couldn't destroy my baby."

"But Strange is so young and so not a father! I can't see how he would be able to take care of the two of you! Besides, it isn't really a baby, not yet."

"Strange?"

"I know you have always loved him. Strange as it seems," she laughed.

"I am not in love with Strange, Carrie." This made me laugh.

"Then who?" she asked.

"You don't know him," I told her. It occurred to me that I didn't know him very well either, but I believed I knew enough.

Knowing I was pregnant changed my center of gravity. I quickly became consumed by the creature who was consuming me. Not once in the weeks that followed did I feel ill or afraid or have a doubt about my future. I was calm, floating inside a pink bubble, waiting to claim my life and announce my news. It did not loom as difficult as one might have thought it should. Perhaps I called Marshall too often, and I was almost always disappointed with the endless rings. We both had crazy schedules and connections were difficult on both ends.

It was a week before the Christmas holidays when Ellie's red head popped into my bunk and said, "Wake up, Lily, Mr. Wonderful is on the phone!"

I ran out into the hall and slid down the wall into a lotus position to talk. There was so much to say and so little to be said at that time. I resorted to the weather. I told him snow was predicted and I didn't know exactly when we'd be leaving for home.

"I want you to be careful, Lily. You are precious, you know."

"I am missing you so much that I want to leave today," I said.

"You are lonely?" he asked.

"Only for you," I said.

"I want you to promise me that you won't leave if it is snowing. If you need to wait, think how we will make it up."

I keeled over into myself, loving the man so much it hurt.

I wanted to tell him there and then about the Christmas gift that was coming, a miracle in the midst of the celebration of that other baby's birth—at least I knew that's how Marshall would put it. If my name had been Madonna I couldn't have felt anymore chosen.

15

Winter break! Carrie drove south through the Vermont countryside with the radio blasting and the Datsun's gears in full throttle. We were both happy to be going home. Last night's dusting of snow was still sitting on the limbs of trees, softening the hills to a lavender haze. It was quietly beautiful. Burlington's terrain is more related to the almost Great Lake to the west and boring compared to the closely knit roll of old mountains that tuck in the little villages to the south where we were headed.

We were giddy with relief to have the burden of tests and papers behind us while the stork in the car stayed present and unaddressed. I loved Carrie for not asking. I knew it had to be hard for my extroverted friend to hold back. We made our way down Route 89 without incident or reference to the third passenger.

Our arrival at Pandora's Box at five in the afternoon was planned as Carrie could leave me with Heather, who planned to drive me the rest of the way home. At the shop, amidst hellos and goodbyes, hugs and promises to call, I once again made the transition from college to family.

My sister had transformed herself yet again. She looked like someone I used to know. But not quite. Now, her very blonde hair was in braids with ribbons wound through them. She had a Heidi look—lots of pink on her cheeks, but no black on her eyes. Maybe Dad had it right. She *should* be a fashion designer. She had already adopted Coco Chanel's mantra: *To be irreplaceable, a person must always be different*. Maybe Heather would follow in her footsteps.

"Oh God, what a weird month this has been," Heather moaned. "I've been working almost every day and Strange has been stranger than ever, his head is lost in books or typing away on the computer. But, he's a great writer. Really! I think he'll be famous."

"What's he up to?" I asked, picking up the jumble of stocking stuffers scattered about and placing them back in their proper cartons: fake glasses with noses and mustaches attached, finger puppets of pigs and ducks and little green creatures, erasers shaped like candy canes and pencils shaped like twigs.

"Mostly, saving Brent." Brent comes here after school three days out of five. Strange puts him in the car and takes him skating—can you believe it? He says Brent is working out his shit on the ice."

"Well, that's good, isn't it? I mean, I know he's always loved to skate. But I had no idea Strange was into it, too."

"Yeah, I'm thinking it's an acquired interest, but nothing compared to the computer. He sits and types every chance he gets. I think he's writing the great American novel. I can't explain it, but something's definitely going on with him."

We turned off the lights on the artificial tree and the star shaped multi-colored lights around the window, then put the closed sign on the door. As Heather helped me toss my bags into the car she said, "You're looking good. Much better than the last time you were home. Pink suits you better than gangrene."

"Yeah, I'm feeling a lot better..."

"I invited Strange to dinner again."

"That's nice. Why don't we invite his brother, too? Make it a family thing."

"Huh? That's a sick joke, Lily. Not only is *our* family broken, but the brothers Marshall and David hate each other. I don't think it would work out. Not a good idea."

"I'm sure they love each other, they've just hit a bump in the road somewhere."

"More like a brick wall. Believe me, it wouldn't work out. I invited Strange because Brent likes him and is more relaxed around him. I did it for Brent."

"That's nice, Heather, really nice. I like Strange, too, you know." I couldn't blame her for not knowing how much I needed to bring Marshall to the family table. He was still only a vague "other". The reality of our baby exploding inside me, claiming the future while his father remained no more than a figment of my family's imagination was my fault.

The Saab felt toasty after the drafty ride in Carrie's car. I was just thinking it was beginning to look and feel like a well-worn shoe when Heather said, "We need another car."

"Yeah, not so good for Mom to have to lend it out to you all the time."

"She's talking about buying a car from your friend Nancy's father, over in Londonderry."

"That'd be good." *I guess I'll have to call Nancy,* I thought.

We drove home listening to the latest Michael Jackson album, *The Way You Make me Feel.*

Despite Marshall's warnings, I loved the music. *I'm shameless,* I thought as I listened. I thought about the way he turned me on—the rhythms we had found together. I knew the weeks ahead would be the most important in my life.

We saw the glow of the house as we climbed the hill. Tiny blue lights outlined its edges and sparkled on the snow under the full moon. It was the first time I had seen the place not as the barn, not as a work in progress, but home. A spotlight focused on the big Leslie Woodhouse wreath on the front door, greeting us with bayberries and the fragrance of pine. A lazy strand of smoke wound about in the air above the chimney. It was as perfect as a Norman Rockwell card.

"Ma, we're home!" Heather yelled.

"Please don't call me Ma, Heather." Mom snapped, coming in from the kitchen and wiping her hands on her apron. They were red from the beets she had peeled for the Borscht we were about to devour.

"Lily! Just in time for some beet soup and your favorite Estonian Breadkringel, fresh from the oven!"

Mom is domestic. I could never match her. Soup and bread should be her middle names. She is happiest with garlic on her fingers and a cloud of flour covering her chest. I wished she had reached for me, but it was not to happen. Those beet stained hands could have been her excuse, but she wasn't much of a hugger; I knew that.

Brent came home in a while with his skates dangling from his shoulders and his cheeks shining from the cold. He took off the red and green stocking cap Mom had knit for him last winter and undid his down vest. "Hi," he said in a voice I hardly recognized. It must have dropped an octave overnight.

"Skating at Olin's Pond?" I asked, stupidly, knowing full well that's where he went.

"Yup."

"I just got in," I said.

"Uh-huh," he answered and fled for his room.

Why was it so hard for me to make any headway with my own brother? I imagined how difficult Marshall must find it to be with Strange, because they had once been so close, but then, Brent and I had once been close, too.

A few days before Christmas, I had a chance to do some shopping. Nancy and I drove all the way to Rutland and rummaged around. I had little money to spend but lots of good intentions. I found Mom a plastic red pepper container for salad leftovers. I bought ponytail scrunchies for Heather, and a puck for Brent. Dad posed a bit more of a problem. He always did. I finally found a t-shirt that read, *I Love My Daddy*. Maybe it would let him know.

Marshall was another challenge. I had only a few dollars left, so I went to a used book store and found a paperback that looked new. It was called *Lives of a Cell* by Lewis Thomas. I remembered Strange had read it two years ago and loved it. Maybe it would become a tool for conversation between them.

I called Marshall too many times that evening and suffered over the rings that kept on ringing. It was upsetting that he was unavailable. He had said how much he wanted to see me and then made excuses, saying the season was demanding of him, that he had to attend to visits and special services. I tried to be patient but he should have called me more often and at least invited me to be with him during the holiday functions. We had to have a long talk, face to face. Excuses were turning into frustration and frustration into fear.

I managed to keep busy. My clothes were now looking for space in Heather's room as she wasn't about to give up my bed or my space just because I was home for a visit. So I spent hours getting control of that annoyance. Then I took on decorating the mantle and hearth with ground pine and cones. I wound twisties around the hooks of blue and green glass balls to attach them to the branches, and placed a few votive candles in green cups for effect. I tried to ignore a growing sense of panic that no calls were coming my way.

After two days had gone by without any word from Marshall, despair began to set in and I turned to prayer for patience. Ernest understood. Wherever I was, he was there beside me, leaning in, pawing and offering his warm furry self. Then there was Mom, busy making holiday treats and lending her steadiness to our household. I had to prepare her somehow for the news I was about to break. She didn't deserve to be left out. She would be hurt.

On Christmas Eve Heather had gone to work, Brent was gathering firewood and Mom and I were in the kitchen frosting cookies. She was lost in sugar and butter and humming a little to herself. *Not unhappy,* I thought.

"How are you and Dad doing?" I asked.

"It's over, Lily. Irreconcilable differences."

"Over?"

"Yes. We are trying to become friends but it's hard. He's being decent about finances and checking-in, but I don't love him anymore." She took a bite from one of the warm cookies, and using the spatula, delicately transferred the cooled ones from the wax paper to a cookie platter.

"I remember loving him. I remember how he loved me. Although he made me up from the start. He saw me at that farm stand and thought I was the Earth Mother he had always wanted, someone as different from his mother as he was from his father. But I wanted to be just like his mother, I wanted her wisdom and confidence, I wanted the beautiful home, the respect, the education. He spoiled all we had with alcohol and bad judgment. It's too late. I hope you'll forgive me, Lily, but I simply need to move on."

Her tone was so matter-of-fact she might just as well have been telling me about a book she had just read. "Mom, there's nothing to forgive. You shouldn't have to live with someone you don't love. We kids are grown up and you tried. We all saw you try. You tried so hard that I...I thought...I just hope you won't mind if I go on loving him in my own way."

"Of course, you *must*. He's not a bad man, he just never grew up. But, Lily, I'm sure you will find a decent man of your own, someday, a man with his feet on the ground."

She was calm, her mind was made up and she wanted me to hear her decision was final. This was a different voice, for her, much different than the one she used a year ago.

"Do Brent and Heather know?" I asked.

"I suppose so, but I haven't told them that I've actually filed for divorce. It doesn't seem quite so terrible now with things becoming clear. Love doesn't die easily, you know," she said, as if she'd been reading my mind.

I was remembering her holding his jacket and hugging it when she thought no one was looking. "I am starting to learn about love, Mom," I said, allowing myself to shift the air in the room.

She put down the spatula and stared at me. I casually licked some of the leftover frosting from the bowl. She folded her arms and leaned against the sink. "Well, this is certainly news. And how are you learning this very hard lesson, Lily?"

"You say love dies slowly, but it can also hit really, really fast. That's what's happened to me. I'm in love, Mom. I'm sorry I didn't tell you sooner."

She smiled in her gentle, accepting way. "Well sometimes things do happen quickly. It certainly did between your father and me. He simply marched in and took over. That's how I remember it at least. Is it a boy in your class?"

"No. It isn't. He isn't even a boy. He's a man I met here in town, sort of."

Her face turned red. She turned to the sink to wash off her hands and spent a full minute drying them. When she turned back to me she was obviously upset. "So it's true. I should have known. You could have at least shared more about this with me, Lily. I count on you to be honest with me; the other two are so secretive."

"I am sharing. I was meaning to all along. I wanted to tell you but...."

She shook her head, picked up the wooden spoon pointing it at me like a long accusatory finger. "It's that...it's not that minister, that man Heather was teasing you about? It's Strange's brother, isn't it?"

"Well, yes, and why not? Why shouldn't it be him? He's a brilliant man. He is responsible and caring and kind. He raised Strange, he helps people find God. He knows who he is and what God wants of him." I didn't mention that he hadn't called since I returned and my confidence was in a kind of free fall.

The buzzer went off and she took the new batch of cookies out of the oven. The spatula shook as she plied them from the tray. I pulled the cooled batch toward me and began to squeeze on some happy faces and sprinkle them with color.

"What do you mean by love, Lily? This is a big word. It may only have four letters, but it can spell out a lifetime. Is this love you are referring to like loving the Beatles or your teacher, Dr. Wolfe, Ernest or your father? Is this unrequited love or a romance novel? A first love usually doesn't have much more to it than fantasy."

It was as if she had a prepared speech ready.

"It's none of those things, Mom. I love him. He loves me. We're going to get married. He is the smartest most beautiful man I have ever met."

"Well you haven't met that many, darling. Maybe you should share him with us so we can take a look at this superman."

"I will. You'll see, you will love him, too, when you get to know him."

"I don't know that it matters whether I love him or not, but, Lily, be careful. At your age you can fall in love with love. This may be more of a crush than reality. You could not have spent that much time with...what's his name?"

"Marshall, Marshall Barry."

"Marshall. How well could you possibly know this man?"

There was no way I could tell her that he was living inside me. That God had already proved our love. I was trying not to act hurt or defensive. It was my fault for not being more honest sooner. "Mom. I know all I need to know. I will never love anyone the way I love him. He has become a part of me and I am a part of him. It's just the way it is. I don't have a choice."

"There's no such thing as only one person you can love. Don't you think I love my three children equally?"

No. No, I didn't, but I wouldn't say it, and she would never admit it.

Ernest jumped up onto the counter and walked between us with his tail standing tall. "Ernest get down!" she said, crossly.

I was sure Ernest was just trying to be a friendly distraction.

"You only loved Daddy. You've been with him forever, haven't you? Did you ever love anyone else?"

"No, but that doesn't mean I wasn't capable of meeting someone else, that there wasn't someone out there who could offer me a new life, love, a new way of being in the world. I was only eighteen, for heaven's sake. I didn't know a thing about myself or your father or life or responsibility."

"I am in love with Marshall. I am going to marry him. He will give me what I want."

"And what is that, Lily? You have already had so much. You won't consider giving up your education? You have wanted to be a veterinarian for so long. He can't give you that. Can you live a life without material comforts? A life as a pastor's wife? Do you realize that being a pastor's wife is like being the mother of the church? Are you willing to give up your dreams for his? Your beliefs?"

"Marshall understands what it means to have purpose and reverence for life. He sees the world through God's eyes. As for me, I have no beliefs. I believe in him."

"Oh, please. Now you are frightening me."

"Mom. This is real. It's the realest thing that has ever happened to me. I need you to understand."

"I understand that you are an innocent, far more innocent than this man you are saying you love. I am not sure you know what love means, Lily. It means sacrificing seventy-five percent of yourself and getting twenty-five percent in return—if you're lucky."

She was snapping the wash cloth, banging the baking pans and shaking her head.

I should have expected as much. She was in the middle of letting love go and I was trying to tell her about the thrill of finding it. I had to stop and lighten the air. It was impossible to go any further.

"These cookies are too good! It's the molasses," I said, munching on one with burnt edges.

"Lily, my darling girl, please just take this slowly, all right?"

I *was* taking it slowly, far slower than I wanted. I willed the phone to ring, waited for a bouquet of flowers, a Fed Ex delivery, a face at the door, anything to show what I had to believe.

16

If a secret camera was hidden in the walls of our house on December 25th, it wouldn't have revealed the reality of our family's problems. It would have seen a mother and father behaving as parents do. It would have shown three siblings acting for all the world like friends. The young male character in the scene, who a year ago would have seemed most likely to fail, was looking healthier and handsomer than ever. Although Brent was his same quiet, monosyllabic self with me, he wasn't glowering the way he once had.

Our friend Strange was not looking strange at all. He seemed like a relaxed version of himself; studs in his ears, black goatee of sorts and his typical black outfit, but less Quixotic. Mom was happy and new, with a short, swingy hairdo and a long black velvet skirt topped with a white blouse protected in front by a red apron. Of course, a potato sack would look good on her. Dad was at ease in his cords and a crewneck, looking for all the world like the happiest guy in town.

Heather, the queen of contention, was moving the conversation along lines she found interesting and had managed to hit a chord with everyone at the table. "Why did you two name us the way you did? I get that you named Lily after Grandma, but why Heather and why Brent? I mean why not Samantha or Thomas?"

Oh my father loved that one. He began another of his soliloquies, this one about the importance of names. He explained how seriously he and Mom took on the responsibility of naming us because a person's name could determine their level of success and acceptance.

"Then why Atticus?" Heather asked.

"Your mother loved it. She thought Atticus Woodhouse sounded like a Pulitzer prize winner. But we knew Atticus was a little heavy for a kid to carry, so we called him by his middle name Brent."

Mom chimed in, "It was solid and unique. We also liked it because it wouldn't be corrupted into a nickname. Like Peter to Petey, or Robert to Bobby or Rob or Bob."

"And, it wasn't a sexually confusing name like Connie or Francis, or Toady or Robin. It wasn't one that could go feminine over time like Leslie or Ashley or Claire," Dad added.

"It's short, too," Mom said. "But mostly it was a way to keep my family's name alive."

"But why did you call me, Heather?"

Dad smiled his most beatific smile and said, "Heather means beautiful, creative, and spontaneous. I think we can all agree we got it right, Princess."

"Oh, right," she said.

Then Dad turned to David. "Now, your name, son, is a Biblical name, the name of kings."

"You don't have to remind me, man," Strange said. "I've heard all I want to know about the little guy who knocked off Goliath and then screwed around with Bathsheba. That would not be me!"

Heather and Brent covered their mouths with their napkins.

"Sounds like you know some of the Bible," said Dad. "We've stayed away from it in this family, although I often think we should have looked at it in the name of cultural literacy."

Strange said, "Cultural literacy? Yeah, but I think it's better to give all the stories equal time. Like, Superman and Siddhartha, Holden Caulfield and those crazy Greek gods and goddesses that fly around in chariots all day. I am not into the Bible, because it was shoved down my throat in my teens and nowhere nearly as interesting as the other things I found to read. Thing is, I wouldn't have minded it if it was taught as myth or fiction, but to call it the Truth? Not."

"Couldn't agree with you more," Dad said.

Ice clattered as Mom raised the water pitcher and poured herself more water. "Were there any other Davids in your family?" she asked.

"Yeah. I suppose I might have been named after my mother's father, but I'll never know, with everyone six feet under. Personally, I think we should earn our labels, the way the Native Americans do it. Live a little and let your tribe do the naming."

"And what would your name be, do you think?" Dad asked, obviously entertained.

"Hmm. I think it might be Strange, like in how the kids in a little backwater town would see a kid from New York who didn't walk in their footsteps. You know what I mean?"

Heather looked at Strange, wide-eyed with Pollyanna innocence. "Hmmm, yes, I see that. You *are* Strange. Let's call you Strange. Strange Barry suits you very well."

Dad pounced. "Not nice, Heather, I don't think so. That's a negative name. You wouldn't want people to think of you that way. What positive word would resonate with you, David, if you were to rename yourself today?"

We all waited for his response.

"Maybe, Solo" Strange said. "I'm flying solo."

"How about Han Solo?" Brent suggested.

"Now there's a definitely positive dude," said Strange.

"What's that brother of yours called?" Dad asked.

"The Very Reverend Marshall Barry."

I felt my cheeks turn red. Again, I was forced to wonder where the reverend was, why he hadn't called.

Dad leaned back in his chair. "Ah, I see. So he got the religion and you got the religious name." He studied the bread he was buttering and then looked up. "Was that your brother's church where you took Lil McGill, back when you two started working together at Pearl's place?"

"Probably," Strange confessed, looking my way for a signal.

"That would be the one she thought would be fun?"

My father had a Velcro memory.

"Fun, if you're into mind games," Strange said.

"And did you think it was fun, Lily?" Mom asked, innocently.

"I don't remember saying it would be fun. It was interesting. David's brother has a lot of power. He makes miracles happen. When Stra...David and I went to the church, we saw a boy who couldn't speak begin to sing. The words just flowed out of him. It was amazing!"

"Was he a plant?" Dad laughed.

"A plant?"

"Your father means was someone set up to make the preacher boy look good?" Strange explained.

"Of course not. You know we saw it with our own two eyes. You were there."

"Well, it wasn't all that amazing, really," Strange said. "P-p-p-people who st-st-stutter seem to do well when they s-s-s-sing."

Brent started laughing. Strange was definitely playing to Brent.

A warm mask of pink covered my face and I prayed no one saw what I felt.

"David's writing a book," Brent said, an announcement out of nowhere.

"Well, how wonderful!" Mom exclaimed. "What is it about, David?"

"It's a science fiction kind of book—about a life form that comes to earth and tries to push new rules on the human race. The humans are too afraid to stand up and proclaim their own authority and soon they're living inside cages and fighting over scraps of food."

"How interesting," Mom exclaimed.

We sat for a long time at the big table loaded with glasses part full and part empty, and a zillion dishes to be cleared. Above us the beeswax candles glowed from the wrought iron chandelier, a rustic counterpoint to the crystal we had once had. Our new space felt more like us, not less. I knew I would remember this meal for a long time. It had all the trimmings of a holiday: scrumptious food, family, laughter, layers of meanings and shades of the future. You might have thought you were in a Wilder play, each of us acting our part and behaving the way either we thought we should or wanted to be, without needing a stage manager to direct us. Whatever, my parents were on their best behavior, we teenagers acted like the emerging adults we were, and even Strange, new friend of the family, was at his very best, playing along with our efforts. The big negative was that Marshall was missing out on this performance. He should have been at my side, enjoying the clove riddled ham and the whipped sweet potato casserole, the sauerkraut and apple sauce, the yummy black pumpernickel bread and the spice pudding.

The very thought of him made me needy. I was wanting to be free of my secret, with him at my side. He was to be my family and I was to be his, and yet these rare moments were still foreign to the person I loved. I put my hand on my belly, reminding myself of the treasure inside, the one that would be sitting on my lap next year.

After dinner we gathered around the blue spruce that was taking up most of the living room. When we unwrapped our gifts, I knew for sure how much Brent meant to Strange. He gave him the perfect gift, a headset he could wear while skating. Brent was silent as he read the card and then gave Strange the most loving look I'd ever seen cross his face. The adorable little boy he once was and the man he was becoming were brought together. He put the card in the box and said in his new deep voice, "Thanks, bro."

Gift giving can be just a ritual. It's the gifts we don't expect that matter most. The gift of the back of a friend's horse, the advice of someone whose heart is open and cares about yours, the butterfly that lands on your shoulder and stays awhile. Or how about finding a lost bracelet, or the sound of a cat purring contentedly on the windowsill? I had all these but couldn't stop thinking about the call that wasn't.

Dad and Mom avoided talking to one another. They talked through us and around us. If they thought we didn't notice, they couldn't have been more mistaken. With a roaring fire and new music to share, we did the best we could at small talk. Finally, I heard the ring of the phone.

"Who could that be?" Heather asked. "Do we have any living relatives, someone we've never heard about? Who calls us on Christmas Day?"

I hoped I knew, but as it turned out, the call wasn't for me, but was for Mom, who grew red-faced and went to a different room to take it.

I busied myself folding up gift paper and tying bows together with ribbons to place in a box for next year. While I was sorting the gifts into piles I looked at the headphones that Strange had given to Brent. The card had fallen out and as I picked it up I saw, *To the next Brian Boitano*. Brian was the golden boy of ice that year, famous for his triple lutz and some kind of outrageous toe loop trick. He was the United States' Olympic hopeful. Strange had to know something the rest of us didn't about Brent's dreams.

Mom came back into the living room still flushed. "That was Carl Kimball. He's got this car for sale that he thinks I should come to see, if I am really interested. He's already had some other calls from people who are."

"Well, geez, he must be desperate to try to sell a car on Christmas day!" Heather said before she thought better about it. In her next breath she begged. "But, Mom, we *need* a car. One of us is always stuck without one."

Dad looked at me and asked if I knew the car.

"How would I know the car?" I asked.

"He's Nancy's father isn't he? Your friend from Al-a-Teen? Is it her car he's selling?"

"If it is, you wouldn't want it, Mom. It's old and stinky. It's not for you."

She turned to me. "Well, I am sure it isn't *her* car as it's an SUV and only two years old. Carl usually trades in his cars every three years but this time he's making an exception. I guess he thinks he'll do better selling it himself. I've checked *Consumers Guide* and the price is right."

"Please get it, Mom, we need that car!" Heather pleaded.

"Well, would you like to come with me in the morning and give me a second opinion?" she asked.

Heather was quick to refuse. She said she had to work on her college applications and Brent was not interested because he wanted to try out his new radio ears on the ice. As usual it came down to me.

I should have remembered that a car is a kind of entrapment. It surely was the next morning when it contained Mom and me for a full forty minutes on our way to Londonderry. "So now tell me. How often do you see your friend the minister?" Mom began.

"Marshall Barry."

"Marshall Berry."

"Barry!"

"Is this relationship a secret that you don't want let out? I think it's high time we met your man. Too much mystery doesn't bode well for a long relationship. It doesn't seem David knows what is going on. I thought you and he were very close. And Heather seems in the dark."

"Well it happened really fast and the time hasn't been right to tell anyone."

"I see. So you do realize you made up your mind very quickly, Lily. We have yet to meet him."

"But you and Dad have always said it was love at first sight..."

"Please, your father and I are not good examples of what works and doesn't work. I was very young, your age actually. I was swept off my feet because of what I saw and not what I knew."

"Mom, I'm afraid you've forgotten all the happy times. You were happy until Dad started to drink too much."

"I was a starry-eyed fool. Now let's talk about this *man* of yours. Just how old is he?"

She was trying to look at me instead of the road.

"He's about ten years older than I am and I can tell you now that he is nothing like Dad. He believes in God, he doesn't drink or smoke or make fun of people. His heart is open to every person. He's got the power to heal, Mom. He does!"

"He sounds a little frightening. A man with no bad habits is a little too rare to be normal. How much do you really know about him, Lily?"

I didn't want to say that I was helpless. That what I was feeling was that I had been placed in his arms and in his life without knowing what was happening to me. It was as if an otherworldly power had taken me from one world and delivered me into another, like he was put in my life to find. She would have squashed that idea in a hurry.

"What does anyone know about anybody?" I cried. "I don't understand my family or my friends or why I'm even here!"

"Lily, I know that the divorce is upsetting. No matter what you saw or knew, it has been coming for years and years."

"But you love him! I love him."

"I had to love him. He was my husband, the father of my children. I had to marry him. I believed that we would grow up together, that there was time for us to become the people we were meant to be. Instead only one of us grew up while the other kept trying to escape."

"What do you mean? Are you saying you had to get married?"

"I mean that I was five months pregnant and broke and scared and he was the only way I had to save the day. My parents would have thrown me to the lions in my condition."

"You married Dad because of me?"

"Well, yes, I guess you could put it that way."

"But you stayed married for nineteen years! It couldn't have been that bad."

"There's a lot you don't know, my darling girl. A lot."

I couldn't speak. I was angry at her for some reason. Did she blame me? They had two more kids after me. What kind of a marriage could they have had if love didn't exist? Why would they stay so long in something that didn't work? Silence sat between us. What a farce it all was, the whole thing—*love at first sight, the best thing that ever happened*— the hugs, the kisses, the way I had seen them together. I felt sick.

"Here we are," Mom said, as we exited the highway in Londonderry and pulled into the Garden Restaurant's parking lot.

And now I would have to put on the act of being the good daughter, behave like Nancy's friend and an interested buyer. It helped that I was curious to meet Nancy's dad. I had no preconceived impressions because she spoke so little of him; it was as if he didn't exist.

We saw him right away. He was hard to miss, waving us in with his long tweed coat and striped college scarf blowing in the wind. His hair was a strange shape; the half of it that was meant to cover his receding hairline was standing up like a rooster's comb. It looked stiff and maybe dyed. His moustache was too dark and too small.

"Here you are!" he exclaimed.

"Carl, this is my daughter, Lily."

"Ah yes, Lily, I have heard so much about you."

"You have?" I asked.

"Yes, yes. Well, here is the car. I imagine you know the Jeep fairly well, Leslie, but I just want to remind you of her good points. She has two new sets of tires and only 22,000 miles of wear and tear. She's got a powerful engine but does fairly well on gas. You should know she has some strange tendencies, too. When you brake, she's kind of clumsy. Her switching of gears isn't as smooth as other cars I've known. They tell me it's a safety feature and I should ignore it, but I thought I should pass that on to you."

I was wondering why we were meeting in a parking lot since this deal seemed all but over and done. And why were we in Londonderry? Couldn't he have come to Purgatory?

"I suppose you are the second driver, Lily? This car is going to feel very different from your Saab, but I imagine you will adjust quickly. It's got a nice high seat and six cylinders to give you plenty of zip. Handles well in the snow, too."

"I like its dark green color," I said.

"Come on now, young lady, sit down and try it out." He opened the door and ushered me into the front seat. "Your mother and I will watch you take a little spin around the lot."

Something felt weird. Alarms buzzed my head, but I couldn't see why. Maybe it was his talking about his car as if it was a woman.

As I settled into the front seat, he leaned over my lap and stuck the keys in the ignition. I could smell his after-shave. Then he stepped back. "Take your time," he said. "Your mother and I will meet you inside the restaurant when you're through."

Did Mom speak? Did she ask a question or give an opinion? I don't think so. I checked the steering wheel, the shift stick, and the mirrors; then put my foot on the pedal and took off as the two of them walked towards the door, his hand on her elbow.

Driving someone else's car is not my thing. I didn't even drive the Saab that much. But this vehicle had some muscle and I felt kind of powerful at the wheel. I did a figure eight, tested the radio, toyed around with the dashboard and pretended it was going to be mine. After about ten minutes, I parked it as close to the restaurant's front door as I could without having to do any fancy maneuvering.

Inside the restaurant, I walked down the center aisle, heading toward the back, past the blue silk flowers in orange plastic pots, past intrusions of idle walkers and highchairs and the hustle and bustle of the wait staff, until I found them in the last booth. He was leaning into her face. She seemed caught up in whatever he was saying.

"Well, here you are," he said, pulling back, and turning toward me when I arrived at their sides. "Have a seat. Some coffee?" he asked.

"I prefer tea."

Mom asked if I liked the car. I nodded.

Mr. Kimball explained that he was only letting the Jeep go because it turned out to be too small a car for the lumber business. I told him it seemed huge to me.

How long we sat there I couldn't say. I looked for Nancy's face in his and was surprised not to see any resemblance. He never mentioned her, but then I might just as well not have been there, either. All he wanted to do was talk to Mom and rattle on about the car and how happy he was to know she would be safe on the highways. His hair was lying down by then, but it remained a distraction.

When we left they made a plan about how we would pick up the car. It seemed much more complicated than necessary, but what did I care? What mattered more was the way he left his hand on Mom's arm a little too long, and the way he stood looking at us as we pulled out of the lot, waving stiffly until we were out of sight. We might as well have been leaving for China.

"That was weird," I said.

"He's offering us a really good deal" she answered.

"Hmm."

"He's quite nice."

"No, he isn't. He's a lousy father and a rotten husband."

"Oh, Lily, what is happening to you?" she frowned.

"Nancy Kimball is one of my best friends. I believe what she tells me."

"Did she say those things about her father?"

"Not exactly. But she implied them."

"Carl Kimball is a hardworking, responsible man. He pulled himself up by the bootstraps and made a good life for himself and for Nancy."

"He told you all that while I was doing loopy-loops in the parking lot?" I asked.

"No. But he has been to AA meetings and I have spoken to him from time to time."

"Does Dad know him?"

"Your father isn't going to meetings anymore."

"I see. How come he's never connected with his daughter when she's been there?"

"Oh, he has. You've been gone."

We took a different route home. Mom pointed to the road sign that said *Woodbury six miles.* "Isn't Woodbury the town where your minister lives?"

"Yes. Did I tell you that?"

"I seem to remember it somehow," she said. "Why don't we drop in and meet him? It might be the easiest way for us to get acquainted. Then I can invite him to dinner this Friday."

"I don't know, Mom, he's so busy. Maybe we should stop and call first."

"Oh, that shouldn't be necessary; ministers have to have their doors open at any time of the day or night. They're emergency workers, counselors, and expected to be readily available for all their sheep."

"What do you know about ministers, Mom?"

"I was brought up in the People's Bible Church."

"A Bible Church? How come you've never talked about that part of your life?"

"I try to forget it. We were taught that just about everything that was fun was forbidden."

"Like what?"

"Like dancing and drinking and sleeping late on Sunday mornings. God was watching with a record book in his hands. Too many sins and you could be sure you'd be punished. I was always afraid of making a mistake, always guilty over the stupidest things. Things like sneaking a second piece of candy or bringing home a gossip magazine or wanting to kiss boys. It was all-encompassing."

"But are you saying you went to a church and learned Bible verses and the whole thing?"

"I had to. It was pretty serious. My parents believed all those stories about Hell and damnation, those lies about death and salvation. So many dark ideas to make a girl afraid, especially if she wanted things she wasn't supposed to have."

"Was Dad one of those things you wanted?" I asked.

"Yes. I suppose he was. He was the most exciting boy I had ever met. He made me laugh and feel free and drove fast and well, he thrilled me." She shook her head as if to get rid of the very idea.

"And did God punish you?" I asked, not wanting to hear her answer.

17

Mom and I drove to Woodbury despite my reservations. I tried to convince myself a visit could be a stepping stone between Marshall and my family. I hoped Mom would help to ease the way. But when we arrived, looking at the church through her eyes disabled my confidence. The building appeared forlorn against the leafless woods, shabby and sad. I was tempted to defend it with descriptions of summer mornings and the welcoming man at the front door, but it would have been wasted on her ears.

I pointed at the trailer. "That's it," I said.

We turned into the driveway and saw another car parked nearby. A teary-faced girl sat in the front seat of what was probably her parent's car. It seemed likely he was counseling whoever was inside.

"Mom, don't go any further. He has company. We can't stop in now," I begged.

"Oh, alright," she said. "I guess I won't be meeting the pastor, today," and reversed our car back out onto the road. "He doesn't actually live in that thing, does he?"

"Just for now," I said. "He's using it until the time is right."

"Well, that's good to hear."

"I could live in a mud hut with him," I said as boldly as I knew how.

"I don't think so," Mom stated.

"Mom, don't you get it? I love him. We are going to get married. I am going to have his baby!"

"Oh please. You hardly know the man. You have years ahead to grow up and decide who you are before you lock yourself into some small miserable life of servitude."

"Mom! Can't you hear me?" She was not only acting deaf, she was acting blind, too. "Slow down! You're going fifteen over the speed limit."

"I hear you very well, Lily, and I want you to give yourself time, plenty of time, time most women don't have, time to explore, to educate themselves, time to decide what's best for them. You're one of the lucky ones, thanks to your grandmother."

"Mom, slow down, please." Her foot went to the brake. As we slowed, I said, "Listen, I need you to take me seriously. You need to know that I'm pregnant."

"You are what?" She pulled the car over to the side of the road and came to a full stop. A truck went barreling by with the driver tooting his horn playfully.

She turned towards me. "You're pregnant?" she asked, trying to make sense of the thought.

"Yes. I've been wanting to tell you."

"What are you saying, exactly?" Her eyes studied mine.

"I am pregnant."

"I don't think so. It can't be true!" She shook her head.

"It is."

"No."

"I am going to have Marshall Barry's baby."

"Well, how on earth did that happen? I mean, you don't actually *know* it's true do you?" Her hands fanned the air, pushing my words away, dismissing me like I was an ignoramus, someone who didn't know the facts of life.

"I know. I have seen a doctor and I am about four months pregnant. Our baby is due in June."

"June?" She shut her eyes and dropped her head while the news set in. Then she began to bang on the steering wheel, making the horn bleat like a lamb. I was helpless as she started to cry in big gulping sobs.

With all the things that had happened to her in the past two years, I had never seen her cry like this. She would try to stop, try to speak but then start to weep all over again. What could I do? I didn't know what to say. I couldn't say I was sorry. No words would convince her not to worry. She wasn't interested to hear that I was happy or sure about my future or that I refused to allow myself to think the baby growing inside me was a tragedy. She had yet to meet the lioness, the warrior rising—the new me. Was my mother going to be just one more person willing to destroy what was sacred? Would she want to kill my baby, her own grandchild, just as my doctor and close friend suggested? Never. I would never.

"Lily, I..." she tried. "Lily, you..."

"Mom it's okay. I am really, really, okay with this. I believe it was meant to happen. There are no mistakes."

"It's not that easy, Lily. A baby determines so many things about your future. It names you before you're even old enough to name yourself. Don't you see?"

"Women used to marry at fourteen; they still marry even younger in many countries. I'm nineteen almost twenty. At least four girls in my high school class were pregnant at graduation."

"Those girls are not you. You have everything ahead, the world to discover. You're a very young and inexperienced nineteen. Why, you have never even had a boyfriend, Lily."

"I see that you don't understand that I am a mother now and I love my baby and her father. Can't you accept that's all that matters, Mom? It's not a tragedy. It's a blessing. Please don't act this way, as if I can't think for myself. You're only thinking of yourself, that you were forced to have me, and things didn't work out. Well, that's not *me*. Things are going to work out and my life is my own, not yours, not anyone else's. As soon as I talk to Marshall we will decide what to do next. He's a man, Mom, not some silly kid."

A passing car slowed down, its passenger looked at us to see if we were in trouble. Mom rolled down her window to wave him on. We needed help but not that kind.

"You...you haven't told him yet?"

"No. It just hasn't been the right moment. I want it to be the best news he's ever heard and I want to make sure it comes at the right time."

"So, you haven't told him?"

"Not yet."

"Well, when in God's name do you propose to do that? When your labor pains start? For heaven's sake Lily, I am not sure your lights are all on."

"Thanks, Mom. Thanks for all your love and support."

"You know you have always had my love and support. I have lived my life for you, for you to have choices. No matter what you are thinking now, this is what my love and support are looking like at this moment. It is probably too late for an abortion, but it is surely too soon for a marriage. We are going to have to think this through. It is not going to be easy whatever you decide to do."

"Mom, *we* don't have to decide anything. This is *my* life. I am driving the car. I am making my own choices. I am parking my car next to Marshall Barry and we are going to make things work out. He needs me. I need him."

"Oh? Oh, he needs you? He needs an innocent inexperienced girl and a baby to help him run his rinky-dink idea of a church. This must not be happening. I am dreaming. I am dreaming this up. Tell me I am asleep."

Our argument went on all the way home. It was the same stuff over and over again, punctuated with tears. We stopped talking at the door and remained silent when we went inside.

I couldn't hang around her gloom and thought fresh air might help. So, I put on my parka and went back outside. The shadows had lengthened as far as they would go before night would take over. I knew I couldn't go too far.

Like an invitation, one by one the lights in the Horner's house came on. I looked up their driveway and considered knocking on their door. Lately, I had been wondering about Amelia and Mrs. Horner. Did they fight when Amelia became pregnant? Did Mrs. Horner accept the unexpected right away? My feet seemed to steer themselves up the road to their front door that was wrapped like a gift box. Wide lacey silver ribbons crisscrossed at its center and a cluster of bright green plastic pine and tiny red bells shook as the door opened.

"Why, Lily Woodhouse, what a lovely surprise!"

I didn't know what to say except, "Merry Christmas."

"Why don't you come in have some tea, dear?" Mrs. Horner said warmly.

"Oh no, thank you."

"Well how about some cider then?"

I followed her to the kitchen and watched her take out the large plastic jug of cider and pour me a glass. She put four glazed Christmas cookies on a dish and said, "Come let's go in the parlor and sit by the fire. You can tell me all about school. How is it going? How is your family? It has been quite a year, hasn't it?"

I didn't want to talk about college and I didn't want to talk about Christmas or my sister and brother but I chatted on and on nevertheless. She began to look at me a little strangely.

"But, how are *you* doing what with the holidays and the divorce and so on? Are you managing to keep your spirits up? I am sure the family changes are not easy for you. I remember how you used to sit on your dear Daddy's shoulders and he took you everywhere he went. It's no wonder you took to horses the way you did. And remember that playhouse he built for you in the crotch of the old oak up by the barn?" She smiled warmly and sat one of her chubby hands on top of the other in an old-fashioned, grandmotherly way.

Such a Nice Girl

I don't know what it was about Mrs. Horner that set me off, but I was very moved by her words. Her simple kindness as she shared the memories of me on my Dad's back and his galloping around the house made her seem like one of my closest, dearest friends, an aunt, maybe.

I began, "Mrs. Horner, I am in a kind of a fix. I wonder if you would mind if I talked to you about a really, really personal problem. Well, it's not exactly my problem, but...?"

Pink bloomed on her cheeks. "Why, of course you can, my dear! I would be very happy to talk to you about anything, whatsoever. I have always had a great fondness for you and your family. You know that. Is something wrong? What on earth is it?"

I nodded, but I couldn't think of a way to begin. I took a cookie and filled my mouth with its sweetness.

She helped. "How is your lovely mother, bless her soul?"

"She's okay, I guess."

"And your sister and brother?"

"They're okay, I suppose."

"Well, then, what is this problem that's bothering you?"

I realized I was forcing a game of twenty questions. I needed to dive in and ask her what I wanted to know.

"You know, I don't really know Amelia very well. She was kind of a goddess to me when I was ten and eleven. I mean she was so beautiful and smart and all the things every mother wants her daughter to be, and any little girl would want to become."

"And she still is!" Mrs. Horner nodded.

"Yes! Yes, of course she is....but I was wondering....just thinking, the other day, what it was like when she....well, you know, when she....when she told you she was pregnant. You see, I have a friend...a friend who...."

"Oh, my!" Mrs. Horner gasped. She waited a moment before she spoke like she wanted to get it right. "Oh, that was quite a hard time. They were so young and so fixed on a life together, but I was not so sure that it would work out. Lordy, Lord I was fit to be tied that things were so out of hand. But, then again, her father and I knew they loved each other and had since they were sophomores in high school. By the time they graduated they were like a pair of old shoes, broken in and too comfortable to leave one another. At least I see that now. And that little Henry is the most wonderful little boy I have ever known. They will all be here tomorrow, dontcha know?"

"Did you tell her she couldn't or shouldn't get married?"

"Why dear, I did not have a sliver of influence. Amelia and Stewie were already married in their hearts and surely I was glad their love was a mutual thing. As far as they were concerned, the baby was simply an early wedding present. I do admit, I wasn't quite so sure at the time."

"Did they know how you felt?"

"Perhaps. I was not very happy. Mothers know what a baby requires. It is mostly hard work and the rewards aren't guaranteed. Why, what if the child is born with three ears? What if it is born inside-out like a baby I read about just the other day in the newspaper? Its poor little heart was outside instead of inside its body. Or what if it has no arms like those innocent little ones born in the 60s deformed by thalidomide? What if it has cleft palette or only a small piece of brain? There are so many things that can go wrong. That's why I am more than just a little grateful for Henry. He's perfect. Praise be."

I saw the room swaying. The bricks on the fireplace became unstable.

I believe I left the house abruptly.

I couldn't go home, not yet, so I decided to walk off my anxiety attack. Irene Horner hadn't meant to frighten me. There wasn't a nasty thing in that lady's head. She was just babbling, revealing how she thought, which was mostly about staying safe and avoiding disasters. She had a basement full of canned goods, a water cooler and bags of change in an old bomb shelter they had set up in the coal cellar back in the fifties, in case the cold war got hot.

I was glad I hadn't said too much. It was just as well she wasn't in on my secret life. Whatever she felt about Amelia's baby had exactly nothing to do with me. What had I been thinking?

At the top of the hill I took the path to Olin's Pond. The sun's meltdown was still lighting the treetops, rabbit tracks crisscrossed my way and fresh footprints packed the dusting of snow we'd had earlier. The pond's ice shimmered in the last light and I could hear the scratch of skates before I saw the boy-man's silhouette. I could hardly believe my eyes. Brent, lost in the music from his headphones, was skating like a professional. As graceful as a crane his long skinny legs moved across the pond, stretching, lifting, leaping into the air, both feet off the ground and landing with only the slightest quiver.

Who was this? It took my breath away to think my brother was this magician, performing an emotional, dramatic dance. I froze in place when he turned toward the granite boulder and bowed as if there were thousands watching. Someone started clapping and from the far side of the stone, out stepped Strange, arms open and feet skidding across the ice to embrace Brent. They hugged, spun around and laughed and I stepped back into the wood to head home, unseen and unsure, of what I had witnessed and why I felt it was wrong to join them in the beauty of that moment.

The blue holiday lights outside were on by the time I reached the house and I saw Dad's truck in the driveway. I figured Mom had called for back-up. I could see them sitting at the kitchen table with cups of tea at hand as I entered the front door; her face blotchy, his, looking grim.

I started to go to my room.

"In here, young lady," my father said.

Without removing my wet boots, I reluctantly trudged in to join them.

His dark brows were meeting above his nose. He couldn't even look at me, but he wasted no time getting to the point. "I hear you have been seeing David's brother," he said. "The wacky minister."

I nodded.

"Seems like you've been doing more than that."

I nodded again, praying for an inspired remark that would tie their tongues.

"I'd like to get my hands on that son of a bitch and wring his fucking neck!" he said.

Not a good opener. I felt rage rising. "Why? You've never met him. You don't even know what a special person he is."

"Exactly!" he answered. "And I am sure he isn't breaking any doors down to meet me! I have his number!"

"What does that mean? You think you know him because you did the same thing to Mom? Because you ruined her life and you think that's what all men do? They are all out to ruin women's lives? Marshall isn't like that. He's a good person who wants to save lives. I love him and I want to be with him and I don't care what you or Mom say about it!"

"Jesus Christ! If you love him so much how come you haven't had the guts to bring him home? If he's such a good guy why hasn't he seen to it that he meets us? If you love him so much where is the son of a bitch?"

"Dad!" I begged. "He is a Christian and a minister. You hate people like him. I couldn't bring him home, and I can't now. I don't want him to be attacked or made fun of. He's special. He's...he's...the man I love."

"Oh, dear God" Mom said. "This is right out of the movies. Let me tell you something my darling girl, you have no idea who he is or what love really is all about. None at all."

"I do. I do know him. I've known him from the moment we met. Maybe before."

"Listen, Lily, this is magical thinking. It isn't real. Marriages aren't made in heaven. They are made out of hard work and sacrifice," Dad said.

"Oh sure. Look at you! What have you sacrificed? You gave up your whole family for beer, and you say you love Mom. You said she was the best thing that ever happened to you?"

"I forgot that *I* wasn't the best thing that ever happened to *her*," he said. "I hurt her in ways you don't need to know and will never know, if I can help it. Love is not a promise of perfection."

Mom said, "This isn't about us, Lily, it is about you. You said so yourself. I just want to help you consider your options."

I felt like I was in a straitjacket. They stared at me, each taking one of my hands. I was their prisoner and their victim. My baby kicked. I jumped a little and pulled my hands from theirs to place them on my belly. "I just felt my baby kick. Is that magical thinking?"

"Lily, Lily, we have to talk this out," Mom said, ignoring the amazing event.

"We sure as Hell do," said Dad. "You are obviously too far along to abort. So we have to think about what happens next. Your school year isn't even half over but you could go back and finish it out."

"Marshall and I will be married," I said.

"Let's talk about that later," he said, as if this was of no consequence.

"The pregnancy may terminate itself," Mom said. "I had a miscarriage after you were born. It happens. You don't have to marry right away. You could wait to see how things go."

"Marshall will want to get married," I said. "I know he thinks it's the right thing to do."

"How do you know this, Lily?" Mom asked.

"He said so."

"But you haven't told him about the baby. What am I supposed to believe here? I don't understand how you can just say we are going to be married and think the crisis is over, and marriage is going to take care of everything. You don't have a place to live, you don't know whether he is to be trusted, you don't even seem to know what it will take to be the wife of a minister. Pastors are married to their church, your family will always come second. My parents were part of a tight religious community. Your father called it a cult. And I suppose it was. Regardless, it was the bane of my childhood. We never had a normal life. The real world didn't exist for them. We were caught in a religious stranglehold."

I was hearing it all now, hearing the dark side when I needed the light. Was my mother telling me this to frighten me? I hated her at that moment. I resented all the stories that had never been told. I wished I had known her mother and father. But she had buried her mother and her father without ever sharing them with us. Why had she done such a terrible thing? It was only now that I wanted to know, only now that their absence became an irretrievable loss.

"Why are you telling me this now? What am I supposed to think? Are you saying that marrying Marshall would be like joining a cult? Do you think a third of the world's people are part of a cult?"

"Cults, tribes. Yes. Yes, most people identify themselves that way," Mom said, quietly.

Dad took over. "You're looking at a life where people believe they can transform bread into flesh and wine into blood and swallow the hero. Does this work for you?"

"Dad, I am not talking about becoming a Christian, I am talking about becoming a mother and a wife."

"You are talking about a way of life," Mom said. "My parents disowned me because they believed in something that transcended family, friends, and reality. They were filled with fear and hate and they called it love. How can I watch my daughter get caught in such a world?"

"I am not giving up my baby," I cried.

"We will never abandon you," Dad said. "But if you marry this zealot you will probably leave us. That's what we fear. You will take our grandchild and go off into some strange land of ghosts and devils, of evil and sacrifice. It isn't for you, Lily," he said.

Then I saw the pain as his Adam's apple heaved and his eyes filled. I got it. I was going to have to think this out with Marshall. It was too fast for them, not for me. My parents could not see beyond their own pain and prejudice.

I faced my mother, "They let you go?"

"When I married your father, they let me go."

"They actually told you you weren't their daughter anymore?" I asked.

"They disowned me."

"Then they disowned me, as well," I said.

"I suppose you could say that," she answered.

"At least they didn't want to kill me!" I blurted.

"No. No, they would never have approved of that. Abortion was murder in their eyes."

"And killing my baby isn't?"

"I will love your baby, Lily. I am not saying she should not exist."

18

By the time Marshall called, I was exhausted. Even though I needed to fall into his arms and hear him tell me he loved me, to smell the perfume of him and experience the oneness, I was too anxious to go to Woodbury. The next day would surely deliver a better me. With my body and mind rested we would figure out a way to show my parents just how right things were, that we were capable of much more than *magical thinking*.

Morning came, and I went downstairs after Brent and Heather had taken off. Mom was watching *The Today Show* in the living room and drinking her coffee with Ernest eyeing her every move. He was less attached to me now that the rest of the family had taken over his care. Still, he did get up and come into my lap when I flopped down on the couch beside Mom. His warm body purring and leaning into my chest, the opening and closing of his huge paws told me he hadn't forgotten our special connection.

Mom looked at me and smiled. It was odd. She seemed different this morning, like the day before hadn't happened.

"Sleep okay?" she asked, her index finger going around and around the rim of her cup. *The Boston Globe* lay opened on the coffee table. The Home and Garden pages read *Planning Spring in Mid-winter*.

"Yeah," I said. "Pretty good."

"We'll have to get you some vitamins. I'll call Dr. Hamilton."

"I already have some, from Dr. Bomson at school."

"Oh, I see. Well, I think we had better get you to Dr. Hamilton, anyway, as he will probably deliver the baby if you are here in June."

Wow. That felt real. That sounded like someone who cared.

We were interrupted by a knock on the door. Ernest jumped up to play greeter. It was too early for company, but when I opened the door there stood Amelia Horner with a tray of warm hotcross buns. "Mom sent me over with these," she said, a big grin on her wind-flushed face.

"Come in, come in," Mom called.

Amelia had changed very little since I saw her last. She was just as pretty and exuded the same positive energy.

Her eyes took in the front room admiringly. "I've been following your progress from a distance for a year now. What a beauty of a place you've put together!" she said to Mom. "I just love the way it feels—so open and rustic and cozy."

"Would you like to see the rest of house?" Mom asked. She clicked off the TV and Dali's surrealist painting of a melting clock faded from the screen.

Together, we led Amelia into the kitchen, where she swiped her open palm across the black counter top. "Oh, I love these concrete counter tops! They should last forever," she sighed.

"Jon made them for us. They better last forever," Mom said.

Amelia looked up at the skylight where rays of sun were melting off a new layer of snow. "It's interesting how well that skylight brightens the room even with the snow cover. This is *so* environmentally correct."

"Well, we certainly try to be," Mom smiled.

She nudged me, "Why don't you show Amelia the rest of the house? I'll put on some tea and we can have one of those delicious buns Irene sent straight from her oven."

Amelia and I walked upstairs and negotiated the rec room which was less about recreation and more about wreckage. She made no comment about the things that were chaotically spread all over the place, but I saw her eyes take them in. She's the neat type.

Inside what was once my room, Amelia asked me in a loud whisper if I'd like to talk.

"You mean right now? Here?" I asked.

"Mom said she thought you might need a friend right now. I'd be happy to be that friend for you, if you'd like. I know we haven't been close over the years, but there was always that difference in our ages. Even so, you know, neighbors are neighbors and I always liked having you just across the way. I watched you grow up, after all."

My mind was darting around like a frightened fruit fly. *What was she getting at?*

I sat down on the bed and patted a spot next to me. "Come, sit," I said. She sat down and I noticed she was looking at Heather's out-of-the-dresser-out-of-this-world wardrobe, scattered about; her ostrich feathered knee huggers now draped on the lamp.

"This used to be my room but as you can see Heather's taken it over."

"Well, I suppose she thinks there has to be some advantage to having you out of town."

I laughed. "Oh I think she's quite happy to see me gone and not just for my space."

"I doubt that," Amelia said. "I'm sure you are her idol."

"Oh I don't think so."

"So what is going on, Lily? Mom said you had stopped in and wanted to talk. She thought maybe it would be a good idea for me to drop in and see if it is something I could help you with. She said you were upset and she wasn't sure what it was about."

This was not good. How was I supposed to react? Hadn't I told her mother I had a *friend* with a problem? What did I say to her, exactly? I couldn't remember.

"Gosh, Amelia, I don't want to bother you with that business right now because I'm not even sure what is happening."

"Uh-huh," she nodded, "I think I understand."

"What do you think we're talking about?" I asked, feeling the heat rising on my cheeks. Blushing is such a give-away.

She tilted her head. "Well, I'm not sure. I guess I should tell you right out that Mom kind of thought you might be expecting."

"She told you that?"

She nodded. "I don't know if she misunderstood, but she felt terrible because later she wondered if she'd said the wrong things. She told me about your visit as soon as I arrived home and insisted I come over and try to fix things up. Sometimes Mom doesn't quite get what's going on the first time around."

It was probably ridiculous not to admit the truth. Why should I be embarrassed, especially with Amelia? She was in the same boat six years ago. I hadn't thought any less of her. Had I? Well, maybe I had. But I was so young and she was the first person I knew who had been pregnant before she got married. Dad had called it a shotgun marriage. Mom had said that it was no such thing.

My hand went involuntarily to the tiny mound of babyhood that I was sure was obvious. "Your mother...I thought our conversation was private."

"She wasn't quite sure what she was hearing."

Of course that's how Mrs. Horner would put it. I was sorry I went over there. Not knowing what to say next, I asked about little Henry.

I learned he liked kindergarten but not as much as she did. She told me how she had cried the first day he went to school and then realized how much easier her life became once he was gone. "No more finding the right sitters and packing all the toys and sundry bags and toting him all over town. And at the end of this summer, I suppose you know, Stewie graduated from college."

"How does that feel now, with him out of school? Are you going to have another baby?" I asked.

"Oh no. I am through with the baby years. My job at the real estate company is pretty good and I think I'll take some courses at night and get myself a license. The work I do right now is boring; filing contracts is not exactly stimulating, you know. But I may have to wait a little longer before I start school, because now Stewie wants to get his Masters. I mean, he's been accepted to grad school and I think it's best for all of us if he goes on. He can't get a decent job until he gets that second piece of paper. It's okay. I can wait another year until he's done."

I nodded. "Have you ever had any regrets, Amelia?" I asked. "I mean, were you ever sorry about the baby and getting married when you were so young?"

"Never. It had to be. I believe in fate and Stewart and Henry are my fate. We belong together. Not that it's easy, really. We live in a one bedroom apartment with no personal space and Henry still needs a lot of attention when he comes home from kindergarten. Sometimes Stewie has to work all night and sometimes we eat peanut butter and jelly instead of salmon, but we are going to get out of all this real soon, start paying back the loans and look for a better place with more room. Just the thought of it makes me excited. Things work out the way they're supposed to, don't you think? We have done pretty well, considering. I think you appreciate every little thing more when you have to work for it. You learn to go with the flow."

"I'm good at that," I said and stood up abruptly. She took my cue and followed me back down to the kitchen where we rejoined Mom and ate buns and you would have thought my situation was forgotten. We talked about the miracle of Ernest's return, the cold weather and the funny way Henry said things. He called trucks, ducks and cups, dups. It was too cute to correct, according to his mother. I did not talk about my little someone or what I was going to do about her.

After she left, I wondered if she went home with enough news to satisfy her mother.

My distraction lifted when Marshall called and asked if I could borrow the car from Mom to come over to see him I cooked a stew for the family as compensation and spent the rest of the afternoon primping for the big occasion. My toes and teeth were polished and hair shining with lemon spray before I left. Along the way, I detoured to pick up fresh veggies, a box of linguini and a package of frozen shrimp, even garlic, in case he had none. Perrier water would make up for the champagne that neither of us drank.

The drive seemed endless. I passed only a few cars as I traveled down that winding, familiar road, imagining the conversation we were about to have. I would time it just right, after the dinner and the loving and when we were as close as we always became during my visits, when his edges grew soft and I felt most myself.

He opened the door before I got out of the Jeep. "New car?" he asked.

"Isn't it nice?" I said.

"Sure is, but you are better." He put his arms around me and I felt myself go weak. He smelled of Old Spice, like Dad, and his body leaned into me just so, so right that it was as if we had been carved from the same tree.

"Inside, now," he said, and I laughed. I was welcome. I was loved. I was his.

We made love before dinner, after dinner and then one more time before I told him the news.

"You're going to be a wonderful daddy," I said, smoothing his hair away from his forehead.

He said, "Someday."

"How about June?" I said, kissing his neck and stroking his furry chest.

"June? The month of weddings? Is this a proposal, Lily?" he smiled. "That's not the way it is written."

"What would you expect?" I asked, being as cute as I knew how.

"I expect you to let me do the asking."

"Is that another old rule from the Bible?" I teased, putting my nose in his hair, smelling the mane that was mine.

"The Good Book says that a man should choose a woman, but it also promises that God will give him the desires of his heart," he said.

"Well, then, do you choose me?" I asked, softly, pulling myself far enough away so that I could see his expression.

He put his face closer to mine. "Well, you are the desire of heart. *My dove, in the clefts of the rock, in the crannies of the cliff, let me see your face, let me hear your voice, for your voice is sweet and your face is lovely.* That's straight from the Song of Solomon. The Bible teaches you what love looks and feels like. It can be pretty romantic."

"So, am I your dove?" I cooed.

"You are more than that, that lame-brained bird who can't build a decent nest to save herself! I choose you, Lily, because you are my bird of paradise, a swan, a golden canary, all things beautiful."

"Are you sure?"

"I am absolutely sure. I love you."

"Good. Because, I'm pregnant," I said, breathlessly.

His blue eyes opened wide and then squinted at me. I saw him take a deep breath as he fell back into his pillow to look up at the ceiling. I waited for the joy to rise up.

"Pregnant? Are you sure?" he asked, his eyes still on the ceiling.

"Yes. I'm sure."

His silence stuck in my eardrums, each second reverberating itself. Before he spoke a quiet humiliation began to seep through me, one I could feel in my larynx, in the arches of my feet.

"And you are sure I am the father? There has been no one else?" he said.

"How could you ask such a thing?" I snapped, in a voice that did not match the scream that wanted to be heard.

"One cannot know these days," he said quietly.

Now the room was spinning. I had to hold on. "But how could you think such a thing?"

"You came to me so easily, Lily. I wasn't sure what to think."

"But you knew you were my first. My only. How could you suggest anything other?"

My eyes began to smart and my heart pound.

"I was afraid when you went away to college that you would give yourself away as quickly as you gave yourself to me. You are a very passionate woman and I am no fool. I know what goes on in colleges these days. I know what is happening among children in middle schools."

I sat up, pulling the sheets around me, leaving him exposed.

"Children in middle schools? Marshall! What do you think of me? Why are you saying these things?"

He knew nothing at all about me. How could he imagine I was anything but his? Where were his thoughts coming from? Who did he think I was, someone hopping from one bed to another? Where did God and all his blessings go? "Have you forgotten you said if I conceived we would know we were blessed?" I sputtered.

A desire to run, to pack myself up and leave him right there, to make sure he never knew his baby or held me again, took over. I rose from the bed, shaking, feeling nothing but rage.

"I'm going," I said, as I began to struggle with my clothes. His trailer was choking me, the furniture, the air, even the floor was changed. It could hardly hold me as I moved to escape.

"Wait! Wait!" he was standing now, grabbing my arms. "I am just...I am just surprised, I have to catch my breath. I never expected it would happen so soon. I have to think, to pray. Forgive me, Lily. Stay. I love you."

I stopped moving, desperate to believe that what he was saying was true, I let him draw me back to the bed, where I sat with my clothes half on and half off until he pulled me down gently to lie next to him.

I awkwardly gave him my back, pulling my legs into my chest, wishing I could make myself very small.

He embraced me from behind and wrapped me tightly in his arms. "I am sorry if I hurt you. Forgive me, Lily. Please. We should get married as soon as possible. That is the only solution."

"Solution? What had happened to God's Grace? What happened to the miracle baby?" How did all this become a problem that had to be solved? I started to cry.

"It will be fine," he sighed and kissed the back of my head.

He didn't ask how I felt, if I was happy or sad; whether I had seen a doctor or told my parents. I never heard words that so much as hinted at being glad about the baby, or God's blessing, either.

My heart was splintered glass. I wanted to shout damn you and damn this and damn that but I became silent and rigid. I think I scared him. I scared myself.

"Lily, Lily, it is alright," he said. "Everything is alright. We will find a way to make it work."

Mom was waiting up for me when I got home. She jumped to her feet at the sight of me. "You told him?" she said. "You look exhausted."

I knew she knew that things had not gone as planned, and to tell her differently would be close to impossible. Besides, I still had to consider Marshall's reaction. Maybe his behavior was not as terrible as I thought. Maybe I was guilty of magical thinking after all. Maybe time would make a difference. Maybe I would hear from him in the morning and know he was glad all over.

I went to her and she put her arms around me. Her soft hands smoothed my hair and she said, "You are going to be all right. You're strong, Lily. You don't have to write the whole story. It has just begun."

That night I didn't sleep well. I had thoughts of running and hiding, thoughts of throwing myself off a cliff, wanting to punish everyone for not supporting this tiny creature now inside me. I imagined her little feet against my belly, her tiny fingers finding her mouth. At some point, in the middle of the night, I rummaged through my dresser and reread the booklets Dr. Bomson had given me, the shiny pamphlet that showed a progression of the fetus from conception to birth. By sixteen weeks old, she was playing with the umbilical cord and sucking her thumb. She was surely yanking on my sides as they stretched to make room for her. I loved her. I wanted her more than anything in the world.

I turned the lights off again and dreamed of mice above my head, climbing inside me, cramps in my groin, a rat being strangled inside my stomach. I heard weeping from some far-off place. Marshall was in bed with me then leaving, Amelia was at the door. Mrs. Horner was putting razors in her hotcross buns, my mother was serving them up with her face beaming with joy. I twisted and thrashed about, became hot and cold, sad and angry and frightened; very, very frightened. After the eternal night ended, I only knew I had slept because I awoke. Still drugged with sleepiness, I rose and stumbled downstairs.

When the phone rang, Mom answered it. "Oh, oh yes she's here. But tell me, is this Marshall?" she asked. He evidently said yes and the next thing I knew she was inviting him to come to the house. "I think it's about time we met, Marshall," she said as nicely as she could. "Why don't you join us for lunch?"

I tried to hear his response but had to settle for hers. "Oh, good. Noon would be fine."

"Mom, Mom, let me talk to him," I said softly.

She waved me back away from the phone. "I will have her call you when she gets up. She seems to need a great deal of sleep right now."

She was probably right, it would be better if I called him after a cup of coffee. I was so groggy and not feeling like myself. She must have known by the looks of me.

After hanging up the phone she said, "Let him wait on it. It's best to give him time to think. You don't want to look frantic. We don't want to give him the impression that he has to make any decision that isn't his."

"Is that what you did with Daddy? Did you let him know that he had a choice?"

She walked away, grabbing a dish towel and heading for the sink. "I wish Heather would think just once about drying the dishes. Actually, it would be nice if she thought of washing them before she's asked. Just once!"

Brent came into the kitchen dressed in long johns. "Are my sweats clean?" he asked.

"You are perfectly capable of opening the dryer and finding out for yourself," Mom snapped.

She threw the towel at the dishes and went to the coat closet. I watched as she pulled out her felted hat and parka and grabbed the ski poles.

"Where are you going?" I asked.

"I am taking a walk. A long walk. I need some time to think." The door slammed behind her.

"Geez, what bug is up her ass?" Brent asked as he came in the room.

"You don't really want to know," I said. "Are you going skating today?" I was willing to pretend we were like any other brother and sister. I wanted to be closer to him, moreso than usual. I wished he wanted the same thing. It would have been nice if we could talk.

"I skate every day," he said.

"Do you always skate alone?" I asked.

"Yeah."

So, I thought, that was how it was going to be; my asking questions, he saying as little as possible. Well, I had my own secrets. Wouldn't he be surprised?

"Strange's brother, Marshall, might be over to visit today, I hope you'll be decent to him."

"I don't even know him, except for what Strange says. He says he's a Jesus freak and a scary dude."

"What makes him scary?"

"It's his attitude. There's only one way and it's his."

"Brent, Strange owes him a lot. Marshall kept him from having to go with families he didn't know or like. He rescued him from child services. Don't you think he should give his brother a little slack? They are both so different."

"He knows all that," Brent said, buttering the toast that had just popped up. "Do we have any jam?"

"Open the refrigerator and look for yourself."

After his breakfast he grabbed his skates and went out into the sunshine. Mom, gone, Brent on his way to the pond, Heather at work, I had a rare moment to myself.

It was as if Marshall was sitting on the phone when I called. He told me he was coming to visit at noon. This seemed good, as food is always a nice diversion when it comes to conversation. Fortunately, Mom and I would be alone and we wouldn't have to deal with one of my siblings as an audience. Not that we could bar Brent from the house, but, lately, he had been eating his lunch at all hours.

Mom came back after an hour or so, flushed and distracted and carrying a bag she acquired on her walk. When I reminded her that Marshall was arriving shortly she said she assumed that such would be the case. "I have some cabbage soup and Irene's homemade jalapeno bread she said. It's still warm."

I set the table, put a bunch of glass Christmas balls in a clear bowl and stuck some branches of pine in the center. It looked quite pretty. I couldn't help but look for a cloth that would tie it all together. We only had the placemats that Mom picked up while we were still using the picnic table. At least they were reddish brown and went with the rest. I folded the laundered red Christmas napkins so they stood like crowns, put ice in our tall frosted glasses and laid out the new sturdy stainless steel utensils. We had just bought red and yellow flowered bowls at the outlet store in Claremont and they looked beautiful on the new clay colored earthenware plates. Two beeswax candles completed the setting.

Upstairs, I changed into a loose sweatshirt and some stretchy pants. My tummy was already obvious in many of my clothes. I could hardly fasten my favorite jeans. But maybe that was just wishful thinking. I loved the idea of growing big enough for the baby to show. As I ran the brush through my hair one more time and gathered it in a tail to put on my head, I heard Marshall's truck.

I ran down stairs and opened the door before he could knock. Not my Mother's style.

He stood looking less confident that I had ever seen him, was careful with my embrace, and quietly waited to be asked inside.

Mom stood behind me smiling politely.

"Nice to meet you," she said, in a voice like one she would use for an insurance man.

That's how it started, tenuous at best.

Our luncheon continued quietly. Mom asked only a few non-committal questions. She didn't reveal she knew anything about the baby or that we were to be married soon. Instead, she performed like an actress looking for words that gave her entry. I was so grateful, so amazed at how careful she was with him, this man I knew she distrusted. Even with anger and doubt, I still wanted him. She must have guessed that.

Meanwhile, Little Someone was about sixteen weeks old, a handful of baby now. In her short life she was already making a huge difference. Frowning and puckering she was stretching her tiny self to join the crazy world Lucille Ball had just left. I hoped she would make us laugh as hard as Lucy had. Everyone loved Lucy. It was a cute name, Lucy, Lucy Barry.

Then again, if I wanted to add historical meaning to her name, the Berlin Wall was coming down. It was a hopeful sign of the future—the hated Wall eliminated without a war. If the Berlin Wall could come down, my family could change. We could become more instead of less. I began to think, Berl Lynn Barry. Maybe that would work. Berl Lynn.

19

I began to pray to that omniscient, omnipotent God that Marshall considered his best friend. On my knees, I asked that my baby be healthy and whole. I believed her tiny tai chi moves were the Holy Spirit answering me. A constant worry was my father's outspoken disgust with all things religious, calling believers weak, empty headed, delusional and worse. If he attacked Marshall, it would be a disaster. I asked God to take away Dad's anger. Mom was no longer my concern.

She had begged me to put off any announcements until I had seen Dr. Hamilton, probably harboring hope that the whole thing was a mistake. But our doctor confirmed Dr. Bomson's assessments, and told me the baby was sound and happily becoming more independent. "Unfortunately," he added, "You are fairly well along. I can't recommend a termination with the fetus so well-established."

One more person had now thought I would consider destroying my child. It was beyond me. Yes, *child.* That's how I envisioned her, in tiny shoes and sun bonnets, a cooing, gurgling, clapping bundle of love. She was blue-eyed, with curly blonde hair and chubby cheeks, just like the happy faces on jars of baby food in the supermarket; just like Heather's baby pictures.

What I didn't see were the machinations of a summit to take place before the New Year. A tribunal of sorts was planned with myself, the Woodhouse parents and Marshall Barry attending. I came downstairs that morning to learn of the event. Mom insisted it was necessary for Dad to meet Marshall in order *to put some reality into the picture.*

My beautiful father, the man whose strong shoulders had once been mine to mount, had not said a word to me since Mom and I told him about my situation. Not a word. I couldn't tell if this silence was another example of his exit from our lives or a temporary reaction. To reduce my tension, I remembered that he considered himself to be a modern man. And it helped to know that my mother and he were once in the same boat. I mean, it was only reasonable that he would have a hard time making me wrong, and yet Dad wasn't always a reasonable man.

We were a silent threesome as we drove over the countryside. I was heavily into prayer and my father must have been rehearsing his tirade. Having my parents as marriage brokers or counselors or enemies or whatever was going to come out of this meeting, was terrifying. I was hating them and loving them and wanted nothing more than to leave them out of the situation, and yet they pushed themselves on us. I couldn't understand why Marshall hadn't warned me of this meeting. Did he think I knew what they were up to, that I was part of a plot?

"Jesus Christ, Lily," Dad groaned as we pulled into Marshall's gravel driveway. "Is this your idea of the good life? What the Hell are you thinking?"

"Dad! Stop! You are already making judgments. If you think I am going through with this in your state of mind, you're wrong. I am not getting out of the car unless you swear to me to be decent."

"Don't speak to me of decent," he growled.

"Jon!" Mom said. "Get yourself into a better place. This is very important. Get on top of your emotions."

"Please, God," I begged silently.

The door creaked open and there stood Marshall wearing a button-down blue Oxford shirt, some chinos and a nice brown belt. His mane was combed back and his face flushed and smiling. He was as handsome a man as I had ever seen.

"Welcome," he said, his right hand pointing to the insides of the trailer as if it was the Governor's Mansion.

"Good morning, Marshall," Mom said, pleasantly.

She made a point to look around the room and sat down at the tiny fold out table Marshall had opened for four folding chairs. She smoothed the placemat and waited. Dad's legs should have been left at the door, there was no place to put them without intersecting with someone else's.

"Hi," I said, reddening furiously. "You seem to have been expecting us. You must have known something I didn't."

"Yes. Yes I did, and I decided that it might be better for you not to be part of this. I don't want you to worry, Lily. I am quite ready to speak for the two of us."

Dad's shoulders hunched and lurched forward. "You don't say," he just about hissed.

"Yes. Yes, I do. It is too bad that we must meet like this, Mr. Woodhouse, with you knowing so little about me and my knowing so little about you."

"And who might we blame for that?" Dad asked.

"It was just a matter of circumstances. But, I want to assure you, I am totally prepared to be a father to your grandchild and husband to your daughter."

"Oh, you don't say?" Dad sneered.

"We are adults, and Lily and I know that God has brought us together."

"The devil you mean! Listen here, minister or not, you have taken a young innocent girl and placed her in a compromising situation. Your God didn't engineer that, your pecker did. There is no father in the world that wouldn't want to make you responsible for an act that is costing his daughter her life."

"Dad! I am not losing my life. I choose to be a mother, I want to be a wife, just like Mom did, just like you and Mom did. Why are you doing this?"

"You can just be quiet, while we sort this out, Lily."

"It is my baby, Daddy. It's my life."

"You are still a child. You are a Woodhouse and you are my daughter and I am not about to turn you over to trailer trash."

The air might have caught fire with the oxygen that was taken from the room but Marshall remained completely calm.

"Mr. Woodhouse, Lily could never be any sort of trash. She is the most precious person I have ever known and will be that way no matter where we live. Besides, she will not be living in a trailer for long. I have an inheritance I can draw on, and I assure you I will find something better for us. God will provide us with everything we need."

"He will, eh? Why you? What's he done for the rest of the world? Have you ever seen a cardboard village? Met a family who lives in a railroad car? This God of yours creates an awful lot of misery. He's great at meting out wars and disease, misery, and corruption. How many innocents has he killed? How many dead have been treated as collateral damage? How much hate and prejudice has he spewed? Why should you and Lily be exceptions to his dirty tricks?"

Marshall lowered his eyes and shook his head. "Because He has spoken to me and I have complete trust in his power. This world is not for us to understand. It is God's and His will will be done."

I swear, I felt faint as I braced for the explosion that was about to wipe Marshall out.

"Jesus Christ!" the veins in Dad's face were popping, "Are you fucking crazy? If God is talking to you we better get the Pope in here to let the people know there's a new Moses on the planet, either that or call the state mental hospital and get you a room, the crazy house is full of your kind."

"Sir," Marshall was even more composed now, his body leaning back in his chair, his big hands folded over one another, calm to the point of looking holy. "Sir, there are many ways in which God speaks. You have only to listen."

"Jon," Mom said, I suppose trying to save my father from a complete meltdown, "We are not here to talk about religion, we are here to discuss Lily and our grandchild. Please, try not to sabotage this opportunity."

Mom was far more prepared than my father. She must have put together an agenda of her own and was not going to let it be bulldozed under.

Marshall upstaged her, however. He, too, had a plan which he announced with confidence, "Lily and I should marry right away. The sooner we do, the quicker we can establish a home and get ready for our child. We love one another and...."

Mom broke in, "My dear, you know very little about one another. There is no need to rush. Love is not *the first time ever I saw your face*, it takes years to evolve. Perhaps you don't know that Lily's trust fund, her college money, will end if she leaves school. Her grandmother wanted to ensure Lily's education. She saw it as a key to a woman's independence."

"We are not talking about Lily's independence, Mrs. Woodhouse. In fact, we are talking about Lily's dependence, on me, and my willingness to provide everything she needs. I can promise you, we will have a Christian home where respect will go both ways. I have no problem seeing Lily as my wife and as a mother to my children."

Dad snorted.

"That's all well and fine," Mom said, "but I would like to propose that Lily complete her freshman year, have the baby, and then you two can talk about marriage. By then you may know each other better and she will have at least one year of education to build upon."

"I believe we should marry now, Mrs. Woodhouse. Our marriage is already sealed in her womb."

"And I believe you should wait," she said. "Then we can have a proper wedding and you will have all the time in the world to build your lives together. Why the rush to marry? Lord, there's hardly enough room for the two of you in this tin box. You will need things like a playpen, a stroller, a changing table and a dresser. Do you have any idea how much room a seven pound creature needs?"

I was emboldened by her question. "I know it needs its mother's breast and its father's arms. There are plenty of families that survive without a roof over their heads. We have to remember the lilies in the field. Mom, Dad, we will work all these things out. Please, this is my life," I cried. "You're not in charge here!"

Dad slammed his hand down on the table, rattling the cups and saucers. I froze, Mom reached out to stop his next move, but he pushed aside her arm and shouted, "I am not going to listen to any more of this bullshit," and went outside.

"Just as well that he go," Mom sighed. "Jon is having too much trouble handling all this. But I have given the situation a lot of thought. I am proposing a sane option to you." She took my hand. "Time will ease the stress and no matter what you may prefer right now, Lily, the next five or six months might as well have a fabric to them that keeps you engaged and gives you both the opportunity to organize your lives. Won't you wait and see your academic year through?"

It was Marshall who responded. "What God has brought together let no man, or woman, put asunder, Mrs. Woodhouse. For Lily and I to marry is the right thing to do according to her beliefs and mine. We would, of course, like your blessing, but that is up to you."

I was so proud of Marshall. He was unfazed by this attack and the determination of my parents to come between us. I imagined most men would have thrown all three of us out the door. He had grown more resolved as they grew more hostile. My love nearly choked me.

I stayed with him that night. It was New Year's Eve and he held a midnight Church service for farewells to the year 1989 and a welcome to 1990. After church, he took out his mother's wedding band. Then he gave me a book of wedding vows and we recited them to one another, alone, in the candlelight. It was as real as it needed to be for me to feel like his wife.

He said I was the most precious gift of 1989 and the most beautiful promise of 1990. I was in heaven. I had a true sense of belonging as I looked into his tender face, through my teary eyes. We were family, forever and ever.

For four days I stayed bundled up in the trailer free of the stress of my parents or anyone else's opinions. It was wonderful when Marshall was home, and boring when he was not, and mostly, he was not. I had many lonely hours to think. It began to look like it would be the next millennium before the baby arrived. I wished we could find another place or trailer long before then, because, just as Mom had said, my few things wouldn't fit in the tiny space now, never mind when we started building a layette for the baby. Most importantly, I had failed to realize the trailer was Marshall's office as well as his home, and he was forced to go out and meet people in strange places, compromised by my presence.

He didn't say a word about being cramped, but it was obvious the lack of an office was a problem. I had no idea so much of his life was about pastoral counseling. In the face of the inconvenience I caused, I began to think more seriously about returning to school. Within three days it became a fact in my mind. I knew it was time to go back to Mom's and prepare for the next semester, no matter how difficult it would be. Love would help us sort out the months ahead.

Although I believed our private vows were sacred, I wasn't prepared to reveal our marriage to my family or friends. It was less necessary than giving them time to get used to the idea of us as a couple, and it would be easier if we just went on as usual until they came around.

I said as much to Marshall and he did not like the idea. He told me this was deceit and God would not approve of the falsehoods that were sure to result. I, to the contrary, felt we had already been deceitful, marrying on our own without my parents' blessing, right after Mom had begged us to wait. I argued that our private vows would always mark our anniversary but we could make everyone happier by planning a formal wedding after the baby was born, one that satisfied my family's traditions.

"We are responsible for ourselves and our little one, now," he'd answered. "We have an authority that transcends what came before. In God's eyes, we are married, Lily. Our vows were real. Our promises sanctified by faith. And you must remember it is not for you to make plans that concern both of us without my approval. That's what a marriage is, a contract for the wife to obey her husband and the husband to honor his wife. It's not that I think your thinking is without reason, you simply must understand that all decisions are *ours* from here on in, not your mother's, your father's, not even yours alone. The Bible is very clear on this."

It was not the best moment for me to ask him how he would feel if I went back to school to finish out the year, but I went ahead and asked anyway. I was shocked at his answer.

"That is what I expected. Of course you should finish. It will give us the time I need to find a larger place to live."

Mom came to get me in the late afternoon of that day. She stayed in the car while I said goodbye to Marshall. I never let on to him that I was happy to be going home, I just promised I'd be back the following night, before I returned to school.

Mom made little conversation as she drove. She didn't seem angry and I was grateful she didn't ask questions. When we arrived at the house, Brent and Heather were spilled on the rug in front of the fireplace. I didn't know what they knew but it didn't take long to find out.

Heather's eyes were full of hurt. She was staring at me as if I was supposed to make a speech or something. "Happy rest of your life," she said.

"You can't marry that dude," Brent said. "He's a Nazi."

"You don't even know what a Nazi is," I answered.

"I think I might know more than you do," Brent said.

"Please, let's not go there. I am his wife and the mother of his child."

"His wife?" they said in unison.

"What are you telling us?" Mom asked.

"We had a Christian wedding. We made our vows."

"You what?" Mom asked.

"We exchanged our vows," I said.

"But that's not legal," Mom said.

"It's as legal as we need it to be. As far as we're concerned, I am Mrs. Marshall Barry, now, and I have come home to get ready for school. That was important to you, right? We made a compromise about my going back so that Marshall will have time to find a more comfortable place to live. Just as you wanted."

I literally heard the air escape from my mother's mouth. She rushed to me and I stood still as she wrapped her arms around me and said I had made the right choice and the whole family would stand by me.

I reacted quickly. "Listen, all I am saying is that I am going back to school and I am married. So let's not pretend anything that's not so. I am really tired and I don't want to argue. Okay?" I felt myself grow weak and then overcome by a need to lie down. "I need to rest awhile."

Such a Nice Girl

The sloshing of my hand-me-down bed felt just fine as I lay my head on the pillow and fell off to sleep. What I had intended as a rest turned into a thirteen hour trip to Neverland. It was the next day when I awoke to a beam of sunshine hitting my face as it streamed through the skylight. The house was quiet. I thought it might still be early, but when I looked downstairs, the breakfast dishes were still on the table and only Ernest was present. Apparently, the family had left me to sleep for as long as I needed. The wall clock, a huge pocket watch, read ten. I couldn't believe that I had slept for so many hours.

I found my terrycloth robe, the lavender body wash and a sponge, and drew a bath that I kept as warm as I could by running the hot water continually until it ran out. It was delicious. I was dreaming in a sea of scented bubbles when I heard Brent skip down the stairs and go out the front door. He, obviously, had slept late, too.

The red cedar that Dad used in the bathroom made the room toasty sweet and I took my time after the bath with my hair and my nails and studying the little mirror that magnified my zits. Surprisingly, there were none. My face was clearer than ever, and the color on my cheeks fairly high. It may have been my imagination but I thought my cheeks were filling out and my nipples were growing darker. On the little mound of my belly, a tiny foot rippled. "Hello, little girl," I said, "I love you."

After a breakfast of hot cereal and heavily buttered homemade Panini toast, I dressed warmly to battle the temperatures hovering in the teens, figures which were actually an improvement over the day before, when Marshall's trailer had been close to frigid. I'd spent the day reading inside his down-filled sleeping bag, turning it into a makeshift cocoon. When he was home, of course, the place felt warmer. He had a body heat that insulated him from cold and radiated out to me. In bed I sometimes had to cool off by untangling myself from his limbs.

I headed up the hill, hoping the effort would warm me up. The woods creaked from the cold, branches snapped, snow crunched underfoot. Some of spring's catkins still hung onto their furry caps, summer's brush was now brittle stalk. Mom had tried to transplant pussy willow cuttings in the fall, but we wouldn't know which ones had taken and which ones had not for another three months. Crimson branches turned black against the sky as I walked beneath their lace. The mid-day sun made intricate shadows at my feet.

I walked toward the pond just in case Brent was there. It would do no harm to try to talk to him, he was my brother and that had to mean something. I could hear his skates on the ice in a rhythmic scraping and then I saw him as he leapt a foot above the ground and landed with both feet and knees bent.

He turned away from me and bowed, shouting "Ta-da!" into the forest.

Strange emerged from the wood's shadows and slid onto the frozen pond without skates, his arms outstretched. Brent skated into them and then I saw them kiss. Not a buddy to buddy kiss but a deep long kiss, the kind I now recognized as love. I stood there stupidly waiting for them to stop, for it to be over. I couldn't move. It was shocking, embarrassing, confusing, queer, and somehow, in the deepest part of me, frightening.

Why hadn't it occurred to me that they might be in love? I had already seen that their friendship had changed them both for the better. But what did this mean? Where would this go? Questions blew through my mind, in a storm of confusion and concern; I turned and ran home, licking the snot from my lips and trying to stop the water freezing on my eyelids. "God, God, what is going on? Poor Mom. Poor Brent with his secrets, poor me with a husband I have to leave at the time I need him most." I prayed, "Please, Lord, help us all do what is right."

Time was crunched in the race to return to school. Arrangements had been made for Carrie to pick me up at Pearl's in the morning, but I had to find a way to spend this last night with Marshall. It took all I had to ask Heather if she would drive me there before Mom got home from work. "I will, if you promise to come back home."

I swore I would. Then she asked if I'd like her to pick me up before she went to school so I could stay the night.

"You're the only one who is willing to move an inch towards my happiness," I said.

"I am not trying to make you happy, Lily. I am trying to understand what the fuck is going on with you."

"I should have known."

"Yeah, you should have known! You should have known you can't screw around without rubbers and you should have known you would freak us all out! Geez. I can't believe you are such a lunkhead."

"Heather, I love Marshall and I believe in him and want our baby. Why is that so hard to believe?"

"It's hard to believe that you are about to leave us all for someone you hardly know. How much can you know about Marshall? How wacky do you think he is? Have you ever heard what Strange has to say about him? Strange only stays nearby because he's afraid the guy will totally lose it!"

"Forget the ride," I said.

"No. I will take you. You may not realize it, but you are my big sister and I always felt I had to live up to you. You were the one who always did things right. Who knew what you were up to? Well, you have just managed to blow everything I thought I knew about you into the stratosphere. And do you know what? I think I love you anyway. I think I love you even more."

I had never once thought Heather had one good thought about me. What clues had I been missing?

20

We drove through the winter evening towards Woodbury with the sounds of the Eagles egging us on. "They're so mainstream," said Heather, turning up the volume despite herself. *You can't hide your lyin' eyes, and your smile is no disguise...*"A lot of old-fashioned crap."

I didn't think so, but then the only song I knew of the group's was *Desperado*. Strange used to sing it to himself over and over. *Better love somebody before it's too late.* I remembered thinking he was singing it for me.

"Mom is still dating that creep," Heather announced.

"I can't see what she sees in him," I said. "How do you know about him?"

"Oh, she isn't too good with secrets. Not like some other people I know."

"Heather, come on! Can't you understand why I felt I had to keep the baby to myself. Mom was really upset about separating from Dad, and, Dad, well, I think Dad would have killed Marshall, especially now that he's drinking again. He's so unpredictable. It's been hard, harder than you know."

"You could have blown me to Pluto. I never ever would have thought St. Lillian was out fucking Mr. Holy Roller himself. Brent is just about out of his gourd over it and Strange, well, he thinks psychiatrists should be called to the scene of the accident. Yup, you have made everyone you know crazy."

"Well, at least *I'm* not crazy. I'm just upset by everyone's reactions. This baby is what I want more than anything in the world. I wish someone would start thinking about her and not me, and stop casting stones on her father. I mean, they don't even know him. Won't anyone believe I have a brain in my head, that I'm capable of recognizing my soul mate when he comes along?"

Heather had nothing to say to that. Could I possibly have caused her to think?

When we reached Woodbury, she begged me to introduce her to Marshall. At first I resisted, but then I relented, because I wanted her to get a sense of who he was and believed she might just get that I was not in love with Attila the Hun.

Surprisingly, it went better than I would have expected. She was polite, held her tongue and said how happy she would be to become an auntie. She deserved an Oscar for her little sister act, wide-eyed, pleasant and an extension of the ribbons and bows of her latest Heidi-does-Purgatory look. Her honeyed breath was practically visible. Honestly, I almost didn't recognize her, and poor Marshall, he could know no better than believe this was the real thing.

After she left, I sank into the chair and said something like, "I'm glad that's over."

"What do you mean?" Marshall asked. "She is quite nice. Having your sister on our side will help in the months ahead."

"Hmm," was all I could manage to say before I domestically scanned the room for what needed doing, ready to act as a good wife should. My eyes landed on the cold, stained coffeepot and I rose to empty out the grounds, wash it and start a new pot. He came and stood behind me, rubbing his maleness into me from behind.

"Marshall?"

"Yes?" he breathed into my ear.

"We should tell each other everything from this day forward, right?"

"No secrets. With the love of Christ, *we will bear one another's burdens and grow strong*—that is the Promise. Now, tell me what is bothering you." He turned me to face him and I could feel his hardness again. His hands pulled me close. His face showed nothing but love as our eyes connected.

"I saw something I shouldn't have," I said, trying to think past his obvious wanting. "I think it was wrong or I was wrong to be watching, and I'm wondering what to do about it or if anything should be done about it at all."

"And what could that have been," he said lustily, grinding into me now, his penis pulsing and hips moving.

"Oh, you, you don't want to hear," I said, weakened, my arms going around his neck, forgetting the dishes, doubts, and the entire world other than our own.

We moved into one another, stripping each other's clothes away until we burned ourselves out. Before we were done, I had visited the counter-top, the chair and the sofa in a dance that needed no music.

Later, as I sat by his side on the sofa, he used his most intimate voice to ask me what it was that I had wanted to talk about.

I hated to spoil the moment. "Oh, it's nothing," I said. "It can wait,"

He sat up and said, "No, no it should not wait. That's not the way marriage works. Proverbs warns us that secrets cause worry." He reached to his bookshelf that sat alongside the couch. "I do not want you to be worried."

"But I'm not sure what I saw. Well, I *am* sure what I saw, but I'm not sure what it means."

He fanned the gilded pages of his well-worn book, and pointed to the words that made his case. You can see for yourself. "Luke says that nothing can be covered up that will not be revealed. In the end there are no secrets. As husband and wife, all should be known between us."

I liked that.

"Well...it has to do with my brother...and yours," I said.

"David and your brother? What do you mean?" His brows furrowed across his forehead, his blue irises darkened.

"You have said they are friends."

"Yes," I nodded.

"Good friends?"

"Yes. *Very* good friends." I smiled a little, hoping I wasn't sounding like a gossip. I was sure there were Bible passages forbidding that, too.

"What are you trying to say?" he pressed.

I spit it out, as if saying it quickly would diminish its importance. "Well, I saw them kissing. A long kiss. I shouldn't have watched but, but it surprised me. I stared at them like a stalker or some kind of pervert. I never saw two men kissing before."

His head went into his hands. "David and Brent. Brent and David. I was afraid. I was afraid something terrible like this might happen when you told me they were friends. Where did you see this happen?"

"At the pond where Brent skates. They go up there a lot. They're really close. I knew they were getting more and more attached, but this was more than that."

He leapt to his feet and started pacing like a caged lion. "The work of Satan! It is perversion, an abomination unto the Lord, that is what it is!"

"I felt dirty watching," I said, not sure why I was excited by his reaction. "I shouldn't have watched."

He stopped and turned, leaning hard into my face. "The problem is not yours, Lily, it is theirs. This is going to have to stop. How old is your brother?"

"Fifteen."

He fell backwards a little. "He is no more than a boy! What David is doing is against the law and he will not only have to face God's wrath but he could be brought up on criminal charges."

"It's against the law to kiss?" I asked.

"It's against the law to take advantage of a minor."

"Oh, I think that Brent was very happy to be kissed. He has been happier ever since he met Strange."

Marshall was not interested in my opinion. "Please don't call him that. That name is part of his aberration with the Devil. He wants to walk on the dark side. He chooses Strange over David, over God."

"You know, he's a very deep and intelligent person, Marshall," I said in a voice too small for my conviction.

"Deep and intelligent is not enough! Judas Iscariot was probably very intelligent but sold his Lord for a few rubles; Adolph Hitler was smart enough to amass more power than he could handle. Genghis Khan was a genius and a monster. The Ayatollah Khomeini is no doubt deep and intelligent but he has executed tens of thousands and held innocent Americans captive. Deep and intelligent is not enough, Lily. God-fearing is all important. God wants goodness and has given us strict laws to live by. When men make up their own laws they are on unstable ground. Our justice system is built on this. Sodomy, murder and theft are all against the law, American law which is based on Biblical law."

"But does the Bible actually say men shouldn't kiss?" I asked.

"It is unnatural!" Marshall all but shouted. "The Bible clearly states that homosexuals will not be welcome in the kingdom. It equates homosexual behavior with sodomy and rape. My brother's relationship with your brother would be condemned in any court in the land and surely at Heaven's gate."

"But rape is against a person's will, I think Brent was very happy to be kissed by David."

"Not to his credit, Lily. We all have to make responsible decisions for our lives. Sex is not meant for anything other than procreation. It is not a sport or an experiment. The suffering of those with AIDS is no accident. AIDS is a bi-product of sin, born to straighten what is bent, to extinguish what is wrong. The Lord is speaking. He is telling us that it is obscene for a man to lay down with a man. That same Lord can make the lame dance, the muted sing, but does not suffer evil lightly."

It hit me then. My brother and my best friend were in terrible trouble. "Oh, God, what can I do?" I wept, my tears spilling into the pillow. "Brent was so sad and so angry before he met David. I hate to see him hurt anymore."

"Let me handle this," Marshall said, pulling on his clothes, our lovemaking now far behind us, but our first real secret shared.

"How? What can you do? They are obviously happy with one another. Stra....David has even begun to be part of the family. Everyone likes him," I said. "They seem so good together."

"Your family would not let David in the door if they knew what he was up to. Trust me. They would make sure he never came near your brother again. This is evil, Lily!" He sat back down on the edge of the couch, shaking his head and trying to get a deep breath. "It is abnormal and one of the worst of the sins. God may have placed this before me to test my will to serve Him. He gives no man a burden he cannot bear."

"You're assuming they're lovers."

"I am. If they are not now, they are headed in that direction. I have worried about David for years and now here he is corrupting your little brother. Our brother."

He's not exactly *little,* I thought.

"They will both burn in Hell if they continue in this direction. It is all over the Bible, from the Old Testament into the New. God burned Sodom and Gomorrah, even their neighboring communities, because of just this kind of deviant behavior. Romans tells of punishments for men doing shameful things with other men. In Corinthians we are told that the homosexual will never know the Kingdom of God. Timothy compares homosexuals to murderers and enslavers. There is no doubt where God stands on this issue."

I started to cry again. This was far worse than I had imagined. I had thought it was just an instinct foreign to mine, one that made me uncomfortable. I wondered if I should feel as repulsed and angry as Marshall, but realized that what I was experiencing was more about fear, fear for my brother and fear for my friend. Whatever happened next was going to hurt them deeply, and it was going to come down just when I was hoping we could become a real family, with Marshall and David, Brent and Dad all getting along. I saw how impossible it is to wish for life to be a certain way when it has a plan of its own.

"You must not cry, Lily. With God's help, I will take care of this situation. Come, we should get on our knees and pray," Marshall said. "God will help make all things right."

Outside the wind was whipping around the trailer pulling the last of the dead leaves from the dormant trees, and a smattering of acorns noisily struck the roof. Despite their rat-a-tat-tats, I began to feel quieter inside. After our prayers and in the heat of Marshall's arms, trust surged through me, drawing confidence from the strength of his body and the clarity of his mind. He would do what was right. I knew that his God would help and things would work out eventually. Then Marshall began to kiss me again, to lend his heat to my body and put his hands in all the right places. This was what my God wanted, for sex to be pure, between a man and a woman, an act of love to create new life and new loves. I was so blessed.

In the morning, before I left, I made coffee, toast and scrambled eggs. You would have thought I was serving up a gourmet soufflé, my husband was so appreciative. The kitchen offered very little to work with, but I would learn. His frying pans numbered one, his dishes six, the sum total of glasses were four, and his knives and spoons were a mismatched assortment of stainless steel.

Before I left we sat at our tiny table like two old folks, he with a pad and pencil, me willing to take on any list he wrote. "I am going to start looking for a new place for us next week. I think two bedrooms and one bath should do, for now, don't you?" he asked. "Then again, maybe we should plan for all the babies that will follow."

How could he possibly know how much I loved him? This was our future we were talking about, matter-of-factly, with ease.

"I was thinking maybe something closer to your Mom's so when the baby comes you have help," he added.

"That would be wonderful," I said, "but I am never leaving my baby with a sitter. She will be tied on my back or my tummy or in my arms from day one."

"She?" he asked.

"Well, I can't imagine having a boy, seeing as I am a girl and all."

Marshall laughed. "Yes. Perhaps boys come from a different planet."

"You think I'm silly, but I should tell you, for years I believed babies were delivered by storks because of a story my mom read to me when I was small."

"We sure do get some crazy ideas," he said. "It takes a long time to learn what is real."

"Well, I think I like the real way a lot better than the stork routine."

Heather knocked on the tin frame of the door. "Yoo-hoo," she said. "You two all done in there?"

21

Heather was in a rare mood for talk as she transported me from Marshall's to the boutique so I could meet-up with Carrie for the ride back to school. Although I smelled weed on her clothes, I decided to play stupid. Between my farewell with Marshall, the mess with Brent and Strange, and anxiety over the months ahead, I didn't want to take on Heather for smoking a little pot. Besides, she probably *wanted* me to challenge her.

"He's a handsome square sort of guy," she said. "Nice voice, too. If he let his hair grow a little and spoke like a human being, he would be dangerous. But he's a Christian soldier, Lily. How can you stomach all that shit?"

"Let's see, I think you said he's good looking, and I believe you implied he's literate. Maybe his confidence and commitment would also be worthy of your consideration. I happen to admire a person who can use language the way Marshall can. I suspect he's not like anyone you've ever met before."

"That's the God's honest," Heather laughed. "Oh well, if you're into him, you're into him no matter what Strange or your brother think. And here's the thing, I have news of my own. Drum roll please."

Did I hear excitement? Pride? I sang a little da-da-da-dat-da-dah, and she shouted, "I got into F.I.T.! Early acceptance!"

"Fashion Institute of Design? Really?" I said. "Dad always said you should go into fashion!" I took a second look at the stocking cap she was wearing. She had made it herself, knitting the hat out of heavy wool and then cooking it in boiling water until it became felt. The deep loden green was striking on her blonde hair, and the cut felt flowers of purple, gold and orange streamed down her back like a winter garland.

Heather exclaimed, "I know, but he didn't mean it! He didn't know I was getting ready for art school this whole year. He was making one of his bad jokes while I was putting together my portfolio in the art room with Dr. Kaplan. I sent for applications from Pratt and Rhode Island School of Design, too, all on my own. I even filled them out by myself. It's amazing to have someone take me seriously. I can hardly believe it. I'm in!"

I wanted to gush like she expected me to, but it wasn't there. Instead, I heard myself give her the big *but,* "But, New York City is a pretty far reach from Purgatory, don't you think?"

She was high enough to ignore me. "Yeah, thank God! I am so glad to get outta here. I'm already getting a new head on, imagining a life surrounded by cement and glass, studying maps of the city, finding out where the cool places are, learning what's in and out. I'll be living in Chelsea, you know, where all the singers and dancers, and people like Patti Smith and Robert Mapplethorpe lived."

Truth was, I'd never thought much about that world. "No, I don't know, not really." I had never heard of Mapplethorpe.

I wanted to tell what I *did* know, what *I* cared about. *My* future was sealed with a man who was clear as glass and as strong as cement. We were going to build something that time could not ruin. I thought how silly it would be to try to explain this. Not in her state of delirium. She wouldn't be the least bit interested that I had a real life, a forever life, in the making.

"I am going to work as much as I can this spring and make a point of reading the *Village Voice* and every fashion magazine that has ever been published. Do you know that fashions cycle? They come back about every twenty years. Fads and fashions are soul mates—they're predictable. If you know what once was cool, you'll be ready to make it reappear in the next round."

"Even at L.L. Bean?" I asked, not consciously trying to blow out her flame.

"I'm not planning to work for them anytime soon, even though they need me," she laughed. "I plan to soak up everything I can, the whole time I'm in the city. I will be in the middle of everything; able to walk to the Empire State Building, Penn Station, Madison Square Garden; but most important, I will be right in the heart of the fashion district. Isn't that phenomenal? I'll be able to observe firsthand what's coming down."

"You sound ready. I like that. Looks like we're both women with a future!" I smiled beneficently.

"Yes!" she shouted, honking the horn and yelling "Right on, sister, right on. I'm in a New York state of mind!"

I said, "Amen," and should have left it at that, but the new me, the pastor's wife, had to add a little sobriety. "I see a lot of challenges ahead for us, but I guess that's how it has to be if you have big plans."

"Are you honest to God choosing to be a Mom and become a pastor's wife?" she asked. "Is this what you want? You know you still have a choice."

"I've made my choice and I feel just as liberated as you do, Heather. I am doing what's right for me. Sometimes I think about my friend Nancy and how stuck she is. She's such a great person and yet so stuck. She's tied to her mom and the farm and the horses. I don't know how she'll get out."

"Maybe you could unstick her. Have you seen her at all during the holidays?" Heather asked.

"Only once. We were both too busy."

"She might end up being your step-sister, you know."

That idea had crossed my mind but it seemed too unlikely to consider seriously. I was not ready to believe in the finality of the divorce and not ready to see her father in my father's place. "Well, she's like a sister now, although she hasn't said a thing about her dad and Mom. I don't even know if she knows what's going on. I just hope we never have to deal with it."

"How come? If she's like a sister, why haven't you said anything? Isn't she curious about her father's sex life?"

"Oh, yuck, don't go there." I said.

"They probably do it, don't you think? You've met him, right?"

"Yup. A dork. Mom wouldn't settle for that."

"Well, it's Mom's life," Heather said. "She gets to make mistakes just like the rest of us, and I am almost out of here, so I won't have to watch."

"Four years at FIT isn't exactly out of Purgatory. You'll still be part of the family and I imagine you will be coming home for holidays for R&R. Look at me! I'm married, pregnant, going to school and I've still got one foot at home."

"Does it feel good, really? I mean knowing you are going to be a mother?" she asked, her doubts showing in her question.

"Yes, it's meant to be," I said, leaving God out of it.

Re-entering school was like moving from the moon to Earth. I felt ingested into my studies, taking tests, finishing what I had started and actually learning a few things. Where my roommates had trouble focusing, I found myself lost in the work. It was something to do, something to achieve and distract. I had no one to answer to but myself. I actually enjoyed the long hours of concentration and felt strangely settled.

My roommates seemed happy to have my illness behind me and a baby ahead. They went about their lives allowing me to be a pleasant voyeur and an occasional confidante. It was not unusual for them to touch my belly and sing songs to Little Somebody. I tried hard not to snack all day, but since the end of morning sickness, hunger had begun to rule. I succumbed to the vending machine's offerings of peanut butter crackers and M&Ms. I kept chocolate kisses under my bed, and couldn't eat enough potato chips between classes.

I spoke to Marshall almost every other night. Our calls were quick and loving. He said he had found a little house in the country that would be vacant after ski season. I couldn't wait for my next trip home to see it. He added that he had made inroads with David and had explained the dangers of his relationship with Brent. I asked how his warnings were working out, but he had no specifics.

The intensity of the fallout didn't reach me until the first week in February when Heather called to fill me in. She said she had been trying for hours. "You aren't in school, you're in solitary confinement," she said. "No one answers the damn phones; either that or they're busy, busy, busy."

I asked what was so urgent and she said, "The shit has hit the proverbial fan. I'm dealing with misery everywhere I look. The old Brent is back, angry and miserable. He's definitely borderline material. Most of the time he's locked in his room and refusing to go to school. Mom wants him to see a shrink but he won't. It's scary. Then, when I go to work, I have to deal with Strange, who has dyed his hair flaming red. I mean Crayola red, Lil, and he's threatening to go to Amsterdam where he says the law is fair, drugs are free and sex is how you like it. He says he has to leave this country."

I waited for at least five seconds before I spoke. "He doesn't have to leave the country. He just has to consider that Brent is only fifteen years old. Brent is too young for

Strange. I think they were having a gay thing going on, and you know that's against the law."

Her voice rose an octave. "Against the law? What are you talking about? How can being gay be against the law? A person is born that way. So what if David and Strange are queer? They're good for each other. You can see that."

"So, you know they had a thing going on? Heather, you should also know it's wrong. It's forbidden by law. We aren't the only country that doesn't allow it. It's forbidden in countries like Italy and Russia and Indonesia and I don't know how many others."

"You can't not allow it. It just is. Some people like people of their own sex. Duh. That's how they're wired! Some people have both sexes inside them and don't like the one that shows. How can you think anyone chooses to be that way? It's like being born with an extra thumb. Gay people are born gay, they don't choose the suffering that goes along with that, and they can't change just because some law tells them they are freaks. Strange is so mad right now he's wearing earrings and swaying his hips like a hula dancer. Honest to God, he's screaming for all he's worth. Neon lights wouldn't say it any louder. I just know he's going to leave, the question is when, and whether Pearl will put up with him acting out like this."

Heather was always so sure, so clear that she knew everything. Now she was an authority on sexual preference. "Heather, there are laws. There are reasons for laws. This whole thing is unhealthy and dangerous."

I could imagine her chin sticking out and her hands clenching the phone. "Only because people like you call people like them sick. We are talking about major injustice here and it makes people sick. It makes *me* sick!"

She was, as usual, championing the non-conforming. I reminded her about Brent's age. "What about Brent? Brent is too young to know what he wants. He's had trouble making good friends and Strange may have just been taking advantage of him. Maybe, maybe we, you know, maybe we told Strange too much."

"Are you crazy? Do you think Strange stalked and seduced and took advantage of Brent? God! Brent was in the store everyday just begging for Strange's attention. He was ga-ga over him. I thought it was wonderful that Strange was willing to give him the time of day. At first he acted a little like a big brother but I saw that change. Not big time and not in a sicky way either. They just got really close. Now, with Strange pulling away, Brent is going out of his mind. He doesn't know what happened or why."

A bell sounded in my head. I had to be careful. "What *did* happen?"

"I think it's obvious, someone threatened Strange and he had to tell Brent *so-long it's been good to know ya*. I don't know. It isn't good, that much I do know. Maybe Dad found out and he went after Strange during one of his drunken rants."

I made no correction to her assumption. I could have said something then. If I had known what to say, I might have spoken, but I didn't. Instead I protested that Dad would have simply spoken the truth as he saw it.

"He's homophobic!" Heather said. "Have you forgotten the thing at the fair? It disgusts him to think his son may not like football. Imagine if he found out his son was into boys?"

"What can I do?" I asked.

"I don't know," she said.

Heather's phone call left me with feathers for feet; a need to lie down, disappear, find candy. I had nothing but questions. I couldn't name the fear, or why I felt guilty or like I had to be or do something to fix all that was wrong. I tried not to think that telling Marshall was anything but right, but if it was right it should have felt right. It didn't. Lying in my bunk, I thought about Little Someone and imagined her tiny feet and hands, her thumb stuck in her mouth, the beauty that was surely hers. I held her as best as I could with my hands warming the bubble in which she lay, caressing the curve of her spine.

I remembered the day when Mom brought Brent home from the hospital and we all examined him. As the older sibling, I was the one who was allowed to sit with his tiny body placed carefully in my arms. I was the one allowed to feed him his bottle when he was being weaned and needy. I was the one who would rock his baby swing suspended from the doorway until he stopped crying, and I was the one who could make him laugh for photo shoots. Jell-O jiggling on a spoon used to make him laugh until he cried. When he was two we exercised together to Mom's Jack LaLanne workout tapes while she rebuilt her body's quadriceps and tightened her abdomen. His little toddler legs would try to do whatever mine did and he wouldn't quit until I did.

It was I who taught him his first word using the kitchen light, turning it on and off. Each time it went on, I would say, "Light," and soon he repeated after me. After that, he knew every light switch in our big old house and every light in the house became his to name. Mom had to cover all the sockets to keep his tiny fingers from exploring their secrets.

When Brent was three he was allowed on the carnival rides for the first time. He did all right on the carousel with Mom holding him on a stationary elephant and all of us waving each time they went by. He held on tight, too frightened to wave. He liked the ride on the pathetic freckled donkey dressed in a bonnet and dolefully suffering the shame of enslavement. Then I took him on the teacup ride and we were whipped around a circle over and over again. I could hear Dad laughing at him, calling, "Buck up, boy!" But Mom saw his fear and had the ride stopped. We had to peel Brent off the seat. He had wet himself and was miserable for the rest of the day.

His best friend in kindergarten was a little boy named Charlie. Charlie had a malformed foot that seemed too heavy to lift. They had also been in pre-school together before they went to the public school. I used to see them holding hands at the end of the line where Brent would take it slow so Charlie didn't get left behind. The teacher told my mom that she thought Brent was the most sensitive, wonderful boy she had ever met.

Charlie and Brent caught bugs together and studied them with a magnifying glass. They named them and buried them, somberly with little tombs to mark the spot. They played dress up as knights of the square table. Mom helped them make cardboard masks and swords. My skirts served as their cloaks. Heather and I would play along like we were anxious maidens in distress. Our goal was usually to ditch them and laugh ourselves silly watching them try to figure out where we were. Every knoll and tree, stair and doorway was our domain. Play and torture were kindred spirits in those days. We girls always had the advantage over poor little Brent who suffered our dominance just for our company.

Did we take away his love and trust in women?

Who knows what makes us become whatever we are. My future was pulling me down a path I had never considered. It seemed to have its own mind, a force behind it that had come from the stars, at least somewhere beyond my control.

22

Things went from bad to worse. The next time Heather called it was about a fire. Someone had set a fire in the dumpster behind Pearl's shop. It wasn't meant to burn the building down, but it was definitely arson, according to Heather. She was afraid the next fire would be worse and even more afraid that someone she knew may have set this one. Using Sherlock's famous method she managed to eliminate the possible culprits. Strange would never do something that could even remotely threaten his own house. Brent was trapped at home every night. Dad was out of town and Pearl had nothing to gain and a lot to lose. She concluded it must have been a local who wanted to scare Strange out of town. Maybe a crazy copycat of the KKK or the Neo-Nazis or some other far out faction. She thought that perhaps Strange was becoming too *bizarro* for Purgatory.

I asked if she and Strange had talked about his separation from Brent at all, and she said the topic was *off limits.* "I don't know how to approach him about his gayness. I mean, I don't know anyone else who's gay except my own brother and who can talk to him?"

A girl asked me how much longer I needed the phone. "Very important," I whispered with my hand over the mouthpiece.

"Well, at least we have each other," I said, to my sister, and realized for the first time that it was true; we were becoming each other's confidantes in the throes of our family's break-up.

She threw ice at my warm words. "Too bad your head is in the dark ages, though. Can't you accept that no two people are the same, that we aren't made out of cookie dough?" she asked.

She was determined to keep up the argument and I took on the challenge. "I can better accept that rules exist and we need them to make the world safe. Do you have any idea how sex can get out of hand, can ruin families, how rape destroys lives?" I asked. "There have to be boundaries to protect us from the mentally ill, from the perverts of this world, the sexually transmitted diseases."

She moaned and interrupted me singing *la-la-la-la*. I could imagine her at the other end of the phone in her yellow braids and latest concoction she called fashion. But I was not going to let her drown me out. "Don't you see that in societies where sex was out of control, lust and greed took over and they collapsed? Just like Rome. Just like Sodom."

"Oh, man you are so having your brain washed. We are talking about your *brother* and one of your best friends. Not Julius Caesar and all his boys and girls. How can you be so narrow-minded. It's about love! Love *happens* to people, they don't really get a choice. Your sexual preferences happen, too. Think about your baby. What if your baby is gay? What if it is born with a uterus and testicles and then grows breasts? That happens you know."

"Oh come on. You're trying to scare me into agreeing with you. Besides, I'd like to know just when you became the authority on all things sexual." I wished I could see her face to face to remind her I was not exactly inexperienced. Instead, her voice reverberated in my eardrums.

"I learned to read before I started kindergarten, remember?" she asked.

I did remember. She was using the mental superiority card. Heather was born wanting to do anything I could do, better. A fluent reader when she was four, she'd grab the storybooks out of my hands and say, "I can do it myself!" when I'd try to read to her.

"So you can read. Big deal," I said.

"Can you?" she asked. "Have you read the *Kinsey Report*, *Masters and Johnson*, or copies of *Psychology Today*? Aren't you curious enough to find out what experts say? It's all in there, on the shelves of the public library—in newspapers, movies, TV. Think *The Odd Couple*. You don't have to be a guru to find out the facts of life, Lily. Look where your lack of knowing has got you!"

I knew enough not to try to mention the laws of the Bible because she would spit or scream in frustration. Plus, trying to use a religious argument was untested ground for me; it would be embarrassing to try, and worse to botch it badly. She couldn't care less about what was in the Bible, anyway. Heather just wasn't one to like simple rules or givens. Her favorite t-shirt said SURPRISE ME and she meant it.

When I was with Marshall the truth seemed fixed, accessible. When we were apart I felt like I had to work to keep my mind on his channel, not to let the static drown him out.

I tried for diplomacy. "All I know is that I want to keep out of this mess, although it doesn't look as easy as I thought. Maybe we should talk to Strange when I get home. Strange and I used to be able to talk things to death. I don't want him to be hurt any more than you do. But, this is such a private thing, where would we begin?"

"You could start by doing some research. You have a brain, college girl, why don't you put it to work?"

I didn't want to hang up at that moment, but the antsy girl from down the hall was pacing ten feet away. I suppose she thought I was using up her time. I pointed at the phone and mouthed *very important*. She looked back with tears in her eyes.

"Listen, I've got to go, really! Someone's waiting for the phone."

"I'm sorry, Lily, I just wish we were on the same page for this one," Heather said.

"We're both worried about Strange and Brent being hurt. I would hate to be the one that made anything worse," I confessed.

"Lily, Strange is beyond hurt. You'll see, *if* he's still here when you get back. Call me and let me know when you're coming."

I promised I would.

Two weeks later we had a long weekend recess. The break fell on the last weekend of February and my housemates were staying put. They decided not to leave campus, opting for snowball fights and skiing dates and other opportunities to play. A nor'easter was forecast. They welcomed the weather because it meant the slopes would deepen, the frat houses would open and they could look forward to plenty of fireside partying.

In order to make it out of town before the storm, Carrie and I hit the roads as soon as my ancient history lecture was over. With my head filled with Taoists, Greeks, and Hindus of the early centuries, my hair was on fire. How could Christianity have thrived in the face of such deep cultures, and in many cases, overwhelmed them?

More importantly, why were my clothes always dirty when I was heading home?

We left as the sky's weight was building. Knowing the great gray shelves of cloud would soon become ruthless, I stuffed my laundry in my duffle bag along with a textbook, the God-awful physics book I hoped Dad would help me decipher. I had to pass physics if I was ever to head into medicine, although that was looking less and less likely.

Carrie was wearing a black and white ski hat with Ying Yang patterns woven in its brim. "Cute hat," I said, "Very Tao."

"Huh?" she asked.

"Symbols of balance and equanimity."

Carrie was not interested in the Taoists or my new wisdom. She was happily headed home to Drew, now past pretending they were just friends. Maybe it was that her experiences at school hadn't produced alternatives, and maybe it was deeper than that. I didn't quite know what to think, but not knowing was so often the name of the game for me.

"How's Little Someone?" she asked.

"She's growing huge. I'd say big as a basketball by now."

"Maybe there are two."

"No. I just popped. It happens around this time. Although sometimes I feel like she has three legs and four arms."

"Are you staying with Marshall while you're home?"

"Some of the time. I need to touch base with my mom and Heather, too."

"What about Brent?"

"Yeah, him, too."

What about Brent? I thought. What would I find? How could I begin to approach him? What did he know about Marshall's warnings to Strange? Guilt sat on the hairs of my neck.

The wind picked up on the way. We had to keep going or be stuck for three days in some nowhere town—not what either of us wanted. About halfway home, snow began to fall earlier than predicted, flying up as much as down. The dry flakes promised many more. I became Carrie's second pair of eyes and ears as we negotiated one curve and then another. It wasn't long before we saw our first accident; a Volvo had spun off the road onto the meridian. Then ahead, a sea of red lights warned of something worse. We slowed down to a crawl afraid of stopping because of those behind us. I tried not to look at the scene of the accident, but couldn't resist the temptation, as I saw other vehicles pulled to the side and people running to help. Passengers were obviously trapped in an overturned station wagon. I imagined the crush of the roof on their heads and doubted they survived.

"Marshall's parents died in a car crash," I said.

"Should we stop?" Carrie asked.

"No. We have to keep going, we have no rescue skills to offer," I pointed out.

We slid into town and Carrie drove me to Pearl's where we surprised Strange and Heather who thought we were coming the next day. Neither Carrie nor I let our eyes rest on the flaming head that was Strange. What was there to say, after all? He looked kind of ridiculous, skinny in black leather, and bold in fire engine red hair with not a natural aspect to him. Even his eyebrows were doing something peculiar. They were painted with kohl into pointed arches meant to frighten. He looked not only strange but evil.

Carrie left us as soon as she could, and Heather asked Strange to cover for her. We were barely out of the driveway when she asked, "Do you get it now?"

"Get it? That Strange needs a lot of attention?"

"Get it that he's angry?"

"Yes. It about hits you on the head. He's a little crazy, don't you think?"

"It's no wonder. How would you like to be told you can't be who you are?"

"This is much more complicated than that, Heather."

"No it isn't."

And so it went; the two of us at it again, back and forth, back and forth. But our divisiveness was not as harsh as it had been, at least I felt we were in a different place, pushing and prodding one another for help.

With my bag over my shoulder and my parka stretched to the max, I must have looked like Mrs. Claus lumbering to the door of the house, but Mom wasn't home from work yet to see such a sight. I assumed the snow building on the roads had slowed her down.

Inside, it took no time to see that Mom was back to herself. The house was a welcoming sight. A perfume of pine wafted from fresh cut boughs placed in the tin milk can by the door; books were piled high on the old traveling trunk in front of the couch. New magazines lay open for grazing. Last year's dry hydrangea were wound together with strings of tiny glass starlights and draping the big mantle over the fireplace. Folded on the brown leather chair was a new quilt stitched in pastel-colored fabrics, swatches probably acquired through fairs and resale shops to replace the reams of material Mom lost in the fire. Recent school pictures of Heather and Brent sat on the side table framed in leather and suede. Heather looked like any other senior and Brent, well, Brent looked like a very thin version of himself.

"Nice pictures," I said. "I have been replaced."

"Not quite and not possible," Heather said. "You are all over the fridge and on Mom's dresser. It's our turn to have the prime spot in the living room."

I called, "Brent. I'm home! Are you here?"

No answer. "I guess he's out."

"I doubt it," Heather said.

She was right. He was hiding in his room and emerged only because we pounded on the door and said we were the police. He didn't find us anything more than annoying. His hair was sitting in tufts on his head, his sweats looked like he lived in them. The room smelled like four day old fish. Fumbling for words, I asked if he was still skating as much as he had been at Christmas—a not very good way to begin. His answer was a grunt.

"The house is cold," I said. "Why don't you bring in some kindling and I'll make us cocoa."

Miraculously, he got bundled up and went outside to do my bidding.

I put a pot of watery milk on to heat, and transferred the dirty clothes from my bag to the washing machine. Meanwhile, Heather put on Jon Bon Jovi and we started dancing around the kitchen to *Livin' on a Prayer.* When Brent reentered, he kicked the front door so hard it smashed into the wall, stomped over to the fireplace and threw the sticks on top of the rolls of old newspapers that were already in place and reached for the long matches that sat on the mantle. With one try, the pile was ablaze. However, the flue wasn't open and in a minute we were gasping from a downdraft of smoke. Although the crisis was short-lived, I had to consciously stop myself from getting mad at Brent, because he should have known enough to check the flue. Heather kept her mouth shut as well.

After I'd loaded the cocoa with whipped cream and served it up, I fell onto the couch, with my baby bundle still dancing. "Want to touch your niece? She's kicking up a storm," I asked Brent.

"She's never going to be my niece," he scowled. "Don't you get it?"

End of conversation. I *did* get it—I was sure he knew it was me who told Marshall, and Marshall's warnings had ended his love life. I fled the room and hid in the kitchen for as long as it took me to throw my clothes in the dryer and decide what to do next. There was really only one way out. I begged for the car keys from Heather and grabbed a few clothes from my closet for an overnight, promising I'd be back in the morning. Mom hadn't been expecting me home until the next day, anyway.

Winter defines Purgatory with its simple palette of blacks and whites. They speak to its ability to cope. I was used to snow. I knew the roads. I didn't bother to put chains on the tires because I wanted to leave right away. I felt little threat setting out on the familiar trek, the roads being less challenging than those in the Northwest kingdom. But somehow I'd forgotten the wind's trickery, how one bank drifts into another and how difficult flat white is to navigate. Between fatigue caused by the trip home and the exhaustion of guilt, I was a nervous wreck. As I peered into the nothingness ahead, Brent's face, his anger glaring, appeared.

I tried to concentrate on the snow. White is beautiful. White is forgiving. It hides a messy terrain and makes the land look pure, innocent. I had to pay close attention to what I was doing. I thought of Karma and wondered if I was reaping the rewards of my disloyalty. It was wrong of me to have put Marshall in the middle. I should have known how he would react. For every action there is a reaction.

But there is also the question about doing what is instinctively right in your heart and mind. This is why Marshall said he feared for me to be under the influence of my Godless family. He said it takes more than most of us have to stand up to people, to confront differences with those we love. He told me I had to let go of the old and be born again, become one with Christ and with all things new. Who was this Christ? I still had not met him. He was an invisible third person in my marriage even though I wanted Marshall to myself.

Normally my heart would be racing in anticipation of seeing him, that face, his eyes and mouth, but this time I was afraid every minute of the way. I wished I had called to alert him. What if I went off the road? There were no cars, no tracks even. In my need to run, I hadn't bothered to let him know I was on my way. He wouldn't know it if I went off the road. I surely couldn't turn around. I wasn't even sure he made it home in such weather. Well, I thought, if he was home or not, it wouldn't matter; I had a key to our place.

But I wanted him to be there. I knew that when I saw him and heard his voice I would be safe, in my real home, my future home, my life. It was only with Marshall that questions disappeared and absolutes made life straight and clear. Away from Marshall there were no truths, no answers and nothing to hang onto. He was my strength and my redeemer.

I saw the church first and then the cluster of weighted pines at the end of his driveway. Lights glowed warmly from his trailer revealing a small, half buried car alongside, with a patch of bright yellow exposed. I hoped it was his. He had been promising to buy us one. I had to get inside immediately, to feel his arms, hear his voice and smell the strength of him or I was going to fall apart. I trudged to his door, each step an effort feeling too great for my tired body, and when I pulled at its knob it opened in a slow, ice-defying motion. On the couch were two people untangling themselves from an embrace.

23

I froze in the doorway, with a white swirl sweeping around me, the snow entering the space I could not. A blur of figures rose and pulled at my arms ushering me inside. Nancy, flushed and red-eyed, helped me to the only chair and I folded into it.

They spoke simultaneously, "It's not, we weren't, you mustn't...." words such as these. Nancy knelt down in front of me and pulled at my sloppy boots, Marshall covered me with a quilt.

"We were just talking about you," Marshall said.

I didn't think it looked like a conversation, not one I would have with someone's husband.

"Oh," I said.

"You are here so early! Why did you risk driving in all this snow?" Marshall asked.

He didn't know? He didn't know that I was not staying away from him for one minute without feeling compromised, without longing, without planning the next time we would be together? I wanted him to lift me into his arms and kiss me as he had done so many other times, when questions needed no answers.

I stayed put, planted in the chair like a pregnant Buddha, allowing myself to be served tea and listening to their excuses for what I had seen. I heard their voices as if we were in a cave, a hollow wet, cold, cell.

Nancy whined that she was afraid we were losing our closeness, she was afraid my mother and her father were growing closer. She suspected it would be hard for both of us, with her loyalty to her mother and mine to my father. I thought of her father's silly hair standing at attention in the wind, his dumb scarf flapping. I saw her pulling herself out of Marshall's arms.

Marshall was very solicitous. He nodded to Nancy's every word. His hands were grasping each other, and his knees were at odd angles, shoved up in the air from his deep position on the ugly little couch. He said friendships were sacred and he knew we would work things out and God's plan was for love to conquer all.

Conquer all left me doubting. I didn't like the word conquer. How would love conquer the love lost between my father and mother? How would love find Brent and Strange? Was love for me the real reason Nancy sat in *my* living room with *my* husband, the father of *my* child? Did I feel numb because of the cold? Did the air that had filled my lungs and promised me undying love disappear? Had they eaten it? I couldn't seem to find any oxygen. "I have to get out of here," I said. "I can't breathe."

"You can't leave," they said in unison.

I knew it was true. I was trapped by the weather and what felt like a great shadow enfolding me in its grasp. Silent, cold and dark.

How the little trailer kept the cold wind out and the three of us warmly tucked in for the next twelve hours is one for the poets. Between tea and talk and touch, I managed to find some warmth within the metal walls, until the need for sleep took over. Nancy and I had to share the sleeper-sofa and Marshall slept in the tweed armchair, watching over us like the Good Shepherd he wanted to be. We were layered in his sweaters and wool socks, sharing two quilts and one another's body heat, and actually found a degree of comfort in the mix. That is, until I realized my newly domed stomach took up more than my share of the bedclothes. I felt like an oaf, my limbs knotted, my hair matted, my back growing stiff and then stiffer while the weight of Little Someone shifted and pushed me around. I couldn't lie still, couldn't find my normal breath. In and out, I told myself, inhale, exhale, again and again, until I drifted off to safety for another bout of the blessed escape.

I awoke when Nancy hit me right in the face. She didn't mean it, but I lay stunned, looking at her prettiness and the wavy hair spilling across her pillow. I sensed Marshall was only pretending to sleep. I almost saw his eyes looking at his captives, one a fat, unhappy responsibility, the other a lovely maiden in distress. Who could blame him for finding her more attractive? What would I do if this thing between them was more than they admitted? But it couldn't be. It mustn't be.

I had to stop the very thought of such a thing or face the risk making it so. They were my soulmates. Weren't trust and love synonymous? I thought of my family and the way I had loved and trusted my parents. I could only hope I would find it possible to love them again with the kind of trust I once knew, beyond the wishes, lies and dreams.

I was in a rumpled mess of exhaustion when I was struck with a dream, an image of my father sitting at the edge of the bed. He was wrapped in his heavy felt blanket centered with the big H for his Harvard days, and confiding to me of his lost causes, the marches in New York and Washington to persuade those who already were persuaded. He was young and sure and singing, "We shall overcome." I woke up wishing he was still with me.

I pushed away the dream. Then I thought of Mom, her hands working their magic as she wound ribbons through pine and returned gilded pinecones to their boughs, her long fingers deftly transforming the ordinary into something more. I ached as I thought of her hugging Dad's jacket, imagined her voice calling us to dinner, trying to make everyone happy at the table. I thought of the big old house, gone forever.

Silent tears trickled down my neck. I would not complain, would not act out of fear, for fear that acting suspicious would only cast me in a more negative light. I had never known jealousy, if that is what I was feeling, even when I saw girls hanging around Marshall at church, or a girl weeping in a car outside the trailer. I wasn't jealous. Why would I question a man who swore he loved me and spoke for God? We were committed from the start. Of course, I hardly knew myself, no less him.

Nancy made a little sound. She was sleeping well, better than I could or would or hoped to. She wasn't upset. She wasn't worried that she did anything wrong. I needed to focus on that, not the darker possibilities, not on the questions that buzzed my head in my semi-conscious state.

I must have drifted off again, as I remember waking at dawn to the sound of the snowplow and the scrapes of a shovel just beyond the door. One of the church members was up bright and early with his plow, earning his stripes for Jesus. Marshall had joined him and was busy at work digging us out of our strange predicament.

Nancy rolled over and looked at me, the blob beside her, sharing a strange bed, and said "Well, hi! Like, what brings you here?" She started to laugh. I did too. It was the craziest situation. I refused to believe she did anything wrong to create it.

We put on our outer clothes and joined Marshall outside. I took a fallen branch to push the snow off the roof of my car and scraped at the windshield. Nancy dug out her buried yellow bug using a plastic platter.

"Here, Lily," Marshall said, "Let me do that."

"I am perfectly capable of doing it myself," I puffed. "I have to get the car back to Purgatory as soon as possible."

"But what is your hurry? The roads will be closed. No one is going anywhere," Marshall argued. His cheeks were red and his jaw stubbly. Behind him only the purity of fresh snow.

"I have to get back home. Mom needs the car, I need Mom."

"Lily, this makes no sense."

"It makes perfect sense to me. I have to go."

He took my arm. "What is driving you away? You know, Lily, the Lord says that jealousy rots the bones. It is not healthy. If you are angry at me, it is the Devil at work. He is the source of such feelings."

"Why do you think I am angry? I am not jealous. Why should I be jealous? I just have to get the car back to Purgatory," I said, praying that the tears behind my lids would stay put.

Nancy shoveled away as I stood my ground, proving that I was not concerned about leaving the two of them together. I had more pressing things to do. I felt a surge of power as I backed away through the walls of snow and left Marshall with his arms crossed watching me, a scowl on his face, but no words to stop me.

I am still not sure of all that transpired in my mind during the long night before, but morning brought a new kind of need, and it didn't include Nancy or Marshall. It didn't lead me back to Purgatory, either. It took me on the wintry roads to Dad's house in Grafton. I didn't know if he would be home, but it seemed urgent for me to talk to him. He was the only man I had ever known, and wise in ways I wasn't. I had to speak to him.

The trees were still being frosted with lightly falling flakes. It was the typical non-threatening flurry action in the pattern of nor'easters, and I knew the break was only that; nevertheless, I had to go. Home was nowhere, what with Brent hating me, and Marshall's place compromised. I wanted to be with Dad. I wanted to have time to understand what happened between him and Mom that was so devastating that he had to leave. Maybe I could find out who he really was. There was too much I didn't know, too many secrets, too many words not spoken.

He was unshaven but relaxed when I arrived, acting like I visited him at eight-thirty in the morning every day of the week. You would never have believed that this was my first time to see his place or that I popped in uninvited.

Grafton gives a person a sense of needing an invitation. It is a perfect little hamlet that is frozen in time, quaintly preserved for postcards and watercolor artists. It was as unlikely a place for a man like my father to choose as Palm Beach. I greeted him saying as much.

"Boy, Dad, you sure chose the corniest village in all Vermont to run to," I teased, as I stamped the snow off my boots on the little porch outside the door.

"It's just a place." He smiled. "So what if every horse is a thoroughbred and every cow has a name! Come in, come in."

I put my coat on the back of a chair.

"Want some home-brewed coffee?" he asked.

I nodded.

His eyes went to my protruding tummy. "He's getting big!" he said.

I smiled. "She."

"For sure?" he asked.

"In my mind's eye."

I scanned the rooms for signs of life. The walls were blank. The floors bare.

"I see. So you want a girl? What are you doing driving around in the worst storm of the year?

One of his hands pulled a chair from the table and the other guided me into it.

"Oh, Daddy. There's so much I don't know," I said, plopping down with the grace of a beanbag. "Just when I should feel most adult I am feeling like a stupid kid. I don't know anything, nothing at all."

"Knowing is not what it's chalked up to be. Voltaire said it best. *Doubt may be unpleasant but knowing is absurd!*" He poured water through his percolator and took two cups down from the open shelf above the lower cabinets. Everything was a shiny white.

He was trying to make light of what I was saying. Was this the way it had always been? I didn't care about Voltaire, I didn't know anything about him or want to at this moment.

"But Dad, I don't know what happened to our family. I don't know the truth. Why aren't we together? Why are we so angry and unable to work things out?" I looked around the bare room. "It's like you want to erase us!"

He picked up the book that lay open on the table, and showed it to me. "I am reading the rabbi's book. You should try it. It explains a lot of things."

Astonished, I asked, "The Bible?"

"No, no, no. *Bad Things Happen to Good People.* You can't fit a square peg in a round hole, unless you whittle it down to next to nothing. Our family will get over this."

"But I don't want to get *over* it. I want to be married and still have a family to go home to. I want you and Mom to be together like we once were. I want Brent to be happy. I want my baby to grow up believing in something, even if it's just a family."

"*Just* a family?"

"Well, I don't mean *just* that way. A family is really, really important and I am not willing to watch mine fall apart and not do anything about it."

"You are quite the little woman, Lily-Vanilli, but it's not for you to fix, and I am afraid it's not fixable."

He took my coat from the back of my seat and hung it on a hook, then he put some milk in our cups, poured the diluted coffee and sat down kind of awkwardly across from me at the little version of a kitchen table.

"Dad. You can stop drinking. Aren't we worth it to you?"

"You are, I'm through with the booze, but it's too late."

"But, have you thought about God? God will help you."

"Lily, don't go there. There's no God waiting to help me out. If you want to believe the biggest sham ever perpetrated on man—I can't stop you, but I can't join you or your preacher man. There's no God, there's only science and fate." He rose and started pacing.

"*Fate* implies God, Dad. It says there *is* a plan. Karma is more than science. It's a spiritual path. Hindus believe in it, lots of other people do, too."

"Uh-oh, sounds like my little freshman is doing her reading." He leaned against the refrigerator and smiled knowingly.

"Please Dad. There has to be more for us than just...just this."

"Nope. This is all there is and that's a lot, Love-of-my-heart. I like the ideas of the eastern religions, don't get me wrong." He sat again. "Maybe they have it right. Maybe we are just recycled until we get it right. But I wouldn't count on it. Let's wait until the physicists have it figured out before we get on our knees."

"Science isn't enough, Dad. Besides I am never going to understand physics."

"Of course you are, if you want to."

"I don't get it and I won't."

"All you have to know is e=mc squared."

"And that tells me nothing."

"It explains more than you know. We are all nuclear reactors. We are pure energy and in the long run simply pushed around by forces we can't see or feel."

"Dad, this thinking doesn't mean anything to me. I am carrying a baby, a love child, and I think she is much more than e=mc squared. She is changing my world, yours and our family's. What will she find when she arrives? Will you love this baby? Will you try to bring Marshall into our family so we can give her a grandma and a grandpa?"

"Lil, your baby's daddy is never going to be my friend." He looked into the bottom of his cup.

"Can't you fake it 'til you make it, Dad?" I asked.

"Don't think so, Princess. I think he's dangerous. Voltaire would agree."

"I don't care what Einstein or Voltaire or anyone else thinks, Daddy. I care about you caring for me, for our family."

He grew tense, his chin thrust at me as he spoke. "That man is not family. I'd rather deal with his crazy brother. At least he is not manipulating people to give up their lives for some crackpot religion."

"Dad, you know nothing about him!" I cried.

"I know he hears voices, wants to turn God into wine and bread once a month to swallow Him. I know he thinks he's right and the rest of world is wrong, that he would ask you to give up your life to live like a vagabond and obey him for ever and ever. Amen."

"Oh, Daddy, you are making this so hard for me."

"I am an angry man."

"Mom loves you," I said, in a desperate attempt to bring him back.

"She doesn't. It's over. She tried. She really did, but I blew it time and again."

"Daddy, there's no reason to give up. Let go and let God. You made me listen to that stuff week after week at AA."

"Wishful thinking, all of it."

"Not all of it," I said.

24

This conversation with my father had been long overdue. It had taken twenty years to take place, and I was more than ready—more than curious—more than heartbroken—and braced. I quietly prayed for rescue.

"There's one truth you can count on, your Dad loves you more than he loves his own breath. You are my princess and always have been. You know that, don't you?" he asked.

I wasn't going to let him hide behind that easy charm of his. Princess was a tired term he used for all the women in his life. He didn't have to distinguish us from one another that way.

"I know that you want me to feel loved, and maybe I did, maybe I still do, but you haven't made enough compromises to prove it. You haven't let me know anything about the parts of you that make you yourself. If you died tomorrow I would have to read your obituary, and depend on other people's versions of your story. Is that how you want it? What bad history don't I know, Daddy? Did you kill someone? Did you steal old man Clarendon's money? What are the secrets you are keeping?

"Gee thanks, Lil. My transgressions look like mere blips along the way compared to your imaginings."

"Well, isn't it time that I know who I'm dealing with? Who the real Jonathan Woodhouse is?"

"Are we playing *"What's My Line*?" he teased.

"Are we what?" I asked.

"Private joke, Princess. Sorry, it's another thing of the past, a stupid TV show."

"I'm trying to be serious, Daddy."

"I know. Speaking of serious, you are looking pretty full of baby there. How are things going for you?"

"I wish...I want to talk about *you*, Daddy. I mean it. I came here to learn about you. I was going to make the excuse that I needed help with my horrible physics class, but I really want much more. And right now, I'm not sure whether you're ever going to let me in."

"What do you want to know? Hasn't your mother told you what a bad guy I am?"

"I've only heard about the drinking. She doesn't bad mouth you, Daddy."

"I'm glad to hear that. But your mother has always been angry with me. If it wasn't this, it was that, or it was about something else before that and before that. I think your mother heard rumors she couldn't forget. I had a life before we met and some of it went on for a few years after. My work was not quite on the up and up. It only cost me my practice and most of my friends, and now it has cost me my family."

"And now you have given me more to question and no answers that help me understand. Dad, I am begging you to tell me more. I need details not vague references. Please let me know you."

He sighed, stood up and walked to the living room's only window, his shoulders sagging and smile gone. The landscape outside was as bleak as the turn in his mood. Memories creased his brow, but were stuck inside his head.

"Enough, now," he announced.

"Are we finished then? Am I dismissed?" I asked. I proceeded to wait for what seemed like hours, while he remained in place, a tall dark shape against the glare outside the window frame. His hands fumbled deep in his pockets searching for lost change.

Finally, I couldn't stand it, I had to break the silence. "Dad. We are still your family. That's what I am fighting for. Can't you see? Why aren't you fighting for us?"

He turned and went to the stove and poured himself some more coffee. "Want some more?" he asked. It was better than nothing.

I nodded. He poured me a second cup and then sat down on the couch patting the space beside him. I almost looked away when I saw his eyes, clouded, their playfulness and challenge missing. They were so sad I was almost sorry I had confronted him.

He began, "There are certain inalienable rights, Lily. A person has a right to say no. No more. Not now. Not ever. A person has a right to declare their independence. That's what your mom is doing. Remember that. This is not my leaving you. It is about my letting go of the reins. You have also declared yourself independent. You have told me so a number of times. I am trying to respect that, along with your mother's choices. I am trying to give you both your freedom."

"But why does Mom need freedom? She was happy enough before you slipped up."

He leaned back and sighed. "I don't know that. Neither does she. She was very young when we met. It was the sixties. Things were a mess. It was coming apart all around us. My friends were getting called up to go to 'Nam, to a war in a place they cared nothing about, to fight against a people's revolution. It seemed wrong for our country to interfere.

"When my best friend got his notice, it hit home. I got involved with the protests and that was the end of my innocence. We were righteous bastards, defying the government we thought was defying us. Ignoring our parents' wishes, dropping out, falling in, crazy. It was the times. Back then, we still believed we lived in a democracy.

"Old man Clarendon was my father's best friend and my best friend's father. You've heard about him, right?"

"No. Not right. I never heard anything about him except that he existed. I have never heard your best friend's name or one other thing."

"Andrew. Andy Clarendon. Well, Andy, he was a great guy, still is. We loved each other. I mean we were brothers, you know, we shared all those rites of passage that kids share, and we made some trouble along the way, but nothing like what came down when he got his orders to report to duty. Then we got mad and became radicalized."

"Did he go off to war?"

"He could have asked his father to help him out, but he didn't, mostly because of his ol' man's patriotic pride and his claims to have saved the world in WWII. He had a medal to prove it. The poor bastard shined up that damn thing and wore it every chance he got. He loved Memorial Day and Armistice Day and the Firemen's parade and the VFW, would travel all the way to Rutland for an event.

"Meanwhile, we ended up with a bunch of guys burning our draft cards and messing up the storefronts of recruitment offices in downtown Boston and Cambridge. We were all adrenaline and righteousness. Then Andy got arrested and his father wouldn't post bail, so I did. He was so pissed off at his dad, he never went back home—even when Carter gave a reprieve to all the ex-pats."

"Did you stay friends?" I asked.

"I suppose. I was the one who found him a way out. I got him across the Maine border, but after that, he traveled west until he ended up in a little town in British Columbia called Nelson. He ended up running a ski resort outside of town. Meanwhile, I had to lay low and play dumb."

"That was brave, Dad."

"It wasn't brave, it was the only way to go, except, without Andy protesting, it was no longer fun. It was damn serious. I joined the underground and hooked up with other resisters; others who were as sure of themselves as I was. We were getting guys across the border in canoes and trucks, in trains and planes and connecting them with each other. Hell, we were helping build a nation up there in Canada. Truth is, they were getting the best guys America had to offer—anything had to be better than ending up in some rice paddy in a place we didn't give a shit about."

"I would be proud, if I was you."

"I was. I am. I still believe we were right, but so many guys died; fifty-eight thousand GI's who had no way out, no understanding of their choices or what they were doing. It was a poor man's war in the end. Not just here but there. Cost more than 3,000,000 lives for the poor peons over there."

"So you didn't have to go?"

"No. You saved my life."

"Me?"

"Yeah, I got a deferment. First it was school, then after graduation I was a sitting duck until I got myself a wife, a baby on the way and meaningful work as a small town lawyer for Ole Man Clarendon. It was enough. Not fair for the guys who had no cover. Not bad compared to what would have happened if anyone had found out my real work was trafficking."

"What happened to Andy?" I asked.

"His father gave up on him. Andy ended up choosing Canada and was probably happier than the rest of us."

"His father never found him?"

"Maybe it was my fault. I never told his father where he was. I figured that was Andy's job. But damned if I didn't have to work for the old man and put up with his relentless questions. It wasn't good for my gut. Then there was Andy's sister who I thought had it figured out. She was nobody's fool.

"It took about eight years before the Feds linked me to the underground and came to get me. Andy's dad put two and two together, fired me and made sure my right to practice law was revoked. I got off easy. It would have been jail time but for Clarendon."

His fingers were white at the tips, pressing hard on his cup. I looked around. The room felt like a cell. He could at least have put some pillows on the off-white couch, a few photographs on his bookshelves. I wondered if he wanted it this way, if he chose to be punished.

"But, you were right, weren't you, Dad?"

"Yes. I was right according to Jonathan Woodhouse, esquire, but there's no such thing, Princess. Right has many colors. I tell myself I would have fought if it had been a just war. I have tried to push the sight of Jessie Bell out of my mind when he came back with half a leg and a lot of anger. Don't want to think about Jim McCormack either, who came back in a body bag. At least I can honor them by saying they were right, too. They fought for the red white and blue, doing what they thought was noble. They had tradition and loyalty and the law on their side. They put their lives on the line, and too many of them paid a terrible price. Andy lives a good life. I lived a good life. Right is a tricky word"

"I'm beginning to think so."

"It takes a long time to learn."

The phone began to ring. "He said, let it go."

"Are you lonely, Daddy?" The rings filled the room with annoying shrillness. They shook up his lonely rooms, rooms he had left as he found them, stiff and unwelcoming. The living room could have been a waiting room in a medical office.

"I'm alone. That's different from lonely. I think I need a break from blame and being the bad guy. Do you understand, Princess? I am just tired. This is a time out for me."

"Time out? Like locking yourself away?"

"Yup. Add to that a little self-flagellating at night."

"But, Daddy, is there more? Are there things you can't tell me? Why is Mom going for a divorce? Didn't she know about you and the war and Andy and the underground?"

"She knew very little. She wasn't political in those days. I couldn't let her know my illegal activities or she would have been liable."

"Did she know I saved your life?"

"No. She didn't quite see it that way. She wasn't aware that I had been called up when we met. It was years later that she realized and it wasn't good. She accused me of knocking her up to stay out of the war."

"Did you?"

"I don't know." He studied the unplugged television set as if an answer might appear on its black screen.

"Daddy!"

"I loved her. I've always loved her. She was the best thing that ever happened to me. Sweet, good, simple and straight."

"But..."

"I wasn't honest. I couldn't tell her certain things. I wanted them left behind. I wanted you. I wanted you and the life we made, and most of all to make the fucking war history."

"Daddy, I don't want you to give up."

"To tell you the truth, Lily-Vanilli, I think I should go see my friend Andy. It's been a few years since we took the trails together. I need to get out of town for a while, have some fun."

"Will you promise to come back?"

"I'm yours Lily-Vanilla, forever and ever."

I wanted...no, *needed* to believe him. The phone had stopped ringing and I hardly noticed.

After I left Dad's, I went home to Mom who was frantic having called Marshall and Carrie knowing I was on the road. By the time I pulled into the driveway, she was about ready to call the State Police.

"For heaven's sake, what are you thinking driving around on these roads, what with the baby and the weather?"

I told her I was lucky enough to have been a small distance behind a snowplow.

"I just don't know what is happening to you, Lily!"

"I had to see Marshall and you weren't here and Brent was in a bad mood. Maybe I was hoping for a welcoming committee after the long ride home. No one here was happy to see me." Couldn't she see I needed a hug not a lecture?

"You came home a day early. How was I to know? And the very *thought* of you driving home in that terrible storm, which is not over, by the way! We are getting two more days of this—on and off. Where has your good judgment gone?"

"Speaking of judgment, I went to see Dad this morning. I needed some help with physics and, well, I just wanted to see how he was doing."

"And?"

"And you may think it's off with Dad, but I don't."

"It's over Lily. Over."

"Well, then you'll be happy to know he is going away—to ski in British Columbia."

She didn't even blink.

"That would make sense. He'll hook up with Andy Clarendon. The two of them were masters of making what was right, wrong, and what was wrong, right. Two peas in a pod."

"Did you know him?

"No. Just some of his history."

"I have decided I know nothing of history. Not *ours* anyway. We don't talk in this family. We're all in the dark, it's like living in a mystery novel. Who done what? What is real? What is not? What is what? For example, are you going to tell me about your boyfriend—your ongoing relationship with Nancy's dad? You didn't like *my* little secrets, why don't you talk about *yours*?"

"He's no secret and I don't like your attitude, Lily. You have had nothing but respect and love in this family."

"That's what you call it? My sister lives to insult me and my brother won't even bother to say hello!" I cried, realizing she didn't understand the constant criticism I took. "You should spend a day in my shoes." I grabbed my stomach.

Her expression changed. "Go lie down," she ordered.

"I won't."

"You must. Your baby can feel how upset you are, you're going to give him colic."

"Her," I said, wishing she would just put her arms around me.

"Mom, things feel weird with Marshall, too. We need to spend more time together this week, you understand that, right? I came over just to touch base with you."

"Well, thank you, Lily. I'm sorry if I was harsh. I do worry you know. I keep waiting for another lightning strike. It seems to be one thing after another these days."

"And what does that mean?"

Her hands went to her hips. "That means your sister has announced she will be moving to New York in September and your brother wants to drop out of school. Brent is all doom and gloom around the house. It's as if he'd like to dig a deep hole and stay in it. Our dear Mrs. Horner has had a stroke, a terrible thing. And I am worried about you. I know you're bound and determined to move in with Marshall come June, but I don't know, it just seems not right. It's all overwhelming, even the weather feels ominous, all those clouds waiting to bury us."

"You haven't mentioned Daddy."

"No. No, I haven't. That book is closed, Lily. Please. No point in trying to open it. You go on and love him as you always have. That is as it should be, although he doesn't deserve it. He plunders on, oblivious of those he hurts and ignores."

"I do love him. If you told me the true story from your point of view, maybe I could understand your anger, but all along I thought the separation was about alcohol and that's curable."

"It's not just about alcohol, it's about manipulation and deceit. Enough said. I am not going there with you. I will honor your loving him unconditionally. That's to your credit. I was never loved that way. I guess I never learned the art."

"Speaking of unconditional love, when did Mrs. Horner have a stroke?"

"Last week."

"How is she?"

"Irene's never going to be the same. No more smiles from that sweet lady. No more cinnamon buns. And that poor man! He is hovering over her day and night. Amelia has come home from wherever. She has brought the boy, what's-his-name?"

"Henry."

"Right, Henry. Hyper little boy, must be stressful."

I couldn't think about Irene Horner for long, I was too distracted, trying to figure out what to do with myself. Should I head right back to Marshall's and confront him about Nancy? Maybe call Nancy first and hear her point of view. Would that do more harm than good? I should get into my physics book. I knew the slippery hike across the street to visit to Mr. Horner and Amelia, would be appreciated, but didn't want to in the worst way. I finally decided to sort my clothes and decide what to keep at the trailer and what to leave at home? I went upstairs to see if I could find baggy clothes that would fit my new torso. What I needed were some of those stretch-banded pants that Mrs. Horner favored.

Tired and heavy, I soon fell on my bed, now Heather's bed, and tried to relax. But my head was tight with stories that had no endings. The sight of Marshall's arms around

Nancy kept showing up. I had to let it go. Tell myself that all that they said was true. Jealousy wasn't going to fix anything. But, I couldn't stop the nagging, gnawing feelings in the pit of my stomach. For a very full person, I was feeling empty. I wanted candy. I lusted for chocolate, a hot fudge sundae. Peanuts. Whipped cream.

The wind was picking up again. A steady shush of pines sounded beyond the windows, sweeping boughs whipping clumps of snow from the branches. It was a typical nor'easter, the storm building its strength again after each blow. How amazing that storms have eyes, I thought, that there is a peaceful heart at its center. I needed to find the same within myself.

After sorting my clothes, I took out my dastardly physics book—a text so abstract my mind got stuck in the grooves of its pages. I saw words like attraction, kinetic, catapult, vertical and horizontal and contemplated the formula, $KE - .5mv^2$ and saw what I hated most. Everything in physics is in code. I wanted the literal, not symbols. I didn't care if symbols made for pure science, they were hard and cold. I tried to relate the vocabulary to myself.

Attraction: I was *kinetically* attracted to Marshall when he touched me, and *catapulted* to another realm. My first response was *horizontal,* but now I am *vertical,* with a new life inside me, and everything *accelerating.* I am being forced to stretch and change as my body discovered *elasticity.*

No matter the metaphors, physics was going to remain my nemesis—one more impersonal foundation of knowledge; more formulas and abstractions to define the world, discussing matter as mass, trying to prove that a prescription determines everything. Does it all come down to this? Is my baby not a miracle or is she simply a by-product of nature?

Dr. Wolfe had turned me on to biology in high school using wonder. I remembered when he asked us if we didn't think it awesome that the earth's first rains continued to move the continents from one place to another; that they traveled around the globe, transforming into new forms, taking whatever shape they needed to, turning into mist or snow or ice or hail to do their work. He said that all the water that ever was, is all there will ever be. "There's no replacement. This is it, it's all we have. We are drinking the same water the dinosaurs drank, it is in our urine and growing our grass and not only do we ingest it, we become it, that after all our bodies are mostly water, we start our lives in water and are drawn to it forever after."

I pictured my baby swimming in her pouch of water, being nurtured by an ancient sea.

I was suddenly thirsty. I could have swallowed a gallon of water for Little Someone. For her, for me, even for Jesus. His last words were "I thirst," weren't they? I was thirsting, too. Am I different or am I just like everyone else? Do all people have such thirst? Instead of gaining wisdom, I felt more uninformed. No matter how much I learned, the less I knew.

25

The storm went on but I did not. With the family cars needed by Mom and Heather and the roads so tricky, it was inconvenient to go back to Marshall's. Also, his days were broken up with commitments, so I waited for a day when he could be devoted to me. I said as much to him and he agreed, "Perhaps that will be best. By then, my surprise for you should be ready."

A surprise? I thought. This was not like Marshall. I wasn't sure I wanted any more surprises.

On the third blustery day with the sun finally peeping out of the clouds, I heard a vehicle turn into the driveway with the very reverend himself delivering his *surprise* to our door. It came in the form of a pale blue Toyota Corolla station wagon. I ran out to examine it up close, forgetting my coat, my boots, my mittens.

"Our first car!" Marshall announced. "The chrome is slightly rusted, but it is as solid as a tank." I could hear the pride in his voice. He held the passenger door ajar as I climbed in. Mom came running out with my coat and hat. I laughed as I slid onto the furry sheepskin seat covers. I ran my hand over the dashboard, took hold of the steering wheel, then checked out the rear view mirror. Something was lodged in the back seat, something blue and green, with little yellow ducks in rows. A baby seat! He had bought me a baby seat. Nothing in the world could have made me happier.

"I want you to pack a bag and come home with me. Is that all right with you, Mrs. Woodhouse?" he asked.

"Of course it is," Mom said, obviously feeling my happiness and maybe even having a moment of her own. "But, come inside for a moment."

Before Marshall sat down, Mom was putting on some tea and cutting up her fresh brown bread. She put a tub of cream cheese at Marshall's fingertips and smiled.

I ran upstairs to retrieve my physics book and a clean pair of jeans, my heart pounding with excitement. The snow had stopped. Marshall was sitting at the Woodhouse kitchen counter, with Mom instinctually serving him, and we had a new, old car in the driveway that included a bumper seat to ensure our baby's safety. What more could I ask?

With bag in hand, I joined them in the kitchen. Mom said, "I have a little addition for your car. Hold on, now."

She went to the highest shelf in the pantry closet and pulled down a plastic shopping bag and handed it to me. I just knew it was holding one of her creations, my hands quickly dug in and withdrew the contents and out came the most beautiful angora wool bunting one could imagine, with squares claiming every color of a pastel palette. In the center was a yellow duck that almost matched those on the car seat. It was soft, yummy evidence that she was thinking about us every day. After all, how many hours had it taken to create such a treasure?

I pressed it to my face and almost smelled talcum powder and baby oil. "Mom, how can I ever thank you?" I asked.

"You just make sure that this bunting goes with your special bundle whenever you get in the car. Okay?"

I thought that my heart might burst. Then another special moment happened, when Mom wrapped me in her arms and said, "You will always be my baby, Lily, even when your hair is turning gray."

As we left I asked Marshall if I could drive and he quickly denied me the privilege.

"I am driving, Lily. You are carrying the baby and that's all you need to do right now."

I conceded. "Maybe I should get myself a rocker and twiddle my thumbs for the next four months."

"I would not object," he said.

"Marshall, thank you so much for the baby seat. It's really cute and really thoughtful."

"Well, I cannot tell a lie, Lily. The baby seat is from Nancy. She bought it when her father was cleaning up the car."

"Nancy?" Fear took a hold of my neck. He was seeing Nancy when he wasn't seeing me.

"Yes, She was there when I met her father. Your mother, as well."

"What do you mean her father was cleaning up the car? Why would he be cleaning our car?" I asked.

"He had taken it as a settlement for someone's debts. He gave me an excellent deal."

My heart was cracking, "Gee, that was nice," I lied. I would have rather he had made a terrible deal than to have to thank my mother's lover or my so-called best friend. I wanted to return the baby seat.

I didn't want my family car to come from that man. Worse, I hated to learn that the car seat was Nancy's idea. Nancy was not part of this family, my family, our family, not related to us in any way. The greatest flaw in our friendship had been her criticism of Marshall. I wanted to tell him that she had called him a con man when they first met, that she did not want me to have our baby.

I was quiet as we drove. At one point Marshall leaned over and shook his finger under my chin and asked, "Cat got your chins?"

He saw then, that fat was beginning to emerge where my chin used to be.

I tried to joke, "You mean my wattle?"

"You are starting to show," he said.

"Starting?" I asked. "I've been showing for months." I was probably the least attractive woman he knew. Maybe he wasn't looking. Maybe I was only a container now.

"Not that much."

"Well, it's true. I have to wear different clothes."

"Hmmm. Should we go buy a few? Maybe we should take a ride over to Claremont or Springfield."

"Maybe, but why so far?"

"Yo would have more choices in a larger market," he explained.

And you wouldn't have to explain my existence to anyone, I thought.

We shopped and when we got back to the trailer, I threw the bags of stretch pants and big shirts on the chair, and collapsed on the couch. He didn't join me but went to the kitchenette and opened some cans of chili and cut up the fresh bread we had bought. He was starving and so was I.

After downing the beans and the buttery salted bread, he pulled a pad of paper out of his briefcase while I rinsed the dishes. His mind was far away as he wrote. His scrawl, dark and angled, spread like spilled needles across his yellow legal pad. Sometimes he reached for the Bible, to find a direct quote.

"Strange says you know the Holy Book from cover to cover," I said. "I'm surprised you still look things up."

"His name is David. How many times do I have to tell you?"

"Oh, sorry, I forgot. You know he says you're a genius," I said, leaving out the fucking part.

"David is in my prayers. God will help him if he just asks."

Strange was not about to bow his head. I knew that. What I was most worried about was that Strange would disappear from us forever. I missed him, missed our easy conversations, his teasing and his caring.

Later, I made our bed, as it was the most comfortable and least intrusive place I could hang out. I smoothed out the teddy bears as I tucked in the sheets. "I am going to replace these sheets the next time I go to the store," I said.

"Waste not want not," he answered.

"Is that from the Bible?" I asked.

He sighed. "No, Lily. That is Shakespeare. You are not the first person to get the two mixed up."

I felt my wattle redden like an embarrassed turkey.

"Well, I'm pooped. Goodnight sweet prince," I said, letting him know I wasn't a complete fool, that I knew a little Shakespeare myself. "Good night, good night, May I not kill thee with my cherishing," I grumbled. "Good night, good night. My body knows such sweet sorrow," and I fell down on the bed with my arms out to each side.

He rose and came to me, planting a very gentle kiss on my lips.

"All right, Juliet. You go ahead and rest. I have work to do here."

I was asleep before he returned to his paperwork. My dreams did not serve me well. I was flying away, with no power over my flight as I was a balloon rising then being taken with the wind to nowhere. Higher and higher I went until I was sure I would burst and the landing would leave me in little fragments. I woke myself up. I turned and found him at my side.

"Marshall, I was flying too high and I was alone and scared."

"You are safe, Lily. I will take care of you," he said, his large, strong hands bringing me back to earth.

When morning broke, he was up before I awakened. Coffee was perking in the metal pot and he had his papers spread out once again.

"You must not have slept," I said. "You're in the same place I left you."

"Have you forgotten your dream, Lily?"

Then I remembered and thought how strange the night had been. Something terribly important was missing. It was the loving.

Wrapped in a blanket and feeling a little clumsy, I poured myself a cup of coffee, sighing as it warmed my insides. I smiled at him, "Gee, I think we are acting like an old married couple," I said.

"And why is that?" he asked.

"Having you put on the coffee and getting to work before I am even up and at it."

"Is that the way it was in your home?"

"Not exactly. Mom is an early riser. Dad, too. She made the coffee, though. It's harder for me to see them separated now than before. I don't know why."

"Marriage is a sacrament, a vow, made before God and never meant to be broken. They need to turn their problems over to God and trust in His love and power to right whatever is wrong."

"I know," I said. "I wish I could make a dent in their thinking, but they seem to be unwilling to budge."

"The Lord works in strange and mysterious ways. He may surprise you. Keep praying, Lily."

"Are you going to kiss me this morning?" I asked.

He rose, and I leaned into him.

"I can feel our baby," he said.

"You can?"

"I think so."

"Maybe that's just my belly."

He stepped back. "Want some breakfast now?" he asked.

I wanted much more but a voice inside my head told me to settle for breakfast.

26

School was a better place when I returned after the long snowy weekend. I was happy to see my roommates, happy to crack the books, happy to do my research for the papers I had to write for American Lit and Soc. II. This semester sociology was elevated from least favorite to favorite class due to a very cool instructor named Dr. Dennis Quinn. His mop of curly, gray hair, seas of freckles and casual attitude eased us into learning from each other.

He divided the class up into "think tanks" of magic sevens. Quinn, (he liked to be addressed this way) believed in sevens. Each week he'd throw out a topic and we had the following week to look at it from a variety of perspectives: personal experience, statistical evidence, tradition, hearsay and authoritative sources like religious principles, professional expertise and the law. Note, seven perspectives in seven days.

He chose deliberately controversial subjects and we drew slips that specified what point of view we had to research to prepare for the discussions. I found myself lying awake at night thinking about what I would say to issues such as gun ownership, the death penalty, monogamy, homosexuality, plutocracy and determinism. These were surely the headiest considerations of my short life and they pushed me to think in new ways.

I learned answers to questions I had never thought to ask. For example, I didn't know that one person commits suicide every forty seconds in this country, and there would be more, but we have laws that prohibit assisted suicide.

Some old folks beg for help to end their lives and yet doctors refuse on the grounds that it's against medical principles. I thought of Irene Horner, and how much her life was compromised by being pulled away from death's door.

When a student said that death should be a right in the case of terminal disease, Quinn asked, "But isn't life itself a terminal illness?"

We explored the thin line between life and death. Is a person really alive who is comatose and being breathed by a machine? Then again, does anyone ever choose to breathe in the first place? It is more like we are breathed. Certainly we can't hold our breath for very long before air pushes itself inside us. If we are being breathed in the first place, who are we to say when life should start or stop? Doesn't every cell, every organism every creature have a beginning, a middle, and an end? Could we say this is a divine order and therefore perfect? I loved the discussions about such things, but didn't speak out because I was more interested in how others thought.

Quinn welcomed questions and allowed them to be explored at great lengths, lengths that stretched across the brief hour of allotted time. Coffee had a way of following his classes, as we continued to hammer out our ideas. One day Sue Beth, a Mormon, was holding forth on her church's position on polygamy. She was the only daughter of her father's second wife, and the sister of four other daughters by his first. She loved both her mothers and thought her father was fair with all his kids and his three wives. "It doesn't seem wrong to me," she claimed.

"Yeah, but coffee and Coke do?" a guy named Peter asked. "You forbid stimulants but not a man's appetite for variety?" He was a know-it-all but he sure added to any discussion.

The other kids at the table shifted in their seats and looked at him menacingly. I noticed a group at the table next to us had grown silent.

He wouldn't back down. "Seriously, Sue Beth, how could you not wonder why your dad has three women and the rest of the world has one? How is that okay with you? Can you have three husbands?"

She reddened. "That is forbidden." Ignoring his commentary on coffee she took up the cause of multiple marriages. "The rest of the world is getting divorced, almost fifty percent of them. How great is that?" Sue Beth asked. "Plus the rest of the world is not America, with their anti-Mormon prejudices. Oriental and Indian societies, Hindus, Africans, Arabs, exotic tribes, the whole world, including Jews have multiple wives."

"No way with the Jews," Peter said. "They gave that up too many years ago to count."

"Well, I think that love is never wrong as long as it's responsible," Sue Beth said.

I was fascinated. No Mormons lived in Purgatory, no Jews or Hindus either. Not that I knew of, anyway.

I think what made me comfortable with Quinn's approach was that he reminded me of Dad. Like Dad, he had been an activist back in the sixties, but unlike Dad he had worked in the civil rights movement alongside Martin Luther King, Jr. He began as a Freedom Rider, putting his white self in a bus filled with blacks and traveled south, dangerously challenging old prejudices. He was also took part in the freedom walk across Selma, Alabama's bridge.

He admitted he was young and innocent. He said he didn't know, at the point where the marchers stopped, if they had won or lost the cause. He didn't even know they were making history. "But we are all making history as we live our lives, aren't we? That is so if we participate in the struggles for justice and peace or not. Each generation gets called; there's plenty of opportunity to choose your cause. Not choosing is a choice unto itself. Ultimately you must get on board. Take responsibility. You want to be able to tell your kids you were on the right side, don't you?"

He called King's death, *inevitable*. "Martyrdom is a necessary factor when it comes to the success of a cause. Look at Jesus. Look at Lincoln and look at Kennedy!

"They were all sacrificial lambs for justice, for the liberation of man. It has always been and always will be. In your lifetimes, monks soaked themselves in kerosene and became burning symbols in the protests against American involvement in the Vietnam."

I thought about mentioning those who gave up family and friends rather than participate in a war they found unjust.

In Quinn's classroom the idea was to argue everything. We were becoming philosophers after only a month of his classes—dialectics. It was so much fun.

He must have sensed my hunger to know. Sometimes he would wink at me, others he would ask my opinion whether I dared raise my hand or not. "And just what do you think of that Ms. Woodhouse?" he'd ask. I was naïve enough to think he thought I had a provocative opinion.

One day he showed us a painting called *The Scream*. "Like this?" he asked. "Want it hanging on your wall?" It was the ghastly face of a terrified person who bore no resemblance to any one I knew.

No one did.

"Well it's worth millions of dollars," he said. "Like it any more now?"

"Not for my living room," someone said.

"For my bank account maybe," joked someone else.

"Some say it's the artist's depiction of his sister's mental breakdown and her institutionalization, maybe it's about his own struggle with insanity."

This led to a discussion about institutionalizing people against their wishes. A boy named Peck Altman said, "There is no such thing as insanity."

Quinn asked him why he believed this, and Peck was ready to explain. "What there are, are different realities," he said. "One person sees and hears things that others don't. That doesn't make them crazy. Maybe they are the sane ones, the ones who are able to see what we can't."

I had thought that many times myself.

Quinn sat back while Peck told us about the aunt who spoke with angels and saw messages in a bowl of soup. "She was the joke of the family until she warned us that Grandpa was going to die. She said a bird came into his house that morning and flew around until it broke its neck on a window pane. That was a sure sign, according to her. But, the thing was, Grandpa died that night."

"So this incident of synchronicity and superstition taught you that insanity does not exist?" Quinn asked. "Have you ever visited a mental hospital, Peck? It might be an eye-opening experience."

"No, man, I haven't had to go, not yet, anyway," he laughed.

"I did," Steve said quietly. "My old man went bonkers after 'Nam. He felt red ants under his skin, said they were eating him from the inside out. He was screaming and begging us to stop them. He seemed pretty crazy to me. He did better at war than coming home to us."

"Some people are a little nuts and some are completely gonzo," said Chloe in the red shoes. I don't think mental illness is always easy to recognize and I don't think most people who have it should be put away unless they are dangerous to themselves or someone else."

"Well, ladies and gentlemen, let's start by listing all the words we have just used to describe divergent behavior," Quinn suggested.

He picked up a piece of chalk and wrote on the board "Crazy, gonzo, bonkers, nuts. Let's think of some more."

They called out, "Manic, off the wall, idiot, lulu bird, weird, sick, scary, schizo, freak, dangerous, whacko, braindead, shit-for-brains, sicko, demented..." The list went on and on.

He stood back and looked at the list. "Not a pretty way to name a human who may be ill, is it?" he asked. "Perhaps you will consider using the term *mentally ill*, today."

The think tank's function worked in many ways for me, but most effectively it taught proficient ways to do research. Microfiche, computers and archives I never knew existed became my personal indulgences. Yes, the library was my haunt. Its quiet seriousness; its depths and even its scent became home to me. I would inhale it as I walked through the doors making my way to the same spot. That carrel near the far windows should have had my name engraved on it.

Homework for Quinn became my obsession. The challenge was to discern fact from opinion and the more technical the language the more difficult to sort. I realized I was a sucker for high language. I was dazzled by sentences like this one from *Lives of a Cell*: "There are neural centers for generating, spontaneously, numberless hypotheses about the facts of life. We store up information the way cells store energy. When we are lucky enough to find a direct match between a receptor and a fact, there is a deep explosion in the mind; the idea suddenly enlarges, rounds up, bursts with new energy, and begins to replicate."

I was in the library one morning, lost in a book, when Quinn approached me. "Hey you," he said. "Mind if I join you?"

He pulled a library chair away from a nearby table, sat down and crossed one khaki covered leg over the other. His dark green and brown hiking boots looked well-worn as did the elbows of his holey crew necked sweater.

"Of course not," I said, flattered to have the great Quinn choosing to talk to me, when there were so many slimmer more intelligent students he could have honored.

"How are you enjoying the class?" he smiled

"I'm loving it! It's the most stimulating course I've ever taken," I babbled, that damnation of color rising to my cheeks.

"Why do you think that is?" he asked.

His hands cradled his head as he leaned back to hear my answer.

I took my time before I responded. He waited patiently.

"Probably because you ask us to think, and we get to decide for ourselves how far we want to examine each topic. In other classes the professors pronounce the truth and all we're asked to do is regurgitate it. You haven't graded our papers, and, still, I want to do every assignment. I'm learning a lot. Learning how to think, for example."

"Your energy is a great asset to the class."

"*My* energy? Wow! All I know is it's really important to me because I don't have much time left before I have to leave. This may be my last chance to take a course like yours. You have taught me a way to keep learning after I leave."

"That's not good to hear," he mumbled into his chest where his chin had lodged itself.

"Oh, I meant that in the best possible way. I love doing research," I tried to explain. "Of course I'll miss the dialogue."

He shook his head. "I meant that you are planning to leave school. Is there a reason?"

"Well, I think the reason is obvious. My baby is coming in June. That will be the end of my college years, I'm afraid."

"A baby? Well, good for you. You might as well procreate while you're young and have that noble act out of the way. But surely it doesn't have to be the end of your education! Life is an education unto itself, and there are many ways to get a degree later. For anyone who loves learning, education is almost mandatory. It's like food; a true student will feel starved without it. I hope you'll find a way, Ms. Woodhouse. You know your baby will benefit as well."

"My husband is a minister and I'll have to work by his side. It's a fulltime job, I'm told."

"Your husband, a minister?"

I nodded.

"I see. You're married, then?"

"Well, we're not married, officially, not yet, but in God's eyes we are. And those are really the only eyes that count."

He lowered himself from his perch on the back two legs of his chair and leaned toward me. "It's *your* eyes that matter most. Has the course widened your vision?"

I tried not to be offended, even though I now realized he had picked me out as a bumpkin and no doubt this explained his interest in me.

Giggles broke out just beyond us. I looked over his shoulder at the group of students exiting the library. Their pony tails waved as they gossiped on their way through the wide metal library doors, a gaggle of girls enjoying each other's company; sweatshirts and jeans, covering their slim bodies, so unlike my own.

Inadvertently, I checked my watch, speculating the amount of time I might have left before my next class. I touched my backpack for no reason at all.

"Got to go?" he asked.

"Not yet," I said.

"So? Tell me more. What else are you taking from the course, other than the lack of constant testing?"

I tried to put it in words. "The thing that comes up over and over again, for me, is that we have so many choices and yet so few of them are right for everyone. How can the world work if we can never agree, if there is no one true Truth to bring us together? With all the approaches we take to each question we haven't come up with an absolute truth. What does this prove?"

"It's entertaining!" Quinn laughed. "Imagine a world where we all had the same answers. Why would we bother to think, to grow, to test the waters, to imagine? How dull it would be!" He ran both his hands through his hair as he tipped back again on the rear legs of his chair.

"And how much safer and saner it would be," I said. "I'm still hoping to discover a Divine plan."

"The obscure, the oblique, the transformative, the ineffable, these are the essences of art, of cultural evolution. The mystery of life is the great seducer. Without it we would have no philosophers, scientists, no rabbis or rebels."

"I know a number of people that turn everything over to God and are better for it," he smiled.

He leaned forward, tipping his chair back into place, all four legs now planted squarely on the floor.

"That's one way to do a life. The beauty of it all is that you get to choose. You can attach whatever meaning you want to your life, to the events of your life. Remember those kids who watched *Wheel of Fortune* everyday looking for word clues to direct them how to live their lives? To me, the best part of their story is that they found what they needed and lived by it. Some have stars, some tea leaves, some find God."

"I think God is quite a stretch from tea leaves."

"As you wish," Quinn said. "And now young lady," he said slapping his knee, "I am sure I am taking up too much of your time."

He stood, buttoned his jacket, arranged his scarf and said, "I'd like to talk to you again in a few weeks. Your theistic question is probably not unique within the classroom. In fact, I will broach it? Would that suit you?"

"Really? I thought we were already doing that by addressing religious views."

"Religious views as they apply to organized religious communities. These don't necessarily represent personal belief systems. The beliefs of others are rarely as interesting as one's own."

"If you have any," I said.

"Don't drop out of school, Ms. Woodhouse. If there's a will there's a way. See me. I will help in any way I can."

He extricated his long body from the chair and I stood at the same time, noticing his eyes travel straight to my belly. My hands went there simultaneously, and he looked up and said gently, "It happens so naturally and yet it's always amazing, isn't it?"

I wanted to thank him. I wanted him to stay longer so I could explain how hard it had been to claim my child, this amazing life squirming her way into the messy world of good and evil, love and hate and all its variables. I wanted to tell him that I knew she wanted to be born.

That she was already dancing, already asking to be loved and nurtured and already making demands of me.

I stayed at the library for a while gathering notes on pacifism, learning that all wars have a way of separating the doves from the hawks. The Vietnam War was only one such war and I wondered if I would have marched against the government or stood firm out of loyalty. I asked myself if I would I have been a Tory or a Patriot? Would I have housed runaway slaves or burned my master's fields? What would I be willing to die for? Kill for? Be tortured for? And I prayed I wouldn't be tested.

That little visit with Professor Quinn was my first personal encounter with any professor.

I saw most of them as unapproachable. After our exchange, I felt more connected to him. When I called Dad and told him about our conversation, I must have sounded enthusiastic because he said he wished he could be with me. "That's my idea of what education should be. Let the instructor step aside and make way for the students."

When I described the class to Marshall during a late night call, he reminded me that all the answers to our questions are written and real and at our fingertips. He also told me to be sure to bring my Bible to class because there was only one man who ever knew it all and his name wasn't Quinn. "This is the very thing I feared for you, Lily. I am afraid that all the intellect in the world will not make you any happier or any wiser. You may end up missing the true meaning of life."

"I know the meaning of life, Marshall. Little Someone reminds me of it every minute of every day," I said, and then added, "I love you".

I can't remember if he echoed my words or not.

27

Ides of March 1990
Dear Lil,

I have given up trying to reach you. How come you aren't in your room? Are you off partying? Only kidding, but remember, I don't know about you. You are not that predictable after all.

The proverbial shit is hitting the fan around here. I am so ready to go to New York I may leave early. Dad has run away from home. Mom is still seeing the dork face. Brent is the invisible man. The last time I heard him speak was when we watched Kurt Browning skate for the gold in Halifax. He's a fan. At least we know he loves something or someone.

School is boring and I am afraid that Strange is up to no good. He has lost his sense of humor, totally. He's become a night crawler, taking off to places unknown and I can see he's hurting all over. I have no idea how to help. I'm afraid he's going to do something really, really stupid, like take bad drugs or get AIDS or shoot himself. I don't want to encourage his leaving town while he's still so messed up. I mean what will happen to the dude? I wish I could let all the gays out of the closet here in Purgatory so he had some decent playmates.

I'm stashing away money and sketching like a future fashionista every day. I show my stuff to Strange and he shows a depth of insight by saying, "Fuckin' A," or "nice shitinski" or "get rid of the foo-foo." I prefer his insults to a deadening silence. His only other friend is iMac, who lives in a blueberry plastic box. He toys with him all the time. I'd love to see what he writes, but that's top secret.

Our relationship was a hell of a lot better when Brent was around. I still don't know why he's knocked him out of his life like this. Pretty soon I could be knocked off too, I suppose. Despite the circumstances, I've been thinking it might be a brilliant move if he came to New York with me. I would have a built-in friend and a guy around, well sort-of, and he would find a world where he wasn't so strange. Come to think of it, maybe that wouldn't work for him because you know how much he gets off on strangeness. In NY he would have to work harder at it. I don't know if I should mention it to him. What do you think? I mean he's not interested in me as a girl, but we usually do get on pretty well. And New York is nothing but artists and writers and gay men. He'll probably fit right in and love being part of the scene.

I am counting the days 'til Easter and your homecoming. You are going to stay with us, right? I mean that little trailer isn't exactly your home yet, is it? We need you. I need you. Mom needs you and you just have to come stay for a while at least.

Mostly miserable,
Heather

Heather's letter sounded desperate, but, despite that, I wasn't persuaded to go home. My role of family liaison, of dutiful ombudsman was over. I was better off at school. Not that I really fit in, since I was more of a voyeur than a college girl. My roommates treated me like an older sister rather than a friend, and it may have been my imagination, but even Carrie was becoming kind of distant. Of course, she was partying on weekends and involved with her sorority activities while I was growing fat. This goes without mentioning choices she made in the past, choices she may not want to be reminded of by the sight of my ever expanding self.

Colleges aren't designed for expectant mothers unless you focus on the academics. That was fine with me. It was a welcome escape from counting the minutes to the next phase of my life, which was starting to look less and less like a fairy tale. Thank heavens Marshall had found a little ski house for us, and thank heavens Mom and Dad were being kind, if not happy, about the prospect of a new baby in the family.

I worked daily to put Nancy out of my mind. It helped that Marshall called me more often, and that each time we spoke we were sharing more than our love talk. He spoke of the need for musicians, the numbers that came and went on Sundays and his plans for the future, while I spoke of grades and stresses and Little Someone's progress. I made a point not to describe how my mind was waking up and finding a world I hadn't known existed.

When I wasn't looking, my baby bump turned into a mountain. I wasn't walking like a duck yet, but Little Someone's existence could no longer be in doubt. What I hadn't anticipated was that my whole body seemed to thicken along with my abdomen. Dr. Bomson told me it was time to be cautious about salted or sweet snacks. Carrots and celery were not offered in the vending machines, however, and although I tried to eat less, potato chips seemed to satisfy my needs between meals. Little Someone was doing better than I. She appeared to weigh at least three pounds and was evidently going to be tall, like we Woodhouses tend to be. She kicked her little feet as she listened to music. I wished I still had my tutus, those lesser victims of the fire.

The second week of April arrived and I was ready for a trip south. Classes ended on Wednesday and Marshall was set to pick me up. He had negotiated my visit with Mom, suggesting I stay with him first and then stay overnight with the family on Easter weekend. His reasoning was an Easter dawn service, followed by an egg rolling contest and then a church luncheon, would not togetherness make. I understood. Easter Sunday had to be about the church and not me. Also, even though I knew no one in the congregation, I knew I would be quite conspicuous, and that my condition might call for explanations we were not prepared to make. Anyway, in little more than eight weeks our marriage would be public and publicly celebrated with our baby in tow.

When I told my roommates he was coming to get me, they were excited to meet him. They kept checking the window for the *blue-mobile*. The truth was, I couldn't wait to show him off, the real thing; the father, husband, beautiful man of the cloth. They would see why I was willing to stay home and study, while they were busy searching for their own versions of Mr. Right.

"Here he comes!" Jennifer said. We all ran to the window. The Toyota cruised to a stop right in front of the building. He must have felt our stares because he looked up as he got out of the car, a prince arriving to take his princess home. We waved and smiled and he did the same, all those white teeth shining, He stretched and we watched his body straightening itself after the long ride.

"Yummy! He doesn't look like any minister I ever met," Jennifer said to Sarah.

"Looks more like a movie star!" Sarah agreed. "He can save me any day!"

"He's gorgeous!" Ellie said.

Possessiveness swept over me. I wanted him all to myself. He was claimed. If I could have put a collar and leash on him and walked him back to the car, right at that moment, I would have.

The girls carried on when he came up to our suite, too. He excused himself for invading their space.

"Anytime!" Sarah offered. "You aren't really a minister, are ya?" she asked.

I couldn't wait to leave. I had planned to use our precious time to show him the campus. We made our goodbyes and I gave each of my roommates a perfunctory hug.

Soon, Marshall and I were tooling around the *shoebox* dorms where a bunch of kids had gathered on the green for the Springfest. This was the weekend when students exhibited ways to participate on campus. It was rah-rah everything from fencing to the campus TV station. Two kids were demonstrating fly-casting on the east lawn, some were dressed in R.O.T.C. uniforms; others were selling shirts of green and gold proclaiming the school's logo.

"Isn't it great?" I asked.

"A playschool as far as I can see," he said, barely looking.

New legs of forsythia danced in the breeze. Tulips and daffodils were trying their best to rise for the show. Spring cannot be any more appreciated or frustrating than it is in Vermont. It's such predictably unpredictable weather. But that day we were blessed with clear skies and a warm sun.

I directed my handsome chauffeur through the city with its busy streets and funky shops, to the shores of Lake Champlain. It lay in a brilliant blue glare, frigid of course, as the waters had just given up their last slivers of ice and the banks were still ridding themselves of patches of snow. I told him, "The beauty of the lake is that it's still a public place and open to everyone. Burlington has a philosophy that keeps the waterfront accessible to everyone."

We looked at it for at least twenty seconds and I realized my chatter was too noisy and too eager. His lack of interest was clear. At this point, I decided to abort my role as tour guide and suggested we could skip the local sights. He made no protest as he revved the motor and turned the wheel to head out of town as quickly as possible. I checked my disappointment by thinking it was me he wanted and not a view of Burlington. He wasn't the only one anxious to get our lives started, away from the distractions and long separations.

Alone in the cocoon of the car, I began to relax and enjoy sharing the air he breathed. Our intimate space was just right for the quiet togetherness I had been craving. It wasn't hard to pretend we were married with our baby behind us strapped into her car seat, my husband and I driving home, content and proud. I looked at his profile and remembered the magnet that had pulled me from everything I had known, to the edge of what I could not.

"You are very pregnant, now," he said.

"Full to bursting!" I agreed. "No matter what the doctor says, I think this is going to be a big baby. It feels like there are two or more in there."

"Twins?" he asked, and I could hear the fear.

"No. I'm just kidding. Dr. Bomson said it's only one, a perfectly normal baby. He also said I'm the one who's growing too much. I guess I'll have to start starving myself. Let lettuce rule."

"You must put the baby first. Eating less will mean less nutrition for it."

"Don't worry. She's on her own now. She takes what she needs and isn't as dependent on me as she was three months ago. What do you think of Hannah for a name?"

"Hannah is Biblical. I like that. But I do not think she was a happy woman."

"Why?"

"She had difficult choices to make. Her husband's second wife was fertile and she was not. She conceived only after she prayed to God to give her a son, and that went along with a promise that she would sacrifice the child to God."

"Well, Marshall, what has changed? Look at how many women are still doing that. Think of all the mothers who wrap their sons in the flag and send them off to war. Anyway, I'm not stuck on a name. If you don't like Hannah, there are plenty of other names to draw on from that old book. How about Jezebel or Salome?"

"Please, Lily. I do not think so," he said. "And by the way it is not an *old* book; it is as new as when it was written.

"Which was a long time after Christ, and by a bunch of men with an agenda."

"Lily, do not do this."

"Oh, Marshall, don't be so serious. I am just trying to make conversation."

At least that's what I think I said. Why was I being so provocative? Was it to prove something to myself? Was it out of boredom? I knew he had no sense of humor when it came to the Bible.

We were on the road for about thirty minutes when I had to stop for a pee break. At the next exit, we got off the highway and found what looked like a gas station, a relic from the fifties, with rusty red pumps, vestiges of lettering on the sides and surely not capable of serving gas. Fortunately, the ramshackle building still had a working toilet available. I ran to the side of the building where a sign said LADIES. The floor tiles were broken, the seat stained from cigarettes, but nevertheless existent, and although the door to the stall's hook was missing its eye, I didn't care. I made use of the bowl gratefully squatting and trying not to touch a thing, or see the spider webs.

When I came back to the car, Marshall was talking to the old man who ran the place. "Got a new'un on the way, looks like," the old man said.

"Yes! Soon, Lord willing," Marshall smiled. "Thank you for letting us use your facilities. God bless you."

"God bless ya' yerseff, son," the old man said, as I got back in the car.

It occurred to me that *we* hadn't used the facilities, it was *my* bladder that needed emptying and it was *me* that should have received the old man's blessing because that place should have been boarded up.

"We are going to take the alternate route home, would you like that?" the blessed one asked, as if he already knew my answer. "We are going to see our house today," he announced.

"You're kidding!" I said. "Oh, that would be wonderful, as long as there's a decent toilet nearby."

"Are you still uncomfortable?" he asked.

"I'm good," I said.

I realized he had probably been distracted by his plans to show me our house. Now the prospect of seeing our love nest was enough to preoccupy me. We slipped into reverie, the two of us, amidst the chartreuse spring buds and the red twigs waking up the landscape. It asked nothing of us but to appreciate the newness of life. Having the baby at the start of summer would be perfect. It meant I could be outside with her, wheel her here and there and we could discover nature together alongside the other new critters in the neighborhood. She turned over, her little foot skittering across my stretched belly. *Love you*, I thought.

Vermont is aptly named. She's graced with verdant everythings; her pasturelands, old hills and forests, everything in her landscape is seeped in green. Well, except for mud, the rundown barns, empty silos and corroding farm equipment. They tell the rest of the story. A lot of Vermonters were once prosperous farmers, but now too many of their progeny are poor, unless they sold out to the newer green, the green bucks of those who buy in, people from New York and Connecticut looking for a Disney version of rural.

We slowed to a stop at an intersection that said YIELD on all four corners. On the right was a little white cottage with a large front porch where a baby sat in a playpen beside its mother. She was reading and slowly rocking in a bright blue rocker. The porch floor was painted the color of slate, with its outer edges tucked in by white Victorian balusters some might have thought too grand for the little house. I thought them a great addition. They gave the house personality. Filigree trimmed the rooftops, too, hanging like musical notes. A stone chimney climbed the far side, and all in all, it looked like a painting by Thomas Kinkade. Heather would have gagged at the thought, but I wanted to move in. I waved at the woman, who had caught me staring. She lowered her eyes.

"Are we almost there?" I asked, turning back to Marshall.

"Soon," he said.

Soon seemed like light years as we drove down roads I had never seen before. At a non-descript street marked Howard's Lane, before an array of multicolored mailboxes, Marshall swerved to the left and we began to climb, passing a lean-to cabin, with a metal shed, and then two A-frame houses sitting like tents on cement pads, the land around them left raw, untended. Beyond these, the road lost its stretch of macadam and our ride grew bumpier. We continued to climb another three hundred yards or so and then a sweep of distance opened the landscape, and tiers of mountains rose, turning from green to blue to lavender-gray.

"Home!" Marshall exclaimed as he turned to see my reaction.

On my right, the angle of a rust colored roof rose above a dark line of firs. A narrow driveway led to a brake of birch trees where a startled squirrel leapt from the branches, from one to another, then another, causing the still naked branches to nod hello.

I really didn't know where we were.

"Home," he said again.

"But where are we?" I asked, hoping my voice was not giving away my disappointment.

"We are in Weathersfield. You're looking at Mt. Ascutney over there."

"I mean, is there a village close by where I can buy milk or eggs?"

"Five minutes or so, by car, maybe ten or fifteen by bicycle. A country store."

"But Woodbury is so far from here, Marshall. Purgatory is even further."

I couldn't pretend. It wasn't in me.

"Come on, why don't we go inside, you will see how nice it is," he said confidently.

I maneuvered my body from the car and carefully placed each foot solidly on the ground as we climbed the rocky grade. Beyond the trees, the house was decent enough. It had two big picture windows on either side of the door, and a faded pink and blue wreath on a dark green door that said, *Welcome.* (Definitely not a Leslie Woodhouse creation!) A filthy mat lay rotting on the front step, where some well-used sneakers were soaking up a piece of the afternoon's sunlight.

Marshall put the key in the lock, rattled it around a bit and managed to open the door. A whiff of insect repellant hit me, or was it moth balls? Or was it old laundry? Inside was a big living room with a brick fireplace, high wooden rafters and wide plank floors. A handwoven rag rug, worthy of Mom's respect, covered some of the well-worn boards but it needed a good cleaning. On the far left, the wall facing the windows, sat an opened Bible on a music stand. Above it was a little painting of Jesus in Mary's arms and a pot of very dry geranium roots waited hopelessly at its feet. Not far away were family photos including a picture of a woman I had seen before, and in her arms, a younger rendition of the boy who could not speak but sang like an angel. Two rocking chairs, still wearing their Cracker Barrel price tags, sat on either side of the stand,

To the rear was a pine clad kitchen with rustic cabinets and open shelves filled with dishes and glassware. The double sink had curtainless windows above it that looked into the woods. Cups, filled with dirt, sat on the sill where little green shoots were trying to emerge from the soil. I opened the fridge and a sour smell made me step back and cover my nose.

To the right was our bedroom with a big sleigh bed and a chest of drawers. A wicker basket held some dirty laundry; towels were draped on pegs on the wall. A sweat shirt lay rumpled on the mattress.

I touched a towel. "Someone or something is still living here," I said.

"Yes. A nephew. He is here for another month or so."

We opened the walk-in closet that led to the bathroom where we discovered a Jacuzzi. I thought a child would be lost in such a tub, but I said nothing.

In the rear of the living room a set of stairs led to a loft with a king sized mattress on the floor and boxes and boxes of Legos, video tapes and plastic bins marked, Do Not Touch. I supposed the time would come when we would need a guest room and this might do. There was no den or alcove for a baby on the first floor but she would sleep in our room the first year, anyway. I wanted to like the place but no good vibes came my way.

How would I endure being stuck up on a lonely road, with a new baby and no store or family and an overworked husband? How could he not see how isolated I would be? Didn't he realize the other houses would be empty for half the year? I could easily believe that the tin house at the foot of the hill was inhabited by an ax murderer. I didn't want to share his neighborhood.

He tried to help me see things his way. "Come here, Lily. I am afraid you are not seeing our home in the light I had hoped. Maybe the college life has taken the idea of a simple Christ-centered life away from you." He held me close and I let the warmth of his arms do their magic. I held on, grateful for the strength they radiated.

He wouldn't want to hear I wasn't interested in a life with Christ at the center, that it was only *he* that I wanted, he that I hoped to build my life around. And why did he bring up college? College had nothing to do with this dirty, isolated, unhappy house. I was looking for a way to respond when he went on.

"Be patient in all things. We were blessed to have this place offered to us until next Christmas. By then we will have found something that suits us both better. You know, we should always give thanks, Lily. Giving thanks is the least we can do. Do not be anxious, as every good gift comes from above and expresses the Lord's love."

"I love *you* Marshall, but..."

"Lily, love Christ first and all good things will follow."

Why wasn't he covering me with kisses, pulling me to the bed, talking about something real? I wanted to scream, "I don't care about Christ, I want you."

28

A scrim of silence hung between us after we left the little house and wandered through the back roads to Woodbury. Shopping at the general store didn't clear the air any. I poked around the food aisles and picked out some mangy, locally grown veggies, and for Marshall's sake, a pound of chopped steak along with a small bag of chips for Little Someone. The necessities, like soap, toilet paper and paper towels cost twice what they cost at the supermarket in Burlington. When I pulled out Mom's charge card, Marshall didn't object, although he did step forward to carry the packages.

During the last leg of our trip, I reached over to turn on the radio. His hand followed my move and took my hand from the dial, saying, "Let us leave WXLV out of this. We need to talk."

We passed a bog where naked trees showed little of spring's offerings. The beavers had returned and were building walls that locked the water in, choking the ponds and re-routing streams. A heron stood as still as a cattail then rose, its great wings mirrored in the still waters.

I looked straight ahead as he spoke to me in his most pastoral voice.

"Lily, I am concerned that you are not happy about living on a hillside, with time and quiet on your hands. I wish you could see that this is exactly what God intends for you. He is giving you time for prayer, time to be with yourself, with our baby and nature. I do not want you to see this home as a bad thing but as the blessing it is. Remember, in God is the joy of the mountain and all that lives therein."

Pinpricks poked my neck. I wanted to say, "*Therein*? No one actually says *therein* unless he's a lawyer or a priest. Why don't you say I want to make love to you, here, now, this minute."

I remembered that Heather had called him, *Mr. Holier-Than-Thou.* At first, I had heard his language as poetry. But in that very short second when he said *therein*, a nerve shot from my ears to my brain. It was then I realized I had once considered him *holier than thou*, a special conduit to God. I had been too ignorant to have recognized the Biblical verse in every other word.

There were so many other things I didn't know. What did he like to do other than preach and make love? Could he ride a bike? Had he ever skied or danced or loved anyone else? Who were his friends? What did he read? How did he see my role at his side in the forever I was imagining? Could I sacrifice my life for his?

The very thought that Little Someone's father was an unknown entity, that he might not be my best friend or the perfect husband, was capable of spoiling the trust that would make our family strong. I had to stop such negative thinking.

By the time we arrived at the trailer, my head was swimming in tears but I couldn't let myself go. Our exclusive time so far had not gone well, and so much rested on this visit's success. If I started by doubting his power and his glory, his kingdom and our kingdom might collapse. I decided I would will myself into believing in the future and rightness of Pastor Marshall Barry. Numbness or dumbness had to be preferable to doubt. No feelings, better than the strange sense of doom knocking at my brain.

Maybe it was the Devil, Marshall's avowed enemy, that wanted to possess me right before the baby was to be born. Here I was, about to begin life with the man I had wanted more than my family, my education, and my friends and red flags were popping up out of nowhere. I *had* to disregard them, to believe in him. He was the new shape and purpose I was counting on to give meaning to my existence; the father of a little person who needed a father as much as I did. What was wrong with me? Where was that magic of the first time he touched me, the first time I lay down with him, oblivious of all else? I prayed silently for God to bring us to back to that place.

As soon as we unloaded the car and the food was jammed into the tiny cupboards and into the so-called refrigerator, I called my mother.

"Mom?" I said.

"Oh, Lily, we can't wait to see you," was all she had to say.

Geysers erupted. "Mom..."

"What is it, Lil?" she asked.

How could I explain that when I saw the heron rise from the bog, its wings spread like sails, I wanted it to lift me up and take me away, anywhere but where I was.

I looked at the wall in front of me, covered with all the notes about pickups and deliveries, scraps of Biblical quotes, handwritten greeting cards by parishioners, some on index cards, some handmade, and children's drawings of angels and happy sunshine faces. I looked at the window blinds, bent and yellowed. I wanted to say I wasn't sure. I wasn't sure I could live in a smelly house with Marshall Barry. I wasn't sure Marshall Barry was my best friend. I wasn't sure I could be the mother I wanted to be. Soon Little Someone would be coming into a world that wasn't quite ready for her. Could I live with a man of the Book? His book, not mine? With no classes, no friends, no car or village where I could find a place? I might as well have been signing up to play Rapunzel.

"I just, I just..."

"Oh, you are alright, Lil. It's the pre-baby blues. Let's put together a plan. Why don't we go to Claremont and buy some baby things, pick out a crib and have a long lunch? Would you like that?"

"Yes, that would be nice," I sniffed.

When I hung up the phone, Marshall put his arms around me and suggested I lie down and get some rest. He said he knew I was carrying a lot of extra weight and I should try to remember that, in a very short time, I would be feeling much better and have that little one in my arms.

I wanted *him* in my arms, but I understood. I was fat and ugly and horribly miserable. Who would want to make love to a weeping cow? He lay beside me carefully, his head turned away. I wondered if he thought about Nancy when he closed his eyes or if she thought about him.

We fell asleep with our bodies gently touching, back to back, and I didn't wake up until early in the morning to the ring of the telephone. He leapt from the bed and cradled the phone on his shoulder as he wrote down the circumstances. "I see. I see. I will. You can," he said. "Just stay where you are and pray for God's help. I will call you when I find him."

He called the fire and police departments, 911 and the hospitals. Then the phone rang again, and whoever it was announced, whoever was missing had been sleeping in a car over on Elm Street.

With that mystery solved, coffee seemed to be the next thing on the agenda. I rose and washed my face and brushed my hair, resenting the unlit mirror over the sink which failed to brighten my face. I practiced smiling before I emerged to load the toaster oven and make toast.

"I bought us some nice fresh oat nut bread. Would you like marmalade or strawberry jam on yours?" I asked, as if the trouble he'd been facing was on another planet. Not important, not of our world. "Either will do," he said.

"Would it be possible not to answer the phone for a while?" I asked, as he was indulging himself in a second cup of coffee and spooning more marmalade on his toast.

"I can't do that. You know I can't. I am the only person many of my people will call when they are in trouble."

"Marshall, I need you. I need you all to myself for a little while. We need to talk."

His eyebrows rose. "What is it?" he asked.

"Who was your favorite friend, when you were growing up?"

He smiled. "Oh. I thought you were about to tell me something serious."

"Marshall, this is very serious. Who was your best friend? "

"The first person that comes to mind was Alfred Koenig."

"What was he like?"

"His parents survived the holocaust and his job was to make their life worth living. He read the Torah morning and night and learned English by reading the St. James Modern Version of the Bible."

"And he was your best friend?"

"My neighbor."

"But, did you play?"

"Not really. He didn't know how to play. We did his homework together and I would drill him on Biblical verses."

"Gee, that sounds like fun," I said.

"It was. I was helping him and learning alongside."

The phone rang. "Please, Marshall, please can't we ignore it?"

He shook his head gravely and reached for the receiver. "Yes? Hello, Mrs. Woodhouse...Leslie. Nice to hear from you....Yes....Here you go."

"Hi, Mom," I said.

29

Late that morning, Mom arrived for our shopping expedition. She had changed plans. After doing some research, she learned Claremont's offerings for baby furniture were meager, so we headed up to Concord instead. I liked Concord better, anyway. Its streets were lined with Victorian houses with nice yards and character left over from another century. The streets were alive with mother's and baby carriages, or was that all I noticed?

Mom lamented, "Remember that beautiful Woodhouse crib we all loved? Just another memory. Gone to ash along with everything else."

I had been thinking about the crib right before she spoke. It had been glued to a spot in the nursery, a reminder of the long Woodhouse line. The hand-tooled cherry spindles were smoothed to a dark sheen by generations of babies who had wrapped their tiny fingers around them. How sad that Little Someone's prints would never be added.

I said, "I used to play house with it. Remember the old pine dresser that sat against the same wall, the one filled with baby things—the soft leather booties that no baby ever wore, and the three baptismal gowns that must have been used by someone in some church, sometime? I would unwrap those lace bonnets, folded into lavender silk and tucked into great grandmother's crocheted blankets. Did you know I dressed Missy with them? How I loved that baby doll. Grandmother said she came from Santa Claus but I knew she was designed for me."

"Of course I knew you played with them. I just let you have the fun of your secret," Mom laughed. "It kept you quiet for hours."

She went on, "I read up on cribs yesterday. I suppose we should be glad that cribs today are much more secure and adjustable," she said. "And they have all sorts of accessories, pads and mattresses, toys, and narrow washable slats where no baby's foot can wedge. Even the sheets are fitted to prevent a child from getting tangled. I hear they have listening devices, too, so you can hear the baby breathing in its crib from any corner of the house. I suppose this means we have come a long way."

"I think it means a baby's bed was a dangerous place. I guess we were lucky to survive. You know, there's no room for a crib in the trailer, Mom, so I have to ask you to store it for us until we move."

"Of course," she said. "It will probably come in a box, like so many things do these days, and need to be assembled. I'll ask Brent to do that."

"I wouldn't. He's not interested in being an uncle."

"Oh, nonsense! You know how tender he is. As soon as he sees that baby he will fall in love. He's always loved kids. I imagine when some girl sweeps him away he will make as many babies as she can bear."

"Mom, you know a different Brent than I do," I said. She was not facing facts.

"Don't you remember Willy, his little doll?" she asked.

"Yes. I remember Willy."

We were quiet for a minute. She broke the silence. "How do you like the house Marshall found?"

"Well, it's a little remote, but it should have enough space. I want the baby to sleep in my room. I don't plan to depend on speakers to tell me when she cries."

Mom smiled, "You may change your mind about that."

"I don't like change, Mom. In fact I keep wishing for something that won't. That's what I want for my baby. A world where she can count on things staying the same."

Mom sighed and shook her head. "Oh Lily, you must know the world isn't put together that way. Everything and everyone is moving on from one point to another. It's just the way it is. Your baby will be better off if you help her to bend and flex. I wanted so much to give you kids some security, some solid ground. I believed I put together a package that was indestructible." She shook her head. "But, I was so foolish. It was corrupted from the start." She negotiated our car into a parking place, and we climbed out and met at the curb.

"If you had a chance to do it over, would you?" I asked, handing her a quarter for the meter.

"How can I answer that? I wouldn't have you and Heather and my darling Brent."

"What would you have done?"

"Well, I will never know, will I?"

"Looks to me like you aren't done yet."

She shook her blond head and made a Mona Lisa smile. "Not that easy."

"Mom, I'm not sure about anything, anymore," I moaned.

"Join the company. Just remember, you don't have to do a thing you don't want to do, Lil, except bring that little creature into the world."

She understood what I was talking about without asking. But she didn't tell me not to worry or say that it was my responsibility to marry my child's father. Her lack of words put the whole thing on my shoulders, just what I had wanted from the beginning. It should have made me feel better. Unfortunately, it didn't.

After window shopping and poking around some dress shops for clothes I could only dream about, we wound up shopping at Sears. The crib we chose was the most practical, white and washable and capable of being turned into a youth bed. Mom bought its furnishings: a mattress, bumper guards, a mobile of colorful geometric shapes, and sheets with yellow and green duckies in rows. I think she was somehow or other coordinating Little Someone's car seat with her bed. Nuts! Right? But that would be Mom.

After browsing around the department store, we returned to the shops on South Street and then went to Chen Yang Li's for lunch. Purgatory was hopelessly limited to American food, well, with the exception of pizza, but Burlington had opened my palette to foreign tastes. Mom said she loved to eat food she didn't make herself, so, we were a happy pair as we downed tea and eggrolls followed by a pu pu platter.

We both had sticky fingers and our mouths full when a man approached our table. He was so out of context that it took me a minute to believe I was seeing who I thought I was seeing.

"Hello, Ms. Woodhouse," he said.

"Quinn?" I asked, with teriyaki staining the corners of my mouth and fingers too messy to touch his.

"The same," he said, bowing a little.

I looked at Mom, "My professor."

He made some small talk as if he had all the time in the world and then Mom said, "Won't you join us, Professor Quinn?"

"Quinn, just Quinn," he said and sat down.

Naturally, we talked about school. I tried to explain to Mom why his classes were like none other. He told her I was a gifted student. Then he began to tell her how many ways there were to get a degree without being on campus. That having a baby didn't have to mean the end to the possibilities.

I am not sure when, but it seemed like all of a sudden the conversation was no longer about me but about Mom. She told Quinn how she had two children by the time most of her friends were graduating from college, and it had never crossed her mind she could go any further in school after that.

He started playing with her mind, the way he does, and soon she was imagining herself going to school and choosing a major. They talked about her interests and how they could be translated into higher education. He said she could get life credits. By the time we left I thought she was ready to sign up.

At home, I quickly hurried to my room for a nap.

Nancy called but Mom told her I was sleeping. The truth was I had completely forgotten my promise to call her and when I awoke my first thought was to call Marshall and tell him about our day in Concord. I half-expected him to come to my mother's house and spend the evening, but it was Good Friday and he had a full service at dusk. In a way, a very small way, I was relieved. I was still tired and anxiety about Brent's attitude loomed like a dark shadow with all things that involved Marshall. I feared an incident when the two actually met.

When Heather came home she was not exactly interested in our expedition. She was more excited about Pearl asking her to go to a buyers' exposition in Boston to choose a few clothes to feature in the store. "She thinks I have *an eye*," she bragged.

"She's one short," I said.

"Where's Brent?" Mom asked. It was then we realized he hadn't shown up after school. It was already growing dark.

"I bet he's up at the pond," I said.

"There's no ice," Heather said. "Why would he go there?"

"Maybe he's hiding because I'm here. That's his private space. He's always loved that spot. Remember when he made the bird cages so the bluebirds would come back. And then how he planted the Mexican sunflowers to lure the hummingbirds. He was going to make it a bird sanctuary."

"I sort of do. I remember the duck, mostly."

"Duck?"

"Don't you remember the winter he found the duck with a broken wing and tried to bring it home in his little red wagon because its family had flown south?"

Mom laughed. "Oh, I do! The duck was almost as big as he was. Your father told him he would take it to the duck rescue league over in Hanover."

"That must have gone over well," Heather snorted.

"Why don't you walk up and find him, Lil? Maybe you two could work on your relationship a little."

"Why don't you go, Heather? He hates me," I said.

"He doesn't hate you, he hates the guy you hooked up with."

"And what am I supposed to do about that?"

"How about you *both* go?" Mom suggested.

We trudged up the hill and even though my feet were swollen, the familiar path and cool air felt soothing. I was twenty pounds above my normal weight and walking took more effort than it should have. Dr. Bomson had warned me and my back said the same.

Spring had always been intoxicating to me. Trillium and crocus were in full bloom and the huge old lilac bushes filling the air with perfume. I went slowly and was happy when Heather took my arm in the crook of hers. She was definitely changing, but I chose not to point it out.

"Brent," she called. "Hey, Bro?"

Silence.

"Maybe he ran off with Strange," she said.

"Do you really think so?" I asked.

"I only wish. No, they're over. Strange is into something or someone else. He's mysterious, that's for sure. One day they were inseparable, the next day, dead in the water."

We reached the clearing and started toward the pond. I don't know who saw first. I don't know who screamed the scream that made the trees shiver. It was a wail, a high pitched wail that should have brought every sentient being to Woodhouse Hill. But we were horribly alone with a corpse suspended from a branch above the pond. His face was gray and his bare white legs lit by a single streak of light.

It looked to me like an effigy of what had been a boy—a heavy sack with a gruesome likeness to my brother. A cruel trick.

"Brent!" Heather screamed, running into the water.

I fell to the ground.

She couldn't reach him. She sank in the mud, in the cold tangle of grasses.

I crawled toward her to help her out. "It's too late, Heather, he's dead. We can't reach him. You can see he's dead!"

We could do nothing but run back to the house to try to find help. I couldn't keep up, I was panting and clumsy compared to Heather. She said, "I'll go. You stay here. Don't go to Mom's. Don't tell her anything, I'll get help from the neighbors. Wait here."

"I have to go to Mom," I said.

"No, no. She can't see this. Wait here. I'll go to the Kleinholz's and call the sheriff."

I nodded and collapsed in a wet heap. I couldn't think. "Please, God, please don't let this be true," I begged.

But it was. It was Brent and he was dead. I knew I should be going to Mom, not to the neighbors. She had to know. I had to tell her, not some official. Not some volunteer who wouldn't know, who wouldn't understand that this boy was her heart. Her soul.

I sat shivering and paralyzed, until I realized my whole body was holding its breath. Breathe, I told myself. Breathe. I looked back and saw his head, slack in the noose, his legs hanging out from the pants that had fallen to his ankles. He needed to be dressed. She couldn't see the shell, the gruesome paleness of it. The emptiness. I thought of his anger and his pain, then his handsome face lit up when he was skating for Strange.

I did it, I thought. *I killed him. I was the one who came between them. I exposed them and helped kill my own brother and destroyed the nerve center of our family.*

30

1-3-3-2. I heard the siren bleating and tried to lift myself from the ground. They would arrive soon and I hadn't reached Mom. My mind was breaking into little pieces. This time the emergency truck's trip up Woodhouse Hill would be easier than that awful night two years ago when our house disappeared. But, once again, due to no fault of their own, they were too late. It didn't matter how would they get through the narrow lane to the pond or how would they get Brent down. It would be better if he fell in the pond and Mom we wouldn't have to see him. I wanted them to hide the evidence, spare Mom the sight.

I had to get to her. I had to be there first. I pushed one foot in front of the other like in a dream where you walk and walk and go nowhere. I was a great tortoise, with my baggage in front of me instead of on my back, plodding on. "Poor Little Someone," I cried, as I sank back down into the grass, no longer able to continue. "What a terrible world I'm offering you. My poor baby."

The sheriff, Claus Hansen, arrived first, with his deputy alongside. He squatted next to me, "Are you Lily?"

"Yes. Lily Woodhouse."

"We are here to help."

"It's too late. My mother, please, I need to get to my mother," I cried. "Could you take me to her?"

"Your sister is with your mother now," he said. "Terrible thing," he added. "Can you take us to the boy?"

"He's right there." I pointed behind me and turned away. They moved quickly towards the pond just as one of the emergency firetrucks came up the lane, plowing down the brush like a bulldozer.

Claus directed the truck to the site.

He returned to me. "How long have you been here, Lily?" he asked, taking a blanket from the rear of the van and wrapping it around my shoulders.

"Just a few minutes," I said. He put an arm around me, lifted me up and walked me toward the car, suggesting I get inside. I obeyed, grateful for directions.

"Sir," the deputy said, "I'm going to take a look around, see if there's a note."

What would the note say? I wondered, burying myself in the blanket's gray wool, deep in the backseat.

Conversations took place all around me while I waited. Nothing was clear. They talked about looking for signs of another person, getting the coroner up there, the type of knot Brent made, how he must have shimmied up the tree and tied his belt around his legs so he couldn't swim if the bough broke. Someone asked about the piles of brush encircling the pond, another mentioned checking for foul play. I wasn't able to take it all in.

Sheriff Hansen startled me when he opened the door of the car and asked if I would be willing to take a look at the things he'd found piled on a nearby boulder. I stumbled out and identified the earphones as Brent's, his old sweatshirt and precious ice skates.

"Any reason he would have his skates up here without any ice?" he asked. How could I know? Then he showed me a book of poetry. It had a weird title, *The Metaphysical Dog.* It didn't look or sound anything like a book Brent would read. But when the sheriff opened it to the cover page, I saw the words, *To my real bro, who needs to love himself.* I recognized the scratchy printing right away.

"Do you know who wrote this?" he asked.

I panicked, afraid that Strange would become a suspect or something, or that exposing their relationship would make things even worse. I studied the handwriting for a few seconds and considered saying it was mine, but it was so obviously not. "I don't know," I claimed.

The coroner arrived at some point as did an ambulance. Pictures were taken before and after Brent was extricated from the limb. "Please don't take photographs," I begged.

"We have to Miss. It's required in a case like this."

Just one more thing for my mother to bear. I saw efficiency on the part of the men, but no signs of grief. They should have been shocked and sad, a young boy, a life gone too soon. I wanted to scream and tell them to go away, to leave us alone.

They photographed the boulder, the rope and the tree and each item left behind. They took pictures of me wrapped in the blanket and took pictures of the piles of kindling someone had arranged. "Looks like some kind of ritual was going down," the deputy said. The fire chief said, "Let's make no assumptions."

Ted Costa, once more the hero, was in charge of the rescue. He ordered a ladder to be spread like a bridge over the pond. One man reached for Brent and held on as two others cut the rope. They took the body gently, one cradling the head and shoulders, the other, the legs. Brent was placed on a stretcher and more pictures were taken.

Someone said to the coroner, "He made sure this was going to work, didn't he?" and dumped the stones he had taken from Brent's pockets. Then he removed the belt that he used to tie his ankles together.

Our neighbor, Mr. Kleinholz, finally arrived with Mom and Heather in tow. They all spoke to the sheriff and were brought to the spot where Brent was laid out. Mom identified him with a simple nod of her head. She was frozen. No tears, no words, a simple nod. Afterwards they began the task of moving him into an ambulance. "Where are you taking him?" Mom asked. The coroner explained that he had to be taken to the morgue because of the circumstances. "But what more can you possibly need to know?" she asked.

I threw myself, weeping, at Heather but she wrestled free of me. "Lil, we have to be strong," she said, her hands holding each of my arms. "Let's get Mom back to the house."

The pain that filled our house was almost visible. Silence ruled. We moved about as if any brush with reality would do us in. Somehow, we saved the newspaper's announcements when they appeared, a coffin was bought and dates were set. Mom decided not to go the cremation route. She wanted Brent buried in the old family cemetery on the hill. "At least that way I can visit him now and then."

Some horrible law stood in the way, one that preserved old graveyards and barred new interments, but Dad saw to it that Mom's wishes were met. When he told her, she said that it was the least he could do. She blamed him for Brent's suffering. "You made things so miserable for him. You helped kill him," she wept. "Please, stay away from here, from us. I can't look at you."

I let him be scapegoated for Brent's misery rather than tell her the part Marshall and I had played.

Dad let her rage. He believed she was right. It was obvious in his agony and grief. It showed in his slow motion and inability to speak. His broad shoulders stooped as they carried the weight of guilt. "I was not the father Brent needed," he confessed, "but, I loved him."

I reminded him of the good times, the campfires they built from sticks and broken boughs, and the s'mores they cooked when we went camping. I remembered a two year old Brent on his double edged skates and how it was Dad who introduced Brent—"I no fall down!"—to skating up at the pond. He had bought him his latest pair of skates, too, settling for figure skates when he couldn't convince him to play ice hockey. I didn't say that no matter how much he wanted him to be more like Drew Piersall, he did the best he could with the son he was given.

The day following Brent's death was perhaps the worst day of my life. Marshall came, uninvited. When I opened the front door, I rushed into his arms despite myself. He held me like a great bear patting my back and saying that he was sorry. We walked into the kitchen where Mom and Heather were sitting silently at the table nursing lukewarm tea, with to-do lists at their fingertips.

"Mom, Heather," I said, hoping for a kind reception for Marshall, "Marshall is here."

"I see," Mom said flatly. Her eyes not lifting and Heather's only slightly.

"I came as soon as I heard. I want to express how very sorry I am for your loss." Marshall began, "I would like to offer my prayers to all of you."

"Thank you," Mom said graciously, leaning back in her chair and closing her eyes. Her head too heavy to hold up and her arms too empty to give herself comfort.

He took her limp right hand and I took her left. Heather's hands remained clasped in her lap.

"Lord we pray for Brent's soul, that it not be cast off, that you will give him rest and forgiveness. That your heavenly doors will open and...."

"Stop that! Stop that right now!" Mom said, flinging our hands away from her own, her eyes suddenly alive with anger. "Forgiveness? For what?"

Heather jumped in saying, "We don't believe that crap here. You don't even know Brent and you don't know us. You can keep all that shit to yourself. There's nothing God has to forgive Brent for and no Heaven or Hell to reward or punish him."

"Our lives are manifestations of God's temple, each of us is part of a Divine plan," he tried to explain, confident in his knowing.

"Marshall..." I begged.

"Prayer is the answer, for you and God and Brent. If there had been God in his world this..."

"Please. I think you should go, *now*," Mom said..

Marshall shook his head sadly. "I understand your feelings, Leslie. Life's lessons are hard to reconcile, but if you can put..."

"Stop!" Heather screamed and stood face to face with Marshall. "Your words don't mean anything here. Do you understand? My mother has asked you to leave, so leave!"

I bowed my head and headed backward to the door pulling Marshall with me.

"Are you coming back with me?" he asked.

"Are you serious?" I asked. "I would never for a second consider going anywhere. I'm where I belong and where I'm needed."

Wasn't it clear to him that I was as much my past as my future? I practically pushed his energy out the door, returned to the kitchen and began to work alongside Heather to plan a dignified farewell for my brother. It took time for the air to clear.

We decided on a quiet, private service, at Purgatory's only funeral parlor, where Grandmother Lillian refused to go, but where no one would mention God or add judgment to a loss that was already almost too much to bear.

31

A few tall bouquets of gladiolas stood like sentinels at either end of the casket. I wanted Mom to close the lid. It wasn't Brent that lay there, after all. It seemed like a waxen image of a sleeping boy. The doll, laid out on white satin, looked peaceful, with all the anger and pain gone, but it wasn't Brent. Brent had gone somewhere else. This shell that was left was dressed in clothes I knew he would not have chosen. The preppy outfit—a pale blue shirt and chinos—was Mom's doing, but what did it matter? What was real was that a boy was dead. What was real was that he was my brother and I had failed him. We had all failed.

Mom was intent on protecting our privacy. She knew the town was driven by gossip and feared the curious might cause a circus. The three of us had worked on the obituary. It began "Atticus Brent Woodhouse, 16, died suddenly on April 20th at his home." And that was followed by the rest of the data about family left behind and the date of the so-called private *family* service. Private was the key word. We had carefully selected who to invite. Among them were, Dad, Ted Costa, Pearl, our neighbors, Nancy and her father, Marshall, despite himself, and of course, Strange, who sat in the furthest corner of the room ignoring everyone.

The funeral director began the service with acknowledgements to the family and friends and then read a few words by Rumi. This is love: *To fly toward a secret sky, to cause a hundred veils to fall each moment. First to let go of life. Finally, to take a step without feet.* And then he added, "This is what we must all eventually do...let the known go and reach for what is beyond knowing. Rumi says to love life one must let it go. And some may say no and others may embrace this idea. We celebrate the life of Atticus Brent Woodhouse today, trusting he has found his wings."

My mind started hearing babble. It had nothing to do with Brent. This funeral director didn't know any more about Brent or the circumstances surrounding his death than some stranger in Burlington. I looked over at Heather. I knew she was in the same place I was, thinking similar thoughts.

Next, Dad rose and made his way to the lectern to try his hand at poetry. His stooped figure leaned before us. "I want to recite a poem by Yeats that keeps coming to mind," he said.

Were you but lying cold and dead
And lights were paling out of the west
You would come hither and bend you head
And I would lay my head on your breast;

And you would murmur tender words....
Forgiving me because you were dead...

He stopped there, mid- stream, and allowed his grief to fill the already grieving room. His tears were caught in a huge handkerchief, and I wondered that he had such a thing and thought to bring it.

After what seemed like five minutes but was probably only one, he began again, this time without the crutch of poetry. My body was rigid as he spoke, fearing his words as his emotions spilled over the rest of us, dimming Mom's almost irrational rage and my unexposed guilt.

"Brent was a boy with great promise. I....He was the heir to the Woodhouse name and so much more than that. He was....he was the new branch on the tree and his talents were many, his aspirations, too. He was a thoughtful, sensitive boy, independent and unique, someone who gave all of us a...a...challenge. We loved him and he deserved that love. His mother and I were so thrilled when he was born, so amazed to have a son, and death cannot take him from us. He will remain with us, our son, whether he is visible or not, he will be here in our hearts...forever."

He sat down, an oxbow of anguish across his shoulders.

Mom did not rise.

It was Heather who stood.

She bravely began, "Brent was my brother. He was funny and sarcastic and moody and brilliant. He was a part of me, a big part of me and I feel that lost part. I am hurting all over and I wonder if this pain will ever end, but I have been told it will, and that I will become a wounded healer because of it. Brent, if you can hear me, I want to say what I never did, I love you. I am grateful for the time we had together, even though it was so short. At least you gave me someone worth grieving for. I am changed now, and sad, and you will always live in my heart. Goodbye."

Mrs. Kleinholz stood up and went to the organ and we all tried to read the printed words on our programs to sing "Blackbird." At first, when I read the words I thought how wrong they were for the service, but then I remembered how much Mom and Dad loved that Beatles song and realized it was a song about injustice and needing to be free.

It was a feeble sound that emerged from my unmusical family, with the exception of Marshall who hummed the tune at first but by the end was able to clearly articulate the lines, "Blackbird fly, Blackbird fly, into the light of the dark black night." Beside me, his rich baritone made a music the family could not.

The funeral director asked that we all have a moment of silence. I could not think to pray. Into my blankness the same man asked if anyone would like to share a memory before the service ended.

Strange stood, went before the casket dressed in his typical black, his hair, now blacker than it had ever been, was held down rolled black and red bandana tied across his forehead. He put his hands over the cold white hands crossed neatly on Brent's chest and appeared to be praying. Slowly, he turned back toward us taking a piece of paper from his pocket, which he opened carefully.

"Poem by Brent," he said, and began to read. He took his time, pausing after each line of verse, punctuating their meaning.

> *I am the fire.*
> *I burn*
> *Wanting to be wanted.*
> *Say so, tell me, beg.*
> *Do it for me, don't make me*
> *Grovel in the dirt where*
> *They would push me*
> *And leave me for dead.*
> *I am dead without you*
> *And with you my legs*
> *Grow strong and fly with*
> *The wings of Daedalus*

He swallowed, remaining in place like he had been turned to salt, stuck in front of us, until Heather rose and took him gently by the arm to the door and they left the parlor.

Mom leaned into herself, gripping her abdomen like she'd been shot. I heard Marshall cracking his knuckles, felt his body shift in the seat, but he stayed silent.

Mrs. Kleinholz knew enough to get back on the organ and the funeral director said some closing words, none of which I heard.

With Marshall at my side, acting for all like he was a part of the family, I realized I was afraid he would not contain himself. And in the end, he did not. As we left the building, he had to say in my ear, "Why bother with a funeral when it is Godless? It is meaningless. What can be learned here? The entire purpose of life and death are lost. Can you see this, Lily?"

No. No, I couldn't see, I thought, resenting his words, wishing him gone. He continued to hold onto my elbow ushering me out of the funeral parlor, away from the others, to the parking lot where I came to, and made up my mind that I would not go home with him. I would go home with Dad.

Just as I was extricating myself from his grasp, Strange lunged at us from behind the rhododendron bushes.

"You bastard!" he spat. "You son of a bitch. You killed him." He thrust his head into Marshall's stomach. Marshall was caught off balance and fell to the ground. Strange kept swinging, flailing about like a wild cat.

"Strange!" I cried, "Not here. Please not here. Stop! My mother, our friends. Think of Brent."

"Brent? Brent's dead thanks to you." He attacked Marshall again, this time with his foot, kicking as hard as he could. "I'm going to take you down. I am going to do to you what you and your fucking God does to everyone else!" he screamed.

Marshall grabbed Strange's foot, lifting him off the ground like he was no more than a toddler. He swung him around and landed him in the eucalyptus.

"Oh my God! Stop it. Stop! Both of you. Please. My family..." I tried.

Strange leered at me. "Your fucking family? They didn't help any. Don't you get it? He died because of your family."

Marshall pulled me back behind him, then he yanked Strange upright by twisting his arm. He said, "David, you are done here. You can talk to me anytime, anywhere else. Move. Move away from this travesty. You, of all people have no right to cast blame!"

"Cast blame? You're a monster. You're the pervert!" Strange wept. "I have your number, you fuck, and I'm taking you down."

Marshall twisted Strange's arm harder, up between his shoulder blades, until he grunted from the pain. I ran back to the funeral parlor's doorway where a few people stood gaping.

Before I knew it, Nancy had her arms around me, then Heather. They brought me to a chair and I remember little of the day beyond that.

The worst thing about loss is that you adjust to it. You keep on living around it, through it and despite it, until you digest it and turn it into a part of yourself.

Long, empty weeks crept by as I moved back and forth between Dad's place and Mom's and became adept at lying as I made excuses to avoid Marshall. Finally, the time came when I had to make the decision to return to campus or drop out of school.

I prayed, begged God to give me a sign, to forgive me for my doubts and fears, for the part I played in making Brent miserable. But God stayed quiet, and offered no divine intervention about what to do next.

Mom was already quietly functioning, weaving spring bouquets into wreathes that she placed all over the house. She was also converting Brent's room into a shrine. His old sweatshirt lay on the bed like a comforter; the beanbag shaped by his weight, remained fixed. She hung his precious ice skates on the wall next to his first school portrait which she had blown up to a much larger size. The Brian Boitano poster remained at the head of his bed. A picture of Han Solo on the opposite wall. On the night table were his favorite Golden books and the earphones Strange had given him at Christmas. She disposed of his game of *Dungeons and Dragons*.

I worried every day that Little Someone was being harmed by our shock and sadness. I had believed Mom when she told me, early on, that a prenatal baby absorbs everything its mother experiences. But, up to that moment, Little Someone was proving herself to be a survivor, still dancing in her bubble, not giving up or slowing down. She was obviously a fighter. She kicked and stretched and reminded me by the minute that she was coming soon, just in case I had forgotten. But how could I forget?

I had not seen Marshall since the funeral, and not spoken to him after his last phone call. At that time he had ranted that Brent and David had lost the war with Satan, and compared it to the entire nation going straight to Hell. "Homosexuals, predators, prostitutes, hypocrisy! This country is doomed. Pay attention: acid rock concerts, demonic raves, drugs and free sex! These are the undoing of our children. We have to rise up and remember that America is under God, and we will be held accountable."

I said nothing, not that he noticed.

"God has called me to lead the battle, to pick up the sword and fight. He asks us all to be born again, to unite and fight for what is right. Empty churches are empty because empty people are in the pulpits. Jesus wants warriors. He wants us to crush Babylon, destroy it and make way for the Lord's will to be done. He wants us to shout and to praise him, and erase the world's filth. We must do this together, Lily. We must glorify His name. Are you at my side?"

My skin shivered at his question. Nothing in me wanted to fight any battles, especially for a God that would create a person like Brent, only to torture and kill him.

I was sure Marshall's fury was dangerous. His was an anger I could never and would never share. But I left my thoughts unsaid, feeling sickened and afraid. I could not be with him in his state of mind, not at the time, maybe not ever.

Nor could I think of being with friends or neighbors, either. I didn't answer Nancy's calls, and stayed indoors despite the beauty of spring. I envied Heather's connection with Strange as they planned their exodus together. I wanted to ask her to find out what he knew about his brother, but I didn't.

I finally chose to return to school for my finals rather than forfeit the semester's credits. I wanted to be with Mom and Heather and needed them as much as I imagined they needed me, but I had already started to realize that grief is a lonely thing. You can't take it off another's shoulders. You have to go it alone.

Back at school, I spoke about Brent not at all. My roommates were as sympathetic as they knew how. They must have been affected by my sadness but made a point not to talk about it. They seemed to want to spare me the details of their good times, too, and consequently we shared a pretty quiet place. If they touched on my personal life at all, it was to talk about Marshall and my wedding. I let on nothing. I engaged their fantasies of the wedding as if it was going to be mid-summer, in the church with the congregation and my family and friends all taking part. Jennifer bought bridal magazines and we poured over the pages. All the time I knew that those girls in the pictures had exactly nothing to do with me. I might as well be selling myself into bondage as to try to carry off a traditional wedding. No white gown was going to make right the messiness or fool anyone that this was a traditional wedding. It was infected by too many questions, strained to breaking by our differences and separations, a distance I now appreciated.

Quinn made a point of taking me for coffee on Fridays after class. Out of sympathy, I guessed. Maybe he saw me as an adult among the dreamers. He definitely was impressed by Mom. I am sure he was. What was there not to like? It was to Quinn I first admitted that I was considering not making my marriage legal. "We promised to love honor and obey, in the eyes of God," I said, "but that was Marshall's God, not my God. I'm not even sure if I have a God."

Quinn smiled. "Maybe you have a Goddess," he said. "Maybe you *are* a goddess."

"Marshall would find that blasphemous," I said. "But then everything is blasphemous to him, even computers."

"He better give that one up," Quinn said, "because they're here for good, and they're going to be running the world someday."

"That's kind of creepy."

"Well, we will always need mothers and love and learning. The computer is just a mirror of knowledge, not knowledge itself."

"Quinn, I know so little. How can I do what I need to do for my baby? I thought she would be growing up with love all around her. I thought Marshall was smart and sure enough for both of us. But things are different now. I think he's anything but stable."

"You will find the way," Quinn smiled. "We all have a way and it opens as we live our lives. That's what life is, after all, a journey. You're just at the starting line."

"I'm clueless."

"You have everything you need to move on. Each moment will bring you to the next. Don't worry. Don't try to write a script that is writing itself. You can try, but you will never stop the world from becoming itself, no more than you can stop that baby from coming."

"God, that's scary," I said.

32

My life at school was simpler than the one at home. I ate in the cafeteria twice a day and doubled my trips to the library. It took a real effort to make up for lost time but I had little else to do. During my solitary moments, particularly in bed, I found myself weighted with grief. I wanted to wake one morning without the pain of it. I needed to be around people, but not *with* them, to feel collegial, but not have to *be* collegial. I wished the greening landscape, the normal sounds of life around me, the food I ate, the most ordinary things could become ordinary again. I wasn't sure if I was punishing myself or being punished as I watched life through a peephole in a highly insulated closet.

It was only in the classroom that my mind worked without the walls shutting me in. Required attendance kept me preoccupied as my womb stretched into an even greater bouncing ball. I tried to resist the potato chips and sodas that sat in the hallways but it was indigestion, not self-discipline, that ultimately worked. Food didn't like me anymore.

By the time exam week arrived, I was ready. I had thrown myself at the books and managed to ace everything, everything but Quinn's exam, which was a wringer. He gave us a take home test where we were asked to state our personal philosophy of life in nine hundred words or less. Really? How could anyone answer a question that involved nothing but an opinion?

I tucked that challenge away for another day, a day when school was over and I was simply waiting. Without ceremony of any kind, I tried to accept closure to my college days. The closest thing I felt to an ending was the group hug I received from Jennifer, Sarah and Ellie, along with their baby gifts and declarations of love. Each, also, promised to come to my wedding. It took the five of us to force my things into Carrie's overloaded Datsun. Fortunately, I had a scarcity of belongings in comparison to hers. "Are you sure you lived here for a year?" she asked.

Carrie and I had quite the ride home. It was as if it was our last chance to be together. She announced she had made a clear decision that she and Drew were supposed to be together after all. But there had been that time when she was not sure, and the time when they were compromised and maybe should have committed and didn't. Now, she was obsessed with the idea that two more years apart might do them in.

She had been with Drew for four years and still had her doubts. *Is that the way it always is?* I wondered. "I don't get it," I said. "All these years and all the stuff you've been through, and you still aren't sure you can make it?"

"That's just it. It's not about all the stuff we've been through, it's that I don't know what lies ahead. I'm sure Drew must be tempted every day. He's such a hunk and there are too many girls looking for their MRS degree. It scares me. I know I've been tempted, but dating has been really miserable. I don't know what Drew is doing. He's a male after all, but I can't stand the thought of him with anyone else. As for me, I don't feel like myself with other guys. He's my best friend, a brother and a might-have-been father. I think if we get married it will make things right."

We were in such different places. I was feeling the only way to make things right was *not* to marry the father of my child. I didn't want to have my baby growing up with a father who had God kicking his sides. No matter what he said, Marshall's God was not my idea of a good guy.

"I am going to have this baby any day, and I have to make some terrible decisions," I confessed.

"Are you thinking about giving it up for adoption?" Carrie asked.

How could she even think such a thing? "She's not an 'it' and there's no way I am giving her away," I said.

"Okay, okay, I probably should have had mine and gone that route. I think about it every now and then. Maybe I won't ever be able to have another one. What if that happens?"

"You went to a doctor and did it right, not in some dirty place where they use hangers or dirty instruments. You'll be alright," I said, sounding to myself like the know-it-all I wasn't.

"Well, what are the big decisions you're facing?"

"I don't think I should get married."

"What? You're kidding, right? You're wearing his mother's wedding band."

"How can I give my life over to someone that makes me uncomfortable? It's just the opposite for me as it is for you. You know Drew too well to give him up, I know Marshall too little to live with him. He isn't really my friend. He's a lot of things, but he isn't my friend."

"Why don't you try it out? Give the baby a name and see how it goes. You can always change your mind later."

"You mean start out with an escape plan? Marry with the idea of getting divorced? I don't think so."

"Well, try living with him for a while."

"I've thought of that, but something died in me."

"Well, you just lost Brent.

"It's not that, Carrie. I almost hated Marshall before Brent died. How can you love someone so much and then hate them the next minute?"

"Two sides of the same coin?"

And so it went all the way back to Purgatory. When we reached town, we vowed to see each other the next week.

313

` Of course that didn't happen.

As soon as my things were transferred to Heather's Saab and my feet returned to the ground, I was caught again in the misery of loss and blame.

At the shop I wasn't surprised that Strange snubbed me. What was very weird was that his language sounded more like Marshall's than his own. He told Heather I was under the influence of *Satan*. "Satan himself ruined her. He's done it before and he'll do it again," he told her. She swore she shook her head and said he was acting as nuts as his brother.

I was frightened; frightened by the anger, the name-calling and the craziness.

I knew the only way we could change things was to talk, and yet, I had seen Strange's rage up close. He was not the same person that I had trusted and cared so much about only a few years ago. But then again, neither was I.

I had been home less than a week when Little Someone seemed to drop from her spot under my breasts to a place on my lap. When I wasn't sitting, I felt like she might fall out. Mom offered to help me set up the layette at the little house on the hill but I wanted to put it off because I couldn't see myself up there, alone, right after the baby was born. I wanted to stay near her, protected from Marshall.

To kill time, I decided to write my philosophy of life. In order to impress Quinn with how much I had learned in a few short months, I used my Thesaurus, my physics book, and made an honest list of my search for truth, starting with magic and ending with its absence. He was going to get all I had. I played around with words to get it just right and when it was done I was satisfied I had said it as it was.

My Philosophy of Life
By Lillian Woodhouse
June 6th, 1990

Such a Nice Girl

At first I wished for magic; a prince on a white horse, winged fairies to touch me with their wands, a jolly man who would come once a year to give me what I most wanted. My first books told me animals talked, skies fell, pumpkins became coaches and witches melted.

Then came the teens and Hollywood fulfilled my longings. Film gave me ET, Superman, and ghosts for every occasion; not to dismiss the interplanetary wars that would save or destroy the earth and time travel for quick fixes. But now I know that such phenomenon belong only in the ganglions of imagination, certainly not in the "real" world. But what is the "real" world? Is there a real world or do we simply make it all up? I think the latter.

Exactly how can we explain knowledge and its acquisition? Life is filled with too many contradictions. It is so skewed that only the most arrogant or ignorant can believe themselves capable of understanding how it works. No philosophy, religion or metaphor can possibly nail it down. Science with all its proofs is no exception. It's constantly changing right along with the dimensions of the universe. Even Einstein's most famous formula is being reconsidered. Science is only true until proven wrong.

Since the most significant forces of our lives, our values, quests, and feelings are invisible, we try to convert them to something visible so we can see what we believe we believe. We build castles, churches and sculptures to point to a Heaven we can only imagine; use corny Valentine cards to confess something as complicated as love; create terror movies to give fear permission to exist. To address spiritual longings we turn to music and dance. But, the truth is, we can't hold on to anything "real" because there's no such thing. Everything is changing, evolving and devolving no matter how hard we try to stop it. Truth is fleeting. We only have religion because we need to add meaning to life. Meaning that's beyond our grasp.

I, therefore, know nothing. I cannot claim a philosophy.

If one was to observe the entire spectrum of time from the big bang forward, it's less than a nanosecond since humans were able to reveal the world of the unseen, the world of germs and atoms, of genetics, microbes and dark matter. We have just begun to realize the invisible things that make up the air we breathe and the land on which we stand. We know electricity surrounds us and travels through us and magnetic gravity keeps us grounded; that we are no more than protons, electrons and neutrons, we have no edges.

We say we are a part of an interdependent web. But we don't care. We forget and destroy the parts of the web that we need for our own survival. Look at how we have rewarded the buffalo, the homing pigeon, the waters, the earth.

At any given moment, catastrophic forces like comets or exploding stars may bombard the Earth, or the molten pressures at our core could pull us under. A madman could press a button that ends life as we know it. But we don't consider ourselves victims. We can't. No, that would be too defeating, as pathetic as being turnips, suggesting we are no more than food fed to a hungry universe.

To quote a great man, "We can never stop the world from becoming itself." At every given moment we are at risk. The sun may explode, our hearts may quit, a madman may blow up a bridge or start a fire, a pandemic could start. Knowing all the variables, it would seem that we, like mayflies, have only come to this place to die, our purpose reduced to regenerate the energy that was here before us and will be here well after. This little planet is no more than a self-generating machine fueled by living things that are formed and reformed as matter. I suspect this happens in the far reaches of space and time, too; that Earth may be no more than a machine part attached to an ever expanding eternal machine. Earth may be no more than a microcosm of the universe which is a microcosm of multi-universes which are mirrors of dimensions too large to ever conjure.

I believe forms of life have always been and always will be, growing, spreading, colliding and collapsing; then colluding and evolving into a new creation, over and over again like bubbles formed in a bath. Watch the water in a tub, and see the bubbles form and meld into one and then float into a new pattern as they move down the drain to yet another reality and another and another until they merge into the great sauce where we no longer can identify the parts. That would be us—bubbles in a stream.

What are we to do with our lives? What good is philosophy or art? What good comes of schemes or theorems? The grand scheme of things reveals so little of its face.

Life wakens our senses and teases our curiosity, but we cannot define it. No Torah, Koran, Bible, Vedas, Shaman, guru or ancient tale can encompass the complexity. We are not meant to know because knowing would be unbearable. How could we face the future if we knew what was in it—a decimating fire, the death of loved ones, the end of dreams, the pains of disease? So we invent. We play make-believe, paint, write, make babies, sing and bang drums. We put on blinders, lie and pretend to know a truth we cannot.

With our best parts invisible, let us call them souls, and with the forces of life necessarily unknowable, is it any wonder that some choose to go back to that place where we were spared the physical pain of life, the trickery, and the heartache? Wouldn't the absence of a life trapped in a body be preferable to the tragedy of life itself, the ignorance and despair?

I once knew a boy who wanted to be accepted and was not; a boy who wanted to be someone else, and could not; a boy who had the ability to create beauty and grace and would not; a boy who loved and tried to follow his own truth and did not; a young man who once lived and now does not, *except in the hearts and minds of those he left behind. This boy chose to return to that world of the invisible. Some say he is at rest. I hope so, but who knows? I only know that, in the aftermath, I will try to look each minute in the eye and continue marching through my time without easy answers. I will fulfill my body's most basic mission, busy myself and play along until I am invited back into the primordial soup. Until then...*

I remain,
Lillian Woodhouse

I stuck my paper in an envelope, addressed it to Quinn and took it to the Post Office.

In town, I stopped at Pearl's to see if Strange would talk to me. He didn't say more than yes and no. I told him that the baby was coming any day and he said he could see that.

"Strange," I tried, "I think we need to talk, a good, long, private talk. I can't do it right now, but, soon, okay?"

He didn't say no.

33

I was looking in at Mom during one of her naps when her eyes popped open and she said, "What's wrong Lily?

"Just checking, is all."

"If you're worried about me, please, don't. I'm fine. I'm keeping busy and, well, doing as best I can."

"I can see that. You're okay, Mom. Like I said, just checking."

"Well if we're just checking how are *you* doing? I've noticed an absence of calls and visits from your future husband."

"I know. It's my fault, not ready yet."

"If things aren't right with Marshall, let's talk about it," she said, sitting up in bed and focusing on me for a change. It was so good to get her attention; I tried to come up with something interesting enough to keep it.

"I am not able to feel much, lately, Mom. Even Little Someone seems to know. She's quieter than usual."

"She's got a big job ahead of her, you know. You, too. I am sorry things are like this—all this darkness," she said, her lips trembling. "You shouldn't have to deal with so many difficult things at once. You've always tried to do things right, Lil. It's no doubt the reason Brent calls you St. Lillian."

Present tense, I thought. *She still thinks in terms of Brent being here.* I lay down on the bed next to her, placed my head on her bosom and she stroked my hair.

"I should think you must be wanting to get your house ready, aren't you? You might as well make good use of the time before the baby comes—which I can see is about yesterday. Let's go up to your house after lunch and look it over. I've packed spices and linens, bought beeswax candles at the boutique and a pair of ridiculously crooked candle holders, silly enough to make even the most humorless person smile."

So like Mom—she used to say where there was candlelight, there was hope. But not anymore; these days she was living her life without any light at all and I wasn't about to find any with the reverend. Despite the onset of spring, Mom and I were like shadows lost in the mist. Not only were all candles on hold, so was everything else. No more Mr. Kimball. No more working at the florist. No more baking Brent's favorite sweets or my favorite breads. No more conversations over tea. She took long naps and the television became white noise that ran morning to night. The house was clean, cleaner than usual, and she managed to dress each morning and move about doing odd things like perfectly folding sheets and cleaning the appliances. I knew she was on automatic, so I was happy and surprised she wanted to do something, anything other than her dreary routines.

Marshall had told me that the nephew of our landlord was long gone, and the house key was under the welcome mat. That was back when he had suggested I move in after school and I had explained why I couldn't, that I needed to be near Mom.

I was happy to ride with her to the new house, just because she was willing. After a slow drive, she turned at Howard's Lane and we climbed the hill. I was silently hoping the shabby lean-to at its base had blown away, but it was still standing. Mom didn't bother to look at it, or much else; her eyes stayed focused on the road ahead. "Most of these places are empty," I said, as if she cared.

When we reached the house at the top, she pulled into the driveway before I pointed it out. We walked to the door together and I awkwardly reached for the key from under what was now a thick, new, woven mat that I guessed Marshall must have bought to replace the earlier rotten version.

Once inside, she spoke.

"Surprise!"

I was shocked. Clean windows, crisp white curtains, new brightly colored pillows on the couch. A Leslie Woodhouse wreath hanging on the wall over the fireplace and one on the table to be swapped for the dirty old thing on the front door. The dank wood smell was gone, the carpet clean, the sink shining and the refrigerator like new. A many-colored quilted comforter brightened the bedroom and a sparkling mirror hung over the dresser. The baby crib was standing against the far wall dressed in its happy coverings. Mom's crocheted baby blanket was spread lovingly over the side and the playful mobile she bought in Concord was suspended above.

"Mom, Mom, it's wonderful. When did you do all this?" I asked, pulling the baby blanket to my face to embrace.

"Oh, I didn't do it alone, Marshall brought me here and asked if I could brighten it up. He left me with a key and we started. Heather and Nancy did more than their share while you were at school. Even your father got into the act by putting the crib together."

I am sure it was the first time she had smiled since Brent died. That was the best gift she could have given me.

"Now, let's fill up the spice cabinet and have a cup of tea straight from your new teapot."

What was I to do? It was too ironic. The world was now conspiring for me to marry Marshall and live unhappily ever after. I had to pretend happiness, to be grateful for what they had done, and stop feeling like a puzzle piece being forced into the wrong space.

On the way home I could think of nothing but how I had to change the future before it was too late. I couldn't run away. I couldn't foist myself on Mom. There was no way to face Marshall to announce what I really wanted to do, which was to have his baby and then keep her all to myself.

I called the only person I imagined could help.

Dad arrived early the following morning. Mom left us alone to visit. He could hardly be described as looking well. Last night's beer was oozing through the pores of his skin and one couldn't miss that his beard was going its own way and that his hands shook. Why could I love *him* unconditionally and feel nothing for my child's father?

I began by thanking him for putting the crib together.

"A piece of cake and my pleasure. How's my favorite girl?" he asked.

"Very ready to have this baby, and not," I smiled.

"Not?"

"No. Daddy, it's a bad time for her to be born. We are all still bleeding. No one is ready to love her like she should be loved. No one, but me."

"You and her father are all that matter, Lily-Vanilli, you must know that."

"But that's the problem, Daddy, I don't want to share her with Marshall."

"A little late, Sweetheart. She's half his. What's the matter? Second thoughts?"

"I'm sort of afraid of him."

His body jerked. "Has he hurt you? I'll break his balls," he flared.

"No, Daddy. He's trying to be nice but he's just not the person I thought he was."

"If he's hurt you, I'll kill him," he promised, staring into my eyes, trying to see inside my head. "Tell me. Tell me the *truth.*"

"Daddy, stop. It's not like that. It's something I can't name. I just know I don't want to be with him anymore. There are things I don't like about him and I think there are worse things I'm going to find out. Things that David implied, things I have kind of felt."

"Felt? That's important, Lil. Your intuition is always important. If someone is lying you can tell, right? Just look at the Capitol. Washington is all lies. These clowns, North and Poindexter, the whole lot of Reagan's men, every damn one of them—liars. You don't need a lie detector to find out, you just know, like I knew that guy of yours was a phony from the start."

"Daddy can you help me? Could I come live with you?"

"But I am a lousy father, Lil. I'm a mess of a man."

"No, no you're not!" I cried.

"Your mother. She will want to have you at home."

"She's grieving and hurting all over. She doesn't need my problems added to hers."

"Maybe she does, Sweetheart. Maybe she does. I think she's trying to work out things. Your baby, your situation is something she wants to be here for. She thinks everything happens for a reason. Maybe she sees it as an opportunity to do something for you that no one did for her."

He twisted in his seat and from his back pocket pulled out a little black book. "This little book helped me help a bunch of guys a long time ago. Some of them actually work for the Feds. Most of them owe me a favor for keeping my mouth shut. Maybe they can do something, for you, now. Let me do some groundwork and find out who this Marshall character really is. I should have done it at the start. What the hell's the matter with me? I'm going to start with David, even though he's a pretty mixed-up kid, I think he might cooperate. He must know his brother better than anyone. He's the one with the roots, the history. Where are they from originally? Do you know?"

I told him New York City, but asked him not to go to David. "I should be the one to talk to David, Daddy. We have a conversation waiting to happen."

Carol St. John

After Dad left, I went directly to Pearl's ready for a confrontation. When I entered the shop with the Indian bells jangling behind me, my anxiety level must have sent out waves of caution.

"Be right with you," Strange called from the back room.

I stood quietly in place for a few minutes until he found me. "Oh, it's you," he said. "Listen, we don't know each other anymore. I thought you had some brains. I thought you were someone else."

"I know, David...."

"The name's Strange."

"Strange...I don't know what happened."

"You traded me in for an asshole, that's what happened."

"Please, please I am so confused and afraid. I need to hear the truth from you, the whole truth. Things are not the way they should be."

"Yeah, a kid named Brent is dead, murdered by stupidity."

"I didn't know, I don't know, what happened. The whole thing is blur, a blur of pain and shock. I hate to think that I had anything to do with it, but I do. I keep asking myself what I should have done."

He didn't need to know what I *did* do, that I ran to Marshall, after seeing them kiss.

"Your lover boy threatened to tell your parents about us. He even called me a child molester. I should have stood up to him but I couldn't. I didn't want to make things worse for Brent. I only meant to help him from the start."

"I know, I know," I said, thinking, he would totally blame me if I told him who fired Marshall up. "But you did more than that, didn't you?" I said, not meaning it to sound the way it did, but hoping to deflect the guilt that was rising in me, knowing now for sure that my words triggered something too terrible to ever fix.

324

Strange took a step backward. "Hey, girl, what's that to you? Your brother was in trouble long before he met me. He was a time bomb when we met. But you want to see something? Do you want to know who he really was? I found out he was an artist and a poet and a person who wanted the same things you do. He just had a different chemistry. Come here, let me introduce you to your brother."

I timidly followed him to the back of the shop, into his space. The wall over the bed was now covered with Brent memorabilia. Black and white photos of Brent on skates, Brent sitting on the motorcycle laughing; Brent in a boa with his hair blowing in the breeze; hand-printed poems; cartoons of Strange signed, *With Love—*.

Strange pointed his tattooed index finger at one of the poems. "This was his favorite. I bet you had no idea he could read, did you? It's his calligraphy, too."

"That's not fair, Strange. I used to read poems to him when he was little, and he would always ask, 'Again?' He loved poetry before he could read."

"It's called Fire and Ice."

I silently reread Frost's poem. It began,

> *Some say the world will end in fire,*
> *some say in ice.*
> *From what I've tasted of desire,*
> *I hold with those who favor fire.*

"O God," I said, aloud, thinking of the mysterious piles of kindling that surrounded the pond. An ache ran through my back and tied it in a knot. I couldn't breathe. Had he meant to set the final fire? Did he try to ignite it and fail?

"He had such a thing about fire." I said softly.

"He was a fucking pyromaniac! He was burning up inside. He had to get it out!"

"You knew?" I asked.

"I knew he almost killed himself biking all the way to Grafton in the middle of the night and back. He could have blown the whole fucking village up."

"He told you that?"

"He scared himself shitless. I'm sure he tried to scare me with the fire at Pearl's. He was crazy when we split up. He didn't know why I had to stop seeing him."

I swallowed hard as I realized he didn't know how I had betrayed them by telling Marshall. But it made no difference now.

"This poem over here is his," Strange said.

I stood before it, not wanting to revisit what I had already heard at the service.

> *I am the fire.*
> *I burn*
> *Wanting to be wanted.*
> *Say so, tell me, beg.*
> *Do it for me, don't make me*
> *Grovel in the dirt where*
> *They would push me*
> *And leave me for dead.*
> *I am dead without you*
> *And with you, my legs*
> *Grow strong and fly with*
> *The wings of Daedalus*

I felt sick. I turned and saw that Strange had turned a pale gray.

Tearfully, I tried to explain. "I didn't know what was wrong; where he had gone. He was such an adorable little boy but he disappeared, and I thought he had just become a miserable person. He hated school, he hated me and just about everything that I loved. I don't think I ever asked him why he was so angry. I wish...I want him back. I want to tell him how sorry I am that I didn't understand. I kept wondering where he had gone, kept waiting for him to...I mean, where is he now?"

"Hey don't go there. Don't start all that bullshit. Brent's a memory, that's what he is. A fucking memory and he's not coming back. Never. It's too late for any of us to apologize."

He lay down on his bed. I thought he was going to pass out. His lips were white and his eyes rolling back in his head. I moved to grab hold of him but he shook his head. "Listen, I gotta take a few minutes off. Would you handle the store?" he asked, his voice flat, his hands on his chest the way I had last seen Brent's. It was like he was having a stroke, a seizure or something that needed to be treated. I didn't know what to do.

Shaking, I went out and into the shop to find the phone, only to be hit by another pain, this one like a great rope wrapping itself from back to front. I had to brace myself for a minute until it passed.

34

I was standing at the Goofy Gifts counter when the mysterious knot tightened itself around my back again. This time it pulled harder and my belly turned to stone. I couldn't move for a minute that seemed like ten. Was this my time? I didn't know. I thought the pain would be lower and longer. I picked up the phone and called Mom. She said, "Walk around, Lil, keep walking, I'll be there as soon as I can." So I walked around and around the store until the next contraction, which felt a little more intense but bearable.

"Are you all right, Strange?" I called, in his doorway.

"Yeah, just kinda tired is all," he said.

Then my water broke and I called for him to help me.

"Jesus!" he said, as he entered the room, "Is that normal? Are you going to have the baby right here in the shop? He looked at the floor and the ceiling, at the walls and then back at my feet.

"I don't know how to deliver babies," he cried.

I suggested he get some towels, one to mop the floor and another for me.

"But how are you going to keep it in?" he asked. "I better call 9-1-1."

Mom, the sheriff and Ted Costa arrived at the same time. Ted told me to lie down in Strange's bed, and although I wanted to go to the hospital, Mom made me lie down so she could check me first. But I don't think it was just Mom checking, my eyes were shut tight. "The cervix is open, the head presenting," Mom said.

I think I started screaming. "It's coming, it's coming." It wanted out no matter what and I wanted it out too.

"Don't push, the medics will be here soon," Mom said.

She could have been telling the moon to go away. I had no choice but to allow the contractions. They were so fierce I thought I was going to die. "Mom, something is wrong, I panted. It shouldn't hurt this much. I'm being ripped apart. Please, Mom."

"Try to stay calm. Count backwards, Honey. Start at a hundred."

"One hundred. ninety-nine, ni-ine- tee-ee- I squealed, caught in the most ferocious pain I'd ever known, before or since. My back arched as I felt the force of all my energy fighting its way out of me. It was a power with its own mind.

"Hold on, hold on," Mom kept saying, placing a cold wet cloth in my mouth and giving me her arm to squeeze.

"I can't. I can't do it. I'm going to die."

"You are doing fine, Lil. It won't be long. You're dilating very quickly, we can see the baby's head."

Ted Costa tried to calm me. "This won't be the first baby I've delivered, Miss. I helped with two of my own and another down in Putney."

"Shi-i-tt! I want the doctor...someone...knock me out, please," I begged.

"You're doing fine," he said, "Try quick short breaths."

"Why don't you?" I asked. "I am not doing fine, I can't get my breath...." A jack hammer was breaking me open from the inside out.

"It's coming! Push," someone said. I felt a split, I honestly did, as I was torn apart.

"I don't have to," I groaned.

Out it had come, a human torpedo, going its own way, ready to get started, to move out and away. I felt enormous relief as the pain ceased and its messy cause was lifted from between my legs and placed on my body.

Help had arrived during the final stages of my ordeal and a stranger was attacking my torn cervix. Everyone around me said I had done very well—all, but Strange—he had fainted.

I had almost forgotten the baby in the midst of the pain; dying and divine punishment were more real. The medic had placed the still wet creature on my abdomen, where it lay like a slab of uncooked meat until the medic lifted it into a white cloth. Its tiny red feet, rigid. I was sure it was dead. Then I saw Ted Costa's large hands take the bundle, with its bloody gray coil still attached to me and watched as the medic cut it, and heard him promise to save it for me.

"No. No, I don't want it," I cried.

Seconds later, my heart burst when the tiny thing's pink crusty claws flailed and its wrinkled feet went into motion. Beneath a flattened nose, two sweet little lips grimaced. And then I saw it, a penis nestled between its legs. "A boy?" I asked, just as he burst into his first song.

While we were both cleaned up I began to shake violently. Mom wrapped me in a blanket and sat by my side wiping my lips with a wet towel, saying, "It's all right, it's all right. He's perfect."

"Mom, Mom," I cried, "Why didn't anyone tell me what to expect? Why is the pain such a secret?

"It's different for every woman," she said.

"But how could you have gone through this three times?

"It was worth it," she said.

"I made a boy!" I said laughing, crying and suddenly filled with the most extraordinary love I have ever known. I reached for him as Ted laid him back down on my breast, loosened the towel that he was wrapped in, and opened the tiny clenched fist with my fingers to explore its pale papery nails. Amazingly, his hand folded around my finger and we shook hands as best we could. Then I studied his little ears that would soon learn sounds that soothed or frightened him. How homely his face was and how raw his skin! I smelled his damp head, felt the softness of its crown and felt his heart next to mine, I embraced the whole of him for those first minutes before this new star in the universe, a miracle like no other, began the journey to become himself. I thought, no wonder Mary believed her son was the Son of God. Isn't every son?

We were placed in the ambulance and taken to the hospital after the fact. But I was glad to go, glad to have the two of us checked out for complications and cared for in that trusted place where one of the wings bore the Woodhouse name, and the births of Heather and Brent and I were recorded and this child of the next generation would be added to its roster.

My only upset was the brief separation upon our arrival, when all of me, shaken and starstruck, wanted to hold him again. It wasn't long before the nurse brought him back, all cleaned up and wrapped tightly in a soft flannel blanket. She asked if I was planning on breast feeding and I said yes. So my sweet boy was laid on me again, this time my breasts bare and ready, and his pink lips pursing like he'd been trained in a heavenly nursery. He suckled immediately.

My nipples were not the spigots I had imagined they would be, but the nurse at my side pressed on them with her thumb and forefinger until the thin whitish liquid appeared and I felt his lips awkwardly attach themselves to begin our life-long love affair.

Little blue cubes appeared on his wrist that read, W- O- O- D- H- O- U- S- E. I was so sure I was having a girl, I had no first name ready.

No one had thought to call Marshall or declare his paternity.

The day after my son was born, I was taking a shower and luxuriating in the warm water running over my body when I noticed that a sac of what was once baby hung like a permanent addition to my stomach. Eight pounds had been removed from me along with water and blood and tissue and yet I was still carrying a pouch.

Later, while I was nursing, a maternity nurse came in to watch our progress. I was still having minimal success while he was trying his best. "I don't seem to have enough," I said.

"Don't be afraid to press on the nipples, and help them along. It's in there," she smiled. "You will never regret the effort. You're doing the best thing you can do for your son and yourself. Nursing not only transfers your immunities, it helps pull your parts back together. You will lose the baby weight faster."

That was a motivating little piece of information. But I needed much more. I had never once considered going to prenatal classes or looking for information about the first days of motherhood. I thought it was an instinct that would appear all on its own. I knew about bathing babies and layettes and following prescribed directions. What I never anticipated was my sense of loss and inadequacy. I was no longer the old me. I was now *less*, empty, and realizing that every thought I had from this moment on would be dedicated to keeping this tiny creature alive. The transfer of him from the inside, out, was almost overwhelming.

I named him Adam Atticus Woodhouse. I did not talk to anyone about my choice. It came to me like a fact. It was his name. I would deal with Marshall later and would make sure the child stayed with me and was my own. I naively felt no obligation to the man who was his father.

Adam and I had hardly begun our journey together when Marshall arrived at the hospital to see him. I still don't know how he learned of the birth.

Mom tenuously let him in, and by some extraordinary coincidence, Dad was visiting us as well.

It was an uncomfortable reunion. Marshall was formal and not so foolish as to think things were right between us. But, like shavings to a magnet, he was drawn to his son.

After tenderly examining him, touching his head and toes, he asked, "There was no veil?"

"Veil? What do you mean?" I asked.

"No covering to his face, no membrane?"

"No. He's perfect," I said.

"Good. God has spared our son from the weight of the world. Now, we must christen him immediately. He is not a Woodhouse, Lily. He is mine as much as yours."

He spoke with the authority of a judge.

My father was ready for a face-off. "Listen here, *reverend,* right now this child is a Woodhouse. He is going home to Woodhouse Hill and I think you would be wise not to get in our family's way."

He sounded like a military commander, the Chief of Police, the final authority of something.

"You have no right..." Marshall started, but Dad was all over him.

"No. *You* have no right. You are unfit to parent this child. You're a sham. An imposter."

"Who are you to say that I am unfit? You, whose son is begging for absolution at Heaven's gate!"

That Marshall had wielded a sword and landed it in Dad's chest was all too apparent.

Dad took in a deep breath, his shoulders bent. "It is good I am not a violent man," he growled. "You are asking for it, and you're going to get it. I know all I need to know to break your back."

"And what do you know?" Marshall asked. "That child is mine and his mother is my wife in the eyes of the Lord. This is a fact."

"Lord? Lord?" Dad sneered.

"You do not even know enough to bow down your head. Who are you to think you can make a better home than I for my son?"

Dad was ready, the prosecutor about to take down the accused. "I know this. Your name is not what you claim it to be. No surprise. I knew from the first you were a phony, a manipulator and it didn't take long to prove. I put some men to work and found out my instincts were right all along. Marshall Barry is some made up name you took to hide behind."

Marshall stood perfectly still. "You know nothing about me," he said.

"I know you have a lot of questions to answer before you even think of being my daughter's husband or claiming her child, *Morris*."

Then I saw Marshall's eyes widen, darken and narrow. He did not appear to be shaken as he heard Dad's words, but I could see his neck muscles flex.

They were two lions about to rip each other apart. "Daddy, Marshall, please. What are you saying? You're not talking about the baby. You're not talking about me."

I felt for the nurse's call button and started to push it again and again.

"I only want what is mine, my son, my wife," Marshall said.

"Marshall, I am not a possession. I am not yours and I don't want this baby to be part of our problems, your problems. I don't know you. Right now, how could I choose you to father my son?"

He fell to his knees. "Lord God forgive your daughter for her sins. Forgive her for trying to keep this father from your divine will. She knows not what she is doing."

"Get up!" Dad all but roared.

Marshall instinctively obeyed my father's command, rose from his knees and faced his foe.

"Listen here, you can stop the act. I've got the proof. Your real name is Morris Baronsky, a perfectly fine name, but not good enough for you, evidently. Why is that, may I ask? Just why did you bury that name to become a sham named Marshall Barry?"

"Your daughter and I are married. That is all you need to know. We are married in the eyes of God."

"*Your* God, not mine, not hers, and not the law's. You're dreaming if you think that phony matrimony will hold up in any court of law in these United States. We can't make things up and then claim them to be legal."

"My name is completely legal, I can assure you."

"There's more to this story and I am going after it," Dad said. "Right now, I want you out of this room and away from this baby until you show me some legal papers. I will get a court order if I have to. But, meanwhile, if you get out of town and out of our lives on your own, I will keep our little secret."

"You are not going to threaten me," Marshall said.

"I already have," Dad spat.

Part of me wanted Marshall to deny whatever Dad was saying, wanted to hear an excuse, an explanation, a declaration of love, give me some kind of hope, but it didn't happen. I had sent Dad off to find a way out of my situation and he found one.

"Marshall?" I asked. "Tell who you are. Tell my father!"

"Save your breath. I know who you are." Dad said. "And we are going to fight you. We will go all the way. That bullshit that you have been feeding innocent people will be no more. You better start looking for a real job."

"I will do God's work as I am told. He has placed His sword in my hand."

"Oh Christ! Get the hell out of here before I call the sheriff and they bring a paddy wagon and put you away."

Marshall's fists locked and unlocked, his temples pulsated and jaw thrust forward. Adam began to cry just as the nurse entered.

"Problem, Honey?" she asked.

"I need this man to be removed from the room," I said nodding toward Marshall.

"I am the father," he announced.

The nurse referenced her chart and calmly responded by saying that his name was not registered and he should come to the desk and record that fact.

"Go, Marshall. Please go. We will talk about this another time," I begged. He left, but I felt sick. I knew there was not going to be another time. I was going to go as far away as I could when Adam and I were released from the hospital.

I picked up Adam and held him to my breast. It was a primal act. A return to sanity.

Incredulous, I asked, "If he's not Marshall Barry, who is he, Dad?"

"You heard it. He's someone named Morris Baronsky. We will know soon enough what his real story is. Meanwhile, I will make sure we get a protective court order and keep him out of here and away from the baby. The less he has access to the two of you the easier for him to make a clean break.

"Am I in danger? Are we?" I asked, trying to grasp the enormity of Dad's discovery.

"We saw what he did to David. Who knows what he is capable of. He tried to provoke a fight, that's as sure as hell. He won't be allowed back in this room. I'll see to it."

A court order seemed extreme, implying Marshall might hurt us or kidnap the baby. But then I didn't know who that man really was. It scared me just to think of it.

Early on the third day as we were released from the hospital, Adam opened his eyes and looked into mine. I had been told he couldn't actually see me yet, but he did. We recognized one another and made that bond no one can understand until they have had the experience. Dad was there to drive us home, and as he negotiated our way through June's radiance, all I saw was the baby in my arms. I had stopped making up the rest of the world.

35

I was feeding Adam when Nancy visited the hospital. She cooed and exclaimed over the baby like an aunt. I forgave her for what might have been a perfectly innocent moment with Marshall, back when I was blindly in love.

She wanted to know every detail of the birth. She asked if she could touch the baby, and called him by his name as she examined his tiny face. "I am declaring myself available for whatever you need," she promised him.

I was saying good-bye, thanking her for fixing the house and coming to visit me, when she said, "You are not going to talk about it are you?"

"What do you call this?" I asked. "Aren't we talking?"

"Not really," she said.

"You mean about that weird night with Marshall? I don't care anymore."

"Yes, you do," she insisted. "You do, anyone would. Come on, let's talk about it,"

"I have let Marshall Barry go, Nancy. He was not the person I thought he was."

"What?" she asked, obviously clueless.

"He isn't even who he says he is," I said. "I can't tell you any more than that."

"But, the baby, the baby is his, right?"

"Of course he is."

"Oh my God. Now what?"

"Now we take it from here."

"That's not good enough, Lily. We have to talk. I don't want you to suspect my disloyalty."

She obviously wanted to explain herself, and clear my doubts. Recreating her visit with Marshall, she told me how they had talked about her father and my mother as the cause of her concern, and added that when she first called Marshall, he had insisted she come to his "office." She claimed she had gone reluctantly, but her curiosity and needs were greater than her resistance. "That was my biggest mistake."

"When I got there," she explained, "he was sympathetic and caring. He said we had a special relationship because we both loved the same woman. He held my hand as I spoke and pulled me to him when I cried. I knew it was inappropriate. I even suspected he did that with every woman that he counseled, but I wanted to be on his good side and not act as if he was anything but caring. I was afraid it would insult him if I pulled away, and he would turn against me. That guy is someone you don't want to mess with," she said.

I thought of Brent, of Strange and of my terrible secret. "No, you don't," I said. "He can be fierce."

"Well, he was gentle and concerned that night."

"I am sure. I believe you," I said. "I think I always did, but it was a shock to see you in his arms, and I suppose I was feeling very shaky back then. But now..."

"Now?" she asked.

"Now, I don't want to ever see him again."

"But?"

"I can't talk about it okay? I promise I will, when things are clearer. But right now, all I care about is Adam."

I looked down at my bundle, at his pouty lips, his little ears, the way he stretched his arms to embrace the air, and I kissed the balls of his busy feet. He was as much as I needed.

In the evening, Heather brought Strange over after work. Quite surprisingly, he arrived as a new and less angry version of himself. He'd dyed the red hair black and had added a few not too horrible tattoos on his arms, but he was almost gaunt.

Heather immediately picked up Adam and kind of force fed him to Strange, who held him as he might have held a lion cub. "Geez, he's real," he said. Then leaning closer to Adam's face he said softly, "Glad you made it, dude. I'm sorry I fainted. Although it looks like things turned out okay for you, without me."

"Yes. He's pure perfection," I announced.

I wanted to take advantage of the moment, wanted to ask him the questions I had stored up inside, but I thought bringing up Marshall might send him away, so I waited.

Dr. Hamilton came in the room acting like a host. "Quite the little man, isn't he?" he asked.

Strange yelped as Adam grabbed a hold of his goatee and held onto it like it was a lifeline, as perhaps it was. Uncle David was surely going to be a part of his future if I had any say.

When Adam was back in my arms, I asked Dr. Hamilton about his nose, "It's still smashed flat against his face," I pointed out.

He assured me it would rise. "It's like putty right now," he said. "He will be fine."

"Oh, good!" I laughed, "I thought he might have to be a prize fighter!"

David spoke. "Well at least he wasn't born with a caul, like my brother was. It messed up his life."

"You don't say?" asked Dr. Hamilton. "Cauls are relatively rare but harmless."

"Yeah. He still has it. My mother dried it and made sure he kept it with him all the time. She believed it was a promise or a sign or something that would protect him. Maybe Jesus reincarnated. She actually became a Christian later on. Of course I wasn't around the first eight years, but

I can tell you it was very crazy, all that superstitious shittola until the day she died."

"Well, young man, your brother being the chosen one must have been hard to compete with," Dr. Hamilton said. "It's nonsense, you know—an old wives' tale."

"Tell that to Marshall," David said. "He fought it at first but bought into it later, when some weird things happened to him like visions and voices."

"Perhaps schizophrenia," the doctor said.

"I thought he was nuts."

"But what's a caul?" I asked, reminded again of all I didn't know.

"It's a mask of membrane covering a baby's face. They used to call it a veil, a blessing," Dr. Hamilton explained.

Strange shook his head. "It was more like a curse."

After the doctor left Heather announced that they should go, too. I asked them to stay. I felt that a door had opened for us to talk and I didn't want it shut. Strange looked out my rain-soaked window while I nursed the baby and Heather watered the half-dead plant they had brought. Without any small talk, I broached the subject of the name Baronsky.

"Strange, do you know anyone named Baronsky?" I began.

He snapped to attention. "Geez," he said as his arms folded and unfolded while he tried to find a comfort zone. I watched his body language travel from denial to truth.

"What? How?" he started. Then gave it over. "Yeah. I used that name for ten years, but Baronsky is definitely not a cool name. It was okay in New York City, back when, but not here, not in Christendom."

He was already making excuses. "Why would you think such a thing?" I asked.

"Because Baronsky was okay when we lived in the projects with a shitload of other Ruskies, but outta the city, we were foreigners. Away from Manhattan you had look and sound like your ancestors came over on the Mayflower or something."

Heather laughed. "Must have been a huge ship, that Mayflower. Really, David, why would you just walk away from your family name, from your history?"

"Because we could. It wasn't cool to be refugees. But, hey, how did you find out, Lily? Did Marshall finally tell you the truth?"

"I want *your* version of the truth, Strange. What really happened?"

"I was a kid. I don't know that much about the decision. I only know a lot of people have done it, people like Cher and Dylan. People like Jennifer Aniston. It's no big deal. Thousands of families lost their names at Ellis Island, when they checked in. My brother said he felt uncomfortable with our parents' roots, because they were not only Jews who left Russia because of the pogroms, but never left their communist sympathies behind. They didn't know any better. In the projects, we were just like everyone else from the Soviet Bloc. The basement get-togethers that took place on Sundays were actually party meetings."

"You have to be kidding! Communists? It sounds so James Bond or something."

"It wasn't. My parents were rah-rah the U S of A, the Land of the Free. They would almost kiss the ground they walked on. But they were still stuck with their beliefs. It was all they knew.

"They didn't know most Americans would have hung them for going through a stop sign. I mean my parents were in the heart of the most hated political scene in America. But it wasn't obvious until we went to commie camp in the summer."

"Commie camp?" Heather asked. "There are such things in America?"

"Yeah. We used to leave Manhattan and go to the *country*, which was about thirty miles north of the city. Our camp was smack in the middle of middle-class white America where there were porches and pools and a swingset in every yard."

I could see the swingsets but not the camp.

"Plenty of hate lived there, too. You know, it was hate that built suburbia, all those pale-faced city folks trying to get away from the *others*. When some of the escapees found out Orange County harbored Jewish communists, they read their KKK manuals and built a huge swastika out of railroad ties, and planted it on the camp's lawn."

Heather seated herself next to me but we didn't look at one another. I patted Adam's back hoping for his satisfied burp. We all seemed to wait, staying as quiet as we could, hoping he would let it go. He did.

"Wow! That was a good Ruskie burp if I ever heard one," Strange said. "He's definitely one of mine."

"But the name? Your real name?" Heather finally blurted. "What is it?"

"David Barry. The original was David Baronsky. I only changed it to Barry for the family. I wasn't as screwed up as Morris. My mother fucked him up. She was always bragging about, *Morris this and Morris that, and Morris says*....from the time he was only a little kid. Even then, she would ask his advice, believing he had all the answers. She'd ask and he'd answer. It was like that for as long as I can remember. If he had said the sky was falling she would have told the neighbors to go inside. As far as she was concerned, God's son spoke only the truth. The one good thing that came out of all that stuff was that he told her she had to stop smoking or it would kill her. She did, and later that year the government banned cigarette ads on television. To my mother, it was only more proof of Morris's *divine* powers."

"But what about the name?" Heather asked.

"When Morris was thirteen and we were at camp he met a shiksa at the local playground, a little girl from a local church; I think he fell in love with her. They were always trying to ditch me. He was a towhead up until then; a real Aryan; blonde hair, blue eyes and tall for his age. He didn't look like Morris Baronsky, a Russian Jew from the projects, that's for sure."

"Then?" I asked.

"So, Morris decides that we should all leave the city and move to the country where my father can start a used appliance business and my mother can make nice new *American* friends."

"He said, '*The projects are not good for us. We will never get ahead. Neither is being Jewish.*'" He argued we were not *real* Jews, because we didn't practice. His number one revelation, however, was that we had to change our names and get away from the city. He warned my parents that it was un-American to be any shade of red and we would suffer for it.

"'*We have to start over. Leave the old world behind,* he announced. *Leaving Russia is not enough. We have to get away from the tribe.*'"

Strange stood and walked back and forth in front of the window. He pointed to the ceiling. "As if God himself had come down to earth and spoken, my mother started to push my father until he gave in. They bought a little split-level house on a hill of new houses that all looked alike, and applied for a new name, Barry. Then they became Lou and Hannah Barry, just like that. No one ever had to know the rest of the story."

"Were they happy?" Heather asked.

"They were shy and afraid of the countryside. They never took a walk in the woods or planted a decent garden. They hated the car. They'd lived a lifetime without a car. To become totally dependent on a machine they didn't trust was terrible. To leave the friends they trusted must have been awful, too. But, they did as Marshall asked. On top of that, Mama drove us to the Community Church every Sunday—the Son of God got to see that little girlfriend of his for a long time, long enough for her to become a woman and ditch him."

"Her father found out they were having sex and just about tore him to pieces. Then we moved to New Jersey and then my parents were killed. End of very sick story."

"Where were you in all this" I asked.

"I was no one. A real nebbish."

"And how about Marshall? What happened to him?" Heather asked.

"Meschugener. After our parents died, he went a little crazy, talking to himself or God or ghosts or something. He was really losing it, at first. Then he heard God telling him to be a preacher. He found a way to be certified through the mail and began. It was really, really, a crazinski time."

"What were you thinking?" I asked.

"I was scared shitless. I thought, he'd gone nuts, I didn't know what to do and was afraid I'd be sent to some relative I didn't know, or to an orphanage, maybe back to Russia."

"You should write a book. This is an incredible story. It's amazing you survived," I said.

"I *almost* survived. Now, I 'm not so sure."

I said, "Dad is going after Marshall. He wants to expose him. He wants to go the church and tell the people who their minister really is."

"Why? What's the point?" He sat on the edge of the bed. "Are you guys really going to let him do that? I mean what about the baby? What about me?"

"Your brother wants to claim paternity for Adam, give him his name," Heather explained.

"So? Why not? He *is* his son. I don't think he's done anything illegal. He's an actor, yes, but sometimes I think he believes his act. He might go off the deep end if he can't claim his kid."

"Well, he's bouncing on the high dive right now. He says he's the new captain of Christ's army," I said. "He's talking about leading the people away from Satan, picking up swords and taking Christ's orders. He's really wired, thinking he's tuned into God, that Christ is telling him what to do."

"More of the old messianic get ready to die shit? What's new?" Strange moaned, his hands in his hair and his eyes closed. "He'll fight for the baby."

"Yes, and he's not fit to be Adam's daddy. I'm a little afraid of him."

"I'm afraid *for* him." David said, his head shaking over his thin shoulders. "He's fucked up and wants to make everyone else to blame. For him there are only two sides, the angels in white and devils in black."

"I know. I don't think I can help him, but my dad is trying to hold him back. Marshall got pretty quiet when he was confronted by a possible charge of fraud."

"People who lose their minds can find them again, can't they?" Heather asked.

David shook his head. "They have to understand that they're sick. They have to sign themselves in to get help. My brother would never see it that way,

He turned to me. "It's my fault. I should have known things were not going to get any better. I should never have taken you to that church in the first place."

"I suppose I should have never gone back," I said.

But, then, what was I thinking, with my beautiful son in my arms?

Dad was unable to get an order of protection because he couldn't prove Marshall had done anything illegal or harmful other than proclaim to be educated as a minister. Independent churches had recently created a set of laws to prevent imposters within their ranks, but Dad withheld pushing the issue as Marshall had seemingly chosen to withdraw from us.

I shouldn't have been surprised to see him disappear so easily. After all, where had he been for those long nine months of my pregnancy?

Dad was sure he would walk away, because he believed men like Marshall were most vulnerable to the threat of exposure and that fear of public shame would ward him off. In fact, he counted on it.

36

David called me a few weeks after our big talk. He was anxious because of what he revealed when he visited the hospital. "I thought maybe we should talk," he said.

"What a coincidence. Adam just told me he's dying to see his Uncle David. Come over."

And so he came and we sat up in my room and visited. He had definitely decided to go to New York, and was going to attend The New School in Greenwich Village to take writing courses. He wondered what I thought about the idea of he and Heather living together. I told him I thought it was great.

"Well, we're not a *thing* you know," he confided.

I assured him that I did know, and that she understood that much, as well.

"Heather gets a lot of things right. She's pretty cool. I'll be there for her if she needs me. I figure we'll do okay. Big thing is that I have to move outta here. I know the city and I know what I want to do. Two plusses against all the minuses."

"You'll find someone, David. I know you will. You're smart and talented and there's someone waiting for you, if you put your real self out there."

"Fuck. I'd like to say the same to you, Lil. But you are such an idiot and so ugly and you already have someone waiting for you, he's just tiny is all," he said.

"Thanks. Want something to eat?" I asked.

"Sure, as long as it's not American cheese."

I left Adam sleeping in his crib, my little sugar plum. My cherub.

We went downstairs and Mom was making tomato-basil soup.

"Are you willing to share that with the hungry?" I asked.

"You could say," she smiled.

I grabbed some bowls and Mom's fresh loaf of boule and put a new stick of butter in a dish.

As we opened our mouths for our first taste, a cry went out from the bedroom.

"Ugh," I said, pushing back my chair, "I'll get him."

"No, sit still. I'll do it," Mom said.

We sat at the table for a good half-hour and I didn't think about Adam for all that time. Instead, we ate and talked about dreams and possibilities, mostly his, and a few of mine. It was sort of like the old days. It wasn't until David left the house that I realized how much that little exchange meant to me. My world had quickly become all about Adam.

I rinsed the dishes and loaded the dishwasher and then took the laundry upstairs, treading lightly so as not to disturb the quiet.

Mom was holding Adam on her lap and looking in his eyes, the wide eyes that so resembled Brent's. She was toying with his long fingers and allowing a baptism of tears to fall. "Hello, little boy," she whispered, "Our little man."

I stepped back, allowing her the moment, a moment that spelled their beginnings.

Later, that evening, when I was filled with thoughts that needed a place to go, I turned on my computer and began to revise my philosophy of life.

I began:

Dear Quinn,

I am sending you an edited version of my philosophy of life despite the fact that you gave me an A on the first. I feel that I have confronted my demons, my naivete, my fears of confrontation. *Childbirth has changed my outlook. I feel now that I have the power and the will to make a difference. Here goes—*

Knowing Beyond Knowing

After Adam was born, my entire body was shaking. I was hot. I was cold. I was ecstatic and exhausted. All at once I knew something to be true. Life wants to exist. It presents itself of its own volition. It is the most powerful force imaginable. My doubts about meaning and purpose were erased in the few seconds prior to my son's first breath, overwhelmed by those that followed. Something more than I had pushed him out, away from my safe harbor into the world; the same world I knew to be at risk, conflicted, callous and beyond naming. I could have been a sow, a mare or a bloody lioness as I pushed that creature from darkness into light. We were one with the eternal force, the great inspiration that asks only that we inhale what is offered. Compared to that first breath, names matter not at all, nor understanding or knowing why.

I wanted him out, to let go of me. I was willing to die in order to find relief and have him breathe on his own. And in that first breath, in the primal cry that emerged from his lungs, I heard the cry of greeting, of release, of survival; the universal cry that we all make as we enter the world, the terror, the joy, the announcement that we are here, for better or worse and for as long as we are given. It is more profound than any sound we can conjure and more demanding. Now all that lies ahead of me will be for his survival and his children's survival and theirs.

Such a tiny creature, and yet he has changed the world forever. No matter how small (seven pounds), no matter how long (21 inches), no matter how scrunched his face and delicate his tiny fingers, he is magnificent. He is all the evidence I need of miracles. No one can know him as I do. He is the flesh of my flesh, the most creative thing I have ever done or ever will do, the Alpha and the Omega. He is it. He is the force of life, the extraordinary reason for consciousness, for future, for work and play, for all things to be considered. He is part of the interdependent web. His eyes are the world's mirrors, his hands the tools. His heart beats to the rhythms of the earth; his mind is a fire of energy asking to be fed.

I watch the cord shrivel where we were once attached, and caress that sacred spot every day as I promise to protect him. I am now one among the Goddesses. I am Aphrodite the goddess of love, Athena the wise. Gaia the earth mother and a new Madonna. I am doing as I am called, learning to be a mother and the source of unconditional love, following all the others who have been down this daunting path.

I hope the invention I make of this world will carry us through; that I can lead us through the danger zones, the dark matter and the unforeseen, and that my son can find beauty and joy of his own making during his allotted time.

With awe and affection,
Ms. Lillian Woodhouse

ACKNOWLEDGMENTS

I wish to acknowledge the inspiration of my friends and family: my husband, Dennis, my children, Leslie Travaglione, John Delamater, Jill Buchanan, Heather St. John and Tamie Claire St. John.

This story evolved slowly with the support of its initial readers, Donna Smith, Kathy Zweig, Kay Rylance, Glenda Martin and Claire Gerus. The professional help of my two editors, Nick Courtright and Chris Anderson, was invaluable as well, and I am grateful for their wisdom.

But mostly I want to thank the readers that have affirmed my writing life over the years, those who acknowledged my columns, who wrote at my side in writing groups and bought and sold my first books. Thank you.

ABOUT ATMOSPHERE PRESS

Atmosphere Press is an independent full-service publisher for books in genres ranging from non-fiction to fiction to poetry, with a special emphasis on being an author-friendly approach to the often-brutal challenges of getting a book into the world. Learn more about what we do at Atmosphere's website, atmospherepress.com.

And of course, we encourage you to check out some of Atmosphere's latest releases, which are available at Amazon.com, BarnesandNoble.com, and via order from your local bookstore:

What I Cannot Abandon, poems by William Guest

That Beautiful Season, a novel by Sandra Murphy

All the Dead Are Holy, poems by Larry Levy

Surviving Mother, a novella by Gwen Head

Rescripting the Workplace, nonfiction by Pam Boyd

Winter Park, a novel by Graham Guest

ABOUT THE AUTHOR

Brooklyn born, Carol Egmont St. John is a mother of four young women, who she claims have taught her more than she could possibly teach them. She is a poet, an artist, a columnist, the author of three novels and a workshop facilitator dedicated to empowering women in their creative endeavors. Her current homes are in Rockport, Massachusetts and Green Valley, Arizona.

CPSIA information can be obtained
at www.ICGtesting.com
Printed in the USA
LVOW11s0405160517
534666LV00002B/325/P